Also by Neal Barrett, Jr.:

BAD EYE BLUES

SKINNY ANNY BLUES

PINK VODKA BLUES

DEAD DOG BLUES

Neal Barrett, Jr.

Kensington Books
Kensington Publishing Corp.

http://www.kensingtonbooks.com

KENSINGTON BOOKS are published by

Kensington Publishing Corp.
850 Third Avenue
New York, NY 10022

Kensington and the K logo Reg. U.S. Pat. & TM Off.

First Kensington Paperback Printing: June, 1997

Printed in the United States of America
10 9 8 7 6 5 4 3 2 1

FOR CHAD OLIVER,
IN LOVING MEMORY

A fine mess you've gotten us into this time, Stan . . .

One

Tuesday started off real fine, then Henry D. called about the dead electric dog. He said the dog was in the Coomers' backyard. It was barking up a storm and Max Coomer didn't care for this at all and could I come and take a look.

"It's six in the morning," I said. "I don't want to take a look. I don't want to see a dog."

"This isn't no ordinary dog, Mr. Jack," Henry said. "This here's a dead electric dog."

I thought about that. I looked at Cecily Benét the yogurt queen. She slept like a three-year-old, a pillow held tight against her breasts, fine legs tangled in the sheets, knees tucked nearly to her chin. Her long hair spread like dark seaweed about her head. She looked slick and tan all over in the dusky half-light and I knew I didn't want to go to town.

"Henry," I said, "this dog, he hit a power line or what, do you know?"

"No sir, I don't think he did," Henry said.

"He's dead, though, right?"

"Yes, sir, he is."

"And he barks. How much does he bark, Henry?"

"He barks a whole lot."

"See, here's the thing, Henry. You're not getting through to me on this. You're not communicating real well."

"Mr. Jack, I think you ought to come on in," Henry said.

"You already told me that," I said. "You don't have to

tell me that again. What I think is, you ought to brush up on your telephone skills."

I hung up and sat on the edge of the bed. Outside, past the yard and the dead peach trees, the cornfield rattled in an early-morning breeze. It was pleasantly cool, but the mercury would climb up to ninety by noon. The sky was oyster-gray, and I could feel the soft silence of the moment when the world holds its breath before it slides on into day. Dawn was on the way, but the room trapped the last of the night, turning familiar shapes into ghosts across the room. I thought if I sat very still I could hear Bob the badger tunneling for mice beneath the house.

I looked down at Cecily again. It's hard to look and not touch and I didn't even try. I kissed the little hollow in the small of her back. She smelled like dusty flowers, like a lazy afternoon.

When I kissed her, Cecily made a pleasant sleepy sound, and I thought about a pre-dawn attack. We could mess around awhile, then cook up some sausage and eggs and fried toast. Cecily's very big on fried toast. What you do, you put a dab of butter on some bread, and drop it in a skillet till it's brown. That's it, the whole thing. Cecily has written this recipe down, and passed it out to friends.

After breakfast, I thought we'd walk down to the creek. We could stand on the bridge and spit at minnows for a while. We could watch Earl Murphy not try to finish up his house. If he wasn't doing that, we could watch him not try to catch a fish.

However, none of the above came to pass, because Henry D. called about the dead electric dog. Instead of fun with Cecily Benét the yogurt queen, my day began to slide downhill.

Cecily opened one eye as I was searching for a Nike to match the one I'd found.

"Whasa-what," she said, "I thought I heard the phone."

"I'm sorry it got you up," I said. "Listen, you sure look tall when you sleep, you know that?"

"I guess I do, Jack. I'm kinda tall when I'm awake. So who was on the phone?"

"Henry D. He's got this dead electric dog. It's in the Coomers' backyard. I guess I'll have to go and see."

"What kind of dog is it, do you know?"

"Henry didn't say. If he did I don't recall."

Cecily gave me a fuzzy look. "I'd go and take a look if I were you."

She turned over then, and pulled the sheet halfway up her hips. Some girls are short when they sleep. Cecily Benét is real tall.

The room was lighter now and I could see to get dressed. I found the other Nike and pulled on yesterday's jeans. In deference to the Coomers, I decided on a clean blue shirt.

In the kitchen, I found one of last night's biscuits, and drank some ice water from the fridge. There were two pork chops in a Baggie, and I took those with me too. Cold pork chops are the key to a long and healthy life.

The sun was still low behind the trees, but the heat was already reaching out to bake the day. A crow rose out of the cornfield to complain, and three or four others joined the fray. As ever, my faded blue pickup was sorely out-classed next to Cecily's bottle-green Jag. But I was sort of semi-retired from sin and crime, and Cecily Benét owned eight hundred Yo-Ho! Yogurts nationwide. You are what you drive, she liked to say, and I hoped this wasn't so.

Alexander the cat was sleeping in my truck. I told him he'd have to move. He pretended he was dead, eyes rolled back and his tongue sticking out between his teeth. I picked him up and set him on the ground.

A terrible cry came from somewhere past the house. It

sounded very much like a chicken whose time has come. This told me Bob the badger was not pursuing mice. Earl Murphy talked me into raising chickens. I bought thirty-two, sixteen white ones and sixteen sort of red. I didn't need chickens but Earl thought I did. He said I'd have eggs all the time. This might have worked out, but every time I reached beneath the hens to get an egg, they pecked my hand. When they did that, I'd knock them off the nest with a stick. This went on for several days, and the hens began to get the idea. If they didn't lay eggs, they wouldn't get hit with a stick. I bought my eggs in town, and told Earl the chickens were doing fine. As near as I could tell, there were maybe seven left. No, make that six. Another week, and I wouldn't have to think about chickens anymore.

Let's hear it for Badger Bob.

Two

The Coomer house looked just like it did when I was growing up in Pharaoh, Texas. It probably hadn't changed a great deal since Elias Coomer built it in 1881, and moved the Coomer clan off the farm and into town. It was the kind of house the wealthy always built for themselves in those days—a three-story Southern Colonial with tall white columns and a broad front porch. The Coomer house differed from the others of its kind in one respect: Except for the stately Doric columns, it was built out of solid red brick from the Pharaoh Brickyards. Brick had made the Coomers rich, and it never occurred to Elias to build a wooden house.

I parked my blue pickup in the circular drive in the shade of ancient oaks and pecans. There were four or five cars already there. I recognized a few. They belonged to the Pharaoh inner circle, men who got invited to the annual Coomer barbecue. Sheriff Deke Glover's car was there, and two black and whites from the Highway Patrol. I wasn't real surprised to find a crowd. When Maxwell Davis Coomer says "frog," everyone in Pharaoh tends to jump a great deal.

I walked up the driveway and cut through the shrubs to the back. Max is the only man I know who still has a pair of those black-face jockeys out front. Max likes the jockeys just fine. They've been there over a hundred years, and they'll likely stay put. Lincoln freed the slaves, but he forgot to ask the Coomers how they felt about this.

The south side of the house has high French doors that lead to a big family room. I caught the glare of Mexican tile and white rattan and then someone moved across the light. I quickly looked away, thinking how it might be Millie and she'd see me standing there. This didn't make a lot of sense, but when you've thought about someone fourteen years and you get a chance to see them again, you're not sure it's what you want to do. Bringing ghosts to life isn't always such a good idea.

Beyond the swimming pool, the backyard slopes past roses and azaleas to the well-kept lawn. Everyone was gathered in a circle in front of the mammoth barbecue. They stood around shifting their feet, hands in their pockets, looking at the ground. It's the way people act when they come upon a wreck and they don't know what to do.

Someone spotted me and nudged Max Coomer, and Max turned around. Max was thirty-six. I knew because his birthday was close to mine. He no longer looked like a Pharaoh High School quarterback. He looked as if he might see forty if he never ate again. He was dressed up for golf in an apple-green shirt and enormous lemon slacks, white golf shoes and a natty white cap.

"Well, sum'bitch," Max said, holding out a beefy hand, "we can all rest easy now, boys, the town constable's done arrived."

Everyone laughed. Just enough to go along with Max. Not quite enough to show offense. I gave them all a pleasant smile. Just enough to show I didn't give a damn.

Phil Eddels, George Rainey, and Eddie Trost were there. I nodded hello. Sheriff Glover showed me half a grin, and pretended he was somewhere else.

"Henry called," I said. "Something about a problem with a dog."

"Problem my ass." Max screwed his face up in a frown. "Fuckin' *atrocity's* what it is. Who'd do a thing like that to a dog, you want to tell me that?"

"Max, I don't know what we've got here," I said. "Henry D. wasn't real clear."

"That boy's a retard. Someone ought to put him in a home."

"Henry's okay. He's a little slow is all."

Max gave me a look that showed what he thought about that. "What we got here's the work of them skinhead South Dallas niggers," he said. "Niggers got no respect for dogs."

"That's the goddamn truth," said Eddie Trost.

"This ol' boy I know in Dallas, he's got him a million-dollar home," said George. "Where it is is up there in High-land Park. This fella's Martin Creel, his daddy's got Creel Oil and Gas. Martin says this beaner of the Mes'can per-suasion is tryin' to buy the place next to his. Says the Mex has got a purple Rolls Royce and his woman don't wear a lot of clothes."

"Jesus," Eddie said.

"Max, about the dog," I said. "You want to talk about the dog?"

"He's real upset about this," Eddie said.

"As I understand, the dog's dead. Henry said we're talk-ing electric power here."

Max turned away. He took a practice drive without a club, then followed the invisible ball with his eyes. Everyone else watched it too.

"Fred, you go on down there with him," Max said. "I haven't got the heart to look at that thing anymore."

"He won't go down there anymore," Eddie said. "Max was real fond of that dog."

"This was your dog then, Max."

Max didn't answer. Fred Newcomb suddenly appeared. I hadn't noticed him before. I left the others and followed him down the lawn. George Rainey asked Max if he knew why Jews wore funny caps. Max said he'd heard it before. I'd heard it too. Max and his cronies kept up with the times. Reds had amply filled the bill for a number of years, but the Communist menace had lost a lot of drive. Now they were back to the old standard villains, always waiting in the wings.

Fred Newcomb was a dried-up scarecrow of a man in his fifties, who looked eighty-five. He'd run the Pharaoh Brickyards for the Coomers all his life. He always looked as if he were coming down with something, but everyone did if they worked for the Coomers very long.

"It's over there," Fred said, "behind the barbecue. Sheriff Glover says they did it back there because you can't see behind it from the house."

I figured Deke was right. Max Coomer's barbecue was built to cook a cow on a spit. It would shelter a family of four, and hide a whole platoon of dogs.

I followed Fred around the high brick wall. Between Henry D.'s bizarre account, and a total lack of anything from Max, I had no idea what I'd find. And when I saw it, when I came face-to-face with the dog, I could see why no one had been a lot of help. It was something you had to see yourself. And when you did, you told yourself you had to be looking at it wrong, that *nothing* could look like that.

The dog was a big black Lab. It was sitting on its haunches looking curiously intent, like the dog you used to see in the old-time phonograph ads. Only this dog didn't like music anymore. This dog was definitely dead. It was stiff as a board, and flies swarmed around its dull eyes. There was awful-looking stuff around its mouth. It was nearly nine o'clock and the day was heating up, and pretty soon this dog was going to smell. A dog that size was going to smell a whole lot.

If you wanted to piss Max off, a big dead dog in the yard would do the trick. But someone had gone to a great deal of trouble to make sure Coomer got the point. Between the dog's legs was a Radio Shack tape recorder, no larger than a cigarette pack. In front of the recorder was a small electric motor, mounted on a heavy steel plate. I don't know a thing about motors, but this one looked as if it might have come out of some common appliance you find around the house. A wire ran from the motor to an outdoor plug by the barbecue pit.

I squatted down to get a closer look. A three-inch wooden disk was attached to the motor's shaft. A small wood screw was on the face of the disk near the rim. Hooked around the screw was a stiff piece of coat-hanger wire. The other end of this wire was attached to the dog's lower jaw. The jaw had been broken so it wouldn't go stiff. The setup was simple but I figured it would do just fine. It would do what someone wanted it to do, which was drive Max Coomer up the wall.

Fred Newcomb was dancing around like he might have to pee. I knew what he wanted. He wanted me out of there, he didn't want me messing with the dog. Fred had lived in Max's shadow so long he never really felt free, even when Max wasn't there.

"Jack, now you don't want to turn the thing on," Fred said. "Max doesn't like it, he don't want it on anymore."

"Max should have thought of that," I said, "before he got me up out of bed."

"Shit." Fred ran a hand across his mouth. "I got nothing to do with this. You tell him that."

"I'll tell him, Fred. You go and sit down somewhere."

"Oh, Jesus," Fred said.

I flipped on the recorder. The tape began to bark. It was the deep, throaty bark of a very big dog, repeated over and over again. I wondered if the bark had belonged to Max's dog. It didn't much matter, but I wondered anyway.

Fred was looking somewhere else. If he didn't look, maybe he wasn't there. I snapped the switch on the motor. The wooden disk whirred into life. The coat-hanger wire bobbed up and down. With each revolution, the dog rapidly opened and shut its mouth.

It was a startling special effect. George Lucas could have

done a lot better, but it worked. I made a mental note to be nice to Henry D. Henry hadn't been confused at all. He simply told me what he saw. What we had here was a dead electric dog. A dead electric dog that barked.

I turned the dog off. I stood and looked for Fred but Fred was gone. He was wandering off across the lawn toward the house. I had probably ruined his day, but Fred was used to that. It happened all the time.

Three

George Rainey and Eddie Trost were gone, and so were the highway cops. I didn't see Max. Phil Eddels was talking to Deke. Phil was sweating like a pig, but he stood there with Deke in the sun. Anyone else would have looked for some shade, but Deke stuck it out in the heat. Shade was for fags and city folks. He had his aviator glasses and his sheriff's straw hat. Real men stood in the sun and got a stroke.

When Phil saw me, he left Deke Glover and started toward the barbecue pit.

"You got a minute, come by and have some coffee," he said. "I'll be down at the café."

"I will if I can," I said. "I don't know how long this mess is going to take."

Phil walked along beside me up the lawn, wiping his face with a red bandanna. He looked back over his shoulder and shook his head.

"By God, if that doesn't beat anything I ever saw, you know what?"

"It's something else," I said. "Where'd Max get off to, you know?"

"Had him a golfin' match. Up at River Crest in Fort Worth." Phil grinned. "That Max is a golfing fool. He's got a game 'bout every day."

"He does, huh?"

"Up at River Crest, or over in Dallas somewhere."

"What that is is bullshit," I said. "Max hasn't played two rounds of golf in his life. Max hates golf. He likes to dress up like that and go sit in the clubhouse and drink and cheat at cards. He wouldn't know a putter from a fucking hockey stick."

Phil looked disappointed. Not in Max but in me.

"Max isn't all that different than he was. He's still ol' Max. You two ought to get along."

"Phil, I get along with Max about as well as I can, okay? And you're right. He's still ol' Max all the way."

Phil thought about that. "You drop by for coffee. I mean, do it if you can."

"If I can," I said. "If I can't, we'll do it another time."

"Sure. Anytime's fine."

"Louise okay? You give her my best."

Phil looked surprised. Maybe a little hurt. "We aren't together anymore, Jack. I thought you knew that."

"I don't guess I did." I remembered as soon as I said it, but I didn't tell him that. "I've been away too long. Guess I'll have to catch up. I'm sorry about Louise."

"Hey, no problem." Phil waved off this major disaster in his life the way people are prone to do. Like it didn't mean anything at all.

"So you doing okay, then?" I said.

"Oh, sure. I'm doing fine."

"Well that's good. You want to try and get on with everything. That's what you have to do."

We didn't have anything else to say, so we stood there and looked at each other for a while.

"Listen," I said finally, "I got to talk to Deke."

"You go ahead. I don't mean to hold you up."

"You aren't holding me up any, Phil. It's real good to see you. We need to get together more."

Phil's face lit up, as if no one had told him that before.

"I'll be at the café. I'll hang around awhile."

"I'll try and see you there," I said.

I watched him walk around the side of the house. It occurred to me that Phil hadn't changed a whole lot more than Max since seventh grade. He was still a big rawboned kid at thirty-five or thirty-six. He still had a thick head of straw-colored hair, and he still got it mangled at Woody's barber shop. Most of all, he still had that totally startled look, as if he'd hatched that morning and didn't know what to make of the world.

"Way I see it," said Deke, "you got maybe two, three counts of creatin' a public nuisance. Plus you got illegal use of a dog. What you got is some really bad shit here, Jack."

"You think I do," I said.

"Well, sure. I don't want no juris-dictional dispute, you understand. Max lives in the town limits, so I figure this here is your case instead of mine."

Deke was enjoying this a lot. We both knew what the town constable did in Pharaoh was check to see the stores were locked at night, and I had Henry D. doing that. A major crime like drunks or dead dogs belonged to Deke.

"I told George Rainey to get Doc Hackley over here," Deke said. "Clyde'll get some pictures, then we'll get that dog in a freezer 'fore it swells up in the heat."

Deke looked down at the barbecue pit, then at me. "You didn't mess with anything down there. Fuck up the prints or anything?"

I had to laugh at that. "You think this joker left prints?"

"I don't know if he did or not," Deke said. "And neither do you."

He gave me that off-center smile like he always did, as if he knew something you didn't and you wouldn't find out. Deke was six feet three in his alligator boots, and most of his weight wasn't flab. The height, the smile, and a boxer's ugly face struck terror in drivers who exceeded fifty-five, but I hadn't been afraid of Deke Glover since I was ten.

"So who you think'd do this?" I said. "Max said he figured a bunch of kids. You buying that?"

Deke took off his dark glasses and wiped them on his shirt. "A kid'll maybe doo-doo on your car seat. He'll break a window or write something dirty on the hood."

"You think somebody else."

"You kill a man's dog, you're getting back for something and that's the end of that. Somethin' like this, it's not the same thing. This perpetrator here, he's got a real hard-on for Max."

"Good luck," I said. "You're talking about nearly everyone in Pharaoh County. I'd bring in the cat lovers first. Check out anyone reads *Popular Mechanics*. That ought to help narrow down your list."

"Jesus, you think this is funny?" Deke stared at me and swelled up like a toad. "What we're dealing with here is a goddamn psychopath. This person's got a de-ranged mind. That isn't real amusin' as far as I can see."

"Deke, it's a joke. Okay?"

"Fuck it is." Deke didn't want to let it go. He might have if it hadn't been me. "Some sum'bitch out there's loony in the head. That's real serious shit to me."

"All right, Deke."

"All right what?"

"All right this is serious shit. You probably got a wacko on your hands. I'm not real surprised. I grew up here too, you'll recall."

"What's that supposed to mean?"

"It means the folks around here don't have enough to do. They get a little weird sometimes."

Deke gave me his official nasty look. "Everyone's crazy but you, that it?"

"Knock it off, Deke."

"Well, is it?"

"You're maybe getting close."

"Shit. You feel that way, why the hell'd you come back?"

"It wasn't much better where I was."

"And where was that? I don't believe you ever said."

"Come out to the place sometime. We'll put a sheet on the wall and look at slides."

Deke's expression didn't change. His neck got a little redder, but that might have been the heat.

"That feeb you got working for you," he said. "You ought to get you someone else."

Deke is predictable as toast. "I take it we're discussing Henry D. Say what you got to say."

"What I'm saying is, it doesn't look good you got a *moron* on the city payroll."

"Deke, in the first place, there's plenty of precedent for that. If Henry was a moron, which he's not."

"He isn't real smart," Deke said.

"No he's not. And you've got a couple of outstanding deputies have to count on their toes to make change. Let's not get heavy into smarts."

Deke's mouth went funny and I thought we'd go at it right there. Instead, he kind of nodded to himself, like he was storing this moment away.

"It might've been better," he said, "if you'd stayed wherever you were. You might not be happy 'round here."

"You may be right," I said. "But I'll decide that, Deke. Not you."

I turned away and left him and started toward the house. I wasn't mad at Deke. Mad was twenty-five years back. When I got sick of getting beat up, and whipped his ass all over Pharaoh Junior High. Deke hadn't forgotten. The look around his mouth told me that. He simply didn't like the idea that I was as big as he was now, and maybe just as mean. He hadn't figured that last part out. He'd let me know when he did.

* * *

I meant to walk back to the car, and that's what I would have done if I hadn't seen the quick blur of motion through the tall smoke trees around the pool. The flash of color was there for a tenth of a second, maybe less than that, but the eye can be very quick indeed when there's something nice to see. I couldn't remember why I'd thought I ought to wait, why I ought to see her some other time. Another few minutes, some other time would be now, and that was close enough for me.

I walked through the shade of the trees and into the turquoise glare of the pool. She was facing me, hands on the bright chrome ladder, shaking the water from her hair as she climbed out of the pool, a tall and rangy girl with broad shoulders and lazy hipbones. Her skin was the shade of dark honey, this color a startling effect against the white string bikini that she wore without a top. She looked up and saw me and tossed me a grin, and there was the hillbilly jaw and the cornflower eyes, and life took a dizzy half-step to the right, a twenty-year lurch and then back, because she wasn't Millie now she was Millie Jean Marks at fifteen, Millie ripe as a peach, turning from a child into a girl.

"Jesus," I said, "who are you?"

A fairly dumb question. Once I bounced back from the *Twilight Zone,* I knew who she had to be.

The girl walked toward me from the pool, semi-naked and totally unconcerned. Her blue eyes flashed and she pressed her lips together and pretended not to smile.

"I'm Smoothy Coomer," she said, "who are you?"

A number of clever lines came to mind. I decided she'd heard every possible play on her name from the boys her own age. Even with her top on, this girl would leave hormonal frenzy in her wake.

"I'm Jack," I told her. "Actually it's John. John Track. But most of the time it's Jack."

"Hey. Jack Track." The girl nodded twice. Once for each name. "I never knew anybody who rhymed. That's great."

"I can't do anything about it," I said. "My father's name was Mack. His father's name was Zack. I have no idea how all this came about."

"Smoothy's not my *real* name," she said. "I guess you figured that."

"I never doubted you a minute," I said.

Smoothy giggled. "I'll bet."

"No. I was completely taken in."

"So you'll believe anything I tell you, right?"

"Not just anything, Smoothy."

"I'm nuts about the beard. Older guys, you know? Sometimes they look real stupid they got a beard. Sometimes they look real good. You're getting kind of red. Do you always sweat like that?"

"Only when I'm having a heatstroke," I said. "I can't take a lot of sun."

"Want to take a dip?"

"Thanks. I don't guess so right now."

Smoothy grinned. "Don't have a suit with you, right?"

I knew better than to try and answer that.

This wasn't real easy. It's hard to maintain a mature attitude when you're talking to a teenage girl without a top. You try not to look or make any sudden moves. She stood about three inches closer than she needed to be, and I could smell the aroma of coconut and female flesh. Smoothy didn't seem to have an idle gear. Some part of her was moving all the time. Sometimes she reached up and fluffed her hair. Sometimes she stood on one leg like a stork, the toes of the other foot flat against her knee. I couldn't tell whether all this was deliberate or not. That lazy little lop-sided smile could mean anything at all.

"My real name's Millicent," she said. "That's my mother's name, only Daddy couldn't stand two Millies in the house. He was the one called me Smoothy. Said I could get away with 'bout anything." That sly smile again. "I can, too. Well, *most* of the time. Sometimes I get caught. That's why they kicked me out of school."

"Smoothy," I said, "I'm not about to ask why."

"What if I tell you anyway?"

"Then I suppose you will."

Another thought seemed to pop into her head. She bit her lip and frowned. "You came about the dog, right?"

I told her I did.

"Yuck. That is *so* gross, you know?"

"Did you see it?"

"I *found* it," she said. Smoothy rolled her eyes in disgust. "Nobody else'd get up. Jesus. I 'bout got sick. You haven't got a joint on you, have you?"

Why was I surprised to hear this? "I've got to tell you," I said, "I am not only Jack, I am Jack the town constable. And I'm duty-bound to uphold the law."

"Oh, wow." Smoothy rolled her eyes again. "Is this a bust?"

"I can't arrest you for talking about it. Smoothy, I know you've heard this before. You shouldn't mess with that. It's not a good idea."

"Leads to the hard stuff, right?"

She turned one hip out of joint and folded her arms across her breasts, a posture of defense that told me to forget about the lecture on drugs.

I looked toward the house. "Is your mother at home? I'd like to say hello."

Smoothy shrugged. "She took off for Dallas. Soon as Daddy told her 'bout the dog. You know my mother, huh?"

"We grew up together. I haven't seen her in a while."

Smoothy cocked her head and watched me, closed one eye, then broke into a grin. "You're an old heartthrob. I bet that's what you are. I bet you thought she was me."

"Smoothy," I said, "I'm not surprised you get in trouble all the time."

"Right. See ya, Jack Track."

She gave me a wink and turned away. She knew I'd stand and watch. She had seen a lot of cop shows and knew how the street girls twitched their bottoms when they walked. She did it just right.

Jesus, I thought, I've got to get out of the sun.

Four

Pharaoh, Texas, was settled in 1872 by malcontents and failures from Tennessee. Most of these hearty pioneers left home one step ahead of unpaid debts. The first to arrive were the Coomers and the Tates. They meant to go a little farther north, but this is where Charity Coomer decided to have her third child. Much to Elias D. Coomer's delight, the child was a boy. Elias found a strange fascination in Egypt and the mysteries of the Nile. No one knew why, but he did. He had named his first two children, both girls, Isis Ann and Delta Lee. He called the boy Pharaoh, and gave the new settlement his name.

The Coomers and the Tates began to grow corn and cotton, which flourished in the rich black soil. Soon, both of these families discovered that nature had left greater treasures in the land. The Coomers found endless deposits of clay that were perfect for making brick. The Tates found immense beds of gravel, ideal for county roads, though no one guessed this at the time.

Other families arrived, including my great-grandparents, in 1878. Pharaoh Coomer grew up to marry Nancy Tate. Pharaoh Brick built thousands of Texas homes, and the Coomers grew rich. The Tates turned out to be poor businessmen, showing more talent for drink and horse racing than trade. This didn't matter, since the Coomers had married in and taken charge.

A generation later, Tate gravel covered hundreds of miles

of Texas roads. The brickyards continued to grow. The Coomers branched out into cattle and real estate. A piece of worthless land some fool Tate had purchased near Midland and Odessa turned out to be resting on a vast pool of oil.

By the time I came along, Pharaoh, Texas, was fading as a town. It would have died if it hadn't been the Pharaoh County Seat, and the home of the Pharaoh Brickyards. There was one main street around the square, with a drugstore, five-and-dime, grocery, and combination hardware and funeral home. The train went through but seldom stopped. The Coomers got richer, and everybody else hung on.

I went to school and played football with Max, Deke, Eddie and the rest. We played Italy and Red Oak, Maypearl and Ferris. We usually got our tails whipped. Maybe the curse of ancient Egypt had fallen on our town. At any rate, the Pharaoh Asps seldom managed to field a decent team, a tradition that stands to this day.

All the good parties were held at the big Coomer house. Max wasn't a total asshole at the time. Still, there was always that invisible line that the rest of us couldn't cross. Max was filthy rich, and we were middle class down to white-trash poor. The only thing we all shared in common was an undying love for Millie Marks, the prettiest girl in Pharaoh County, and possibly the state.

Everyone wanted her but Max Coomer won. They went together all through school, and married the day after Max finished Texas A&M. The prettiest girl and the richest boy in town. No one else had a chance. Max worshiped Millie Marks, and Millie never looked at anyone else.

Except for me. I don't know how it happened, but it did. It was my first encounter with lust, and Millie's too. Max Coomer got her, but Millie was mine for one glorious summer afternoon. It happened that once and never happened again.

And now there was Smoothy, who looked so much like Millie it was hard to avoid immoral thoughts. She was clearly Millie's daughter, but she was something else besides. At Smoothy's tender age, Millie had had an innocent animal grace, a sexual presence as natural as breathing in and out. She drove a generation of Pharaoh men and boys to self-abuse, but she couldn't help that.

Smoothy was different. Smoothy knew exactly what she had, and what all the parts were for. I thought it was truly a wonder that she didn't look a thing like Max. Not anything at all. I decided maybe Millie's genes had made a deal with Max: I do the outside, you do the rest. We'll do a little sexpot that looks like me, and give her a shitty attitude.

Driving back to the farm, it occurred to me that Pharaoh hadn't changed a great deal. Max was pretty much the way he'd always been. All Phil had done was get tall. Deke the school bully grew up to be a cop. I didn't know about Millie, but I was willing to bet she was the same.

Maybe I'd changed more than the rest. I'd gone away for fourteen years and come back. I'd put on twenty hard pounds, and done some things I'd like to forget. I'd lived another life and had a name that wasn't Jack. I hid my face behind a beard, because I couldn't let anyone remember where they'd seen that face before.

What I wanted to be was Jack Track. Jack Track who likes to watch the grass grow and listen for Badger Bob. And, whenever she has the time to drop around, make some fried toast for Cecily Benét. When I wanted excitement, I could maybe hit a chicken with a stick.

I was nearly back home before I remembered Phil was probably still at Audie's Café. With Millie and Smoothy and Cecily Benét in mind, it was easy to forget about Phil. I forgot to pick up a loaf of bread. I almost forgot about the dead electric dog.

Five

Around noon, Cecily and I walked down from the house along the narrow dirt road to the creek. The sun bored through the canopy of big pecans and oaks, trees a hundred years old or maybe more. Earl was building his house on the rise to the left of the old iron bridge. At least that's what he said. What he was doing was accumulating neat stacks of lumber and brick, shingles and shiny copper pipe. The only thing he'd actually built was a shed to house his awesome collection of power tools: drills, ripsaws, band saws, the works—one of everything the Black & Decker folks had ever made. I worried a lot about Earl's power tools. If he ever turned them on, I was certain he'd saw himself in half.

In the meantime, he cooked on a camp stove and lived in his white Aston-Martin Lagonda. If you really had to rough it, this was the way to go. I knew the first "U.S.-legal" Lagonda had come into this country in 1983. I knew because Earl had told me several times. The asking price then was a hundred and fifty grand. God knows what it is now. This one was worth a little less, because Earl kept it right beneath a cottonwood tree, and it was covered with bird shit all the time. I told him he ought to take care of this very fine machine. Earl said a car was just a car. This totally appalled the lovely Cecily Benét. Cecily believes maltreatment of cars is the same as child abuse.

* * *

The first thing I did when we reached Earl's unbuilt house was stop and rip the mailbox off its stand. The second thing I did was take it out on the bridge and toss it in the creek.

"Oh dear," Cecily said, "we're not going to start this, are we?"

"Damn right we are," I said.

Earl was watching all this from a worn-out camp chair by his car. He didn't say a thing, he just watched. Cecily walked up to the site, and I brought up the rear. Earl stood and gave Cecily a hug.

"You look especially lovely today," Earl said. "You want to go overseas or what? Stockholm's nice, unless you'd rather go to France."

Cecily grinned. "I'd love to, Earl, but I've got a bunch of business stuff to do."

"She's busy," I said. "She's got a lot of stuff to do."

"I was speaking to the lady," Earl said. "I don't believe I spoke to you." He looked toward the creek. "I will have you arrested for that."

"You do that," I said. "You try and put it back up, I'll tear it down again."

"It is going back up," Earl said.

"You two don't mind," Cecily said, "I'll go and get a cold drink."

"There's some Taittinger in the fridge," Earl said. "There's some Pepsi there too."

"Pepsi's fine."

She walked off toward the power-tool shed. Earl and I watched her go.

"I see the house is coming right along," I said. "I don't believe I've seen that stack of pipe. That pipe's new since I was here."

Earl looked straight ahead. "Is this your house?"

"No, this is your house. My house is back up the hill."

"You going to live here at all?"

"No, I'm not."

"Then shut the fuck up about my house."

"I like the weathered-wood effect. Of course, some people, they put the wood *on* the house first. This is probably something new that I don't know about."

"There's a lot of things you don't know about," Earl said.

"That's very true," I said. "Proper care of cars, I don't know a thing about that."

"You want a cold drink?"

"Some of that champagne would be nice."

"Would if I was offering you some."

"Pepsi's fine," I said.

Earl looks like a young George Foreman, if George were five-three and weighed a hundred and twenty-five. He has sad beagle eyes and no hair, and skin the color of polished teak. Today he was wearing bib overalls, a custom-made shirt, snake boots and an old straw hat. He came back and sat in his chair and handed me a drink. His was in a glass of ice. Mine was in the can.

"Listen," I said, "I know you don't care, but I really want to talk about this. You got to cool it with the box. It is simply not right. And it's real embarrassing to me."

"It's my house," Earl said. "It is my protest movement, not yours."

"It's my road," I said. "And it's not a protest. It's racist is what it is. See, it's a protest thing to you, but other folks see it, they get the wrong idea."

"It is my mailbox," Earl said.

"I don't give a shit it's your box. You want to say something, say something else. 'The Nigger of Wall Street,' it doesn't look right."

Earl smiled at that. " 'The Afro-American of Wall Street' just doesn't have a ring to it, Jack."

"What about Earl Murphy, Route 6? That's what a lot of people do. They put their name on the box. It's a real common practice everywhere."

"Most folks got no imagination at all," Earl said.

* * *

There was no use arguing with Earl. He made sense most of the time, but when it came to the mailbox he was totally obsessed. Three generations of Murphys had worked on the Track family farm, living in the shack that used to stand on the site where Earl was building his house. We played together by the creek when we were kids, but our worlds were far apart. We both endured being poor. Earl and his family put up with being black.

Earl made it out of Pharaoh County, the only member of his family who ever did. Now, though it certainly didn't show, he probably had more money than anyone in town except Max. The mailbox was his payback, his own peculiar way of flaunting his success to the white folks who'd plagued his early years. Maybe I didn't blame him, but I wasn't about to tell him that. He'd keep putting up the mailbox. I'd keep tearing it down. In between bouts, we'd cool a case of Dortmunder Kronen in the creek and get whacked.

I'd already told Cecily about my adventures in town. At any rate, the part about the dog. I left out the Smoothy part. Cecily made a big thing about our open, adult relationship, but I'd noticed that she didn't care to hear about any other women in my life, past or present tense. Smoothy wasn't either one, but why mention that I'd had a close encounter with a teenage girl without a top?

Earl was silent for a while when I finished the story of Max Coomer's dog. He looked off toward the creek and waved gnats out of his drink.

"That is a most bizarre event," he said finally. "I don't guess I ever heard of anything like it before."

"Well, I think you'd remember if you did," I said. "Something like that."

"You say it barks and everything."

"Smells bad, too. 'Course a dog that big, your bigger dogs tend to smell pretty bad when they're alive."

"I bet old Max didn't care for this incident at all."

"Max took personal affront."

"Max takes personal affront, it's July, he thinks it ought to be May."

"If you're saying he likes his own way, that's nothing real new. He's kind of used to that."

"About time he had a little trouble in his life," Earl said. "Everybody's been getting *his* share."

A trace of a smile crossed Earl's face. It was easy to see that he took some pleasure in Max's distress. That, and something else. More than Max's dog was on his mind.

Earl caught me looking at him. He studied the ice in his drink.

"I don't much care for Coomers," he said. "I guess you know that."

"I expect I do. The Coomers have always been just a little right of the Klan. Which is not real unique around here."

Earl shook his head. "It was the Coomers who handed out the jobs. You're black in Pharaoh County, mostly you worked in the Coomers' brickyards. At twice the hours and half the pay. My people didn't have to do it. I know plenty who did."

"Some of 'em still in Pharaoh, no doubt."

Earl frowned at that. "You saying what?"

"I'm not saying anything. Max did. First thing he said was, South Dallas niggers killed his dog."

"He said that."

"I take that back. He said South Dallas *skinhead* niggers did his dog."

"An interesting combination," Earl said.

"I thought it was. Deke Glover seemed to like the idea. Of course Deke likes just about anything Max Coomer says." I stopped to sip my drink. "Deke and I almost went at it, by the way. We will sometime. I just don't know when."

"When you do, take an ax handle along," Earl said.

"Why's that?"

"Because Deke's got one in his car."

"How you know he does?"

"Everyone in Pharaoh County isn't white, they know about Deke. Deke likes to discuss the situation awhile, before he takes you in."

"Jesus," I said, "is that true? Hell, I guess it is. And no one's done anything about it?"

"Someone maybe is," Earl said.

"Like who?" I caught a slight glint in Earl's eyes. "You mean you, right? You're doing something. You want to tell me what?"

"Did I say me?"

"Not exactly, no."

"That's right," Earl said.

I thought about that. Earl wasn't big on brag. Earl always did what he said, he simply took his own sweet time. Like building the house. When he was ready, then he would, when he'd thought it all out. When he knew exactly where every nail and board would be. I was sure this was how he'd made a fortune on Wall Street, taking his time while a lot of other people hurried up and went broke. That's the way it was when we were kids. My fishing line was always tangled up. Earl's was always ready to go. If Earl had it in for Deke Glover, Deke was in very deep shit. Earl could wait. He might do something tomorrow. He might do something next year. I was glad this skinny little short guy wasn't mad at me.

We talked about the dead electric dog for a while, and who'd do a thing like that. Earl agreed with me. It was easier to figure who wouldn't like to get back at Max than who would. I said it was getting time for lunch, and Earl said he thought it was amazing that I always showed up in time for meals. I said this wasn't true at all. Earl said since I'd brought along Cecily Benét, he'd whip up a Veal Papillote and Mushrooms Florentine. I said that would be fine. Either that, or I'd treat us all to peanut butter and white bread up at my place.

Cecily appeared on the bridge, tossing rocks at something in the creek. She was wearing a very skimpy pink T-shirt, and cutoffs that were likely against the law.

"That is one fine-looking lady," Earl said. "I got to say that."

"Watch it," I told him. "That's a white woman you're talking about."

"I'm willing to overlook it," Earl said.

Cecily had to fly to L.A., so we said good-bye with the shades pulled down against the afternoon sun, the air turned up to high. It ended too soon, as it always does when you know someone has to go, and by six I was alone.

Earl's fine lunch was still with me, so I opened a can of soup, made a grilled cheese, sat out on the porch for a while and watched the night and went to bed. Cecily's perfume was on the pillow, and I went to sleep thinking of clever ways to keep the scent. Science could work on these things if they would.

In the morning, I got up early and drove to Waxahachie in Ellis County, and ate breakfast there. I read the *Dallas Morning News* until I lost count of murders, drug busts and rapes, then I drove over to the hospital to see my Uncle Will.

Will was the only surviving relative that I ever really wanted to see again, and the reason I was temporary Town Constable of Pharaoh Township. I took the job because Uncle Will had asked me to, and I didn't have the heart to turn him down. He was seventy-nine and he'd held this dubious post for forty years, until he had a massive stroke. The stroke came from age. It wasn't job-related stress. Stress on that job wouldn't kill you in four hundred years.

Will was in fairly good shape, which meant he knew who I was and didn't sleep all the time. I told him everything was fine. I didn't mention the dead electric dog. I did not tell him that I'd hired Henry D., that he was checking doors at night instead of me. Will wouldn't understand that the job he'd done with pride, dressing up every day in a black suit and tie, could be handled by a handicapped kid. He had enough problems as it was. He didn't need to know about that.

By the time I got to Pharaoh, it was five. I meant to pick up a few groceries and drive back to the farm. I meant to see if the drugstore had some new paperbacks or magazines. I never got to either place. Instead, I ran into Millie for the first time in fourteen years. She came out of the courthouse, wearing a pale blue dress. She saw me and waved, and ran toward me across the green lawn.

I learned two things, and the first was no surprise: One, she was even more beautiful than I'd imagined she would be. And two, I learned what she was doing downtown. She had come to see Deke, and tell him that the girl who came to clean at the Coomers' had apparently disappeared. She wasn't home or anywhere. She had started off to work that morning, then dropped right out of sight in the full light of day.

Six

Smoothy had hit it on the nose. My heart still throbbed for Millie Jean. I know it sounds silly as hell, but that's the way it was. The moment we came together on the lawn, I knew I hadn't wasted my youth on carnal thoughts. The thrill was still there.

And, as an extra added bonus, it was very clear that Millie felt it too.

This was a big surprise to me. Except for our moment of lust some twenty years before, she had never given any hint at all that she thought of me as more than just a friend. Our kiss on the courthouse lawn said this simply wasn't so. That is *not* the way you kiss a friend. You do not press your body parts together like you're sweat-hand dancing in a corner somewhere, but that's exactly what she did.

Jesus, I thought, what's happening here? It's Archie and Veronica, together again at last. Let's run down to the malt shop and talk about the big spring hop.

Which is exactly what we did, or close enough. When we got through the part about how fine we looked and how long it had been, we walked across the street to Buddy's for a Coke. It was the same drugstore we'd all flocked to after school when we were kids. The same soda fountain—possibly the last soda fountain in the world. It had marble-top counters and white tile floors. The floors smelled freshly mopped. There were wire-back chairs and a lazy fan turning overhead. The shelves were dark wood, and they still held remedies no one had ever heard of before.

With the fading summer day and Millie Coomer by my side, I was approaching nostalgia overload. Any moment now, LBJ and James Dean would appear. The TV up front jerked me back to the nineties with a scene from Bangladesh.

"You 'bout had me with the beard," Millie said. "You sure look different, Jack."

"So how come you knew me?" I said.

"Because you look just the same. You haven't changed a bit." Millie gave a nervous little laugh. "Lord, does that make any sense or what?"

"Not much. I didn't have any trouble with you. You're just the way you always were."

"Bullshit, Jack." She shook her head and lit another cigarette. She seemed to smoke a lot. I had an idea she didn't do this all the time. She crushed out her butts about as fast as she got them lit. The rest of the time she played with that little blue cellophane strip, or turned the pack at one angle, then the next.

"I'm not just saying that," I said. "You look the same to me. Maybe not Millie Jean Marks at fifteen, but close enough."

"I've changed a lot more than you think," Millie said. "I'm not that Millie anymore. I'm not anywhere close."

It wasn't simply what she said. It was the expression that went with the words, the sudden turning away, the quick look of desperation in her eyes. She was there, with me, and for a moment she was somewhere else. I felt as if I'd gotten a glimpse of something I wasn't meant to see.

"Millie," I said, "you okay?"

" 'Course I'm okay." She looked right at me and forced a smile. She reached across the table and squeezed my hand. "I'm a little worried is all."

"I can see you are."

"About Emma, I mean. I am real concerned about her, Jack. People don't just up and disappear. Not people like Emma Stynnes. That girl is solid as a rock. She wouldn't just—wander off somewhere."

That wasn't it, but I decided not to pry. Millie was worried about her maid, but whatever was eating at her, it wasn't Emma Stynnes. And whatever it was, it wasn't my business to try and drag it out.

"What did Deke say? He give you any help?"

"You know Deke." Millie shook her head. "Deke said *niggers* are going to take off now and then. He said that's what they do."

"Good old compassionate Deke."

"Deke is Deke. You can't expect anything else."

"Huh-unh, that's no answer, damn it. That isn't any help."

I was a little surprised at how quickly my anger rushed up out of nowhere at the mention of his name. I was letting this bastard get to me, and I didn't care for that. Maybe it came from something Earl had said. The fact that I knew how Deke handled Pharaoh County's blacks. Or maybe I just didn't *like* the son of a bitch.

Millie was a little surprised but not much.

"You and Deke still close as ever, huh?"

"I am getting tired of this—everything's okay because it's always been this way," I said. "Deke is Deke and that makes it all right."

"Hey, I didn't say it was okay, hon."

"I know you didn't. But that's the way it is, here in ol' Pharaoh, Texas."

Millie gave me a look. "You've been away awhile, Jack."

"I guess I have. You want another Coke?"

Millie said she did. I stood and walked over to the counter. The lady behind the soda fountain gave me a sour look. She knew who Millie was. She knew I wasn't Max. Word would soon spread through Pharaoh at twice the speed of light.

I watched Millie Coomer while the Witch of the East took her own sweet time with our drinks. I wondered what was going through Millie's head. You see someone like Millie Jean and it's hard to imagine that trouble could intrude upon her life. It is foolish to believe that the rich and the beautiful don't have problems like ordinary folks, but our culture has set them apart, and we have come to believe our own myths and fairy tales.

Maybe I was still too awed at just seeing her again, to remember she was real. I can't say she hadn't changed because she had. The last time I saw her she was just twenty-one. Now she was nearly thirty-five. Still, the years had stolen nothing from her. Time had taken youthful good looks and turned them into full-blown beauty. She still had that incredible skin, a willowy figure, and the legendary Millie Jean legs. Nature had given Millie a lot of imperfections, mixed them all up, and stuck them back together in a manner that put all the Miss Whatever contestants to shame. Taken one by one, all of Millie's features were flawed. Her china-blue eyes were a little far apart. Her button nose was too small and her mouth was too wide for her prominent Texas jaw. Bring all of this together and you had something wondrous and rare. There simply aren't any more Millies anywhere.

Correction. There was a fair-enough copy prancing about the Coomer pool. But Smoothy wasn't Millie, she was Millie Coomer's daughter, and in spite of the way she looked, she was only fifteen. Or so I kept telling myself, as I tried to put unwholesome thoughts aside.

I took our drinks back to the table. Millie was watching the fan turn around, crushing out another cigarette.

"How's Max," I said, for lack of anything to say. "He doing all right?"

I didn't really care how Max was. If Max took off for Mars, that was okay with me.

"Max is fine," Millie said.

"He in town, or what?"

"It's still daylight. I imagine he's whackin' a golf ball around somewhere. That's what Max likes to do."

Millie stared off into the distance. It was fairly clear she didn't care to talk about Max any more than I did. I thought about that. Maybe things weren't going well. Maybe that's why Millie seemed strained. I tried to think good thoughts, and wish their marriage well. I guess I didn't try very hard because nothing came to mind.

"I understand you met Smoothy," Millie said. "I understand she didn't have a top."

This from left field somewhere, catching me completely off guard. Hesitation is a sure sign of guilt, so I answered as quickly as I could.

"Yes. That's right," I said. "We sure did. Yesterday. Now that you mention it, she didn't have a top."

That's how it came out, totally transparent and too late to think how I could have said it right.

"My Lord, Jack." Millie sighed and looked at the ceiling. "You don't have to act like I caught you with the cookies. I *know* how she looks, and I know how she acts in front of men."

"She's a very, uh—precocious young lady," I said.

"Precocious, my ass." Millie's eyes turned nearly black. "You want to call gettin' kicked out of every school there is *precocious,* I guess that's what she is. Max has spoiled that child rotten. That's what's wrong with Smoothy, you want to know. He thinks acting like a little hooker is *cute.*"

"I guess fathers have got a kind of blind spot, it comes to their daughters," I said.

"Max isn't blind, he's just dumb," Millie said. "That girl's got a criminal mind. Wait'll she holds up a 7-Eleven store. See how her daddy likes that."

Millie paused, closed her eyes a moment and shook her head.

"Christ, Jack, you don't want to hear all this. I get goin' on Smoothy sometimes and I don't know how to stop."

"Hey, it's okay," I said. "And I don't guess anyone can blame you for being upset. What with everything sort of hitting you at once. This stuff with your daughter's enough, without that business with the dog. And now Emma Stynnes on top of that. I haven't had a chance to say it, but I'm sorry about the dog."

"Me and the dog weren't close," Millie said. "The dog belonged to Max." She decided that didn't sound right. "I'm sorry what happened, I don't mean it like that."

"I know what you mean."

Millie shuddered. "God, that's a sick thing to do. Do something like that to a dog."

"There's all kinds of people," I said. "Some of them haven't got their heads on straight."

Millie made a quick, dismissive gesture that told me she didn't want to talk about dogs. She glanced down at the table and played with her cigarette pack. When she looked up again, the tiny lines of strain around her mouth had disappeared.

"And how 'bout you, Jack," she said. "You back to stay or what?"

"Maybe so," I said. "I'd like to think I am."

"I guess it's kinda dumb to ask what you been doing with yourself. It isn't like you've been gone overnight."

"I hopped around some. Saw a lot of places I thought I ought to see. You get there and find out it's mostly like where you were before."

"You going to say where?"

"Now that'd take a while."

"Uh-huh." Millie showed me half a smile. "That is a polite way of sayin' bug off, Millie Jean."

"It's not like that at all."

"Okay."

"Well, it's not. Really. It isn't that interesting, you want to know the truth."

I didn't want to get into this, but I didn't know how to get out. Millie grinned and let me hang there awhile, then she reached across the table and squeezed my hand.

"I'm glad you're back, all right? I really am, Jack."

"It's good to see you, Millie Jean. It's been way too long."

"I'll call you, all right? We'll get together and I won't pry into your dark and lurid past. That okay with you?"

She was still holding on to my hand, and the look that she gave me went all the way down to my toes. What it said was her kiss on the courthouse lawn was no mistake. She wanted me to be real clear about that.

"I'd—like that," I said, "that'd be fine."

Or maybe I said something else, I don't recall. I know I said something like the fan isn't working real well in here and it probably never did. Millie said she hadn't noticed, that it seemed just right to her. She said she had some things to do, and I walked her to the door.

"I'll drive out by Emma Stynnes's place," I told her. "See if I can learn anything. If I do I'll let you know."

"I'd appreciate that," Millie said. She gave me a mischievous wink. "I'll tell Smoothy you said hello."

"You do that."

"Smoothy thinks you're pretty cute. She's crazy about the beard."

"Smoothy's got taste."

I looked at her another long moment. The afternoon sun turned her skin to dusty gold. "She'll likely straighten out some, Millie. Kids that age, they do a lot of crazy stuff."

"What age is that?" Millie said.

"She's what—fifteen, sixteen?"

"Smoothy's twelve, Jack."

"Holy shit . . ."

"My sentiments exactly," Millie said.

Seven

Millie had told me Emma Stynnes was twenty-five, un-married, and lived with her mother. She had worked for the Coomers seven years. She walked to work every morning, cleaned, cooked the evening meal, and left around five. This morning she hadn't shown up. She didn't have a phone, so Millie drove out to her place around noon. Emma's mother said she'd left home at seven like she always did. She seemed more irritated than alarmed, and Millie thought Mrs. Stynnes might have some idea where Emma was—that there might be a man involved.

I asked Millie why she thought that and she said she didn't know, she just did. Still, she didn't think Emma would run off with a man. That simply wasn't Emma's way. Millie told Mrs. Stynnes she'd ask the sheriff for help, and Mrs. Stynnes said no, she didn't want to do that. She'd ask around first. She was certain that Emma would show up or call real soon.

Emma didn't. Her mother called Millie from a neighbor's phone a little after four. She had checked everywhere. No one knew where Emma was. Millie said the woman sounded scared. That's when Millie went to see Deke Glover. And, a little after that, we met on the courthouse lawn and did our big reunion act. Passion on a Pharaoh afternoon.

It was hard to get her out of my mind. She had been there for quite some time, and unrequited lust has a way of hanging on through the years. Okay, so we'd requited that once, if that's a word, twenty years before. That only added fuel to the fire, and Millie's drugstore look said things could heat up again soon.

I wondered how I felt about that. It gets a little scary when your dreams come home to roost. I wasn't sure I was ready for a rich and steamy fantasy life. Besides, I cared for Cecily a lot. And, moral issues aside, I didn't know about Millie, but Cecily was a damn good shot.

Pharaoh's black community was on the north side of town. Seven blocks down Fifth, the white folks' houses came abruptly to a halt, along with sidewalks, streetlights, and Fifth Street itself. A quarter mile down a dirt road was a collection of clapboard houses that rambled down the slope toward Antelope Creek. The creek had dried up, and was full of rusted-out appliances and bald-face tires. Many of the houses were empty, and some had simply given up the ghost and collapsed. Up until the fifties, there were three hundred families living here. Since then, any black family that could possibly get out of Pharaoh had gotten up and gone. Max Coomer blamed this exodus on "niggers who didn't know their place." In other words, people who could get decent jobs somewhere else and didn't have to work for him.

I didn't have any trouble finding Emma Stynnes's house. Deke's car was parked out front. This surprised me a little, then it struck me that he wasn't there for Emma, he was there because a Coomer was involved.

The house was well-kept, neat and freshly painted. There were flowers in pots on the porch. The porch looked cool, but I decided to wait by the car. I didn't mind aggravating Deke, but if I wanted him to tell me anything it wouldn't hurt to pretend to be polite.

At first I thought Deke was in the house. Then, a few moments later, I saw him walking toward me down the street. He looked unhappy and hot. He glared at me from under his broad-brimmed hat.

"Afternoon," he said. "What the fuck you doin' here, Jack?"

"Nice to see you too," I said. "Find out anything?"

Deke lit a thin cigar and nodded vaguely down the street.

"Hasn't anyone seen her, don't know where she is. Or that's what they all say. Niggers won't tell you nothing. They all got something to hide. So you playing town marshal or what?"

"Just keeping my hand in," I said.

Deke frowned at that. He wasn't going to push it, but he let me know he didn't approve.

"Nobody knows anything, huh?"

"Shit, how do I know they do or not?" Deke studied the end of his cigar. "What I figure, this Emma took off with some buck. Picked her up this morning and took her up to Dallas somewhere. She goes with this boy named Harlan Duke. I know him. Works at an Exxon over at Waxahachie. I called over there. He's at work and don't know where she is. So it's likely some other ol' boy."

"But you don't know that."

Deke glared. "No, Jack, I don't know that. I don't know if it's going to rain, but I'm pretty sure it's not."

"I understand she's pretty steady," I said. "This doesn't seem like something she'd do."

"Where'd you hear that?"

"I asked around. That's what people say." He'd hear about my afternoon with Millie soon enough. I didn't intend to give him any help.

"Folks are going to tell you what they figure you want to hear," Deke said. "Someone thinks they got to drag-ass down to the courthouse awhile, they'll tell you most any kind of shit, it'll make you go away."

I thought Deke was likely right about that. No one likes

to mess with the law until someone swipes their color TV.
Then they want a cop right on the spot.

I looked past the side of Emma's house. The lady who
lived behind her was hanging out her wash. Everything the
family owned was red. Red sheets, red towels, red underwear. I had an aunt who did that, only everything she had
was blue.

"You don't think this business with Emma's got anything
to do with Max's dog, do you?" I said. "I mean, both coming so close together and all."

Deke looked at me like I'd suddenly grown antlers on
my head. "What are you talking about? Why the *fuck* would
I think anything like that?"

"Boy, I don't know, Deke. Maybe because they happened
a day apart, and they both have something to do with
Max?"

"A nigger maid takin' off's got nothing to do with that
dog." Deke did something with his teeth. It might have been
a snarl. It probably worked if he stopped you for going
ninety-five. "And don't you go spreadin' crap like that
around town. You'll get everybody worked up and I don't
need that."

"I'm not spreading it around," I said. "I'm asking what
you think."

"You get my answer straight enough?"

"I guess I did. See, what I was thinking was the last
crime wave in Pharaoh was Mrs. Deaver's runaway cat. Now
that's an isolated event. Then these two things come along
a day apart. Someone kills the Coomer dog, and the girl
who works for them disappears. If I was an ace crime
fighter, I could see this was just a coincidence. I understand
it better now. What I did I lost my head."

Deke stretched himself a good inch, the way he does
when he thinks about taking me apart. The urge seemed to
pass, and he settled for another nasty grin.

"Why don't you go check a few doors somewhere," he said. "Go help that re-tard of yours."

"I thought I'd have a word with Mrs. Stynnes while I'm here."

"You thought wrong, then. She's over staying with a friend who's got a phone." Deke looked straight at me, and his mouth twisted up like he'd tasted something bad. "You see that rich nigger friend of yours around, you tell him to keep away from me. You tell him that."

"Just who are we talking about?"

"Who the fuck you think? How many rich niggers you know in this town?"

"What did he do, try to vote? By God, we'll put a stop to that."

Deke looked disgusted, then turned and stomped off toward his car. Halfway there he stopped and faced me again. "You tell him. He messes with me, I'll slap his black ass in jail."

I watched him drive off. He left a quarter inch of rubber on the road. I wondered what Earl had done to get Deke fired up. It wouldn't take much, I knew that. In Deke's mind, there were two things worse than being black. One was being rich and black both. The other was being rich and black, and driving a car that cost more than Deke's house.

Deke was itching to take Earl down. He'd had his eye on Earl since Earl came to town. I knew Earl Murphy, and I knew that he'd never give an inch, and that worried me a lot. Deke would lie in wait for him and stop him some night, then make up a reason why. Earl wouldn't wait for the ax handle Deke kept in his car. Earl would pull out the .44 Magnum he kept beneath the seat, and shoot Deke Glover in the head.

Earl knew I'd seen the gun. He told me he kept it there for snakes. A gun that big would give a dinosaur pause. Earl knew that, and I knew it too. He didn't keep it there for snakes. He kept it in the car because he knew as well as Deke who he was: A rich black man with a fancy foreign car. I didn't like to think about it, but they still give prizes in certain parts of Texas if you bring in a trophy like that.

Eight

When I got back to the farm, I stopped by Earl's but Earl wasn't there. He was off somewhere in his bird-shit car. Earl didn't leave home a lot, and I didn't much like him being gone when there was clearly some trouble between him and Deke, but I couldn't do a thing about that.

I read for a while, and listened for his car passing by. I fell asleep about one. At nine in the morning I drove by his place and he still wasn't there. What the hell, I thought, Earl Murphy's a full-grown man, he can drive off anywhere he wants. Still, it pissed me off some that he played everything so goddamn close to the vest. Sometimes that's a good idea. And sometimes it's not.

A little after ten, I stopped by Doc Ben Hackley's to see what he'd learned about the dead electric dog. Ben said Deke had told him not to let me see anything, but Ben didn't like Deke Glover any more than I did.

The dog had been killed with poisoned meat. Ben said whoever had done it set the dog on its haunches like we found it, real soon after it died. The dog had been kept in a freezer overnight, before the perpetrator hauled it back to Max's lawn. Ben said the dog killer had done a good job, cutting the masseter muscle behind the jaw so the mouth would hang loose just right. He also said this didn't mean a thing, that you wouldn't have to be a surgeon or a vet to figure out something like that.

Ben had talked to his nephew, who worked as a part-time deputy for Deke, and learned they hadn't found any prints. The tape recorder was an item you could buy anywhere. The motor came from a blender four or five years old. In other words, no one knew a thing that would tell us who had killed Max's dog.

One of Pharaoh's charms is its leisurely style of life. The town went to sleep about 1956, and it's been that way ever since. No one seems to mind. Lethargy takes the pressure off the local businessmen. There is limited trade to be had, and there's no use scrambling about for any more. If you've made it in Pharaoh, Texas, you can sit around and wait. The customers know you're there. If they want anything, they'll drop in.

So while the Dallas wheeler-dealers had been up since dawn courting cardiac arrest, Pharaoh's movers and shakers were still drinking coffee at Audie's Café. It was ten forty-five. At eleven, they would take a work break and get back in time for lunch.

I pulled up a chair between Billy McKenzie and Eddie Trost. The conversation lagged long enough to acknowledge I was there. Roy Burns looked slightly out of sorts. I had cut into the middle of his speech and he didn't care for that. Lawyers don't talk or discuss. Lawyers make a speech. Say hello to Roy, and you'd better be ready for a major address on the topic of the day.

"It's right clear to me what happened," Roy said, taking up where he'd left off. "The boy got scared, or maybe him and the girl did both. He picks her up and they scat. The cops'll spot 'em pretty quick. They'll run into Dallas and shoot up in a cheap motel. Niggers got to have that dope. I expect the boy'll stop and rob a store."

"That's the thing," Eddie said. "They got to have that dope."

Roy gave Eddie a sober look. "That's what I said. I just said that."

"I know you did," Eddie said. "You said they got to stop and shoot some dope."

Roy shook his head. He'd never liked Eddie Trost because Eddie liked him. That's the way a lawyer is. You act too friendly, they know you're not up to any good. Eddie didn't just like Roy. Eddie liked everyone. He ran Trost's Hardware & Funeral Home, and his business was making lots of friends. He didn't look like he belonged in such a trade. He should have been cadaverous and grim; instead, he was chubby and happy as a clam. Roy wouldn't go into Eddie's store. If he wanted a hammer or a nail, he'd pick them up somewhere else. He said Eddie Trost would get his business in the end, and he wouldn't spend a dime before then.

"Why'd he have to kill that dog?" Phil said. "That's a goddamn awful thing to do. Go in a man's yard and kill his dog."

"Maybe it wasn't entirely him," Roy said. "Maybe he did it, it was Emma's idea all along. She got pissed off at the Coomers somehow, she had this ol' boy do the dog."

Phil nodded. "She couldn't hang around after that. She got scared and took off quick."

Phil glanced at George Rainey, then at me, as if he might have something to say. Whatever it was, he decided to keep it to himself.

"Damn right," Roy said. "That's the way it had to be. They took off and ran. That's what a nigger's going to do. A nigger's going to run ever' time."

"Bull*shit*," said Billy McKenzie. He set down his coffee cup. "You don't know what the fuck you're jabberin' about, Roy Burns. You're just blowing to hear yourself talk."

Roy Burns laughed, and so did everyone else. Roy and

Billy had a friendly running feud. Insulting each other was a part of their everyday routine.

"Why don't you go sell some poor sum'bitch one of those lemons you got on the lot?" Roy said. "Why don't you go and do that?"

"Like the one you sold me," Phil said.

Billy stared at Phil. "There is not a thing wrong with that car a little pre-ventive maintenance wouldn't cure. That's what's wrong with that car. It isn't nothing more'n that."

Roy grinned and nudged George Rainey. "You're supposed to put *oil* in 'em, Phil. Every hundred thousand miles, whether she needs it or not."

Roy's remark brought another swell of laughter to the table. The color rose to Phil's face, then he forced a weak grin. It always worked out that way. Roy and Billy would start on each other, then gang up on someone else.

Annie Keller waddled around the counter and brought me a cup. She refilled everyone else's, and Billy McKenzie told a semi-lewd joke to make her blush.

"Where'd all this stuff get started?" I said. "About Emma and her boyfriend, I mean. Is that just talk or what?"

"Shit, it's a lot more'n talk," Roy said. He folded his hands and gave me a courtroom look. "Anyone with good sense can see these two things have got to be connected somehow. The dog gets killed one day, and that gal hightails it out the next."

Roy glanced around the table for support. Everyone nodded assent except George. George Rainey hadn't said a word since I'd arrived. He sat there and looked out the fly-specked window, letting his coffee grow cold.

"You see this kinda stuff all the time in the law," Roy went on. "One thing always ties in with something else. What'll happen, what'll happen is, a teller or someone'll start stealin' money from the bank. See, that's your isolated event. The next thing you know, this dummy in the bank, he shows up with a brand-new car. He's wearing those nigger sport coats like Billy here does, he used to wear a black suit. You don't have to be a fuckin' rocket scientist to figure something's going on that isn't right."

"That's for damn sure," Eddie said. "Something's going on that isn't right."

"Jesus," said Roy, "that's what *I* said."

Phil and Billy laughed. George didn't crack a smile.

"It sounds good," I said, "but it doesn't prove a thing."

"Sure it does." Roy looked at the others, then at me. "This isn't all my idea, you understand, I won't take credit for that. I was thinking on the very same lines, but it was Deke put it all together first."

"Deke did."

"Uh-huh. Me and Billy saw him in here last night, after he came back from talking to Mrs. Stynnes. Deke's right on top of this."

"I can see that," I said.

"Well, don't you think it is?" Phil said.

"Don't I think what is?"

"One thing related to the other. The dog business and Emma Stynnes."

"Might be just a coincidence," I said.

"Coincidence, my ass," Roy said. "It's an event-related crime is what it is. I've seen it happen a hundred times."

I stood and dropped a dollar on the table. "Deke's the high sheriff. He ought to know. All I do is check doors."

"Shit," said Billy, "the re-tard does all that."

Everybody laughed.

"Hey, now Jack's real busy," Roy said. "Y'all leave him alone."

I knew what was coming with that phony somber smile. Roy's cheeks sagged, and he looked like a beagle that someone had beaten with a stick.

"Jack's got that long-legged ice cream lady comes out to the farm," Roy said. "He can't be checkin' on doors."

"It's yogurt," I said. "It's not ice cream."

Roy grinned and made a show of licking his lips. "She taste like vanilla or strawberry, Jack? Which one?"

Everyone laughed, but not much.

"A little like that girl in your office won't let you in her pants," I told Roy. "A little like your wife."

Roy turned red from his collar on up. I could see the venom clouding up his eyes, but everyone was laughing and he had to let it pass.

I left, then, stopping at the counter to drop another dollar in front of Annie. She gave me a gap-toothed grin and went back to scraping grease off the grill. Annie and the grill were about the same age, seventy or seventy-five. Together, they had served up several generations of cholesterol burgers and fries. If you dropped dead in Audie's they didn't have to take you very far. Trost's Hardware & Funeral Home was next door.

The sun was nearly straight overhead in a washed-out summer sky. The heat rising up from the sidewalk was strong enough to crack cement. I thought I'd pick up a few things from the store and get back out to the place. I tried to remember if I'd turned on the units at home. If I hadn't, the house would be as hot as Annie's grill.

I heard my name called and turned around and saw George. He was walking real fast to catch up, and he stopped and caught his breath.

"You got a minute," he said, "we ought to talk."

"Sure. Let's not do it out here," I said.

We walked half a block down to Buddy's, and took the same table where Millie and I had sat the day before. There were two kids at the counter wearing Nikes and jeans. They were sucking up sodas and reading comic books.

George went up to the soda fountain and got me a Coke, and a Dr Pepper for himself. The same old lady was there.

She didn't look at me. She didn't care if I was in there with George.

If anyone had changed a whole lot in the fourteen years I'd been gone, it was George. I remembered the Raineys from my youth, George's worn-out mother and his scarecrow father, who had scraped out a living on four hundred acres east of town. Something was wrong with the Rainey land. Everyone else could make a crop in the rich black soil, but whatever the Raineys grew, it came up stringy and spare.

As a boy, George had been a gangly, red-faced copy of his father. When he got out of high school, he went right to work on the farm. There wasn't any choice, that's what he had to do.

That's how I left him. When I came back to town, he was still a skinny redneck farmer but he certainly wasn't poor. George had turned his worthless land into a prosperous catfish farm. The whole place was full of pools, and the pools were full of fat, white-bellied fish. The catfish rage was rampant in the land, and George couldn't raise enough to meet demands. The money poured in and he was thinking of buying more land. He still wore overalls and drove an old pickup truck, but now his wife shopped at Neiman Marcus instead of Sears, and his kids went to a private Dallas school.

So, I thought, if everything's going real fine, why does George look like half a million catfish just went belly-up and died?

George wasn't any Roy Burns. He sat down and got right to the point.

"Nate Graham called," he announced. "He's up in Dallas. He called me and Phil both. Three or four times."

I waited, to see what came after that. George looked at me like I was supposed to know the rest.

"Nate *Graham,*" he said. "You remember Nate. Kinda short guy. Wore the same clothes every day . . ."

"I know who he is," I said. "What about him, George?"

George frowned and wet his lips. "Like I said, he called me and Phil. Started maybe ten, twelve days ago. I think he was drinkin' when he called. Hell, I know he was. Phil thought so too."

George paused and looked at his hands. "Phil said he was going to talk to you 'bout this. You and him were going to have coffee. After that—stuff with the dog."

"We didn't make it," I said. "What did Nate Graham say?"

"He wanted to know if I remembered who he was. I said sure I did. He rambled on some, like you do when you're soused pretty good. Went on and on how his family'd left town before he got to finish school, how things hadn't been real good in his life and how he'd thought a lot about the guys he knew back when. He asked about everyone. He asked about you."

George finished off his Dr Pepper and wiped his sleeve across his mouth. I could tell he was having a hard time with this. He wanted to get there and he didn't. He figured if he went there the long way around, he could buy himself some time. I remembered how Phil and George had looked at each other in Audie's, the funny way Phil had looked at me.

"He asked about you," George said. "And Roy and Billy and everyone else. Mostly—he talked about Max."

He got the last part out and looked away. "He said, he said Max was a son of a bitch. He said Max had treated him bad. He said if *he'd* had money like Max, he could've made something out of himself. That things wouldn't be like they'd been."

"Nate was a whiner," I said. "I remember that much."

"Yeah, but he's right. I mean about Max." George shook his head. "Max liked to pick on Nate. Real bad."

"He picked on a lot of guys, George. Anyone who wasn't his size."

"He told Phil something I'd forgot. I remembered, when Phil told me. How Max caught Nate one day talking to Millie at her locker. He didn't say a thing. He just waited till after school and caught Nate out behind the gym. He made him take off all his clothes. Everything, even his underwear. Shit, I can see the poor guy now. Max chased him out front where everyone was hanging out. Nate was crying and trying to cover himself, and all the kids were laughing up a storm."

"I remember it," I said. "I wasn't there, though. I don't remember where I was." I looked at George. He was still back there with Nate Graham.

"I knew something was bothering you at Audie's," I said. "This business with Nate has really gotten to you, George."

"I guess it has."

"How about Phil?"

"You know Phil." George shrugged. "Phil keeps a lot of stuff bottled up inside. Like Louise taking off. He doesn't ever talk about that. He talks about his sister sometimes. He won't talk about Louise. But yeah, Nate's calls got to him too."

The witch behind the soda fountain was giving the two boys hell. She said they'd spilled stuff on *Spiderman* and they'd have to buy it now. The boys laughed at her and ran out of the store. The old lady muttered to herself, wiped off the comic book and stuffed it in the rack.

"I don't know what we ought to do," George said. "Phil says we ought to just forget it, and I say fine, leave the poor bastard alone, except now there's this thing with Max's dog. Hell, I don't know. Graham callin' up and all and bad-mouthing Max . . ."

"Are you asking me if I think you ought tell this stuff to Deke?"

"I guess I am."

"Why?"

"Because Phil says he trusts you. He doesn't trust Deke."

"What about you?"

George looked down at his hands. "You and me weren't ever real close. We just know each other is all. You're Phil's friend. So am I. I'll go with what you and Phil—"

"Huh-unh No way. I'll talk to Phil if you want, but you can't put this on my back. You two'll have to decide what to do about Graham."

George blinked. "Well, sure. You feel that way about it. I can understand that." He looked surprised and disappointed. Maybe a little pissed off, but he didn't let it show.

"You see what I'm saying, don't you, George? I didn't talk to Nate Graham. You and Phil did."

"I don't want to get the guy in trouble," George said. He left it hanging there awhile, then studied his empty glass. "I keep thinking, you know, if Nate *was* mad enough at Max to— do something . . ."

He looked at me again, still hoping for an answer. "Jesus, Jack. Now there's this business with that nigger girl."

"I've got some shopping to do," I said. I stood and looked at George. "You've both likely figured out what you want to do, so go ahead and do it. Quit fucking around with this."

George pumped his head up and down. "You're right. I know that. That's what we gotta do."

He showed me a feeble grin. He looked like an overgrown weed that was wilting in the sun.

I walked across the street to the courthouse and climbed the stairs to the second floor. Deke wasn't in. I told his overweight deputy what I knew about Nate Graham's calls, and who he'd made them to. The deputy took it all down. I didn't have any idea whether Nate Graham was mixed up in this business or not, but I knew Phil and George would take a week to decide what to do. Indecision is a way of life in Pharaoh, Texas, and those two had been here too long.

Nine

The asphalt road to the farm was ready to boil and melt away. A million years from now, they would find me in a tar pit and put me on display. This was a Honda, we think, and this one was a pickup truck. As you can see, the driver was a male and he is partially intact.

A radio station in Dallas said the temperature at two was a hundred and four. Just out of town, there were casualties on the road. Someone had smashed a rattler flat. A car had lost a tire, tearing it to pieces in the heat, leaving dead clots of rubber everywhere.

Half a mile down the road was a very tight curve to the right, just before you got to the Pharaoh Cemetery. There used to be a clump of cedars at the curve. They totally hid the road ahead. If you kept to your side of the road, you had to slow down to twenty-five. At Pharaoh High, this was a cowardly thing to do. If you had any guts, you hit the gas and took the outside lane, and hoped no one was coming the other way.

Roy Burns's older brother Hal guessed wrong one afternoon. He took the outer lane at sixty-five and hit a Texaco truck head-on. Hal, two other boys and three girls exploded in a pyre you could see a good ten miles away. The truck had a full load of gasoline. Gravel-sized pieces of Hal, his friends, and the driver of the truck were scattered everywhere. Enough remains were found to fill half a shoe box. The highway department came and cut the cedars down.

Trost's Hardware & Funeral Home divided the remains into seven equal parts. The truck driver's portion was sent down to Waco where he lived.

All six funerals were held in one day, but school closed down for a week. We weren't supposed to go out to the wreck site but we did. Everybody claimed they found burned bits of bone, but they could have been almost anything. The earth for a hundred yards around was charred black,

It was one of those real peculiar years when fate or whatever seemed to save stuff up and toss it at you all at once. The Pharaoh Asps won three games in a row, a record that still stands today. Mr. Hack, who taught geometry and shop, got caught in Corsicana in a strapless evening gown. Phil Eddels's little sister was raped and sliced up, and tossed out in a ditch. The guy they said did it was a vagrant, a mental case passing through town. They caught him in Dallas and tossed him in a cell. Before they could send him back to Pharaoh, he found something sharp and didn't have to go to trial.

Cotton prices were good for a change, and everybody paid their bills. Four girls from Pharaoh won 4-H prizes at the Texas State Fair.

On Christmas Eve that year, Billy McKenzie's mother bought a 12–gauge Remington pump, walked in the house and blew up the Christmas tree, shot the turkey in the oven and Billy McKenzie's dad, then turned the weapon on herself. Billy went to live with an aunt.

This was also the year I walked down to the creek and found Millie by herself and we had our one magic afternoon. I also didn't flunk algebra like I figured I would. Those two events loomed equally large at the time. Which shows you that a kid doesn't know a whole lot about life the way it is. I still remember how great Millie looked that day. And I haven't used algebra since.

* * *

I was right about the air. I hadn't left it on. The house was shut up tight and it was hot enough to bake biscuits on the floor. I turned on the units, took a quick shower, and found some cutoffs underneath the bed. I also found one of Cecily's lacy bras. It smelled awful good. I wondered what she might be doing right then. I wondered who she might be with. I decided not to think about that.

I iced down a six-pack of Czech Pilsner beer and retreated to the porch. The pecan trees shut out the sun and stirred up a little air.

I wondered if Earl was back. I could ride down and see but I didn't want to get in the truck. The truck was hotter than the house.

At four o'clock I ran out of beer and walked around to the back. Murder had struck the chicken house. There were feathers and blood everywhere. I raked up the mess and dug a hole and tossed everything in. Jesus, I thought, who could eat six chickens all at once? Maybe Badger Bob had a friend.

The house was cooling down, and I made myself a burger and sliced up an onion and tossed it in the pan. I found a tomato outside that the bugs had left behind. By the time I'd finished off half the burger, I heard Earl's car go by. It is truly a sensuous experience to hear a Lagonda pass your house. Even if the engine needs a tune-up it's a rich and soothing sound. If I had one, I would keep it looking nice. I would drive through town, and they wouldn't say Jack's got bird shit on his car.

Earl looked bad. I don't mean bad like sick or anything, I mean *bad*. Mean mother head-stomping bad. When he looked at me his eyes were the color of river mud. A mean-eyed, skinny Othello in bib overalls. He was ready to kick some ass or he already had.

"I can stand out here in the road," I said, "it's okay with

me. I come in peace. We're on our way to Oregon, we mean your people no harm."

"Don't be an asshole," Earl said.

"Yes, sir. I'm trying to quit. You got any beer?"

Earl slumped down in his camp chair and nodded toward the shed. I got two Coronas, opened them, and brought one back to him.

"I can ask you what's wrong," I said, "but I won't. You'll sit right there and do your Darth Vader act or you'll maybe open up. I never can tell which."

"Why don't you take that beer and go back up to your house," Earl said.

"I could do that."

"I don't see you gettin' up."

"It sure is a nice afternoon. Maybe a little hot. You people of the African persuasion seem to take the heat better than other folks do. That's because of the high degree of melanin in your skin. Melanin comes from the Latin 'watermelon,' or maybe it's the Greek—"

"Jack, just shut the fuck up." Earl glared at me, then stared off toward the creek. A swarm of gnats circled about his head and he swatted them away.

"Leola called me up, she got word to me quick about her girl. I been asking a lot of questions over in the black part of town. Is that all right with you?"

"Who's Leola?" I said.

"Leola Stynnes. Emma Stynnes's mother. Leola's my cousin. My daddy was her brother."

"Jesus, Earl. Listen, I'm sorry . . ."

"You got a bad habit, Jack. Your mouth takes off before your head. You mean well most of the time but that doesn't do the trick."

"I'm sorry," I said. "You want me to write it on the blackboard or what?"

"Shit. There you go again."

Earl looked at his empty bottle and frowned. It was clear

that he wanted me to get up and get him another beer. Something moved in the big pecan tree across the creek, and I watched a squirrel spiral around the trunk, then leap up to a branch. He froze there, looking wide-eyed and startled. Squirrels always look surprised. They never have the slightest idea where they are.

"I wondered what it was got Deke Glover frothing at the mouth," I said. "You were stepping on his toes."

"I was asking people questions. People going to tell me things they won't tell Deke."

"Sure they will. That's what pissed him off. He says you mess with him, he'll slap your black ass in jail."

"He said that."

"Deke's got a serious problem with your economic status in life. He thinks you ought to trade that car. He feels you'd look better in a sixty-two Ford."

"Uh-huh." Earl gave me a weary look, and rested his hands on his knees. "I talked to a man lives close to the tracks. The way Emma walks to work. He wouldn't tell Glover anything. He told me he saw Emma go by. There's a path along the creek, you can go to the brickyards on the right, or you can walk across the tracks into town."

"I know where it is," I said.

"That's the way Emma went every day. She didn't run away with anyone like they're talking around. Everyone knows her knows that. She went to work like she always did. She just didn't get there is all."

Earl paused. "I got out and walked the way she did. I did it half a dozen times. There was nothing there to see."

Pharaoh's black community had used that route for years, working for the whites in town. "There's a dirt road goes right by there," I said. "A few yards west of the tracks. I drove down there after I talked to Deke."

"I went down there too," Earl said. "So did Glover, but he figures that's where she met this fella who took her on a spree."

Earl's dark eyes were nearly lost beneath his brows. "That's where someone got her, Jack. Right there. The brush is real thick. You can't see a car on that road from anywhere."

I lit a smoke and offered one to Earl. Earl shook his head.

"There's something I think you better know about," I said. "It likely has nothing to do with Emma Stynnes. I don't think it does, but right now it's hard to rule anything out."

I told him what George had told me about Nate Graham. About the phone calls he'd made to George and Phil. I told him everything George had said, and that I'd told Deke's deputy to pass the word to Deke.

"Goddamn," Earl said. He gave me a hard and ugly look. "That son of a bitch won't do anything and you know it. He's got this thing figured out the way he likes."

"I know he won't. The Dallas cops could check Graham out. I don't know anybody up there—"

"I do," Earl said.

"Who?"

"Nobody you know, Jack."

"Fine," I said. "Fine with me."

I wasn't about to push it any more than that. When Earl closed down, there was no use wasting your breath. All the doors slammed shut. Besides I didn't want to talk about cops. In Dallas or anywhere else.

As I walked back to the truck, he was stomping past the various components of his house, heading for the shed where he kept his power tools, fridge, items of personal care, and his telephone. Earl had everything he needed close at hand. All the comforts of home except a house.

It was getting close to dark when I drove back up from the creek. Several lights were on in my house. A bright-red

Mazda Miata with the top down was sitting in my drive. Jesus, I thought, it's Millie Jean. Millie's here. Inside. In the house. I'd seen the car before, parked in the Coomers' circle drive.

My adolescent heart skipped a beat. I felt a brief moment of guilt, an image of Cecily Benét. The image went away. Reason said I was a victim of circumstance. I hadn't asked her out here. Betrayal implies intent.

The lights in the kitchen were on. The hallway was dark, but she had turned on the bedroom lamp. The radio was on, and something smelled peculiar in the air. Something very much like funny cigarettes.

Smoothy was sitting buck-naked on my bed. She was smoking a joint and reading a *Batman* comic book.

"Hi there," she said. "Where you been, man? You're out of beer, you know that? Boy, this is really a weirdo house."

There was an awful lot of girl there, an awful lot of honey-brown skin. "Get out of there," I said. I tried to sound like an adult. "Get up right now and get dressed."

Smoothy giggled and kicked her legs. *"C'mon,* Jack. Who's going to know, okay? You think I'm going to tell Max?"

"Smoothy, get up and get dressed and go home. Right now."

"You don't want me here, huh?"

"That's right. I don't want you here."

She gave me her impression of a grown-up leer. "Oh yeah? Then what you lookin' at? Your eyes are 'bout to drop on the floor."

"You are a very disturbing sight," I said. "You already know that. All of which is very much beside the point."

That sly look again. "Even if you *don't* do something, I can tell Daddy you did."

"Good idea," I said. "Let's tell him right now."

I turned and walked out of the room, leaving Smoothy

looking shocked and surprised. I picked up the phone in the kitchen and punched the numbers in.

"You wouldn't," Smoothy yelled, "you wouldn't do that!"

I heard her padding down the hall. She appeared in the doorway as Millie picked up the phone.

"This is Jack," I said. "Your daughter's out here at my house. She doesn't have a bottom or a top."

"Christ," Millie said, "how'd she get out there?"

"She *drove* out," I said.

"Why, that girl doesn't even have a license. She's not supposed to drive a car."

I looked up at Smoothy. She stood in the kitchen looking stunned. One long leg was wrapped around the other and she had one hand across her mouth. I tried to look at something else.

"Millie, I wouldn't worry too much about that, okay? An underage driver's not exactly the major problem here."

"What are you doing?"

"What?"

"Right now. What are you doing with Smoothy right now?"

"I'm whipping her into submission. Soon she will be all mine. What the hell do you think I'm doing, Millie Jean?"

"Can she drive all right?"

"She got out here. I imagine she can find her way back."

"Let me talk to her."

I looked at Smoothy. "She wants to talk to you."

Smoothy shook her head.

"Millie, she doesn't want to talk. I'll get her in the car right now."

Millie was silent for a while. "Jack?"

"What?"

"I want to talk to you."

"All right."

"I don't mean now. I want to *see* you, Jack."

My throat clamped shut. Millie's voice was all lazy and soft. I didn't have to ask, I knew exactly what she meant. This is absolutely fucking crazy, I thought. Millie's making out on the phone, and her daughter's stark-naked in my house. This didn't seem right. It didn't seem socially correct somehow.

"We'll—talk," I said. "I'll call you tomorrow." I looked up. "About Smoothy, I mean. I'm sure it'll all work out."

" 'Bye, Jack," Millie said.

I hung up. Smoothy struck a pose, one hand on her hips and her head tossed back.

"How do I know that was *her?* You could've made it all up."

"That's right," I said, "I could."

I walked past her down the hall to the bedroom. I picked up all her clothes, her Minnie Mouse wallet and her keys, and her *Batman* comic book. I tossed all her stuff in the hall and locked the door.

I stood there and waited. In a moment, Smoothy started pounding on the door.

"I'm scared to drive home," she said. "I don't like it in the dark."

"Night driving is a part of growing up. I imagine you'll do just fine."

"What if I burn down your fucking house?"

"I would take offense at that."

"Shit," Smoothy said.

In three or four minutes, I heard her drive off. I unlocked the door and went out and watched her lights down the road. Then I locked up and checked the house. Nothing seemed to be on fire. I fixed a bowl of hot cereal and went to bed.

I couldn't go to sleep. I put Cecily's bra beneath my pillow but it didn't seem to help. I didn't feel it was right that

I should spend the night alone. Offers were pouring in from several age groups, but none of them were here.

Fun erotic dreams should have followed this event. Instead, I plunged into hoary nightmares where furry things chased me through the dark, screaming and biting at my heels. I woke up at two in a sweat. I wondered what the hell was wrong. I hadn't had dreams like that since I was a kid. It was a pepperoni pizza nightmare, and all I'd had was Cream of Wheat.

I got up and got a drink. I smoked and walked around, got back in bed and started on an Elmore Leonard book. The phone woke me up. The clock by the bed said four-seventeen and I'd been sleeping real fine.

"Okay," I said, "this better be good."

"Mister Jack? I'm sorry I woke you up."

"Henry D.?" I frowned into the phone. "Henry, do you know what the hell time it is? It's *four*."

"Mister Jack, we guh-guh-guh—"

"Calm down," I said. "What's wrong, Henry?" The kid sounded awful, like he might be having a fit. "Take it easy," I said, "okay?"

"Listen, Mr. Jack—"

"It's all right, son."

"Sh-sh-*shit!*" Henry said. He started bawling and it all spilled out. *"We guh-got us a dead electric Max, Mr. Jack!"*

Ten

It took me twelve minutes to get to town. I thought that was pretty good, considering the pickup usually reached critical mass at forty-five. Twelve minutes, and everyone in Texas was already there. The big floods at Pharaoh Field were burning bright. The streets around the stadium were clogged with honking cars. People drove by. People got out and left their cars anywhere.

I pulled up in someone's driveway and walked. The cops had parked out front, stopping at crazy angles the way they like to do, leaving their light bars screaming blue and red. I spotted three black and whites from the Highway Patrol. A sheriff's car from Ellis County, locals from Maypearl, Wilmer and Waxahachie. I wondered how all these clowns had managed to get here so fast. Maybe they slept in their cars.

Two cops from out of town were on duty just past the ticket booth. They closed in fast. One of Deke's deputies came down the rampway and told them to let me through. He was a fat boy, maybe twenty-one or twenty-two. I couldn't remember his name.

"What happened here?" I said. "Where's Max?"

He stared right through me. Little black birdshot eyes. "This is—bad shit, man . . ."

"Right. What happened?"

Nothing came out. He went white around the mouth, turned and hurried back down the ramp. I left him and walked toward the field. I never watch people throw up. Even if it's me, I try to look somewhere else.

I saw a pileup once on I-35. A bus hit a car head-on and there were fucked-up people everywhere—in the wreck, on the road, torn up in a ditch. You come on a thing like that, you tighten up your gut because you know how bad it's going to be. You're going to find some awful stuff, you know that's what you're going to see.

Seeing Max was worse than that because Max looked fine. He looked better than he had in twenty years. He was dressed in bright green and gold, the colors of the Pharaoh Asps. Gold pants, green jersey, a shiny gold helmet on his head. The crowd roared. Max held the ball close to his chest. His legs churned air, running for glory and Pharaoh High.

The illusion was fine if you stood off a ways and didn't look at Max's feet. His feet were wired to pedals, and the pedals were attached to a bicycle wheel. A chain ran back to a motor and the motor hummed away, pumping Max's legs up and down. He must've been clocking eighty-five but he wasn't going anywhere at all. He was stuck there forever on the two-yard line because the big steel rod held him back. One end was rammed up his backside, the other end was planted in the ground. The rod gave Max nice posture, but tended to slow him down.

There were maybe twenty cops around Max, guys in tight khaki, faded blue or brown, guys who spent a lot of time at Dairy Queens. Deke looked up at me and frowned. No one else seemed to notice I was there. No one seemed to know what to do, so they didn't do anything at all. One of the cops had a video camera. A guy I knew from Ferris sucked on a long-neck Coors. The harsh light of the floods ate up every shadow on the field. The tape-recorded roar of the crowd bounced around the empty stands, and Max ran as fast as he could.

I felt like I was stuck in a bad Italian movie, where everything you see means something else. I always have to ask Cecily who everybody is.

"He sure looks natural, don't he?" someone said.

"Damn sure does," said someone next to me.

I walked around the back of the crowd to Deke. He knew I was there but he didn't turn around.

"You going to what," I said, "let him run all day? Don't you think you ought to turn him off?"

Deke moved his head half an inch. "Billy Cace from over at Wilmer's takin' pictures for evidence. I asked him to do it. That okay with you?"

"Sure. Everything's okay with me."

"I'm fuckin' glad to hear it."

"When did it happen?" I said. "I got a call a little after four."

"A quarter till, somethin' like that. Guy driving by saw the lights. So who called you?"

"Henry D."

"He know how to dial a phone?"

"He can phone as good as anyone else."

"Shit. You could've fooled me."

Deke stared at Max. It was a mean and sour look, even for Deke. As if Max had maybe done this to screw up Deke's day.

"I figured that fuckin' dog was it," Deke said. "I didn't figure on some crazy sum'bitch doin' this."

"I don't guess Max did either," I said.

I noticed he didn't mention Emma Stynnes. He hadn't worked for her, he'd worked for Max. Emma Stynnes had never slipped him a twenty or a hundred now and then. He wasn't pissed off at Emma, he was pissed off at Max.

The clown with the video camera was working his way

around Max. He went down on one knee, zoomed in a minute, and then pulled back. A real artsy shot. Maybe he liked Italian movies, too.

"I left word with your deputy about this Nate Graham business," I said. "You check him out or what?"

Deke looked irritated. "Now why the hell you botherin' me with that? I look like I don't have anything to do?"

"Maybe he's involved in this, Deke. I don't know if he is or not."

Deke pulled one of his little thin cigars from his pocket, changed his mind and put it back. "I called an ol' boy on the Dallas police. I told him 'bout Graham."

"And what did he say?"

"He said he'd look into it." Deke showed me a nasty grin. "I had Phil and George Rainey in for a talk. They aren't real happy with you."

"I can live with that."

"George said you broke a confidence."

"George doesn't understand us lawmen. You and I know duty comes first. We can't be worried about our friends."

"I don't think I have to listen to this," Deke said. "I'm pretty sure I don't."

"He's got the same jersey," I said. "You notice that?"

"He's got what?"

"The same jersey. Number 15. The one he wore in school. That's a real nice touch."

"Jesus H. Christ." Deke walked off and talked to someone else.

The crowd seemed to be getting louder outside. The guy with the video camera was standing on the goal line, getting a close-up shot. A couple of hairs climbed the back of my neck, and I turned and walked off across the field. I didn't want to think about that. The last thing I wanted was a look at Max's face.

* * *

I wondered if Deke's fat deputy was still throwing up somewhere. I heard the siren moaning outside, stopped and looked back, and saw the ambulance skidding through the north entryway beneath the stands. Red lights flashed on and off as it raced around the track. Doc Hackley sat next to the driver, squeezed in beside Eddie Trost. Doc Hackley looked tired. Eddie looked like Eddie always does. I could guess what he was thinking. He was thinking how this was the big one—maybe the biggest he'd ever had. Max Coomer's funeral would buy a lot of barbecue and beer.

It was awful out front. The entire population of Pharaoh was eager for a look inside. Deke didn't have enough people for a thing like this. Even with outside help, it was a struggle to keep everybody out.

As I walked by the ticket booth, three kids broke through the line and headed for the cyclone fence. A deputy yelled for them to stop. The crowd cheered the boys on, the deputy panicked, drew his pistol and fired off a shot in the air. A woman screamed. The boys froze, turned and darted back into the crowd. Everyone booed. Someone threw an empty bottle. It smashed near the deputy's feet. He jumped back, shook his fist, and shouted something I couldn't hear.

Halfway to the gate, a blinding white light turned the bleak early morning into noon. I turned and saw the big Chevy van making its way through the crowd. Two guys were on top. One worked the camera, the other aimed the lights.

I stood there a second, caught in the glare like a deer on a back-country road. I knew how the poor bastards felt because the same fear reached out and clawed me in the gut. It happened. I couldn't help it, it was there. I ducked into the crowd, running from the lights. Someone called my name, but I didn't look back.

I sat in the truck a long time, waiting for my heart to

slow down, waiting for it all to go away. Knowing it could hit me like that scared me more than anything else, because I thought I had put it all behind me, I thought coming home would do that. I was Jack Track now. I wasn't that other guy. They wouldn't look for me in Pharaoh, Texas. No one would pass me on the street, look behind the beard and see my face.

Great idea. Only now we had a dead electric Max in a goddamn football suit. When the sun came up, Pharaoh would rise from obscurity to headline the national news. By late afternoon, every media hound in the country would be in town.

Christ. A busload of nuns would be a better place to hide in than here . . .

Eleven

What I wanted to do was go to bed and flake out but I knew I couldn't get away with that. I probably wouldn't ever sleep again. I was wired up tighter than a junkie on the street. Seeing Max like that was bad enough, but the shit with the TV truck had shaken me up a lot. There are rooms in your head you don't like to open up. That's what doors are for. To keep things in or out.

Breakfast didn't interest me at all, but my stomach had other ideas. I fixed a ham sandwich with a slice of tomato and opened an import beer. I took the sandwich and the beer to the bedroom, found the remote and turned on the TV. Max was already on the news. Fort Worth and Dallas had cut into the network shows and they all had people on the spot. No one could get inside, so they did what they always do, which is talk about everything else. Every channel was the same, grim-looking people still half asleep, framed against the entry to Pharaoh Field. They told us how this was where the brutal pre-dawn slaying of a prominent state figure had taken place. They said "brutal slaying" a lot.

I switched between 4, 5 and 8. This was a good time to get your big break on TV. Everyone was marking time. They'd talk to anyone who'd stand still. They interviewed Billy McKenzie and Roy Burns. Billy was stunned by the loss. Roy Burns was shocked beyond belief. They both made it clear that Max Coomer had been their closest friend.

Channel 4 interviewed a lady who thought there'd been a highway accident. She said drinking was a sin. Before they could stop her, she said Satan pissed in every can of beer. I believe this is very likely true.

Now and then Channel 8 cut back to their "exclusive early-morning shot, taken moments after the grisly crime." We saw the ambulance rushing to the scene, and the washed-out faces of the crowd. I was pleased that I didn't see myself.

For lack of anything to do, they started showing pictures of Max. They showed him with senators and presidents. They showed him holding up a fish, and pretending that he liked to play golf. They even dug up some old high school shots of Max in his football suit. One of the channels had a black-and-white picture of Millie, "the attractive blond widow," at a party in Houston somewhere. They had caught her with a drink, a strap falling off one shoulder, a silly grin frozen in the flash.

That seemed to be about enough. I turned off the set, got another beer, and walked out to the porch. Alexander the cat was asleep in the rocker, so I sat down on the steps. It was hot and there wasn't any breeze. Bugs were starting to chatter in the trees. It was only ten-thirty, and I felt like I'd been up for a week.

I wondered how Millie was taking all this. I knew she didn't care a lot for Max, but even if you're not real close to someone anymore, a thing like this, it's got to hit you pretty hard. Your loved one has a stroke, he gets clobbered by a truck, you can kind of live with that. Some clown comes to the door and says, "Sorry, Miz Coomer, your husband, he's running down the football field, he's got this rod up his ass," that's got to be a shocker and a half. You're not expecting something like that.

I thought I ought to go and see her, then I thought how the TV people were likely laying siege to the house, and I decided I could pay my respects some other time.

* * *

Cecily Benét called at noon from L.A. She said she'd be
back in two days. She said she had the TV on, and what
the hell were we doing back here. I told her she could see
for herself, that I didn't know any more than that. I didn't
tell her that I'd been into town and seen all there was to
see. She wouldn't want to hear about that. I told her I was
having an affair with her bra. She said she wasn't real surprised. She said she might stay in L.A., and mail me un-
derthings from time to time.

Earl Murphy showed up around two. He brought a sack
of barbecue, and half a case of good German beer. He put
his stuff on the porch, tossed the cat off the rocker and sat.

"I wouldn't be lettin' some cat take my chair," Earl said.
"A cat doesn't need to be sitting in a chair."

"He got there first," I said. "I try to be fair."

Earl opened up a beer. He kept an opener with him all
the time. He kept it on a long gold chain, the way men
used to do with a watch.

"I see you're not watching TV," Earl said.

"That's right, I'm not."

"You're missing all the news."

"That's what I had in mind. Missing all the news."

Earl sat back and tasted his beer. "Pharaoh's a fucking
circus. You never saw the like. You can't even drive through
town. Dan Rather's sittin' right in Buddy's, big as life. Everybody knows what happened to Max, but they don't have
any shots. They're real pissed off about that. He's still out
there on the field. They got him covered with a tarp. A
special team's coming in from the FBI."

I looked up at Earl. "You got to do this, right? I don't
want to hear it, that's okay with you. You're going to give
me all the news."

Earl frowned. "What the hell's wrong with you?"

"Nothing's wrong with me."

"Yeah, there is, too."

"I was in there, Earl. This morning. I don't need to see the news."

"I know you were."

"Well, that's why. There's nothing more I want to know."

"A man ought to keep informed."

"What for?"

"He just should is all. He ought to know what's going on."

Earl tore open his sack and exposed two or three pounds of ribs. They were big beef ribs, the size of barrel staves. Dark and moist and rich, covered with pepper and fat. If you ate just one of those mothers, your heart would flat stop.

"I don't guess you want to hear about the dog," Earl said. "I doubt you want to hear about that."

"That's right, I don't."

"That's what I thought. See, they haven't got a picture of Max. What they got, they got this picture of the dog. One of Deke's deputies bootlegged a picture of the dog. Deke's madder'n spit. Little fat guy, I don't recall his name. Deke ran him out of town, which is fine with the fat guy, 'cause ABC gave him five thousand bucks."

"For a picture of the dog."

"For a picture of the dog. Guy I know, a black guy clerks down at the courthouse. He overheard this judge who knew Max tell a lawyer how someone had tried to sell a picture of the dog. This wasn't today. This was right after the business with the dog. The man who runs the paper in Dallas, the guy knows Max, so he calls up Max and asks him what's going on. Max tells him forget about the dog. He doesn't want any shit in the paper about the dog. The guy says okay and that's that. 'Course it doesn't matter now. A guy's dead, he hasn't got a lot of clout."

I threw a rib bone down in the yard. The cat sniffed at it and backed away. "I hadn't thought about it," I said, "I guess that's what he'd do."

"You guess who'd do what?"

"Max. He'd make sure nothing got out about the dog. He liked to get his picture in the paper, but he'd be real embarrassed he got in the news over something like that, like a dead electric dog."

"Well sure he would," Earl said. "Joker like Max, he's got this image, wants to keep it lookin' fine. Man sure fucked up this time. People already forgetting who he was. What they're going to remember's how he *went.*"

Something in his voice made me turn around and look. Earl had a big wide fuck-you grin on his face. Earl is Earl, and he wasn't pretending it was anything else.

"Jesus," I said, "the guy's *dead,* Earl."

"I know he's dead." Earl's dark face was hard as stone. "I'm supposed to do what? I *like* the guy now because he's dead?"

"I don't think you have to do that."

"Damn straight I don't." Earl leaned forward and pointed a skinny finger in my face. "You want to know what I like about Max? Him gettin' killed means the law'll start looking for Emma Stynnes. She's not just a missing nigger girl anymore, she's tied in with Max. Those bastards'll *have* to look."

The phone rang in the house. I counted the rings. It rang seventeen times. I didn't feel like any more ribs, so I had another beer.

"You don't know for sure Emma Stynnes has got anything to do with this," I said. "I mean, my personal feeling is she does . . ."

Earl glared. "What are you talkin' about? You know damn well she does."

"That's what I said. Isn't that what I said? No offense, pal, I know you're related and all, but this looney tune doesn't just knock his victims off, he's into special effects. If he carried Emma off, I think we'd all know it by now."

"You think I haven't thought about that?" Earl growled into his beer. "Hasn't done anything yet, that doesn't mean he won't. Christ, Emma's mama isn't talking 'bout anything else."

I could read the awful pain in his eyes. I wanted to tell him that we might be wrong about Emma, that she might show up just fine. I knew that wasn't so, and Earl knew it too.

We sat on the porch a long time and didn't talk, then Earl stood and went inside. I picked up rib bones from the yard and threw them under the house for Badger Bob. Earl came up behind me and watched. I thought he might ask about the chickens, and I didn't want to get into that.

"I turned on the tube," Earl said. "Peter Jennings is going on about Max. Says a small Texas town is reeling in shock this afternoon."

"He said 'reeling in shock.' "

"Uh-huh. He had a guy on from the FBI. The guy said he had no comment to make at this time. They had Deke on after that. Deke said it was real clear to him there was some kind of madman on the loose." Earl grinned. "He got this real serious look. Like no one had figured that out before him."

"Deke doesn't care for these big fish swimming in his pond. He isn't going to go for that."

Earl eased himself down in the rocker. "Peter Jennings says the funeral's day after tomorrow. He says the Vice President's planning to attend. Says folks from all over going to be descending on a grief-stricken small Texas town— Jack, you listenin' to me or what?"

"Sure I am," I said. "Funeral. Vice President. What, there's going to be a test after this?"

I tried to look pissed but Earl wasn't buying that, because he'd seen me kind of jerk up straight like something hit me right between the eyes. Christ, I hadn't even *thought* about the funeral, it hadn't crossed my mind. Maybe I thought they'd just dump Max Coomer in a Hefty bag and that'd be that. Or maybe it was something I'd tossed in a corner of my mind so I wouldn't have to look at it again.

Earl peeked in the neck of his bottle, like there might be a message inside. "You don't want to talk about it, fine. I don't pry into another man's affairs. My daddy didn't raise me like that."

"That's good to know," I said.

"You got something troubling you, that's no concern of mine."

"*Nothing* is troubling me, Earl, all right?"

"I can see that. I can see you're just fine."

"Okay."

"You don't go to that funeral, what you think folks are going to say? You give any thought to that?"

That stopped me cold. "Who says I'm not? I say I wasn't going to the funeral, I tell you that?"

Earl finished off a rib and wiped grease on his pants. "Man sitting moping on the porch, he's not watching TV, you know he's got something on his mind. That's not natural, a man's not watching TV."

"Jesus," I said, "why don't you get yourself a talk show, pal? People could call in, you could tell 'em this shit you're tellin' me."

Earl stood and stretched. "Might work out. Black people got a lot of insight. What we got is your ancient tribal genes. You mind if I borrow your truck?"

"What for?"

Earl gave me a weary look. "I need to haul something, Jack. That's what you do with a truck."

"I know what you do with a truck. I don't need you to tell me that."

I tossed him the keys. He asked me if I wanted the rest of the ribs. I told him no. He was so pleased at that he forgot about the beer.

I took the phone off the hook and went to bed and slept until a little after four. Then I got up and fried an egg and fed the cat and got one of Earl's beers and walked down to the creek. Earl wasn't there, and neither was my truck. The day was hot and quiet. The squirrels were crapped out somewhere, and even the locusts were keeping still.

It occurred to me I ought to be worried that Earl could see right through me, that he knew I didn't want to show up at a national media event, which meant I surely had something to hide. I wasn't all that concerned about Earl, but I was damn sure concerned that it showed. If Earl figured something wasn't right, maybe someone else could see it too. Someone who'd be real pleased to bring me down if he could figure out how. The name Deke Glover came to mind. Deke would like that just fine.

There had been a few times, late nights and early mornings, when Earl and I had OD'd on single-malt Scotch, when I thought I'd maybe tell him all about it, knowing that he'd likely understand when I told him how it was. It's not good to drink if you've got things to hide, because you get to a point where you think it'll help if you get all the bad shit out there and lay it off on somebody else. I almost did it two or three times, but I couldn't think how to say it right. You got to lead up to something like that. Even if you think you know a guy real well, you got to tell him how it happened first, and how you kind of had to do what you did, you didn't want to but there wasn't much else you could do, the situation being what it was. You had to kill the two guys and the money was there and you could walk away from somewhere close to two million bucks, but after you'd whacked the guys out it didn't make a lot of sense.

Which explained why you came back to Pharaoh, Texas, and you didn't want to ever go anywhere again, and the last thing you needed was your face on the ten-o'clock news.

You have to get real drunk to spill something like that. Maybe I would sometime, but I wasn't ready yet.

Twelve

A little after six, I fixed another gourmet meal, crackers and Campbell's Tomato Soup. Then I called to check on Uncle Will. A nurse said Uncle Will was fine, or as fine as he was likely to get for a man who was living somewhere in 1939.

Those are two things I did. Two things I didn't do was call and talk to Millie, and watch the TV. I wanted to talk to Millie, see how she was, but I kept thinking later was a better time than now. I didn't need a shrink to tell me why. *Why* had to do with my afternoon nap. The nap had included a dream in which Max Coomer's funeral was held at Buddy's Drugs. Everyone was there. Tom Brokaw sang a medley of Willie Nelson hits. Dan Rather spilled a Coke on his *Predator* comic book. The dead electric dog began to cry. Sometime during the service, the grief-stricken widow and I went at it on the cold marble floor. The Pharaoh Asps were playing CBS, so no one seemed to care.

What the dream told me was I didn't want to offer my condolences to Millie. What I wanted to offer was me. I should have felt bad about that. I didn't, but I thought I maybe should. Which is why I didn't call. Instead, I called Cecily Benét in L.A. We could have a little kinky conversation on the phone, or I could read myself to sleep.

Cecily wasn't in. I fed Alexander the cat and called again. Jesus, I thought, it's seven-thirty on the coast and she's not in her room. What the hell's she up to out there? You think you've got a solid relationship, you think you've got someone you can trust. A good-looking woman owns a bunch of yogurt shops, she's going to get out of town and go nuts. She's going to cheat on you every time.

Earl showed up early the next morning, a little after six. I hadn't slept much and I was up having coffee and cold tomato soup when I heard the Aston-Martin throwing gravel out front. I walked out on the porch and he came up the walk carrying a big paper sack.

It's easy to tell when Earl's on the sauce. He takes slow and careful steps like there might be mines in the ground, and he tries to look extremely dignified. What he looks like is a drunk pretending that he's not.

"Where's my pickup?" I said. "I don't see my truck."

"Don't you worry 'bout your truck," Earl said. "That ol' truck's doing fine."

"It is, huh?"

Earl reeled past me to the kitchen, smelling like Glasgow on Saturday night. He lifted the lid on the coffee pot, sniffed and made a face.

"Looks like you could learn to make coffee," he said. "Isn't all that hard to do."

"You don't have to drink it," I told him. "You can go back down to that lumberyard you got and make your own. Where's my truck, Earl?"

Earl poured himself a cup and leaned back in his chair. He was wearing his L.L. Bean hunting boots, the pants to an eight-hundred-dollar Italian suit, and a T-shirt that read, "Nuke the Whales."

"You're okay," Earl said. "I got you all fixed up. It's going to go real good."

I set down my cup. I didn't like that funny little smile.

"I think I missed something here. *What's* going to go real good?"

Earl went blank. "I don't know, what?"

I sat down at the table and looked at Earl. He was doing these focus exercises with his eyes. He could do just fine with the left eye or the right. Two at once seemed to be a chore.

"Earl," I said, "is this just an ordinary drunk or something special? You mind me asking that?"

"Jack, your truck's okay." Earl picked up his cup, missed his mouth and spilled coffee on his shirt. "Don't worry 'bout your fuckin' truck."

"You know where it is? Right now?"

"It's in the creek," Earl said.

"In the creek."

"Hey, that's where I saw it too. It looks to be totaled pretty good. You don't have to worry 'bout a thing. What happened, some guy ran you off the road. This was late yesterday afternoon. I got a eyewitness to that. I called a friend I know in Waxahachie. Dr. Sam Watts is who it is, he's white but he's a stand-up guy. Anybody asks, he's got it all written down. I drove you up there 'bout five. You got a fractured wrist and contusions of the head but you're going to be fine."

Earl laid his paper sack on the table. "I got the bandages and stuff right here. I can help you put 'em on. Shoot, you can go to all the funerals you want. Won't anybody know who you are."

I got up and went to the sink and washed my cup. I didn't say a thing for a while. I didn't look at Earl.

"I want you to know I'm not angry about this," I said. "I read in *Psychology Today* what you do. What they tell you, what they tell you is a guy flips out you don't get him upset. You don't want to piss him off. I'm not pissing you off am I, Earl?"

Earl sat up straight. "Well, *fuck* me. Can't anybody help you, can they? You got to do everything yourself."

"That's it, that's what you think you did?"

"Someone tries to do something for you, this is what they get. I should've known better. You want to get kicked in the head, do somethin' for a friend."

Earl scraped back his chair and stood, an action that took some time. He grabbed the table for support, then swayed to the window and stared out at the yard.

"I don't see any chickens," he said. "I gave you a— whole bunch of chickens one time."

"Fuck you and your chickens," I said. "What you did, you totaled my goddamn truck. That's the only truck I've got. How am I supposed to get anywhere, I haven't got a truck?"

Earl turned from the window and showed me a lopsided grin. "Where you need to *go?* Man eats cold tomato soup for breakfast, he doesn't have anywhere to go. Wouldn't *learn* anything if he did."

"Is that right?"

"Tha's right." He looked around the kitchen, searching for the door to the hall. "You think about someone else besides yourself, I'll be down at the house."

"You haven't got a house, Earl."

"Hell with you. I don't have to take a lot of racial abuse."

"Just listen to you. You're talking, you don't even know what's coming out. When did the drinking start, Earl? Before or after I had my accident? I don't want to intrude on your personal life, I'd just kind of like to know."

Earl didn't answer. He held on to the wall and stumbled out of the kitchen. I followed him down the hall. He slammed the screen door, then turned on me and glared.

"You think be-bein' poor and black's a lark. I can tell you that it's not."

"You're not poor."

"I used to be poor. I used to be *real* poor, Jack."

"Will you stop this? You've got more money than Switzerland, Earl. You've got more money than the Pope."

Earl's eyes filled with tears. "What good's it do me?

Money doesn't matter, your friends don't want you around anymore."

"Get in your car," I said. "I'll drive you to your house."

I stepped off the porch. Earl backed away, swung at me and fell on his ass. He picked himself up, muttered to himself, and cut a twisted path back to the car. He missed the driver's side twice, finally made it to the seat. I watched him spray gravel and disappear.

I walked back to the kitchen and heated the coffee up. I wondered what this was all about. If you didn't want to think too hard, it looked like Earl had gone on a toot and then smashed up my truck in a misguided effort to help me out. It looked that way, but that wasn't how it was. There were two things going on here. The truck was one thing— Earl Murphy swacked out at dawn was something else.

That wasn't like Earl at all. Earl drank with purpose, the way he did everything else. He drank because that's what he wanted to do at the time, and he always drank with someone else. Someone else was usually me. Correction: It was *always* me. No one else would put up with Earl Murphy but me and a woman in Tulsa named Marie, who may not actually exist.

So if this wasn't fun-time boozing, something had shaken Earl up. And I couldn't buy that because if something bothers Earl, Earl gets even, he doesn't get drunk. Only this time maybe he did. Hell, what do I know? I can't get my own self straight, how can I figure out Earl?

The day seemed to go on forever. It does when you haven't got a truck. I didn't want to go anywhere, but that's beside the point. You like to decide that for yourself.

I cleaned up the house for the first time in four or five weeks. Then I made a list of things I needed to get, if I ever went back into town. Late in the afternoon, I went out in the yard and tore down the chicken coop. It's the kind of work that satisfies the body and the soul. I formed a happy image in my head. Earl comes up and says, "Where's the chickens, Jack? Where's the chicken coop?" I smile and say, "Earl, all the fucking chickens are dead. What do you think of that?"

Not a big reprisal, and it didn't make up for the truck. But sometimes you go with what you've got.

Supper was a minor event. I read awhile and dozed off around eight. The phone rang at ten. I stumbled out of bed and padded to the kitchen in the dark.

"It's me," Phil said. "Jesus, Jack, I been trying to get you all day."

"I had the phone off," I said.

"What for?"

"Because I didn't want to talk to anyone."

"Why not?"

"Phil, you going to tell me what you want?"

"We got to talk, George and me are coming out."

"No, you're not," I said. "I'll call you tomorrow sometime."

"Damn it, Jack, it's important. We got to talk *now!*"

Phil was clearly agitated, but that didn't tell me a lot. Both Phil and George Rainey thrive on the fretful side of life. That's why they're together all the time. If one of them doesn't have a problem, he knows he's got a friend to help him out.

"Phil," I said, "you want to tell me what this is all about, I could be thinking on it some and then—"

"I can't talk about it on the *phone*," Phil said. "It's real— confidential, Jack."

"I'll meet you at Audie's for breakfast. Nine-thirty or ten."

"You say you will, Jack, but you won't."

"Christ, Phil, I missed one time. You going to hold that against me, I missed one time?"

Phil hesitated. I could hear him talking to George. George

said something to Phil. Then Phil said something to George. Then Phil got back to me.

"We think we ought to come out," Phil said. "We think we ought to do it now."

"No," I said, "it's got to be tomorrow. I can't see you now."

"Why not?"

"Because I—" I spotted Earl's sack on the floor. "Because I had an *accident,* that's why. I don't feel like it right now."

"My God, you kidding?" Phil sucked a breath out of the phone. "You all right, you hurt real bad? Jack's been hurt," he told George. "He had an accident. He's banged up awful bad."

"Phil. I am not banged up. A guy—a guy ran me off the road. My truck's in the creek. It's totaled pretty good. I got a fractured wrist and contusions of the head. I'm just fine."

"You're just—oh, shit!" Phil's voice exploded in the phone. "I didn't even think about that. It could've—been the same guy!"

I frowned at the phone. "The same guy what? You're losing me, Phil."

"Nate Graham," Phil said. "I bet you a dollar it was him!"

"Nate Graham."

"Hell, who else could it be? He runs you off the road, then he takes a shot at Deke. He's up to his neck in this. He's behind the whole thing."

Something caught in my throat. I took a breath and counted—one . . . two . . . three . . . It didn't help at all.

"Phil. Someone took a shot at Deke. At Deke Glover. When was that?"

"Last night. You saying you didn't know?" Phil gave me a nasty little laugh. "You answer your phone, you'd know what was going on. Caught him out on the farm road. Shot out all his tires. Pinned Deke down for an hour and a half.

That car looks like a sieve. Bullets went right through the block. That motor was a rebuilt, good as new. Deke is sure pissed. He's got a all-points out."

Jesus, I thought, *I am not hearing this . . .*

"Listen," I said, "the guy ran me off the road, it couldn't have been the same guy. This was some Mexican, maybe twenty, twenty-five. He had a carful of kids. Eight, if I recall."

"You sure it wasn't Nate Graham?" Phil was clearly disappointed. "You get a license plate?"

"He didn't have a plate. See, that's the thing. He didn't have a plate. Isn't any way of knowing who it is. But I know it wasn't Graham."

Phil conferred with George again. "George says he could've been wearin' a disguise. He could've borrowed those kids."

"Phil, it wasn't him. Okay? We'll talk about it in the morning. Nine-thirty. You and George get some sleep."

Another moment of silence on the phone. "You're going to be there, aren't you?"

"I'll be there, Phil."

I hung up before he could tell me anything else. I sat down at the table in the dark. I thought about Deke. I thought about his fine-looking car full of holes, and I thought how a .44 Magnum would go through a block like butter, and I knew someone who had a gun like that. Of course a lot of people did. Clint Eastwood had three or four, but I didn't think he'd ever heard of Deke.

Alexander the cat came and rubbed against my leg. I wondered if I had any beer left in the fridge. The phone rang again. I grabbed it off the hook and said, "Goddamn it, Phil, I'll set your *house* on fire you call me up again!"

"Jack?"

I stared into the little black holes. "Millie? Is that you?"

"Well, my lord, you 'bout broke my eardrums, Jack."

"I'm sorry," I said. "I thought it was Phil. That man's

flat irritating, he doesn't even try. You all right, Millie Jean? I mean, of course you're not all *right,* what you been through, are you doing okay?"

"Jack, I've had a real shitty day," Millie said. "And yesterday wasn't real swift."

"I know that's true. You've been through a whole lot."

"Jack?"

"What, Millie Jean?"

"I'm feeling real low, Jack. I've drunk everything in the house and thrown up about a hundred times. Drinking isn't doing any good."

"You had anything to eat? You ought to eat, Millie Jean. You got to keep your strength."

"I tried that. I can't keep anything down. Jack, what I was thinking is I'd like to get fucked. I can come on out, that'd be all right with you. Smoothy is driving me absolutely nuts and those TV folks are camped out on the lawn and I—Jack? Jack, you still there or what?"

Thirteen

It doesn't matter how old you get or who you are. You take a guy drives a truck, he goes to Omaha and back. That's all he ever does. He gets real lucky, he nails a pretty waitress now and then. You take a duke from Paris, France, he's done about everything there is. He's been to bed with models and stars and he's tired of doing that. One day he finds he's about to get the girl of his dreams, a girl he's been wanting awful bad. He isn't ho-hum anymore. All that sophisticated shit goes out the door and he's acting like a high school kid. He isn't any different, he's just like the guy drives a truck. That's the way a man is. He's got these backseat drive-in movie genes just waiting to spring up again, and he can't help acting like a fool.

I didn't know how long she'd be. A woman says she's on the way, you don't know what she means. I took a quick shower, got on some jeans and a shirt I'd worn once, and found some clean sheets. Cecily had left a good bottle of Puligny-Montrachet and I stuck it in the fridge. I found a nice candle, lit it and put it on the table by the bed. My watch said three past eleven. I flipped through my CDs. Something like this, you've got to get the music right. Millie Jean after waiting twenty years, that's too big for your ordinary sounds. Too big for Barry Manilow. Maybe even too big for Frank.

I went through the stack again. What the hell, I decided, why not? When in doubt, go all the way out—the Brahms Violin Concerto in D. That sucker slings you around, then stomps you on the floor. I'll bet Johannes drove those German honeys wild. It works wonders on Cecily Benét. Half a bottle of wine, and that double-stop Adagio sends her into acrobatic fits.

I was slapping on some Old Spice Lime when her lights swept into the drive. Brushing my teeth real fast, I walked out on the porch. As she slid out of the car, the very short cutoffs climbed up her crotch, and the legendary Millie Jean breasts tried to poke through a Harley T-shirt. I watched her as she came up the walk with that long-legged country-girl stride, hipbones swinging just right, everything lazy and serene, and I thought, my God, I bet this girl didn't come straight out, I bet she went through a Jiffy Lube somewhere.

Millie breezed past me, glaring straight ahead, leaving a trail of perfume, looking sullen and out of sorts.

"Jesus," she said, "I thought I wouldn't never get those TV fuckers off my tail. I had to double back twice." She kicked off her shoes in the hall. "I am not real big on your car-chase scene, I'll tell you that. Those old boys'll just—"

Millie stopped, blinked at me and stared. "My God, look at you. What'd you *do* to yourself?"

"I had an accident," I said. "A guy ran me off the road. I'm okay. I got a fractured wrist and contusions of the head."

"Well, bless your heart." She came to me and kissed me on the mouth. "Didn't damage any vital parts, I hope?"

"Everything else is just fine."

"That's good to hear." She reached out and took my hand. "The bedroom's this way, right? Smoothy drew me a map."

She caught my expression and grinned. "Jack, I appreciate you sending her home intact. She doesn't get turned down a lot."

"It seemed like the right thing to do." I thought about

Smoothy prancing naked down this very same hall. "I'll tell you what," I said, "that girl doesn't look twelve to me."

"That girl hasn't looked twelve since she was six," Millie said. "You got anything to drink?"

I aimed her at the bedroom and went back to the kitchen for the wine. Alexander gave me a look and hopped off the counter to the floor. There was only one wineglass left. I could give that to Millie, and I could use the Spiderman. Still, it would look a lot better if both glasses matched. Social decisions. I decided on two Peter Pan jars just alike. A girl like Millie's used to going first class.

When I walked back into the bedroom my stomach turned a flip and I nearly dropped the bottle and the glasses on the floor. Millie was peeling the T-shirt up past her ribs, her arms held high, body sort of twisted at the waist, the skin of her tummy a miraculous shade of gold in the yellow candlelight. I stood there and watched, more or less stunned, dazzled by the sight of the T-shirt catching for an instant on the tips of Millie's breasts, a curtain going up on a show you knew had to be a hit. My throat began to close up tight and those wonders sprang free, nodded a little, then looked right at me. They seemed to say, "Hi, there, Jack, it's sure good to see you again, it's been a lot of years."

"My God," I said, "you're better-looking than you were at fifteen." I set the wine and the glasses on the floor. "I didn't think anyone'd ever be prettier than that."

"I expect you've seen a tit or two since," Millie said. "Still, that's a nice thing to say." She snapped the top button of her cutoffs, paused to light up, then made a face at me.

"I'll tell you what, I cannot get used to you all wrapped up. I can't hardly see your head."

"This stuff'll be off in a couple of days. The doc says I'll be just fine. That's Dr. Sam Watts. Over in Waxahachie. I don't know if you've heard of him or not."

Millie shook her head, sucked in a lungful of smoke and

blew it out. "You're awful spooky-looking, pal. I feel like I'm hopping in the sack with Frankenstein."

"The Mummy," I said.

"The what?"

"The Mummy. You said Frankenstein. The Mummy's the one wrapped up."

"I didn't get to go to scary shows. Mama said it'd mess up your period if you did." She tossed her T-shirt on the bedside lamp, wet her fingertips and snuffed my candle out. "You mind a whole lot? I got an allergy to wax."

"No problem," I said.

"You got a bathroom here, I guess."

"First door on the right."

Millie padded out. I poured two glasses of wine and set the Peter Pan jars by the bed. I had to pull a bandage aside to take a sip. I hated the damn things more than she did. Still it struck me right after she called it was that or not show up at the Max Coomer Show, and I couldn't risk that. I could've put them on in the morning, but I'd already opened my big mouth to Phil. I couldn't change my story now. What really pissed me off was the bandages were Earl's idea. Even worse, the idea worked and I really hated that.

Millie came back, humming to herself and looking great.

"That child is flat driving me nuts," Millie said. She reached in her purse and got a brush, stood before the mirror and started stroking her hair. "I don't know what the hell I'm going to do now, with Max gone. He's the one fucked her up and I got to live with that. You know what that sum'bitch did? He enrolled her in SMU when she was four. I got this picture of Smoothy readin' a college book, she can't hardly get through the alphabet. She wants to be a major dope fiend, that's what she wants to do. You don't need a degree to do that."

I sat on the edge of the bed. I couldn't take my eyes off Millie Jean. I loved her bony shoulder blades, the way her hair frizzed up at the back of her neck. She had a little Band-Aid on her heel. I liked that Band-Aid a lot.

"Maybe you and Smoothy ought to try and get away somewhere," I said. "For a while, anyway. Until they catch this nutcase, I mean. I think that'd be a good idea, and a trip might do you both good."

"Go where?" Millie paused in her brushing, and frowned at me in the mirror. "Where you think we ought to go?"

"I don't know. Europe. Go to Italy or France. Wherever rich people go."

"Great," Millie said, "that's all I need, haulin' Smoothy Coomer off to France. She can act like a slut right here, I don't have to take her overseas."

"Okay, maybe it's a bad idea. It just seems to me you'd be a whole lot safer if you went off somewhere awhile. Millie, you going to brush your hair all night?"

Millie twisted on her hips and gave me a lazy grin. "You not getting horny are you, Jack?"

"I don't know why you'd say that."

Millie tossed her brush away. Her hands went to her waist and I heard a little *zip!* and she skinned out of her cutoffs in a flash. Catching the cutoffs on her foot, she flipped them across the room.

"I believe I'm naked," she said, "and you're not." She put her hands on her hips. "What you plan to do about that?"

Millie was right. I had never seen anyone more naked in my life. The flutter in my stomach worked its way straight down. I sat there and stared at my teenage dream, at the Millie Jean legs and the flare of her hips, at the patch of duck down in the shadow of her thighs. I sure did like that little patch of down. She'd trimmed it up nice and left a neat little strip, like the part you always miss when you mow the lawn at night.

I didn't say a thing. I got up and tore my clothes off in eight seconds flat. Millie bounced her lovely butt on the bed, put her hands behind her head and grinned. I crawled up toward her like a snake sneaking up on a mouse. I wanted that mouse real bad. I kissed the little Band-Aid on her foot. I kissed her ankles and her toes, I kissed my way up to her knees. She smelled like perfume and soap. She smelled like a teenage Millie Jean.

"Jack . . ."

"What?"

"You mind turnin' that off? Violins are real irritating to me."

"Sure. That's fine." I got up and went across the room. "You want to hear something else?"

"I got a stereo at home," Millie said. "I can listen to it anytime I want."

"Right. I don't care for music all the time. Sometimes I do. I don't like it all the time."

I crawled back on the bed and started in where I'd left off. My lips reached Millie's thigh. Duck down tickled my nose and I remembered that hot afternoon by the river, when I'd fumbled at her clothes, learning as I went, uncertain what to do when I reached that mystic nest, wholly unaware at the time of the other fun things that one could do. It hadn't occurred to me then, but duck-down glory was straight ahead now, and I wouldn't let it pass me by again.

"Jack . . ."

"What, Millie Jean?"

"Listen, I appreciate the thought, I really do, but I kinda got the foreplay done on the way out in the car. I'd like it if you'd just get it in, okay?"

I looked up over the dusky expanse of Millie Jean. "Well sure, that's fine," I said. "I just thought we could, you know, sort of do something else first."

"Now I know you did, hon." Millie gave me a thoughtful smile. She sat up and took my hands and drew me down to her and I felt like I'd landed on a stove.

"We can do that pervert stuff some other time, okay, that's what you want to do. You're not mad or anything?"

"No. Of course I'm not mad."

"That's good. 'Cause I am real fond of you, Jack, and I got an awful need."

"I've got an awful need too, Millie Jean."

"It's a whole lot better if you do. I mean, one person hasn't got a need, it's not going to work out good. *Cosmo* had a article on it month before last."

"I missed that," I said.

" 'Course you did, silly. It's a girl's magazine. Lord, Jack, I want you to do it real bad!"

Millie's legs snaked around my waist. Her hand slipped between us. Suddenly, as they say, the two of us were one. Her private parts slammed against mine. She squeezed her eyes shut. She said, "Oh, *shiiiiiit,* oh wow!" She trembled all over, let out a breath, and opened up her eyes.

"Boy, that was a keeper, Jack. Was it okay for you?"

I looked down at her. "Are you through, that's it?"

Millie gave an apologetic sigh. "I should've said something. That thing's got a hair trigger. I get off real quick."

"Three seconds," I said. "I'd say that's kinda quick."

"Now see, you are mad, Jack. I can tell somebody's mad."

"I'm not mad."

"You are so." She tightened her legs again. "You go ahead, hon."

"What?"

"Go ahead and finish up. I know you got needs same as me. A man's entitled to pleasure too."

"Christ, Millie."

"What's wrong?"

"Nothing. Everything's fine."

Everything wasn't. I realized I now had nothing to pleasure with. Millie, who was in a position to know, realized it too.

"Don't you let that bother you, hon." She kissed me on the cheek, and stretched to the table for a smoke. "That's something happens now and then. It doesn't mean a thing."

"Yeah, right."

"God, look at the *time*." Millie rolled me off and scooted out of bed. I sat up and stared.

"Millie Jean, what are you doing?"

"I am looking for my pants."

"You mean you can't stay?"

Millie picked up her cutoffs and gave me a puzzled look. "You talking spend the night? Lord, Jack, I got my husband's funeral tomorrow. I don't feel that'd be right."

"I'm sorry. I didn't think."

"We got plenty of other times, you and me." She zipped up her cutoffs and crossed the room, fluffing up her hair. "We should've got together 'fore now. I can't see why we waited so long."

"You were sort of taken up to now."

"And you were sorta out of town." Millie stopped and leaned down and took my face between her hands. "Honest, Jack, if you'd've ever asked . . ."

"I didn't know that."

"Well you know it now, okay?"

"Now's fine with me," I said. I reached real fast and got hold of her zipper and pulled it down.

"Jack . . ." Millie grinned and backed off. "I *told* you I had—*Jeeeeeesussss . . . !*"

Millie bit air like a fish, her mouth twisted out of shape as her eyes rolled back and her hands came up to her face, all this in the slice of a second before sound exploded in the room and the window shattered in a thousand darts of glass. I came off the bed and put a shoulder block into Millie's legs, driving her roughly to the floor. Lead plowed into the mirror and splintered the bedroom door. The shots came so fast they might as well have been one, but I'd heard that sound before and I thought not as fast as a fully automatic, just trigger-pull fast, which is plenty fast enough.

Millie found her voice and screamed and tried to roll me off her back. I grabbed her waist and dragged her to the shelter of the bed, then I kicked out and hit the table lamp. The bulb went out, and three more shots came through the dark. I pulled the drawer out of the table by the bed, brought it to the floor and found the Charter .38, leaned up on the bed and emptied the revolver at the window. Nothing came back. I grabbed a handful of shells, told Millie to stay where she was, and snaked out of the room, cutting my feet on broken glass.

Common sense said stay inside the house but I was too pissed off for that. I went out the front door and around the right side of the house. The night was fairly black. I could see the backyard and the ghostly square of the garage and the darkness of the cornfield after that. Whoever had been there was likely gone now, but I couldn't know for sure. Maybe he knew I'd be dumb enough to come outside where he could take another shot. No way, I decided, that's not the way it is. If he'd wanted us dead he could have finished us off in the house. None of the bullets had even come close, they'd all gone overhead, and no one's as bad a shot as that. What he wanted to do was let me know that he'd stood out there and watched, that he could shoot us or not or do anything he liked. That's what your hard-core loony wants to do. He wants to let you know he's in control and you're not.

Jesus, I thought, a nice quiet life on the farm. Norman Rockwell out of Mickey Spillane.

Car lights swept around the house and I flattened myself against the wall. Tires whined on gravel out front, and someone took off fast, winding up the rpms. Which didn't explain why the lights still flared around the corner of the house. Someone was gone, but someone else was there.

"Jack, you in there or what? If there's someone else inside you better get the fuck out real fast!"

I let out a breath. "I'm not inside, Earl. I'm out. By the side of the house."

Earl didn't answer for a while. "You sure that's you? It doesn't sound to me like you."

I stepped out into the open. "It's me, okay? You want to turn off the damn lights?"

The lights went off, but they stayed on longer than they should. Earl stepped from behind his car. He was wearing jogging shorts and no shirt. His pistol was three or four times the size of mine.

"You get a good look?" I said. "I hope you didn't miss anything."

Earl made a face. "I didn't look at all. Isn't anything I less want to see than a naked white man." He nodded down the road. "Jeep pulled out of here fast, nearly ran me off the road. Looked to me like Millie Jean."

"That's who it was. Millie Jean."

"She had some pants on. She wasn't wearing any top. What you been doin' up here besides that?"

I wanted to put the .38 somewhere, but you can't if you don't have pockets on your ass. "Someone looked in the window. He got off thirty or forty shots. Didn't hit anything because he wasn't trying to."

"I heard about ten."

"Okay, about ten. Ten's enough for me."

Earl grinned. "Your bandages look real nice. Told you that they would."

I turned and started for the house. "I'm going in and have a drink. I might have three or four. You can join me if you don't say anything I don't want to hear."

"You going to get somethin' on?"

"Fuck you," I said.

Earl had an answer, but that was the moment a deep and pleasant sound filled the night. Earl and I stopped to look.

Lights came down the road and I thought for a second Millie Jean was coming back, but I knew that a Jaguar doesn't sound at all like a Jeep, and I realized my luck, which hadn't been terrific up to now, had finally run completely out.

Cecily caught us in her lights. She stepped out of the Jag and slammed the door—she never slams the door—and stopped about ten feet away.

You just drive up like that, you don't have the whole picture in your head, what you see isn't going to look right. You got two men standing there, one stark-naked and one in jogging shorts, both fully armed and one with a whole lot of gauze around his arm and on his head. What you're going to do is get the wrong idea right off.

"I'll tell you what," Cecily said, "this looks like real kinky shit to me. You guys having lots of fun?"

"I thought you were still in L.A.," I said.

"You fucking wish."

Cecily stepped out of the glare of the lights and I could see the way her chin thrust out and the cold blue look in her eyes.

"Cecily," I said, "don't go getting the wrong idea. Things aren't always like they seem."

"They're not, huh?"

"No, they're not. People see something, they take it out of context sometimes. My life was in danger tonight, you didn't even know about that."

Cecily let out a breath. "You're pathetic, Jack. You really are. I'm surprised at you, Earl. I'm not surprised at him."

"Cecily—"

"I passed your little friend coming out. She was driving buck-naked in a Jeep. I thought, say, I wonder where she's coming from? There isn't anyone out here but Earl and Jack."

"She wasn't fully naked," Earl said. "She had some pants on, she didn't have a top."

Cecily glared at Earl. She wouldn't look at me. "I've got

some personal things in the house. It won't take me long to get 'em out."

Cecily turned and stomped up the walk. She slammed the screen door.

"I guess I better be getting on back," Earl said. "You going to be all right?"

"Oh sure," I said, "I'll be just fine."

"Hope you don't keep another gun in the house."

Earl got in his Lagonda and drove back down the hill. He didn't use his lights. I wished I had a drink. I wished I had some pants.

Cecily came back out, carrying her things in a pillowcase, the kind of stuff you leave around when you stay a lot at someone else's house.

"It wasn't anything," I said. "I know that sounds real dumb, but it's something just happened is all."

"My fucking wine. You even used the same CD. You ever have an original thought or what?"

"Cecily, that woman was absolutely the worst lay I ever had in my life. That's the honest truth."

"That makes it okay."

"No, it doesn't make it okay. I didn't say it made it okay. That's all you care about's her, you see what happened in there? You didn't even ask about my head."

"What happened to your head?"

"I had an accident."

"Good. Have a nice life, Jack."

She turned and walked back to the car and got in and drove away. I walked back in the house and got a sheet and went to bed out on the couch. I drank half a bottle of Scotch and went to sleep about six and got up and tossed everything around eight.

The bedroom looked even worse in the full light of day. There was glass everywhere. Bullets had cratered the wall and there was wine spilled on the rug. I found Millie's T-shirt tangled in the lamp.

I got a flash and went outside and looked for tracks, but the ground was too hard and there was nothing much to see. Back in the kitchen I put some coffee on and made some toast. I wondered who had shot at me and why. Everyone knows a few people who really don't care for them a lot, but I couldn't think of anyone pissed off enough to do that. At least, not anyone around here. Back when I wasn't Jack Track for a while, that's something else again. But none of those guys would stand outside a window and fire a bunch of shots into my room. What they'd do is just walk right in and put a bullet in my head. If they felt real good that's what they'd do. If they were kind of constipated, or they'd had a little spat with the wife, they'd leave me with my dick in my mouth. Guys like that, they can think up a lot of real cute things to do.

Fourteen

How I came to be Wayne Grosz of Philadelphia instead of Jack Track is a matter of chance and a shitty attitude. It didn't have a lot to do with planning and intent. I didn't do planning back then. My only effort was to make as little effort as I could. After two fairly hazy college years, in which I learned to smoke pot and attend major sporting events, I cast myself adrift on the aimless tides of life, taking one job and then the next, moving on quickly at the first hint of success. If I found that I liked what I was doing, if I gained a sense of pride, I got myself out of there fast. Often, just in the nick of time. I nearly got promoted twice.

Lack of purpose seemed to suit me just fine. I got to see a lot of the country, and meet girls from regions I was not familiar with at the time. It worked out well for six years. Impulse ruled the day, and the nights took care of themselves. I thought I was safe, counting on random events. Instead, it was an impulse that betrayed me, and brought great change into my life.

On December 21, 1984, I quit my job selling cars in Tulsa, Oklahoma, drew everything I had out of the bank, and flew to Las Vegas Christmas Eve. Why not? It seemed like the right thing to do at the time. I was in Las Vegas an hour and a half when I met Lloyd DeWitt and Mary

Zee. In a single afternoon, Lloyd introduced me to the pleasures of criminal life. In one long weekend of pornographic bliss, Mary Zee taught me I had only imagined there was nothing that I hadn't done twice.

I told myself I stayed around because I couldn't get enough of Mary Zee. Which is true, but Lloyd was a part of it too. I couldn't stand the guy. I thought he was a pompous little hood. Lloyd would borrow a quarter for the toilet, then piss in the corner of your room. I didn't like Lloyd but I liked the way he lived. I liked the way he dropped ten grand at the tables and didn't give a damn. I liked the fifty-dollar steaks and the hundred-dollar wine. Lloyd knew showgirls and stars, and everyone in Vegas knew him. I thought he was an asshole in alligator shoes, and I was flattered that he let me hang around.

I know what happened. At least I do now. I fell victim to America's romance with gangster life. *The Godfather* taught us that wise guys are folks like us. Life seems more exciting on the edge, and you can watch it with some popcorn and a Coke. I think it helped that I'd grown up dumb and semi-poor, that all I had to show for my twenty-eight years was a dull résumé and a polyester suit.

So I stayed close to Lloyd. I stayed real close to Mary Zee, who was always ready to commit some unlikely act anywhere or anytime. I told myself I could live the good life for a while, that I wouldn't have to stay. I could make some good money, and I wouldn't have to get in very deep. Which goes to show that travel hadn't broadened me a lot. I was still a jerk from Pharaoh, Texas, and I learned there was a lot about crime that you're never going to see on TV.

Anger is the key. Things happen and you start getting hostile inside. Hostile builds up and you need to get it out. I'd been saving it up for some time. Since 1956, to be exact, the year that I was born.

My folks got divorced in the summer of 1973. They endured each other for eighteen years. From what I recall, eighteen was more than enough. I was seventeen at the time. Dad died two years later from an overdose of mean. He couldn't stand being mad all by himself. Six months later, my mother met a sleazeball lawyer from Dallas and took off for the Coast. She said she deserved a little joy in her life. She said she'd be back and I could stay with Uncle Will. That was in the spring of '75, and Mother hasn't been back since. She sold the house long-distance and sent me what she got. I gave the money to Uncle Will. There was plenty to get me through college, but two years was all that I could take. The stored-up anger was beginning to affect my daily life. I couldn't see much future in the history of Rome, and I'd pissed off all my friends. That's when I left and caught the first plane out.

Mother and I have seen each other four or five times through the years. She got rid of the lawyer, and married a guy who makes beer in Saint Paul. She said she was sorry, just leaving me alone and taking off, but she'd had about all she could take of family life. I told her I sort of understood. I didn't at all, but what's the use in saying that?

How I got to be Wayne Grosz is a strange happenstance. As I said, when I abandoned college life I took the first plane out. It happened to be for Philadelphia, and that was fine with me.

I got there and looked at the Liberty Bell and the U.S. Mint. I saw Independence Hall and the Betsy Ross House. I wasn't sure what to do next. What I did was find a bar and get a drink. What I did was have maybe six or eight.

Whiskey gives you insight, or that's how it seems at the time. Here I am, I thought, in the cradle of the nation's independence. There's got to be an omen in that. Our country's free and so am I. No one in Pharaoh or anywhere else knows where I am. That's pretty deep stuff, and I was fairly impressed with myself. And if that was not enough, a little while later as I threw up in an alley out back, fate stepped in again, this time with a sign that I couldn't ignore, because you throw up on a guy, the guy's dead, there's got to be a message in that.

I sobered up quick. A dead guy's better than an ice-cold shower every time.

I did something then and I don't know why, I still can't explain why I did it but I did. I should've gotten out of there fast. The normal thing to do, you go somewhere and call the cops, you hang up when they ask you for your name. Instead, I squatted down and went through the guy's jacket and his pants. I'm guessing it was fate behind that; it's not the kind of thing that I'd ever done before or I'd ever do again.

The guy was maybe twenty-five, three years older than I was then, but he'd been through some pretty rough times. He was dressed like a bum. He needed a haircut and a shave. He had two dollars in his wallet, and a Social Security card. His driver's license had expired the year before. He had a picture of a woman and a two-year-old boy. He had a worn and folded clipping that told how Mrs. Anna Grosz and her infant son, Will, wife and child of unemployed welder Wayne Grosz, had died in a tragic house fire. The date on the clipping was two years back.

It wasn't hard to picture what happened after that. Wayne got distraught with his grief and everything, and started going downhill and ended up on the streets. It happens all the time.

Standing there in that alley I think it's the first time I really understood how angry I was at everyone. Angry at my folks for splitting up, then running off or dying and leaving me alone by myself. I was mad at myself for wasting two good years, because I knew I would never go back to college life. It was something I couldn't do again.

What I knew was I didn't want to be Jack Track. I didn't want to be from Pharaoh, Texas, or remember what had happened to me there. Which is why I got to be Wayne Grosz, who lost his family in a fire and ended up in an alley fairly dead.

The next day I rented a safety-deposit box. I put everything in it that said I used to be Jack Track. I found a cheap room and got a job selling shoes. I showed them Wayne's Social Security card. I told the people at the driver's-license place that I'd moved out of town and let my license run out. They said I'd have to take the test again and I told them that was fine.

For six months I sold shoes. Then I moved to Newark and sold aluminum siding for a while. I forget where I moved to next or what I did. Six years later I was in Las Vegas doing gymnastic tricks with Mary Zee and hanging out with Lloyd DeWitt.

For a while everything went fine. I got a Buick and some wing-tip shoes. Crime didn't seem that different from your ordinary legal enterprise. It paid a lot better, and you didn't have to fuck around with tax.

It was going real good. Wayne Grosz was having himself a time. Then, as they are often prone to do, things went from good to really bad. I don't mean bad like you're down to your last hundred grand, or the blonde in the chorus is making it with somebody else. I'm talking *bad,* like a guy named Vinnie thinks you'd look a lot better if you didn't have a head.

Lloyd had assured me that we wouldn't get into any shit that was hazardous to our health, that someone was taking care of that. Maybe they were and they forgot. Or maybe Lloyd lied to me a lot. Maybe I should've stayed in Tulsa with what's-her-name who had the squinty eyes. My life would've turned out different if I had.

Fifteen

Max Coomer's funeral was a little more subdued than "The Circus of the Stars." There weren't any elephants, or any I could see. There was plenty of everything else. There were tycoons from Dallas, Houston and New York. Both the senators from Texas, and a whole herd of mourners from the House. The Governor came, and everyone in Austin who could get the day off. The Vice President was late. He came in a big black car. He brought along twenty guys in shades. They all had haircuts to match.

The media was an army in itself. *Time, Newsweek, U.S. News & World Report. Playboy* and *People* magazine. All the major networks, and several looney tunes from overseas. There were maybe only half as many people in town as they sent out to cover the Persian Gulf War. Which seems fair enough, since Pharaoh is smaller than Iraq.

Someone pointed out a reporter from *The National Enquirer,* a tall and scary dude who looked a lot like Vincent Price. Now we would all learn that Lee Harvey Oswald was alive, that he and Elvis had had it in for Max.

None of the above were on hand for the small church service, which was just for "the family and friends." Good thinking on the part of the widow, and funeral director Eddie Trost. The Pharaoh Methodist Church only seated a hundred and ninety-six, and there were that many people here from CNN.

* * *

I have tried to think what they left out at the cemetery site. Surely it was not a whole lot. The Reverend Henry Plank said we'd see Max Coomer by and by. Many of us gave some thought to that. The Governor told us we couldn't bear a loss as great as this. The Vice President read from a little blue card. He said something-something sorely missed. A platoon of bagpipers squealed through "Amazing Grace" twice. A Broadway star sang "Memories" from *Cats*. Full-dress marines fired off a bunch of shots. Buglers, a hundred yards apart, did the echo rendition of "Taps." Two marines snapped to smartly and folded up the flag, baring, for the moment, a casket grand enough for Tut. They presented the flag to Millie Jean. Millie just looked at it, unsure what to do next.

This military tribute seemed a bit pushy at best, since Max had dropped out of Cub Scouts and, to my knowledge, hadn't worn a uniform since.

Still, no one seemed to mind. It was all part and parcel of the fantasy at hand, the myth we created that God, through some unfathomable error, some momentary lapse, had snatched a great man from our midst. For an hour and a half at the Pharaoh Cemetery, this was not Max Coomer, the asshole no one knew and loved. This was Max the third-act player, shed of all his sins. We gave him all the best lines, the final white lies we grant the just and the unjust alike, before we drop them in the ground.

All this while the sun blazed down from a bleached Texas sky, not a sheltering tree within three or four miles, the temperature steady at a hundred and three. The natives were used to the heat, but the Eastern folk were dropping like flies. There were personnel on hand to handle this, and the droppees were quietly carried off and out of sight.

Finally, it all came to an end. I am certain even Max must have felt it was time to call it quits. I wished I had the cold-drink concern for this crowd, but some enterprising high school lads had thought of that. As soon as the funeral began, they set up a stand in a pickup truck, halfway up the road back to town. Pepsi went for three bucks a pop, snow cones for two and a half. This merchandising coup put the finishing touches on an already hopeless traffic jam. Deke Glover found the heart of the problem, and made the boys stop. The parched and irritated mourners didn't care for this at all. They pelted Deke with tire tools and rocks. A dozen state troopers forced a wedge through the crowd and got him out. When they were gone, the motorists rushed the drink stand and emptied it in thirty seconds flat. Thirst had driven them beyond good manners, and the everyday pleasantries of life. They took what they could get. No one seemed inclined to pay.

Phil had picked me up that morning. George was already in the car. Coming out to get me was a neighborly act, but there was somewhat more to it than that. Phil made it clear, through less than subtle hints, that he knew, if given half a chance, I would bug out on breakfast again.

I couldn't argue that. I had planned all along to avoid these two at any cost. I could tolerate either George or Phil; together, they would likely drive me nuts.

There was nothing new in this. Phil and George had paired off in third grade and they had been an irritation ever since. Maybe they liked each other, maybe not. They really didn't have a lot of choice. Kids instinctively know their place. Max was always at the top. Roy Burns and Eddie Trost had fathers who were semi-affluent, so they ranked right after Max. Billy McKenzie was in the running for a while, until his mother went berserk and shot Mr. McKenzie in the head. Billy's income and his status dropped to nothing after that.

I was as poor as Phil and George. I was even as poor as Deke. But Deke was a good offensive guard, and I was a star running back. A jock can overcome his natural station in life.

When the funeral was over, everybody left. Phil and George and I sat. Phil said he didn't want to get in the traffic back to town. That he wasn't about to drive two miles an hour and wear the air-conditioning out. I didn't want to argue and I didn't want to walk back to town, so I kept my opinion to myself.

Phil and I sat in the front. George sat in the back. This was fine with me. Phil had picked him up at his farm, and even with the car doors open it was clear George was heavy into fish.

"What I wish you hadn't done," Phil said, "I wish you hadn't broke our confidence. That was real humiliating, Jack. Deke setting me and George down and asking all kinds of stuff. Like we were maybe New York mobsters or such."

"We were grilled is what it was," George said.

"Deke likes to watch a lot of cop shows," I said. "I wouldn't let it bother you much."

"Well, you weren't there," George said. "He gave us all this shit about obstructing justice and withholding this and that. He mentioned criminal intent."

"I think I get the picture, George."

"It wasn't up to you, Jack." Phil looked as if I'd hit him with a stick. "Telling Deke was up to George and me."

"Except you weren't going to do it," I said. "You were going to sit around and talk it to death."

"You don't know if we were or not."

"Yes, I do, Phil." I scooted around in the seat so I could see them both at once. "I don't know if this Nate Graham stuff is worth anything or not. But we've got a man dead and a woman who's flat disappeared. That's why I broke your fucking confidence. I couldn't see messing around while you two waited for it to snow."

"Well, you don't have to talk like that," Phil said.

"Yeah, I do too. I got to talk like that. You get me on the phone with this real important shit, you can't talk about it on the phone. You pick me up, you can't talk about it then. We're sitting out here baking in the heat, I still don't know what I'm doing here."

Phil muttered something I couldn't hear.

"I didn't get that," I said.

"I said, it's not a telling thing. It's something we gotta *show.*"

"Something you got to show."

"That's right."

"Okay. Fine. Let's go."

"Well, we're kinda—already here." He wouldn't look at me. "I mean, that's sort of where we are."

"What is?"

"Where we got to go."

I couldn't think what to say next. Phil didn't wait to hear. He opened his door and got out. George got out of the back. I could get out or I could sit there in the car.

It hadn't rained in two months. The black earth had cracked around the dead summer grass. The sun hammered down and I didn't have a hat. The last of the mourners had left, and the TV people had run out of interesting angles at the open grave site. No one was left except the cemetery crew and a guy from Eddie Trost's who was folding up the chairs.

Phil and George led me through the oldest section of the Pharaoh Cemetery, where the tombstones were leaning and stained with red rust. I read the death dates, and the latest I could find said 1902.

We crossed a gravel path, and Phil stopped to let me

catch up. The graves were newer here. George took a bandanna from his overall pocket and patted down his face.

"It's over there," Phil said. He nodded to the left. "We spotted it yesterday afternoon."

"And just what is it I'm supposed to see?"

"Just go and look," Phil said.

I walked past him and stopped where George was standing by a polished gravestone. The deep-set letters read:

EDNA LEWIS GRAHAM
1936–1988
—RESTING IN THE BOSOM OF OUR LORD—

"It's Nate Graham's mother," said Phil. "His father's still alive. I talked to some people knew the family. He's out in Arizona somewhere."

Phil didn't have to tell me. I knew what he wanted me to see. The gravestone had a fluted marble urn attached to either side. Each urn held a mix of red and yellow zinnias and white daisies. The flowers were only slightly burned. They hadn't been there very long. I squatted down and picked out the flowers on the left. I sniffed the water inside, then scooped a little out and touched it to my tongue. The water tasted like plants but it clearly wasn't stale.

"I did what you're doing," Phil said. "Flowers aren't going to last too long in this sun. I figure yesterday morning 'fore noon."

I looked up at him. "Why before noon?"

"Because I was here right after that. Me and George both, a little after one."

I stood and dried my hands on my pants. "You think Nate Graham was here."

"Who else would it be?" Phil squinted past me at the sun. "His old man hasn't ever been back. There isn't any other kin."

"He's here in town," George said. "Likely hiding out somewhere."

"That's not real easy to do in Pharaoh," I said.

"I didn't say he's here," George said. "He's been here, though."

"It could have been someone else. It didn't have to be him. Phil, you said there were folks in town who remembered Miz Graham."

Phil didn't bother to answer that. He looked at me a moment, then turned and walked back to the car. I know he caught the lack of conviction in my voice. I was protesting out of habit, simply because it was Phil. He knew I believed in Nate Graham because I'd seen the new flowers on the grave. Sinister phone calls were one thing, flowers were something else.

I guess I could've said I was sorry I'd hurt his feelings, that I hadn't meant to doubt, but I figured he was pissed off enough and whatever I said wouldn't help. I could have said the reason I believed a lot more in Nate Graham was a bedroom full of bullet holes, but I wasn't about to tell him that. It didn't have to be Graham who'd done the deed, but he was earning a spot on my list.

Phil was standing by the hood of his car, kicking at the gravel in the road. George had his bandanna out again, running it down beneath his collar and up around his throat. I was baking beneath my bogus bandages, and I envied George a lot.

George looked at me and sighed and shook his head, a silent commentary on the heat. "We ready to go?" he said. "I could sure use a cold drink."

"Sounds good to me," I said.

Phil didn't speak. He continued to show great interest in the ground.

I looked across the road at Max's plot. They had the tent down now, and they were smoothing out the dirt.

"You said you were out here, when?" I asked Phil. "Right after noon?"

"A little after one," Phil said. "I told you a little after one."

"That's right, you did."

"Why you want to know?"

"If we were sure about the time, I was thinking we might get lucky and turn up someone else who'd been around. Before you were here. Maybe someone saw Nate Graham."

"Yeah, you ought to do that, all right."

"Now damn it, Phil—" That hangdog look was plain enough. "You *said* you didn't see him. That's all I meant by that."

Phil looked down at his hands. He found something under a fingernail. "I been coming out here every week since we were kids," he said. "Maybe I missed one or two. I pass that grave every time. There hadn't ever been a flower on it yet. I got a little sister buried out here, Jack. I expect you forgot about that."

"No, now I didn't," I said. "I know that, Phil."

Phil looked up at me then. Getting mad was what he wanted to do, but Phil always had trouble with that. Anger was too much effort, and he never seemed to get past sad.

"No, you don't," he said. "That's what you do, you forget. You forgot Louise and me wasn't together anymore. And you forgot about my little sister too."

"No, I didn't forget about her, Phil."

"Doesn't matter," he said. "Don't give a fuck if you did or not."

The air conked out the minute he started the car. It was a hot and silent ride back to town.

Sixteen

I thanked Phil Eddels for the ride, and told him I'd get off at the square. He didn't volunteer to take me home and I certainly didn't ask. I think it was clear that we'd both had enough of each other for a while.

After the funeral, a lot of out-of-towners had headed out at once, but Pharaoh was still jammed with people and cars. It doesn't take much. Twenty people on the square is a swinging Saturday night. Forty is a full-scale riot.

I walked across the courthouse lawn, into the cool, dark halls and up to Doc Hackley's second-floor retreat. Doc was stretched out nearly flat behind his rolltop desk, more or less seated in an object of wonder that had once been a standard executive chair in some forgotten former life, and was now a disaster laced together with rope and baling wire. Somewhat like Ben Hackley himself. He had come from somewhere just before I left town, and he'd been here ever since. Ben was an A-one doctor but he lacked the drive to make it to the top. Private practice proved too great an effort, even in a lazy Texas town. After several years, he got the county coroner's job, mostly by default. He was into his forties and looked sixty-five. He wore ill-fitting suits and had thinning sandy hair. He drank too much and smoked cheap cigars. He chased after women when it seemed worthwhile. If they ran too fast he'd simply quit.

When I opened his door, Ben peered at me over his dirty reading glasses and frowned.

"Jesus," he said, "what the fuck you do to your face?"

"I had an accident," I said. "I ran my truck off into the creek."

"I don't recommend driving. People get killed all the time. Sit down and have a drink."

He pulled himself up with some effort, opened a drawer and set a bottle of bourbon on the desk. "You want a glass, you got to find it," he said. "Used to be a couple here somewhere."

"No, thanks," I told him. "I never take a glass, I'm in a doctor place. You don't know what they've been using it for."

"Good thinking." Doc took a long swig and made a face. I took a drink and then made a face too. I didn't turn the bottle around. I didn't want to see the brand.

"I went to the funeral," I said. "It was something else to see. I take it you didn't attend."

"I don't like 'em. I try to miss as many as I can."

"I can understand that."

"I strongly doubt you do. It's a hazard of the trade. You cut these fuckers open and diddle with their parts, you get sick of having 'em around. You've got no desire to look at them in a box."

Doc took another drink, reached out and grabbed a folder and dropped it on the desk. "You don't have to get social 'less you like. This is what you came to see."

"What I come here for's to drink your booze."

"Now that's a lie, Jack. You got better taste than that."

When I opened up the folder, the photographs took me by surprise. Previews of a bad horror show. Full-color shots of the eviscerated Max. I quickly turned them over but it wasn't quick enough.

The autopsy report was chock-full of things I didn't want to see. There were diagrams and charts. Drawings of this and that. I learned how the killer had cut Max up so he could pedal his way to glory down the field. What you do is, you incise the fibrous joint capsules at the hip and knee joints. At the knee, you cut into the joint and separate the tibula and the fibula bones. Then you slice in between the femur and the hip.

The pictures were still in my head, and I took another drink.

"How hard is this to do?" I asked Doc. "Would you have to have some kind of training to know just where to cut?"

"You'd have to know *some*thing," Doc said, "you want to do it right. If you're asking if this perpetrator's some kind of pro, no, he's not."

Doc paused and gave me a nasty grin. He knew I didn't care much for people's messy parts. "It's just like you cut up a chicken," he said. "Same thing. This ol' boy did a fairly neat job. I expect he's cut something up before."

A sobering and slightly queasy thought. I'd assumed that our killer was someone who didn't like Max. Clearly this was so. Which didn't mean he hadn't been pissed off at someone else before. Maybe he'd been pissed off a lot. If the phantom Nate Graham was our man, he had been out of town for some time. I knew these people didn't suddenly appear and take up the loony trade. You're into shit like that, you've probably been at it for a while.

"I guess they're checking this out," I told Doc. "The cops or the F.B.I. See if this joker's just local or what."

Doc shrugged me off, like he didn't much care. "This impaling business, now . . ." He stopped and lit a cheap cigar. "He wasn't real swift about that. Stuck that rod up the rectum, through the abdomen and into the thoracic cavity. That's the chest, you don't know. He got kind of impatient. Went off-center twice, had to back off and start again."

"And what does that tell you?"

"Doesn't tell me a thing. Except what I said before. This fella isn't Dr. Kildare."

He took the file from me and turned back another page.

"Something real interesting over here. Shows you how the killer did the act. We've got blood pooling in the dependent areas of the body. In this case, Coomer's big ass and his legs. Our boy set him down in a chair. Wanted him to settle that way so he'd be upright for his pedaling routine. Set him there and did his cutting, then stuck him in a freezer for a while."

Ben Hackley grinned again. He was clearly enjoying this a lot. "You look a little peaked, boy. I don't recommend you pursue the surgeon's life. I expect you'd throw up all the time. That wouldn't look good, you get in the O.R."

"I dated a nurse once," I said. "She worked for an asshole doctor, in Waco or Mineral Wells, I forgot. I didn't care for her dinner-table talk."

"That wasn't Wendy Simms, was it? Dark-haired girl, kinda short?"

"I don't know, it might've been."

I studied the report for a minute and took another drink. The whiskey didn't help. I was down to page six when something caught my eye. "Jesus," I said, "he *shot* Max too? I didn't know that."

"One bullet at the base of the skull," Doc said. " 'Bout a fifty-two-degree angle, up into the brain. Caliber thirty-eight, soft-nosed slug. Went right out the top of his head. Nothing you could see when they found him out there—he had that football helmet on."

"That kind of surprises me," I said.

"What's that?"

"A psycho like this guy, Doc, you've got enough hate, you're going to do something like this, you're going to make your victim suffer, you want to see him squirm. It doesn't sound right, this guy letting Max off like that with a bullet in his head."

Ben Hackley gave me an irritated look. The way doctors do when some uppity patient wants to know how long he's got to live.

"You poor at reading, or what?" Doc said. "I never said he let him off. Where'd I say that?"

"You saying he didn't?"

"Hell no, he didn't. Next paragraph, if you'd bother to look. He gave Max a local. Made him watch while he started slicin' into his leg. Max's heart quit like *that*." Doc snapped his fingers to show me how. "The bullet was for kicks. Likely made him mad that Max was dead. What he did, he *scared* that poor son of a bitch to death . . ."

Seventeen

Ben Hackley's office smells of stale cigars and old socks, cheap whiskey and several generations of dust. There is also the musty aroma of mice, a traditional odor that permeates the courthouse itself. The mice have been around from the start, arriving with the first pioneers. They have raised countless families in the walls and in the floors, feeding on mortgages, warrants, and suits of every sort, a diet that has seeped into their genes to form a sly and cautious breed. Now, they are as cunning as country lawyers, and cannot be caught by any means.

Ben does not keep cadavers in his courthouse lair. He does his grisly work in the Pharaoh County Hospital, two miles out of town. Still, I always leave his office with the feeling I have picked up the gamy scent of death, along with the more familiar smells. No doubt this is only in my head, but that doesn't seem to help.

I was glad to get away and breathe the still and humid air outside. I grew up here, and I don't mind the weather that much. In Pharaoh, Texas, stupefying heat is what you get. It's there between June and December every year. It was hot when the Comanches were here, and it will still be hot when all of us are gone. Nevertheless, everyone you meet says, "Lord, it's a scorcher," like they truly expected something else.

Crossing the courthouse lawn, I thought about a tall cold

drink. A chocolate Dr Pepper came to mind. An RC Cola or a Delaware Punch. Drinks of yesteryear.

Not a real good idea. The drugstore was packed with out-of-towners. Audie's Café would be chock-full of locals, I didn't have to look. Everyone I knew would be in there, rehashing Max's release from worldly strife. Phil Eddels and George. Billy McKenzie and Roy Burns. And, with my luck, our illustrious lawman, Deke.

No one I really cared to see. What I needed to do was go home, get in the shower with a full bar of Ivory and a Dortmunder beer. A sensible plan indeed. If Phil hadn't brought me into town. If Earl hadn't run my fucking truck into a creek.

I turned and walked back the way I'd come, past the courthouse to the far side of the square. There is not much over there to see. Most of the storefronts are empty, and have been since 1966. There is a real estate office with a dentist upstairs, a dime store struggling to stay alive. If Pharaoh is dying a slow and easy death, you can see the open wounds right here.

Herb's Exxon & Auto Repair was on the corner, next to an empty shoe store. Herb was close to Uncle Will's age, and they had been boyhood pals. If Herb remembered who he was, he might remember me. If he did, he would let one of his snot-nosed grandsons run me home. He had five or six, and they pretended to work in the garage; what they really liked to do was steal cars and strip them down for parts. They weren't very good at this trade and they usually got caught. I was hoping maybe one of these country crime czars would be out on bail at the time.

Herb was fixing a tire when I walked into the shade of his garage. The tire was an old Goodyear and had no tread at all. It might make a good mosquito net, but it would not do much for a car. Herb stopped and blinked up at me with dishwater eyes.

"I'm closin' up," he said. "Whatever it is, I haven't got the time."

"Herb, it's me," I said. "I'm Will Track's nephew, Jack."

"Is that right?" Herb blinked again. "What the fuck happened to your face?"

"I had an accident. I ran my truck off in the creek."

"You want to sell it, I can get you something for the parts. Will dead yet or what?"

"No, he's doing pretty good right now."

"Uh-huh." Herb thought about that. He stood with some effort, and wiped greasy hands along his pants. "I mean to get over and see him 'fore he's gone. I don't expect I will. I never cared much for Will but I doubt he's smart enough to know that. You'd be his brother Mack. One married the Hailey gal."

"No, now I'm Mack's *son,* Herb. I'm Jack."

"Mack's boy."

"That's right."

"What the fuck happened to your face?"

It was fairly clear to me this wasn't working out too well. I was putting out on FM, and Herb was back there with Tom Swift. There weren't any grandsons around, and it suddenly struck me that even if they had been lurking about they wouldn't be here now. I am no Deke Glover, but those boys don't like a badge of any sort. This hadn't occurred to me before. Everyone else thinks my job is just a hoot, so I am used to ignoring it myself.

It made me feel kinda good—Herb's boys running at the sight of Town Constable Jack. Of course they might have been out stripping cars. This would be a good time, with all the extra folks around.

I didn't say good-bye to Herb. Herb had forgotten I was there. He went back to his tire, and I walked out of the garage and into the glare of the late afternoon and wondered where I'd left my shades. Maybe up at Ben's. If I had, Ben would claim them as his own. Anything you left up there belonged to him.

I had one foot off the curb when the Caddy came out of the alley going maybe forty-five, kicking up boxes and empty oil cans, coming right at me like a goddamn tank and missing me by an inch and a half. A miss is not as good as a mile when you're hugging the wall and your belt scrapes paint off the Caddy's front door. The car whipped by in a blur and the driver jerked the wheel over hard, hit the curb and made sparks, bounced back into the street and burned rubber and fishtailed south onto Elm. I watched until it made a quick Indy to the left and disappeared. I heard it squeal again, likely heading east and out of town. I leaned against the alley wall and shook for a while. I wished I had a drink. I wished I had three or four. I had gotten a look at the driver as he passed. The driver was Roy Burns.

Maybe Roy saw me, maybe not. In the quick half-second I saw his face, I saw a man frightened and possessed, a man with a single blind purpose in his head: to get the hell away from where he was. Roy right then could have run down a whole herd of orphans and never looked back.

And there was something more than that. Someone else was in the car. I don't know who, I didn't get a good look. But someone was there hunched down beside Roy with his hands up tight against his face. His face or hers, I couldn't swear to that.

I stood in the street for a moment and looked up toward the square. Grackles were landing in the courthouse trees. Before it got dark, there would be about a thousand of them there. They would roost in the branches and shit until dawn. When we were kids we would run across the lawn, zigzagging this way and that. Whoever came through unscathed was the hero of the night. Hardly any of us ever won.

I walked back up the alley, tracing the path of Roy's car. There was nothing much to see. The back of Herb's garage;

a wooden door at the rear of the real estate office that hadn't been opened in years. Doors to empty stores. The back of the dime store, with boxes and garbage cans. Roy had somehow missed them in his kamikaze dash across town.

I knew that's how it had to be. That he hadn't come from somewhere in the alley itself, he was merely passing through. All the doors were locked up tight, and the far side of the alley was an old stone fence choked with trumpet vines and weeds. The backyards of houses past that.

So what the hell was going on here? Roy is an asshole at times, but this goes with the lawyering trade and you sort of have to overlook that. I've known him all my life and he's not the type to race around in cars. Billy McKenzie, I can see him doing that, but not Roy.

Maybe someone got hurt, I decided. Roy takes the victim in for help, his eyes on an injury suit. Something like that made sense. Except he wasn't going that way. The hospital's out on the other side of town.

I heard a car door shut and I turned and looked back. Deke was getting out of his car. Not *his* car, which someone had shot full of holes, but another just like it that said "401" on the side. Someone who didn't know better might imagine there were four hundred other Pharaoh County Sheriff's cars instead of six.

Deke tugged his hat down tight so it just touched the top of his mirror shades. He came up the alley in his lazy Western walk and stopped a good ten feet away. Gary Cooper, *High Noon,* 1952.

"Jack, what the fuck you doin' here," he said, "you want to tell me that?"

"Someday you're going to ask me something different," I said. "You do and I'll likely have a stroke."

"That doesn't answer the question," Deke said.

"I am checking out doors. That's what they pay me for. That's what I do."

Deke showed me a nasty grin. "This your re-tard's day off?"

"Crime's out of hand in this town. Every man's got to do his part."

Deke dropped his cigar stub and ground it in the dirt. "A car come screeching through this end of town a while back. I was up on Main, you could hear it up there. You see it go by?"

"I heard it," I said.

"You didn't see it, though."

"I was in the Exxon. Talking to Herb."

"What for?"

"I might get into stolen parts. Farming isn't what it used to be."

Deke took off his glasses and wiped them on his shirt. He looked at the ground, then he looked up at me. I had seen the look before.

"Everything's a fucking joke to you," he said. "I'm getting awful tired of that."

"Deke, I am awful tired of you," I told him. "I wish there was something we could do. I don't know what that'd be."

Deke was trying to hang on to his cool but it wasn't working out. I could see the skin getting real tight around his neck.

"What I'm thinking is I ought to run you in. Take your sorry ass up there and toss it in the can. Shit, I thought you had better sense. A shootin' in your house, that's a felony's what it is. Something like that, you get on the phone and call *me*. That's an obstruction of justice if you don't. Who the *fuck* you think you are?"

"I was thinking Injuns," I said.

"You were what?"

"Injuns. They chase a deer or something up around the house. A couple of shots go astray. Hey, I bet the same thing happened to you. Some pesky redskin saw your car and thought he had a buffalo. You can't tell a thing in the dark. Filled it full of load before he—"

Deke's big fist came at me in a blur. I saw the blow coming and I had time to think how I should have known something when he took his glasses off. How I'd waited half my life to get him pissed off enough to get me back for that afternoon at Pharaoh Junior High. And when he finally did, where was I?

I decided to lie there for a while. I looked up at the afternoon sky. I wondered why Millie had felt a great need to share our adventure with Deke. That girl needs to watch her mouth. This is good advice for one and all. A stray dog came and sniffed my feet. I wondered if he knew anyone who had a car. I still didn't have a ride home.

Eighteen

I washed up at Herb's, pulling sweaty bandages aside and splashing cold water in my face. The water smelled like Goodyear tires. I left and walked back up toward the square. My jaw hurt bad. I sat down on the curbside to rest. I should have been watching Deke closer, but that's beside the point. There's a question of fair play here. What kind of person hits a man who's got gauze wrapped all around his face? The same kind of person who carries an ax handle in his car. You can't trust a person like that.

Grackles squawked among the trees. A TV truck rattled by, heading out of town. The driver looked at me and opened up a beer. My watch said a quarter after six. Cecily Benét's green Jaguar turned past the courthouse and purred up to the curb. Cecily tapped a finger on the wheel. She looked straight ahead, like I wasn't even there.

"You got a little knock in there," I said. "You might need a tune-up. It could be just a plug."

"If I need maintenance advice, I expect I'll ask somebody else," Cecily said. "Come on, get in. You look like a wino waiting for a bus."

"We don't have a bus," I said. "Pharaoh is a very small town."

"It's not small enough for me."

I wondered what she meant and decided not to ask.

The air was on high. The seat felt good, like you're sitting in a fine expensive chair. I sure like foreign cars. Cecily looked real nice. She was wearing those cutoff jeans, the same ones she'd worn down at the creek. Her legs were slick and brown. The sun caught the downy little hairs atop her thighs. I remembered hot lazy afternoons and carnal nights. Cecily caught me and showed me her razor-blade eyes.

"This isn't a show of affection," she said. "Don't go thinking that it is. I am giving you a ride. I do good works from time to time."

"I appreciate it, too. I ran my truck off into the creek. I guess you heard about that."

"I have heard a lot of shit lately," she said. "Most of it from you." Her voice was calm and easy, no trace of anger at all. I took this as a very bad sign.

"What I thought, Jack, I thought we had something kinda nice. This is how it looked to me. I seem to do this to myself. I think something's good, I turn around and see it's not."

"Now that's not true," I said. "I think we've got a misunderstanding is all. I know we can work this out."

Cecily turned and scorched me with a look. "Don't you *tell* me that. You tell me that, I'll throw up!"

She jerked the wheel around hard. I slammed into the door. The rear end snaked to the right and we nearly hit a truck.

"Now we're not going to get anywhere we don't talk," I said. "Talking's how you work things out."

Cecily ground a gear into third. "What you better do, you better shut the fuck up."

"No, I won't do that. That won't straighten out anything at all. Cecily, I don't blame you for feeling like you do. You're sure entitled to that. What I'm saying is, there's stuff to consider. Things aren't always how they look."

"Jesus, Jack." Cecily turned to me and stared. She shook her head and looked back at the road. "You know how stupid that sounds, you say something like that? I see this lady, she's driving this Jeep, and her tits are hanging out. I catch you and Earl half-naked in the yard, I think, boy, I wonder what's going on here? The *hell* things aren't the way they look. Don't you tell me how they look."

"I'd like to explain about that."

"You do and I'll toss you right out of this car."

"Cecily, I care for you a lot."

"Oh, shit."

"Well, I do. I think you know that."

"Uh-huh. You care a whole lot when I'm in town. Thanks a lot, Jack." Cecily made a funny little sound. She went "hmm-hmmm-hmm," like a show tune was floating in her head.

"This extracurricular fun, that works two ways, you know," she said. "It isn't just *here,* it could be about anywhere else. You might want to think about that."

I was two, maybe three beats back. It took me a while to catch up. When I did, I felt like someone had kicked me in the gut.

"What," I said, "you got some guy in L.A.? Cecily, you telling me that?"

Cecily let out a little sigh. "Things *happen,* Jack. I mean, things do. I believe it was you told me that."

"Well did you or not? I bet it was one of those stars."

"I don't know a lot of stars."

"It was one of those businessmen, right? Some jerk in a suit. You're a sucker for a guy's got a suit."

"Well I'm sure not likely to run into one around here."

"I know what you're doing," I said. "Don't think I don't. You didn't do it. You want me to think you did."

"Do you?"

"Do I what?"

"Think I did or not."

"Cecily, I don't want to talk about this."

"Good. Let's don't."

"I'm real disappointed if you did, I'll tell you that."

"Fuck you, Jack."

"I guess we're even now. I guess that's the point."

Cecily gave me a phony smile. "You don't know if we are or not. That's what's bothering you, right?"

"Nothing is bothering me at all."

"Oh, right. I can see that. You're just— What are you *doing,* Jack? You supposed to take that off?"

"What I'm doing," I said, "I'm getting well real quick. I am tired of being all wrapped up."

I had sweated underneath that thing long enough. The last little drop came rolling down my nose did the trick. I tore that mother apart. Gauze went flying like a toilet-paper roll in the wind. I rolled the window down and tossed it all out. The air felt good. I scratched everything that itched.

Cecily looked appalled. "My God, you've got a big blue bump on your jaw. It sticks out about a mile."

"That isn't from the accident," I said. "I had a fight with Deke."

"Did you win or him?"

"He did."

"Good. Saves me the trouble," she said. "He can probably hit harder than me."

There wasn't a lot more talk. I sat and scratched, and Cecily drove about a hundred on the narrow gravel road out of town, the purpose here being to scare me into saying "Slow down." I knew the Jag would go a lot faster, so I wasn't about to do that.

I thought about the double standard for a while. I had tackled this problem once or twice. I suppose it occurs to every right-thinking man at least sometime in his life. It hurt me to imagine that Cecily Benét might have shared her lovely self with someone out of town. In the big moral picture, this would cancel out my night with Millie Jean. Men grab a quickie and think it's just fine. Why shouldn't women do it, too? I didn't know why, but it didn't seem right.

What's sauce for the goose is sauce for the gander, as my mother used to say. I never did like these folksy observations, they seldom seem to make any sense. That one always bothered me a lot. Why would geese or ganders—either one—care what kind of sauce the other got? If sauce is a problem in your life, it means you're Christmas dinner and you're sitting in a pan.

I dozed for a minute, then Cecily Benét hit a rock. Hit one, or found one that she liked. We passed the Collier place and then old man Hunt's, and home was only moments away. The day had beat me down. Phil and George and Roy and Cecily Benét—not to mention Deke—had left me frazzled to the bone. Max Coomer's funeral already seemed a distant event. Only the high points came to mind. I recalled that Fred Newcomb, who worked maybe thirty years for Max, actually had smiled. Probably for the first time in his life. Smoothy had winked at a marine. The Vice President had peed in his pants. Either that, or the man had devised a most peculiar way to sweat. You would think the Secret Service had a way to handle this.

I thought about Max. I wondered where he was. If he was anywhere at all, he was pleased the way everything had gone. Hardly anyone gets a better sendoff, unless you're the President himself, or a major movie star. The only thing missing was the darkies coming in from the fields, solemnly gathered at the Big House to sing a few hymns for Massah Max. Max would have liked that a lot. Which only goes to show that even in our most outlandish dreams, a little bit of truth can prevail. I am certain that every black person who ever heard of Max broke into song at the news that he was gone. Some, I am sure, considered this called for a drink.

* * *

I didn't ask much. All I wanted was a bath and a beer and a bed. The latter with Cecily Benét or without. For the moment I was too tired to care. The Jag pulled up into the drive. The lights of the car swept the house. I saw the shadows of the trees on the wall. I saw someone had sprayed FUCKYOU on my door. Right below the spot where they'd nailed Alexander the cat.

Nineteen

Cecily made me a drink, a very tall Scotch in a Mickey Mouse glass. She made another for herself and we sat at the table in the kitchen in the dark. Light from the hall slanted in across the worn-out linoleum floor, a lot more light than I needed at the time, a dull yellow square that found the corner of the fridge and Alexander's water dish. I thought about him hunched over there, as far from the bowl as he could get, thoroughly disgusted that he had to consume this stuff, knowing there was always a chance that he might get a little on the outside of himself as well as in.

I tried to keep my eyes off the floor. I looked at my Mickey Mouse drink. A glass that big would dull my senses pretty quick. I didn't want to get dulled. What I wanted to do was fucking kill someone, I just didn't know who.

"What kind of person would do a thing like that?" I said. "Do something like that to a cat? I have known some real sorry-ass bastards, I don't think I know anyone who'd do that."

"You've led a very sheltered life," Cecily said. "People do a lot of bad stuff. They do it all the time."

"Thanks. See, I didn't know, this is the first time I heard about that."

Cecily showed me this look that she gets, like you're working with the handicapped, you ought to be nice. "Jack, I don't want you sitting here thinking all night about your cat. I want you to finish that drink and go to bed."

"Listen," I told her, "I am real upset right now. I was awful close to that cat. I don't know if you understand that, it's like losing a person to me. I knew who did this, I'd shoot the son of a bitch on the spot. Why, I wouldn't even blink."

I got up and walked to the back screen door and looked out at the dark. What I wanted to do was go and cry somewhere but I wasn't sure how she'd take that.

"You know what I don't get? I don't get what any of this shit has to do with *me*. Someone doesn't like Max, okay, he kills Max's dog and then Max. I guess he probably killed Emma Stynnes too. So why does this asshole want to shoot up *my* bedroom and do something awful to my cat? I haven't got any connection with Max. I didn't like Max in second grade. He's dead and I don't like him any more now."

"Uh-huh."

"Uh-huh what?"

I heard her behind me, heard the noises in her throat as she took a stiff drink and set the glass back down.

"Pardon me if I intrude on your personal private life," she said, "but you're looking for *connections,* you and the lovely widow come to mind. I mean, you and her connected in the biblical sense, I guess that ought to count."

I turned back to face her, expecting those taut little lines around the mouth, around the eyes, something to complement the bite in her voice, but there was nothing there at all, possibly a slight touch of sadness and regret.

"Cecily," I said, "I wish you'd go back to being mad. I can sort of work with that."

Cecily shrugged. "Too bad for you. I'm past being mad. I'm into something else."

"Like what?"

"Like cool and collected. I am setting my self-respect and hormones aside. I got to think for a while."

"This is bad for me, right?"

"Jesus, Jack." She gave me a chilling look. "You're not

even in this, pal. I know you think you are, but you're not. This is just about me."

I started to speak, but Cecily waved me off. "Let's get away from me, all right? Just leave it there, Jack. Did you hear what I said back there? I *saw* that bedroom. You've got a piece of this action, you like it or not."

"Well I don't know what it'd be." I sat back down. Cecily had finished off her drink and started on mine. The whiskey line was down to Mickey's knees. "You think, what? This maniac's pissed about me and Millie Jean? That seems awful far-fetched to me. If Nate Graham's in on this, I doubt he ever spoke to Millie twice."

A thought suddenly hit me. I remembered what Phil or maybe George had said.

"Hey, maybe you're right. Max caught him talking to Millie Jean. I don't recall what grade we were in. It might've been the ninth. Anyway, he made Nate take off all his clothes, then he ran him around in front of the school so everyone could see. My God, you suppose he's still mad about that? Dumb question, right? If he's crazy enough to kill Max and his dog, the man's not thinking real straight."

Cecily set down her drink. "Jack, who is Nate Graham? What the hell are we talking about here?"

"I forgot," I said. "I guess you don't know about that. Nate Graham's been calling George and Phil. You don't know them either. What happened is, Nate left Pharaoh but he's back. He's been out at the cemetery. Phil just missed him. He might've been the guy who killed Max. This doesn't make any sense to you, does it? I can tell."

"Well, shit." Cecily clamped her lips together tight. There were angry little sparks in her eyes, but for once they weren't for me.

"I got an earful from Earl," she said, "but I didn't get that. He kinda left some parts out. I would like to know why he's messing with my head."

I looked at Cecily. "When was all this?"

"When was what?"

"Earl messing with your head."

"Today. While you were off doing your funeral bit." Cecily paused, as if she wasn't sure exactly what to say. "I wanted to talk to Earl. I knew you wouldn't be around."

"About what happened at the house."

"Yes, damn it, about what happened at the house." Cecily made two little fists. "If you think that means I'm concerned about you, well you're right. It does *not* mean this is a *personal* concern, so don't you dare go thinking that."

"Okay, I won't." A big lie, because I did.

"Earl told me about the shooting. How the guy wasn't trying to hit you or he would, and what you two were doing semi-naked in the yard. He didn't say a thing about Nate what's-his-name, I don't know why he left that out. Mostly, he talked about Deke."

"About Deke."

"Earl thinks it might have been Deke shot up your house. He thinks maybe Deke did Max."

I stared at Cecily Benét. "He thinks what?" I had to laugh at that. "That's the dumbest thing I ever heard. What was Earl drinking at the time?"

"He wasn't drinking all that much. Jack, he's got a point. He says Deke doesn't like you nosing around on his turf. Doesn't like you playing cop. Two, he doesn't like you because you're Earl's friend. And three, he doesn't like you anyway, never mind one or two."

"I guess I already knew that. Deke and I were never real close. But that doesn't mean he had anything to do with that business last night." Everything started to itch. I closed my eyes and scratched. Maybe it was permanent. Maybe it wouldn't stop.

"Listen," I said, "I can see Deke Glover running over a cat. Or just about anything else. I don't see him nailing my kitty to the door or shooting up my room, I don't see him doing that. I sure don't see him killing Max."

Cecily made a slightly tipsy face. "Yeah, why not?" There wasn't much left in her glass or mine.

"Because Deke's not entirely stupid's why not. Deke would kill Max about the same time he'd burn his bank account. Deke was Max's personal law and order in Pharaoh County. He did what Max wanted done and he got paid for it. Real well, too, I understand. Cecily, Earl's got Deke on the brain. He's got it in for Deke a lot more than I do. I'm not saying anything I wouldn't say to him. I think it's real likely he shot up Deke's car."

Cecily grinned. "I heard about the car."

"Earl told you about that?"

Cecily shook her head. "Earl didn't. You stop for gas or buy a loaf of bread in this town, you're going to hear about Deke's car. You think he did that?"

"I certainly do."

"Why don't you ask him if he did?"

"I intend to. As soon as I see him I will."

Cecily looked slightly amused. "And what do you think he'll say?"

"I don't know what he'll say. Not with Earl I don't."

That was the honest truth. Sometimes I could tell what Earl would say and do. Sometimes I just thought I could. I'd been right and I'd been dead wrong. I didn't think I was wrong about the car. An ambush wasn't Earl's style, but there are times when we all must compromise. Earl had a lot of anger inside and he'd simply let it out. It wasn't just Deke and his ax handle, what he was doing to Earl's people now. It was Pharaoh itself—now, and for more than a hundred years past. Shooting up Deke's car was Earl's way of getting back. A little stronger, maybe, than his "Nigger of Wall Street" mailbox act, but not as permanent as shooting Deke himself.

Cecily stood and washed the glasses in the sink, a little unsteady, I thought, but that woman had had a lot to drink.

"If he did it," I said, "that's just fine with me. As long

as he doesn't get caught. You can bet he's at the top of Deke's list. Deke doesn't care for anyone who's slightly black. He sure doesn't like 'em if they're rich."

"But you don't think he's got it in for you. Deke, I mean." Cecily didn't turn around.

"Yeah, he's got it in for me. You take a look at this jaw? But he isn't mixed up in this thing about Max. And he sure didn't take a shot at me. That stuff's all in Earl's head."

Cecily turned and leaned against the sink. "There's something I need to tell you, Jack. Earl said he would, he just wanted to think about it some."

"Think about what?" I said. Cecily's eyes drooped a little and her face wasn't working just right.

"Doesn't anybody know this in town, I don't think. I mean, anyone who's white. Earl went back to see this Mrs. Stynnes, Emma Stynnes's mother? Apparently, Emma saw everything that went on in that house, and told her mother about it. Deke Glover was having a red-hot romance with Millie Coomer, Jack. I mean, they've been going at it for three or four years. Right in the house upstairs, whether Max was home or not. In the back of Deke's car out front. Emma said she saw 'em do it underwater twice. Earl says maybe that's the reason Max Coomer and his dog got dead, and poor Emma's vanished out of sight."

Cecily gave me a cold-eyed, straight-on look, or as straight as she could manage at the time. "It *sure* as hell explains why someone took affront to you humping Millie Jean. Lovers don't like that kinda shit. I can personally attest to this, Jack. You might want to think about that . . ."

Twenty

It's funny how people react sometimes and how they don't. You hear about something like Deke and Millie Jean and how they fuck like rabbits all the time and maybe Deke's a looney tune on top of that. You got any sense, something like that it ought to get your attention real fast. You ought to say something like, "Holy shit, I sure didn't know that!"

What I did was just sit there and look at the table for a while. The pattern on the tablecloth showed different kinds of ducks. I had looked at that tablecloth a thousand different times and never noticed this at all. You get to thinking that a duck is just a duck. The truth is, a pintail and a mallard aren't anything alike.

I grabbed up my bottle and left. There wasn't much there, but it was possibly enough. Cecily gave me a bleary-eyed look, the kind of look that says: I am lost in an alcoholic fog; for a while I will have the IQ of a semi-conscious moss.

In the bathroom I opened up the cabinet where I keep the sheets and towels. There was one towel left. One pillowcase and a towel. You live by yourself, things tend to run out. You run out of glasses and your last clean socks. I found a solid cardboard box in the closet in the hall. The box showed a picture of a VCR, made by our neighbors overseas. I thought Alexander would like that a lot. He was very fond of videotapes. They are nearly impossible to open, but he had somehow managed this twice.

Outside, the night was hot and still. I got Alexander off the door and I don't care to talk about that. I buried him in the dead peach orchard out back. He liked to roll around out there and look for bugs. He thought he was a lion and the beetles were gazelles. When I thought about that I sat down and started bawling like a kid because I loved that cat. There is nothing wrong with that. If he wants to, a grown-up man can love a cat.

I started on the Scotch and I thought about Deke and Millie Jean. I didn't want to, but I did. I wondered how Deke liked sex with Millie Jean. Maybe they were both real quick and it worked out fine. Fucking Millie Jean isn't all that fun but it sure does save a lot of time. That, and you cut down the odds of somebody finding out. You spend maybe two or three seconds in bed, it's not like a nooner or a no-tell motel afternoon. There's a good chance you won't get caught.

Getting caught's something you have to think about. Betrayal is the key to your average romance. A sad commentary on life, but that's pretty much the way it is. Millie Jean messed around on Max. Max likely played around on Millie Jean. Millie Jean cheated on Deke, and I betrayed the yogurt queen. It is not impossible that Cecily Benét messed around with a guy in a suit, but I would rather not think about that.

I didn't hear Earl walk up. I noticed these broomstick legs poking out of yuppie shorts, and Earl was on the other end of that.

"Good thing I wasn't an assassin or something, you'd be awful dead," Earl said.

"If you are," I told him, "go ahead and get it over with. I don't really give a shit."

Earl sat down cross-legged in the dark. He reached out for my bottle and took a healthy swig.

"I saw your lady inside. She was able to talk a little bit.

I'm real sorry about your cat. I tried to keep an eye on the place. I wish I'd seen the son of a bitch."

"Thanks," I said, "I appreciate that. Is Cecily okay? She wasn't looking real good."

"She's okay now. Mumbled for a minute and passed out on the couch."

"I hope you didn't touch anything."

"I've done that maybe once. Molested a lady in her sleep. I enjoyed it a lot but it didn't seem right. What the fuck happened to your face?"

"Me and Deke had a fight."

"You hit him back?"

"This was one of my slower days."

Earl looked disgusted at that.

"Listen," I said, "this stuff you were talking to Cecily about. Why didn't you come and tell me? You told her about it, you didn't tell me."

Earl shrugged. "Wasn't much *time* to talk about it last night. You had a lot going on around here. Cecily still pissed off about you and Millie Jean?"

"What do you think? Earl, I'm not real shocked about Deke and Millie Jean. Nothing either one of them did would surprise me a lot. What I'm not buying is all this crap about Deke doing Max. That doesn't make a bit of sense."

"Doesn't, huh?" Earl plucked a thin cigar out of his shirt. He struck a kitchen match on his shoe and lit up. "All that fine Coomer money just lyin' around, maybe half a billion bucks. Get rid of Max, you get the gold and the lovely young widow Millie Jean on top of that. Seems kinda simple to me."

"Jesus, Earl." I took my bottle back. Earl had sipped his way down to the bottom and there wasn't much left.

"You are pushing it, pal. Now you got a conspiracy going, right? Deke and Millie Jean. I can sure see that. Minnie Mouse and Goofy off on a murder spree. Isn't either one of 'em bright enough to walk and chew gum."

"You don't think? How bright you gotta be?"

Earl pulled on his cigar. The glow lit the dark planes of his face. I heard the heavy beat of wings, and saw an owl swoop low against the branches overhead.

"*If* they did," I said, "which they wouldn't, they'd knock off Max in some ordinary way. Deke'd just shoot him in the head and say a burglar did it. They sure wouldn't do that weird electric shit, that and cutting people up. What we got here is a fucking maniac. I think we got Nate Graham is who we got."

I filled Earl in on my graveyard adventure with George and Phil. I told him I had not been overly convinced about Nate and his funny phone calls until I'd seen those flowers on the grave. Nate Graham seemed a lot more real after that.

"Apparently, he's got this long-standing hard-on for Max. Your maniac type, he's going to do something like that. He's going to let his hate fester for ten or twenty years. Then something kinda snaps and it all comes out."

"All right," Earl said.

"All right what?"

"I didn't say this fella wasn't in it. You didn't hear me say that."

I tried to see his face in the dark. "Wait a minute, now. What's all this?"

"I said, I didn't—"

"I heard what you said. I might have a hearing loss, Earl. What I thought you said was Deke and Millie Jean. I didn't hear you say Nate Graham. I thought *I* said that."

"That's what I'm saying too," Earl said. "I'm not letting the crazy dude out. But that doesn't rule out Deke."

"Deke and Nate Graham."

"Uh-huh."

"What about Millie Jean?"

"Might be she doesn't know about Nate. If I was to guess, I'd say no. She doesn't know about that."

"If I was to say, I'd say you're into hard drugs. I'd say we're looking at substance abuse."

"That's one of those ethnic slurs is what it is," Earl said. "I'm willing to let it pass. I know you got a recent loss. Come on inside. Something I want you to see."

"I think I'm fine right here."

Earl stood and brushed off his knees. "Good. I'll just check on Cecily, see if there's anything she needs."

"The hell you will," I said.

Cecily was sprawled out on the couch, one hand hanging limply to the floor. She was lying facedown, and her mouth was pooched up and her nose was squashed all out of shape. She didn't look like your average yogurt queen. She looked like a lady got strapped in a rocket off to Mars, taking nine or ten Gs.

I walked in the kitchen and opened up cabinets to see if there was anything to drink. There was nothing but some Llano, Texas, wine, and I didn't want that. I thought I had a six-pack in the fridge, but there was nothing there but a stone-dead tomato and some cheese.

Earl went off to the john. When he came back in he had a book in his hand. He dropped it on the table, and I saw it was a yearbook from Pharaoh Senior High. It was a sickly sea-green, a pebble-finish vinyl with a gold-embossed Pharaoh Asp about to strike. The asp looked awfully fierce. We had worn this mean-eyed serpent on our helmets, but we seldom managed to scare the other team.

I got a glass of water and sat. "Looks like fun," I said. "A stroll down memory lane."

Earl gave me a look. "Yours, not mine. Didn't do this kinda shit in my part of town."

I didn't comment on that. I remembered the black high school. Ours was two stories high and made of Pharaoh brick. Theirs was a clapboard building that always needed paint.

"After Cecily and me talked, I walked her back up here," Earl said. "She drove off, and I took a look at your books."

"That explains the missing beer."

"I got the place marked." He opened the yearbook and slid it across to me.

"And what is it I'm supposed to see?"

"Just look." Earl tapped his finger at the open page.

I studied the picture. It was in that section they call "Candid Shots," supposedly catching boys and girls off guard, which they seldom ever are. Mostly they are obviously posed, grinning at the camera, hamming it up the way kids are prone to do. I recognized Deke. He wore his letter jacket. His shirttail hung outside his pants. He looked a little thinner in the face and his hair was cut short, shorter than he wears it today. The guy next to him was soft and fat, not as fat as he might get later on, but he had a good start. His hair was parted in the middle and slicked back close to his head on either side. Thick, gold-rimmed glasses magnified his eyes, and made him look like a constipated owl. I remembered him the moment I saw him again. I remembered how he talked and how he waddled through the halls, hugging his books against his chest, knowing he would not get far before one of us knocked all his belongings to the floor.

I don't remember what we called them then. The word they use today is "nerd" and it still describes the same kind of kid. Book-smart and different, a funny-looking guy who didn't fit. He lacked what passed for social graces at the time. He was out and we were in. The caption beneath the picture said, "Buddies Forever, Deke and Nate."

I set the book aside and looked at Earl. "Okay, granted, I'm surprised to see Deke with Nate Graham. I remember him now. He wasn't anyone Deke, or anyone else, for that matter, would likely hang around."

"Pictures don't lie," Earl said. "Those two mothers were *friends*."

"So they were friends. I don't remember that but it's obviously a fact. At least they knew each other, all right?" I stopped for a minute, trying to figure how to say it. "Earl, you've got it in for Deke. I sure don't blame you for that. But you are *way* off base on this. Two guys together back then, it doesn't mean anything now."

"Hell it doesn't." Earl leaned in toward me. His eyes were nearly shut. "They were buddies back then, there was some *reason* for it, right? You said it. Deke wouldn't spit on a kid like that. 'Bout as much as he'd have spit on me. Picture here tells me something going on with those two. Maybe something's still going on now."

Earl pushed back his chair, stood and jammed his hands in his pockets and stalked about the room. When he walked like this, his head and his shoulders beat his body by a mile. He looked like a rabid black stork.

"You think I'm crazy as shit." This without turning around. "Go ahead and say it, that's what you're thinking in your head."

"I don't think you're any nuttier than usual," I said. "Not any nuttier than me. I think you've got your head up your ass. I don't think it's anything that'll last."

"I appreciate that." Earl turned and faced me again. "Isn't anything I said any crazier than the rest of the stuff going on around here. Fucking *dead* man runnin' down a football field. That makes sense and I don't."

"What I think we got here is two separate events. You got Deke and Millie Jean. That's one event. The other thing you got is Nate Graham. *Maybe* Nate Graham, maybe not. Deke knew Nate when they were kids. I knew a guy named Toomey Fields. We hung around a lot. We both had the hots for *Wonder Woman* at the time. I doubt I'd even recognize him now."

Earl stopped pacing. "You get your picture taken together? You and Toomey in this book?"

"That was fourth or fifth grade. I don't remember which. We didn't have a book."

"I'm going home and go to bed," Earl said. "I feel irritation setting in." He aimed a skinny finger at my chest. "What you ought to do, you ought to keep an open mind about stuff. You ought to try and work on that."

"I don't think I will," I said. "A cheerful and receptive attitude has screwed up my life so far. Listen, you shoot up the sheriff's car or not? I got an idea that you did."

Earl gave me a curious look. "Now why you think I'd do a thing like that?" He nodded toward the living-room couch. "Cecily's going to wake up feeling bad. You send her down, I'll fix her something that'll make her well quick."

"An old darky potion, no doubt."

"Hangover cure from one of my Wall Street pals. White guys got a lot of cures, because they don't know how to drink."

I heard Earl's car start up. The valves were still giving him a fit. The question I had asked didn't bother him at all. If it did, he surely didn't let it show. I knew Earl as well as anyone, but the man didn't give away a lot.

The bedroom was a disaster. I couldn't sleep in there. I got my trusty revolver and a blanket and camped out on the living-room floor. I was there about a minute when Cecily Bénét woke up. She watched me with one wary eye in the dark.

"Don't go thinking you can edge up here in the night," she told me. "I'm not quite drunk enough for that."

I said, "The idea never crossed my mind."

"Yes, it did, Jack."

"I have real strong feelings for you, Cecily, and they don't always have to do with that."

"You've got feelings for me in your shorts. You don't think about me in your head."

"That's the way you're looking at it now, because you're all upset. You think about what happened, you keep an open mind about that, you could see it another way. I am hoping you'll give some thought to that."

Silence from the couch. I could hear my stomach rumble in the dark. I tried to remember when I'd last had something to eat.

"Jack?"

"What, Cecily?"

"You still awake?"

"I guess I am."

"You didn't hurt yourself, did you? All those bandages and stuff."

"No, I didn't hurt myself."

"I didn't think you did."

Gentle snoring after that. I wondered why I'd answered right off. It wouldn't have been that hard to try and make something up, something with more appeal than the runaway truck. Apparently, Earl was quick on the draw and I was not.

I tried to get to sleep. A floor is not a mattress, a floor is for your feet. I dozed off about four. I dreamed of Deke and Millie Jean. They were going at it doggie-style at Pharaoh Field. The crowd cheered. Nate Graham sat beside me in the stands. He was eating hot dogs. He shoved them down his throat at a dizzying pace. He never seemed to stop. His jaw was hinged like the dead electric dog. His teeth were rows of razor blades. Each time he bit down, the blades went *schlick!* like a French guillotine. It was not a pretty sight.

I woke up fast about six. Blue and red cop lights were flashing in the drive. Two or three officers were stomping about the yard. Another was pounding on my door. The revolver would give me five shots. I could kill all the cops, and save the last bullet for myself. Cecily Benét would take affront. She was mad at me now, and this would damage our relationship a lot.

Twenty-one

It was the sound I'd been dreading since I shed my secret life, the past rushing in on enormous cop feet, sweeping me away into penal servitude, into white coveralls, into a cell with a guy named Tiny who would take me for his wife.

I panicked, fell apart. I wasn't wearing anything but shorts. You see it on the "Top Cops" show all the time, they break in the house, the guy is always in his shorts.

Cecily sat up on the couch. "Whassa-whassit?" she said. "Whossat?"

"About ninety-nine years," I told her, "you better get up."

The pounding came again. I shoved the .38 beneath the couch, yanked on yesterday's jeans, and stumbled to the door.

"Mr. Track?"

"That's me." Stoppage of the heart.

"I'm Aaron Hess. Special Agent, Office of the Governor. Mind if we talk for a while?"

He stuck a wallet in my face. An ID and a badge. The badge was blue and gold. The card had a nice state seal. He didn't wait for me to say yes or no, he snapped the wallet shut and stepped inside.

He was fifty, maybe fifty-five. Stocky build, nice tan. Wheat-colored summer-weight suit, blue shirt and paisley tie. Horn-rimmed glasses and the scent of Ivory soap. A winning smile and kindly eyes. A warning bell went off inside my head. A friendly cop is a very bad sign.

"Nice place," he said. He took the room in in a glance. Cecily's blanket on the couch. Mine on the floor. What kind of arrangement did we have around here? He'd seen the green Jag outside. Heard Cecily Benét slam the bathroom door.

"That's a new one on me," I said. "Special Agent for the Governor. Is that like the Rangers or what?"

"You got any coffee, Mr. Track?"

"I can make some up."

"Say, that'd be real nice."

I sure didn't like that smile. It said we were going to be pals, that everything would be fine.

Hess followed me into the kitchen and sat. I put water on the stove and spooned coffee in the pot.

"We sure got a tragedy here," Hess said. "It's an awful thing to happen in a nice little town."

"That's a fact," I said.

"You know the deceased very well?"

"We grew up together. I didn't know him very well after that."

"You like him or not?"

"Not a whole lot."

"Why's that?"

"I got to have a reason?"

"No, you don't. I'd like to hear it if you did."

"Max Coomer was an asshole and a half. He had a good start as a kid and he worked hard at it all his life. He brought assholeness to an art. He was damn near perfect when he died."

"*Ass*holeness. I got to remember that." Hess grinned and shook his head. "I have to hand it to you, Track. You're about the only man in town hasn't said Max Coomer was a personal friend of Jesus Christ. I like a man tells me where he's at. That coffee water's boiling on the stove."

"Right." I poured water over the filter and watched the grounds turn into sludge. I looked in the cabinet and found two matching cups.

"Truth is," Hess said, "I don't think this Coomer *had* a real friend. He had plenty of people hanging 'round. You got your wealthy types, you're going to see some of that. Honey draws a lot of flies. Everybody's got a weakness and money draws it out. Listen, where the hell have you been the last fourteen years, Mr. Track?"

I nearly dropped the coffee on the floor. I was glad I was looking at the wall and not at him.

"I've got sugar," I said. "I hope you don't want any milk."

"Black'll be fine."

I handed him a cup and put the pot on the table and sat.

"You can see why I might ask," Hess said. "That's a real peculiar thing to do, flat dropping out of sight. You recall if you filed with the Infernal Revenue during that time?"

I saw him coming this time. It wasn't a question, that shit about the tax. I was certain he'd already checked me out.

"For fourteen years I was a tramp," I told Hess. "I hitch-hiked some and rode the rails. The trains aren't what they used to be and people don't like to pick you up, but you can still get by and I did. I did odd jobs when I could. Mostly when I worked I worked for food. If I'd made any money, yeah, I would've filed. I didn't plan to be a hobo all my life. I didn't want to come back and find someone breathing down my neck."

"Someone like me?"

"Yeah. Someone exactly like you."

Hess caught the irritation in my voice, and granted me a smile. "You don't much want to get into this, do you? It sorta riles you up some."

"It was not the most satisfying time in my life. It's something that I did. I didn't know exactly who I was at the time. I thought dropping out might give me the answer to that."

"You think it did?"

"I don't see that's any concern of yours."

"True enough. It's a free country, Mr. Track."

"I heard that it is." I refilled my cup. I didn't bother his. If he wanted more coffee he could pour it for himself.

"Is that what you came out to see me about? The Governor wants to know where I've been?"

Hess shrugged. "I don't know, she might." He looked at his cup, picked up the pot and changed his mind. "Mostly what I want to do is catch this fella that's hacking up rich folks and dogs. Names come up when you're working on something like that. Yours seems to come up a lot."

Hess looked up to see if I was worried or impressed. "That sheriff of yours, he's not real happy with you, Track."

"Good. I'm not real delighted with him."

"You and him had a fight."

"He hit me. I didn't hit back."

"You had a shooting out here. You sorta neglected to report it to him. Why's that?"

"There was a lady here at the time," I said. "I didn't want to get her involved."

"That'd be Mrs. Millie Coomer," Hess said. "I spoke with her yesterday afternoon."

"Fine. You know all about it, then."

"Not *all* about it, Mr. Track." Hess leaned back in his chair. He stuck a finger underneath his glasses and scratched at the corner of his eye.

"I'll tell you what we got here, friend. We got some loony on the loose, he's murdered this rich ol' boy had a whole lot of clout in this state. I don't personally care if he did or not, but the powers that be get real upset about shit like this. They want to know about every twenty minutes have I caught this killer yet. I got to tell 'em that I'm getting real close, which I'm not. I can handle that. I'm a lawman and this is what I do. What I *don't* like's the side effects, Track. People that mess my routine because they're doing something doesn't look right and I got to check 'em out. Some ol' boy's been gone out of town and come back and doesn't anyone know where he's been. Soon as he gets here he has an illicit relation with the widow of the newly deceased. Then you see him at the said deceased's funeral rites, he's got his face all bandaged up. He's told a couple friends that his doctor's Sam Watts, who it turns out never even saw this fella in his life. What he *did* see was a black guy named Earl Murphy who gave him a hundred bucks. Which would've worked fine, if one of my boys hadn't asked around some, and reminded Dr. Watts about pulling out his pecker in front of little boys back in 1986, a charge that was dropped at the time but might just come to light again.

"Jesus, Mr. Track." Hess stood and gave me a weary look. "You are a fucking irritation to me and I don't much appreciate that. What I'm going to do is ask around about you, see if something doesn't turn up. I find anything, we'll have another talk. That's sure good coffee. You got a vanilla bean in it, or what?"

"Hazelnut," I said.

"Hazelnut. I got to remember that. You object any if some of my boys drop by this afternoon and go over that bedroom of yours? Normal procedure is to visit the scene right after the event but you kind of fixed that."

"Be my guest," I said.

I walked him to the door. He went outside on the porch and sniffed the morning air.

"I love those big old pecans," Hess said. "I bet they're a hundred years old. Tell Miss Benét I like her yogurt a lot. I go for that apricot-peach. Who you figure wrote 'Fuck You' on your door? You're a real interesting man, Mr. Track."

Halfway up the walk, he stopped to pick up a pecan. His

buddy cops were waiting by the car. I supposed they'd been snooping around everywhere while we talked. Maybe they found the site of Badger Bob's chicken massacre. Maybe they'd take me in for that.

I watched the car turn around and head down the hill for Earl's place. I decided there wasn't time to call him, and it wouldn't much matter if I did.

Cecily joined me on the porch. She looked a little shaky and alarmed.

"Jack, you all right?" she said. "You look a little white around the eyes."

"I'm just fine," I said.

"You don't look fine."

"Thanks. Neither do you."

I set her aside and hurried back inside the house. I could feel it coming on, everything rushing up, an eruption on the rise. I barely made it to the john. Everything arrived at once. Whiskey and yesterday's lunch. Cheeseburger and kosher pickle bits. Oatmeal cookies and anger and regret. Jesus, I am sorry for my sins. I never meant to get into crime and vice. My daddy went and died, and my mother ran off to pursue a better life. It's true that I offed those guys, but neither one was very nice. I took the money but I didn't have a choice. I wish all this hadn't happened but it did . . .

I washed my face and tried to remember if anyone had snapped my picture in my life as Wayne Grosz. Cameras weren't encouraged at the parties I went to with Lloyd DeWitt and Mary Zee. There were always people in Vegas from Chicago or Detroit. A lot of these people had names that end in vowels, and they didn't want their faces in an album somewhere.

Which didn't mean the law couldn't have me in their files. I have seen enough cop shows to know they hide in vans that say "Water Department" or something like that, and they snap you as you're walking down the street. Still, there was a very good chance they'd passed me by. When it comes to your big-time criminal enterprise, Lloyd was a very small fish. The cops wouldn't spend a lot of time on a minnow like Lloyd. The cops would go after a barracuda or a shark. Besides, I wore my hair long back then and I didn't have a beard.

Or maybe, I reminded myself, that's how I want to think it is. Maybe they've got me out in front of Caesar's, grinning down Mary Zee's front. Maybe Hess will put a beard on that face and he'll nail me right off.

Like I say, Lord, I wish I hadn't gotten into this.

"I've got a meeting up in Dallas," Cecily said. "I'm late right now as it is." She was sitting in the Jag, tapping a finger on the dash.

"I'd like to know," I said, "if you and me are okay. I mean I know we're not *real* okay, I know that. Say you took it on an 'okay' scale from one to ten, we'd be a what? You think a six? All right, a four. It wouldn't be lower than a four."

"I told you, Jack, this doesn't have to do with you." She looked straight ahead. She wouldn't look at me. "It has to do with my own inner self. I don't know who I am anymore or where it is I want to be."

"I can sure relate to that."

"Don't you do that to me. You always do that."

"Do what?"

"Say whatever it is you're doing that too. You just— Fuck it, Jack. I don't want to talk about this. You and that cop, is everything okay?"

"They're talking to everyone," I said. "It's no big deal."

"It's big enough to throw up."

I started to answer but she shook her head and reached

out the window and squeezed my hand. Then she took off, spraying gravel like she always did.

I watched her until she disappeared down the road, then I went back in the house. I was hungry but I didn't feel good enough to eat. The phone rang while I was standing in the kitchen. I picked it up and Roy Burns said, "Jack, I got to talk to you."

"Okay," I said, "go ahead."

"Christ, I don't mean on the fucking phone." It wasn't hard to read the tension in his voice. "Can you get into town? My office, say right after noon."

"I can manage that."

"Good."

"The thing is—"

The phone went dead and he was gone. I didn't have time to say I'd happened to remember that my truck was in the creek. That I didn't have a way into town. I thought about calling up Billy McKenzie and talking about a truck. I decided there really wasn't much to talk about, I had to have something to drive. Earl would take me in, but he was tied up with the cops. I wondered if they'd ask him if he shot up Deke's car, and what he'd say to that.

I was thinking about a bowl of Grape-Nuts and how they'd go with water instead of milk. I heard a car sound and ran out on the porch. Hess and his cops roared by, churning up dust. Good. I could call up Earl. We could go into town and I could buy a new truck and have breakfast or lunch and then talk to Roy Burns. I already knew what he wanted to talk about. He'd seen me in the alley and he knew I'd seen him. He had a good story that would tell me what that was all about. It might even be half true. With a lawyer you couldn't ever tell.

And while I was thinking on that, Earl's shit-covered Lagonda came up the hill fast, stripping gears and eating Hess's dust. I ran out and shouted and waved my arms. Earl didn't stop. He knew damn well I was there and he didn't even turn and look back. I thought, what the fuck is *this?* and the answer came at once. God wants you stuck out here, Jack. Jesus doesn't want you to have a truck.

Old man Hunt's place was only a mile, but it seemed like ten in the sun. His boy was sixteen and not overly bright. His eyes were awful close, and I was sure I'd never seen him with his mouth completely shut. There was royalty back in this family somewhere, a set of fractured genes.

Still, the boy was sharp enough to work my three-buck offer up to seven eighty-five. You didn't have to be smart as toast to sense I didn't want to walk into town. We talked about grain on the way, and did I like Madonna's tits. I said I hadn't dated her much, but I was pretty sure I did.

He stopped the car on Second, two blocks from where I wanted off.

"What's this?" I said. "I want to go down there."

"I need another dollar for that," the boy said.

"Are you holding me up? We settled on seven eighty-five."

"That's trip money. The dollar's for gas."

"You little crook. That's fraud and extortion. I could take you in for that."

"Shit, you don't even know her," he said. "You never went out with no star."

I got out and watched him take off, then I walked the two blocks. It occurred to me that kids these days don't know their place. I don't suppose they ever did, but we would've never had the nerve to talk to a grown-up like that. We might've come back later and pissed on his seat, or let all the air out of his tires. But that's not the same as talking back.

I stood on the sidewalk awhile, watching commerce and trade at Billy's place. There wasn't a whole lot to see. There were banners draped all across the front of Billy McKenzie's Pharaoh Ford. Colorful streamers snapped in the breeze outside, and a string of balloons trailed up to the summer sky. It was a circus atmosphere, but no one was buying any cars. All the salesmen stood inside drinking coffee and telling jokes, a gathering of discount plaid and bow ties. There was a time when people came from Fort Worth and Dallas to towns like Pharaoh to get a better deal. That was before hard times. Now, they didn't have to go that far. The big-city dealers were dying on the vine, and they were overcome with joy if you'd just come in and *look* at a car.

They saw me at once as I walked up the drive. The whole covey scattered, like someone had tossed a grenade inside. Everyone pasted on friendly salesman smiles. They would gladly sell me any car I wanted, bottom dollar, fully loaded, and payments wouldn't start till next year.

I was nearly to the door when the siren whooped into life and the car came gunning past the corner of the building from the back, rear wheels sliding, tossing gravel at the windshields of Subarus and Hondas and Chevrolets and Fords, the light bar flashing blue and red and the son of a bitch coming right at me. I turned and made a leap for a Cadillac hood, went flat as a roach and held on, looked back and saw one of Deke's deputies at the wheel. He wailed out of the lot onto Second, burned rubber and headed north.

I eased down off the hood. My right knee hurt a lot. In less than a day and a half, I had nearly been run down twice. The law of averages was clearly out of whack.

Billy McKenzie ran around the corner, wearing Black Watch plaid and no tie. He looked at me, then frowned at the Cadillac.

"You all right?" he said. "I hope you didn't dent that hood."

"Fuck your hood," I said. "What the hell was all that?"

"Gary Lyle, works part-time for Deke? He was looking at an '82 van, Deke got him on the radio. That nigger girl was missing, Emma Stynnes? Her mother got a finger in the mail."

"Oh, Christ," I said.

"Isn't that something or what? Listen, Gary doesn't want that van, I can make you a price. It's got a ladder rack and new tires."

"Billy, I got to get over there, can you give me a ride?"

"Sure, we'll take the demo," Billy said. "You ever thought about a van?"

"I don't want a van, I want a truck."

Billy grinned. "Shoot, I got a honey in mind. We can fix you up."

Twenty-two

We didn't get close to Mrs. Stynnes's. One of Deke's deputies had angled his car across the road. He stood in the street maybe three or four blocks from the house, turning people back. Who it was was Gary Lyle, the jerk who nearly ran me down in Billy's lot. He looked real official now. The sun blazed off his mirror shades, and he rested one hand on the pearl-handled .45 revolver that hung at an angle at his side. Billy leaned out the window and waved. Gary Lyle didn't wave back. He was Matt Dillon now, and he'd vowed to keep the vermin out of Dodge. He had never seen Billy in his life.

"Well, fuck me," Billy said. "I was doing that little shit a favor, taking that wreck of his in and nothing down. What do you want to do now?"

"Forget it," I said, "let's go."

I thought about flashing my town constable's badge, and decided that would only give Deke a big laugh. It would be a lot easier to call Doc Hackley later on. Deke could screw around all day at Mrs. Stynnes's and probably would—but in the end, the grisly evidence would get to Ben.

I wondered what Earl would do when he heard Emma's finger had turned up in the mail. All that stored-up anger at Pharaoh was boiling inside, looking for a place to come out. Shooting Deke's car had helped a lot, but that wouldn't cut it now. Earl would flat lose it. Go totally berserk. He'd have to kill something besides a motor block.

I thought if I could get to him first I could maybe get him drunk and chain him to the bridge for a while. It would piss him off a lot but it would keep him out of jail.

On the way back, a state trooper passed us going eighty, eighty-five, churning up a cloud of dust. Behind him came the car that had stopped outside my house. Two guys were in the front, and Hess was in the back. I ducked out of sight, hoping he hadn't seen us pass.

I did it, I didn't even think, and when it hit me what had happened my face got hot and I turned and looked at Billy to see if he'd noticed what I'd done. It made me mad as hell, reacting like that. I had let that asshole shake me up, and I didn't like to see that in myself.

"What I want," I told Billy, "is a plain-vanilla pickup truck. I don't want a truck from overseas I want a Ford. I'll take any color that you got. I don't want a brown. I won't drive a brown truck."

"I've got a real nice blue," Billy said.

"Blue's fine. Long as it's not a powder blue. I don't want the color you guys call teal, that's not a real blue. I want air and FM, I want tires. I'm not talking your Daffy Duck factory tires, I want something won't go all to pieces I maybe hit a tack."

"I got a sweetheart," Billy said, "it's out in the lot. Previous owner, low miles."

"You mean used."

"We don't say that anymore, Jack. You say *used,* that's got a bad taste to it. Your previous-owner car, the kind you're going to find in here 'cause I don't handle anything else, you're going to have a driving experience, you get into a car like that."

"I don't want an experience," I said. "What I want is something new."

"That's the smart thing to do. You're thinking real straight on this." He nodded toward the lot. "I got seventeen pickups out there, Jack. Fuckin' *all* of 'em blue. Pick out the one you like."

"You do it," I said. "Fix up the papers, whatever else you've got to do. I can pick it up, a couple of hours, what?"

Billy looked hurt. "You don't want to see it?"

"I am not a car person, Billy. This is a sensuous experience for you, not me."

"Couple of hours," Billy said, "you can drive her right out. You got time for lunch? I'm buying, seeing as how you're springing for a truck."

I looked at my watch. I could eat and walk over to Roy Burns's. "Fine, I can do that," I said.

Billy walked across the showroom to get someone started on my truck. His salesmen didn't look pleased. The boss had made a sale, which meant he would get the commission, plus what he took off the top. No one ever said that life is fair.

"That's real awful. About the nigger gal," Billy said. "Shit, something like that, I guess you got to figure that she's dead."

"I'd be surprised to hear different," I said.

"Things don't pick up back there, I'm going to be in deep shit, Jack. This country's going to the dogs, you know that? It's the government's what it is. Listen, I got something worrying my head. I haven't told this to anyone else. I don't even know if I should."

We were walking the three blocks to Audie's. You saw Billy McKenzie very much, you got the idea he'd gone to the same plastic surgeon where all the dealers go, and had his salesman's smile permanently sewn in place. He'd

maybe dropped a stitch somewhere, because he wasn't smiling now.

"I'm listening," I said, "I don't know if I can help."

"Everybody knows about those calls Phil and George
have been getting," Billy said. "Word gets around in a place
like this."

"I guess it does."

"You think there's anything to it?"

"I think it's something ought to be looked into. You've
got a psycho person running loose, they ought to check out
everything they can."

"He called me," Billy said. "Last night. Twice. Scared
the pee out of me, Jack."

"Nate Graham."

"Midnight, and two in the morning. Elona, she'd sleep
through a nuclear attack, which is all right with me, she's
awake about all I can take as it is. Only I'm the one has
to get the phone, it's two in the morning, it's Billy gets the
phone. You don't want to hear about my marital bliss with
Elona, right? *I* don't want to hear about it. Anyway, this
Nate Graham calls about twelve. I say, 'Who the fuck is
this?' and he says, 'Nate Graham, Billy, I guess it's been a
while'—like, you know, we been out of touch two or three
weeks? I said, 'Hello, Nate, how you been?'—somethin'
real brilliant like that, my throat's clutching up, I can't
hardly even talk. And he says, 'You didn't ever treat me
real bad when we was kids, Billy,' and I know enough to
keep my mouth shut, and then he says—Christ, this is the
spooky part, I 'bout crapped in my pants—*he* says, 'I don't
want to do any more of this stuff but I *got* to, Billy, I got
to go and finish it up.' And then he starts—bawling, like a
little kid crying. That's what it sounded like, a little kid
crying. I'm sittin' there listening to this, I'm not about to
hang up on this loony and piss him off, you know? So
finally *he* hangs up, and I'm not getting back to sleep after
that, I sit up and watch an old Tarzan on TV, it's the one

used to have Johnny Weiss-what's-it in it, the guy looked like he didn't have enough sense to know which end of Jane to stick it in. Shoot, I sure as hell would."

Billy stopped on the corner to light up. The match shook a little in his hand. I thought I saw Smoothy in the red Miata cross Oak, but it could have just as easy been Millie Jean. I'd mistaken the two a lot closer than that.

"You sure that's what he said. He said *more*."

Billy looked at me. "You think that's something I'm likely to forget? He sure as hell did. Like he's got a damn *list*."

A vivid image came to mind. Probably the same one haunting Billy's head. A crazy with a pencil, the pencil's worn down to a stub. He's sitting in a room somewhere with a 20-watt bulb, crossing out names on his list. I tried to see if my name was there, but the light was too dim.

"And you haven't talked to anyone about this?" I said. "You know you've got to do that, Billy. This guy isn't through, he's planning on hacking some other people up. Christ, he's maybe got half of Pharaoh on his list."

"I know that," Billy said.

"Good. You know it, do something about it. What about the other call? You said he called back about two. What'd he say then?"

Billy shrugged. "I don't know, bunch of stuff."

"Like what?"

"Just stuff, shit, I don't know. Crazy stuff!"

Billy turned away, muttering to himself. His voice, the expression on his face, said pissed off and mad. What I read there was *scared*. Whatever Nate Graham had told him, he'd stuck it in deep and then twisted it around.

"Okay," I said, "fine. You be sure and see Deke. Let's get something to eat."

"Jack, I didn't mean to fly off like that."

"It's all right. Forget it."

"Okay if we do this some other time? I don't feel much like eating right now."

"Huh-unh, no way," I said. "You're not pulling that car-dealer double-reverse on me. You're paying for a lunch." I put a smile on it, but he wasn't buying that. He wasn't faking this. He looked a little clammy, kind of white around the eyes.

"You going to be all right?" I said. "You want to sit down for a while?"

"I got an ulcer is all," Billy said. "Selling cars and living with Elona, it's hard to top that. Jack, you're not thinking 'bout making any waves on this shit, are you? I mean, talk to Roy and all, he can tell it better than I can. It wasn't any big deal, Roy'll tell you that."

"Roy will."

"Just talk to him. That's all I'm asking, Jack."

I looked at Billy McKenzie. I wondered what track we were on and decided not to ask.

"Sure," I said, "I can do that."

Billy looked relieved. "I mean, I got enough on my plate, I don't need any hassle on this. It was a dumb thing to do, but didn't anybody get hurt. You know? See, that's the thing. It's over and done, and didn't anybody get hurt. Listen, I want to give you something off on that truck. I'm thinking, what, couple of bucks over wholesale, I don't make anything, what the hell, the business is shot to shit anyway."

"You want to give me something off. Why do you want to do that?"

"Hey, why not?" He tossed me a silly little grin. He looked like a man trying not to throw up. He took a few steps to the right, decided he was slightly off course and tried again. One foot made it, the other stepped right off the curb, and Billy fell flat on his ass.

I went to him and helped him up. He shook me off and sat there in the street. He started crying and covered his face with his hands.

"You know what the motherfucker said to me, Jack? He calls me at two, he doesn't even say hello, he says, 'Billy, what did your daddy look like when your momma went and shot him in the head?' He said, 'You remember that? Was his brains all over everything, did he shit in his pants when he was dead? Was that a fun Christmas or what?' He said some . . . dirty stuff about my mother and I hung up after that. Isn't a day I don't think about it, that son of a bitch has got to call me up and talk about that."

"Jesus, Billy."

Billy looked up past me somewhere. He didn't see me, he was seeing something else.

"I don't need any more shit, Jack, all right? I got plenty as it is. I'll *give* you the fucking truck!"

Twenty-three

Whatever you're doing, you tell yourself it's okay to do it and you give yourself a lot of good reasons why it is. The reasons I dreamed up for hanging out with Lloyd and Mary Zee were so clearly transparent it's hard to imagine I actually believed them at the time. Later, when I stood in a tortilla factory in South Miami with a very large gun in my face, I began to see the light. As it always seems to happen in my life, timing is the key.

For a while, I wondered about Lloyd and Mary Zee. Mary and I went at it like crazed wolverines night and day, and Lloyd never blinked an eye. As far as I could tell, they were partners in crime and nothing else. Still, it did not seem possible that any healthy male could be close to Mary Zee for a minute and a half without being stricken by terminal lust. She was that kind of woman. Men looked at her across the room and spilled their drinks. They forgot about their girlfriends or their wives.

I decided Lloyd was gay. When I learned this wasn't so, I was glad I'd been smart enough to keep that opinion to myself. The truth of the matter was, Lloyd lived to make a score. Greed was his passion, and everything else took second place. When his gut began to growl, Lloyd ate. A steak, a banana, it didn't matter what. A stirring of the loins, same thing. A showgirl, a waitress, whoever happened by. Bodily needs simply got in Lloyd's way. He took care of them as quickly as he could, and got on with the important things in life.

Lloyd DeWitt lived on Vegas Time. He thought I was a wimp because I often liked to go to bed at night. He didn't know anyone who did that.

"You sleep, you get fucked," Lloyd said. "You aren't doing bidness, some other guy, *he's* doing bidness instead of you."

For a while, my part of the "bidness" was hanging out with Lloyd. We'd go to a club or a bar and meet a guy. Lloyd and the guy would have a drink and insult each other for a while. Then we'd go somewhere else. We'd drive around in Lloyd's car and he'd tell me all the big shots he knew in Chicago and Detroit. Then we'd stop and meet another guy. I didn't handle any dope. Lloyd did all of that. What I did was hang around. I was Lloyd's audience. He seemed to get a kick out of that.

When Lloyd didn't need me, I did kinky stuff with Mary Zee. These were always exciting, and sometimes scary, interludes. Romping with Mary Zee was like bungee-jumping on a yo-yo string—a thrill every minute if you didn't kill yourself.

I had been in Vegas maybe four or five months when Lloyd thrust me actively into crime. No big deal, I was already there. I knew what Lloyd did. I was used to meeting guys named Sal. The transition seemed easy at the time.

As the drug business goes, Lloyd was fairly small-time. What he did was bring stuff in from Mexico. Strictly marijuana. He wouldn't deal in heroin or coke. Pot was fine with me. College kids and yuppies smoked pot. It wasn't like selling crack to fourth graders. You didn't see marijuana addicts lying in the streets. I was getting very good at justifying me to myself.

Lloyd went with me on my first time out. He said it was to show me the ropes, but we both knew better than that. We flew into Tucson, rented a car, and drove across the border at Nogales. A Mexican met us in a bar. Lloyd and the Mexican talked. We bought some tequila and some crappy souvenirs and drove back. Lloyd kept the tequila and dumped the souvenirs in the trash. He said it looked funny if you just drove over and didn't bring anything out.

At two in the morning we were sitting in the car west of Tombstone, Arizona, on the San Pedro River. At nine past two, an old Buick pulled up behind us without any lights. Lloyd said relax, it was the guy from Mexico. At two-fifteen on the nose, a plane screamed out of the west, ripping away the desert silence, and missing the car by a foot and a half. It scared the shit out of me and every rattlesnake and owl for miles around. Lloyd looked at me and laughed. He got out and talked to the guy in the Buick and told him I'd shit in my pants. Not true, but close enough.

On the ride back to Tucson, Lloyd told me how the deal worked. A guy who worked for him put money in a bus-station locker in San Antone. Lloyd gave the Mexican in the Buick the key. The plane dropped the dope, and two of Lloyd's people picked it up.

"It comes in low," Lloyd said, "you don't need a parachute, you kick the stuff out. The guys pick it up, they're gone."

I thought about that. It gave me a real bad feeling in my gut. The border patrol or the DEA gets the plane on its radar, the plane makes a drop and we all get neatly scooped up. I told Lloyd what I was thinking and he gave me that look I get from Cecily Benét: Teacher loses patience with the handicapped child.

"Are you fucking nuts?" Lloyd said. "They don't *drop* it where we're *at*. The plane comes out of Mexico eighty, a hundred miles from here. The drop is in *New* Mexico, for Christ's sake; you think I'm sittin' under a fucking drop?"

"So anybody gets picked up, it's the guys on the ground somewhere."

"They're getting paid," Lloyd said.

"Right."

Lloyd turned and gave me a look. "Hey, jerk. You rather them get caught or us?"

I didn't answer that. Lloyd grinned and got a station from Mexico. He said he liked a greaser band because you didn't have to listen to the words.

Later, he told me the rest. There were three planes buzzing the desert that night, all three flying in different directions at once. Only one dumped its cargo on the ground. The narcs were always short of money and men. We weren't the only dealers out that night, and there was no way to cover every mile of the border with Mexico.

Lloyd liked to do this, hold something back and then hit me with it out of the blue. I should have remembered that, stored it away in my head. Only Wayne Grosz, formerly Jack Track was having too much fun humping Mary Zec and playing gangster on the side.

Some of it was that. Some of if had to be the suits. There are two things we didn't have at Pharaoh High. We didn't have girls who could cross both legs behind their head, and we didn't have silk Italian suits.

Twenty-four

Lunch at Audie's no longer seemed a good idea. Everyone there had a ringside seat to Billy's looney-tune review. If I joined the luncheon crowd, I would turn into a prime source of news and I didn't care for that. I walked to the drugstore instead, sat at the counter and ordered a burger and a Coke. Someone had run a hasty mop across the floor. The fans overhead whipped the smell of disinfectant in the air. I thought about catching up on *Batman* while I ate, and remembered this would violate the rules. This is how chaos begins. One lonely rebel reads a comic book free, and soon the whole world joins in.

I couldn't get Billy off my mind. I had watched him come unraveled, nearly lose it right there on Main Street. Whatever he and Roy didn't want me to talk about had shaken Billy good. Then, there was Nate Graham's call on top of that. Billy McKenzie came closer to the rubber-sheet gang than I ever care to get. You know a car dealer needs psychiatric help when he says he'd like to give you a truck. That's a sure sign right there.

Maybe, I decided, Billy was never quite the same after what happened to him as a kid. Watching your mother blow your dad's head off, then do it to herself, is a good way to fuck up Christmas Eve. Something like that, it's going to stay with you for a while, it could make a big impression on your life.

As I finished off my burger, a caravan of cops descended

on the courthouse square. They stopped in the middle of
the street, drove up on the lawn, double-parked, and took
up all the handicapped zones. I counted thirteen cars and
maybe twenty-five cops. Deke and his deputies were there,
a flock of state troopers, and some overweight bozos from
several surrounding towns. I was proud of myself. I looked
right at Hess and didn't twitch.

How many lawmen does it take to bring one finger into
town? I waited for the punch line but nothing came to mind.

"My thought on this, I mean, you think what you like,
that's up to you, I'm just expressing what I think, sorta
opening up to you, Jack, I feel I can do that with you, I
feel like I know you pretty well. I'm looking at the overall
situation here, what I'm seeing is I don't see bringing this
out it's going to do anybody any good. Something of a
delicate nature like this, it's got ramifications of every sort.
You know what I mean? Someone looks at this thing, there's
going to be people want to blow it up a whole lot bigger
than it is. You got folks in this town, they got closed minds
is what they got. Some do-gooder bastard he's singing in
the choir, he's screwing little dogs on the side. This puppy
fucker's going to get real pious he hears about this, he's
going to be first in line to start throwin' bricks at me. Listen,
I fix you a drink? I got a little bourbon, I bet I got a beer
in the fridge."

"I'm fine," I said.

"Well, you don't mind I'm going to have one myself."

It appeared to me that Roy had already had one himself.
Or maybe three or four. He looked a little frazzled around
the edges, a little red of eye. He had missed a spot shaving,
and spilled scrambled eggs on his natty lawyer's vest. His
hands shook as he poured a stiff drink. The bottle was handy
in a right-hand drawer of his desk. He drank better whiskey
than Doc Ben Hackley, but almost everyone did.

"Jack, you're a real smart fella," Roy said. "A whole lot smarter'n Pharaoh gives you credit for."

"I guess that's a compliment, Roy."

Roy frowned and shook his head. "That sensitive crap doesn't cut it with me, I see it all the time. You pull that stuff in court, why I'd knock you down quick. Let's get straight to it, friend. You going to fuck us up or not?"

"That depends," I said, like I knew what we were talking about.

"Depends on what?"

"On a lot of things, Roy."

"Uh-huh. Right." Roy Burns showed me a cagey lawyer look, a sly little smile. "I get it, I am reading you loud and clear. How much? And don't try and hold me up. Man, I'm surprised at this. I don't mind telling you that."

"Forget it," I said, "Billy already offered me a truck."

"He did?" Roy made a face. "Jesus Christ, I told that fucker to stay out of this." He set down his glass. "All right. What are we talking 'bout here? What kinda deal you got?"

"I want to know the whole thing. All of it. Without the lawyer two-step, Roy. You're asking me to help. I know . . . some of it, I want to hear the rest."

Roy looked irritated. "What's to know? You saw that gal in the car. I would've waited till night but this broad's getting antsy, you know? Says she wants to go *shopping* or something. You picture that? I say no fucking way, you're staying right here till we go. Hey, didn't mean to run you down, pal. I 'bout shit, I see you huggin' the wall, I'm saying what's old Jack doing there? What *were* you doin' there, you got a thing for alleys or what?"

"You and Billy," I said. "Who else? You weren't keeping her here, I know that. I doubt if she was over at Billy's place."

I was guessing, but the look on Roy's face said I was right.

"You got to dig it up, right? Okay. Eddie. Fucking Eddie was in it too."

"Eddie Trost?"

Roy shook his head. "Hey, we didn't have anyone else, and Eddie's place was safe. No one pokes around in a funeral home, you don't know what you're going to see. We kept them up there. A back room upstairs he doesn't use for anything else."

Them? My God, I thought, we're talking multiple bimbos here.

"So you brought the girls in, and kept them at Eddie's place. You're saying what? Lots of girls, two or three, what?"

Roy gave me a sour look. "What the hell difference does it make?"

"You called *me* up, Roy. I didn't call you."

"Two. Maybe three one time. Mostly it was two."

"And this was going on how long?"

"About a year. Little less than that."

"I'm assuming this was personal recreation for you and Billy and Eddie Trost. You weren't running a bawdy house here."

"Hey, you hold it right there." Roy poked a finger across his desk. "Those girls were professional entertainers. We didn't pull 'em off the street. Why, one of 'em's taking a college credit course."

"Oh, well, see you didn't mention that. *I* thought you were keeping a bunch of hookers upstairs at Eddie's place."

"Fuck you, Jack."

"Roy, what do you want out of me? You want me to keep my mouth shut, you got it. I don't think you're worried about that. I think it's something else."

Roy looked down at his empty glass, considered another drink and changed his mind.

"You're not getting the picture here," he said, "I don't think you're seeing that. It wasn't supposed to be this . . .

live-in kind of thing. What it was, it was a weekend now and then. I mean, it started out like that. We brought a girl or two down, they went back. It worked out fine. Shit, you aren't married, you got no idea about needs. You've got that ice-cream lady, you can do it 'bout anytime you like."

"Yogurt," I said, "and we aren't discussing my social life, Roy. You better remember that."

"I'm just giving an example is all." Roy decided on a drink. "You don't need to take affront. I'm just saying . . . what I'm saying is, you get into somethin' like this, someone isn't whining all the time'll do anything you like, that's a . . . it's a comfort to a man."

"All right. I won't argue that."

Roy gave me a bleary look. "I 'ppreciate it, Jack. That's no . . . that's no bullshit, pal."

"Okay, Roy."

"I got an idea you're going to . . . what I'm thinking is, you're going to do me right. 'M I wrong or what?"

The whiskey line on Roy's bottle was shrinking fast. So was Roy. He kept getting lower in his chair. His head and his shoulders would slide an inch or so but his coat stuck to the chair. He looked like a man who'd hung his suit up and forgot to take it off.

"You said there was . . . something else to it, and there is," Roy said. "We had a kinda . . . party, is what it was. Just me an' Billy. Eddie wasn't there. Thelma made him take her to a show. Thelma doesn't miss a movie it's got a . . . it's got a horse in it somewhere. Eddie doesn't know why. Woman won't get near a horse that's live, she likes to see 'em in a show . . ."

"So you and Billy McKenzie were there. You and a couple of girls."

"Just one. That was the . . . she was the one in the car. This was after ol' Max got killed."

Roy paused, and tried to get his eyes working right.

"What happened is, someone peeked in the window one

night They saw me and Billy an' the girl. We were . . .
sorta engaged in something at the time."

"Someone looked in. You see who it was?"

Roy shook his head. "I didn't see it. Billy didn't either.
The girl . . . the girl was who saw it, and by the time she
tol' me, whoever it was was gone. See, what there is there's
a real little window up there, it's got a curtain on it you
could maybe peek in about an inch. The room's up on
the . . . on the second floor, you'd have to get a . . . damn
ladder you wanted to take a look."

"But she saw someone there."

"She said she did. I don't . . . see why she'd make it
up."

Roy slid down another inch. He didn't seem to notice. If
he did he didn't care.

"After that we decided to shut the thing down," Roy said.
"I'm thinking . . . I'm thinking, shit, all this stuff with . . .
with Max and the dog, I don't need this. Asshole cops and
those TV folks all over the . . . place, you don't know what
they're going to find. This girl doesn't like it, she's all
freaked out, you know how they get? She wants to get *out*
and I'm telling her she's got to sit tight a couple days, I'll
get her . . . outta town. 'Bout driving me nuts. She wants
a TV, she wants a bunch of fashu-fashion magazines."

Roy gave me a sly and crooked smile. I could see the
little whiskey gears turning in his head.

"What I'm thinking, it's maybe that retard of yours. I
doubt he's getting a . . . a whole lot of pussy himself. That's
what a kid like that'd do . . ."

"Forget it," I said, "it wasn't Henry D. He's got more
sense than Pharaoh gives him credit for. Just like me, Roy."

"What I don' want, see that's what I'm saying here, I
mean any of this came out, Mary Jeanette'd go through the
fucking roof I'd prob'ly get my ass disbarred, I'm selling
fucking *cars* on Billy's lot. Jeshus, anyone even *thought* this

thing had anything to do with Max, I don' want any part of that."

"Why would they?" I said.

"Why would they wha'?"

"Think this circus of yours had anything to do with Max getting killed. That doesn't make a lot of sense."

"Hell, it doesn't." Roy brought his chin up off his chest. "You're not . . . thinking straight, Jack. Whole damn town is going nuts. Some jerk runs over a . . . a *squirrel*, they're going to tie it in with Max. You know? You jus' wait. National whatchacallit, they'll do a story 'bout the squirrel. Might be about a . . . about a duck. We got any dug . . . ducks in Pharaoh County? My daddy used to have a goose. No, I take that back. He had a . . . had a chicken, he didn' have a goose. Sum'bitch wouldn't buy me a bike . . ."

Roy Burns slid out of sight. I got up and went behind his desk and hauled him to his couch. His eyes were still open. He lay there with his hands across his chest, talking to himself. He said he sure wanted that bike.

The summer sun was threatening a meltdown afternoon as I walked back from Roy's up to Main. I wondered if the law had cleared out and I could call Doc Hackley and see if Emma's finger had any dark secrets to tell. I decided that could wait, that I ought to look for Earl. I knew how he'd react when he found out about Emma Stynnes, and I wanted to be there if I could.

I had a carnal thought about Cecily Benét, and then another after that, a little sorrow and regret, how she looked tangled up in my early morning bed, and then the other thing hit me, caught me unaware, sorta *wham!* like that, slamming like a migraine semi through my head, tossing happy thoughts aside, leaving something harsh and ugly there instead.

I stopped in the middle of the block and got the sweats.

I knew why Roy Burns was scared, why he didn't want anyone to tie his little playhouse into Max. There weren't just three of them in it, there were four. The other one was Max. Roy wasn't drunk enough to tell me that, but I knew that's how it had to be. Those three goofballs together couldn't open a loaf of bread. They wouldn't have the nerve to bring tarts into town, but Max would. Max would work it all out and the others would go along, do anything he said, happy to be a part of this Max Coomer fun enterprise.

Only now Max was dead, and someone knew what these good ol' boys did over Eddie Trost's Hardware & Funeral Home. Maybe, Roy figured, whoever it was had peeked in that window before, when Max was there. Nobody knew where Max was or what he was doing the night he got killed. He could have been there. With Roy and Eddie and Billy and the girls. If he was, those three weren't about to tell the law about that. Or maybe Max was up there with a professional entertainer by himself. Maybe the one who was taking a college credit course.

It came to me then why Billy McKenzie was ready for a butterfly net. Roy and Billy and Eddie Trost would have talked about the peeper, all of them concerned about that. But worry is one thing, and being scared shitless is something else. Billy knew something he hadn't told his friends. He'd had two phone calls in the middle of the night. He didn't think the peeper was Henry D. or anyone else. He thought Nate Graham had looked in that window and seen him up there . . .

Twenty-five

I picked up my brand-new truck at Billy's lot around two. I talked to a salesman named Al. Al said Billy wasn't there. No big surprise, considering the last time I saw him he was sailing without a rudder down Main. Hopefully, he would land somewhere intact.

Al said the papers weren't ready, I could come in and sign them anytime. I said fine, I just wanted to know the price. Al played around with his numbers and added in the license and tax. It was certainly more than fair, but nowhere close to free. Apparently, Billy wasn't entirely around the bend. He still had a hold on the solid world of commerce and trade.

A shiny new car is a wonder to behold. There is no finer tonic for the soul. My senses were assailed by the manly smell of clean motor parts, by the sweet scent of vinyl unsullied by pizza stains and cigarette burns, by accumulated farts. A new car is free of dents and there are tits upon the tires. It is much like starting all over again, another chance to get it right. I drove a few times around the square. I am sure there was awe, I am certain there was envy and applause. People could see that Jack Track knew how to live the good life.

Henry D. came out of the five-and-dime clutching a paper sack. I hit my new horn twice. Henry looked perplexed.

He knew it was me, but the truck did not compute with the Jack Track image in his head. Finally, he put the two together and broke into a grin.

"Hop in," I said, "I'll give you a ride. You on your way home, Henry D.?"

Henry D. climbed up in the cab. He buckled up at once, and folded his hands around his sack.

"This is nice," he said. "This is a real nice truck, Mr. Jack."

"I just picked it up," I said.

"I'm going to get me a truck, too. But I gotta learn to drive. You got to drive good 'fore they'll let you g-get a truck."

"That's a good idea."

"I know it," Henry said.

I turned south on Main. Henry D. lived with his mother on Oak. Oak starts off fairly nice, and then begins to go downhill. At the far end of the street the clapboard houses are in a state of near collapse. Windows are patched up with tape, and the yard decor leans toward dead refrigerators and rusty auto parts. I know the neighborhood. I grew up there myself.

Henry D. looked about seventeen, but he might have been older than that. His mother did sewing for the ladies in the better parts of town. With Henry working too, they scraped by. Henry D. made it through the third or fourth grade, but gave up schooling after that. There were places that could have helped him, but Henry D. was all his mother had. In Dallas or another big city, some agency would have frowned upon this. In Pharaoh, we tend to let people decide these things for themselves. This is a good idea sometimes. Sometimes it's maybe not.

Looking at him sitting there holding his paper sack, I tried to imagine him peering in a window at Eddie Trost's. I couldn't get a picture in my head. Even the simple act of window peeking calls for planning and rudimentary skills.

First you have to figure out there's something there to *see*. Then you have to know that a ladder is required. You have to get the ladder, hide it somewhere out of sight, be there at the proper peeking time . . .

No, this was a project beyond Henry's grasp. Henry could organize breakfast if the Wheaties and milk were close at hand. He could do as he was told, like checking out doors, but not a great deal more than that. It occurred to me that Henry was not that different from anyone else. People give us more credit for our skills than we deserve, and they also give us less. No one ever seems to hit us just right.

"You want to see my socks?" said Henry D. "I g-got some new socks."

He didn't wait for an answer. He pulled them out of the sack and proudly held them up for me to see. They were white athletic socks with red stripes around the tops.

"They got red stripes around the t-tops," Henry said.

"I see they do."

"I'm going to get me a j-job, Mr. Track."

I turned to look at Henry D. "You've already got a job. You work for me."

Henry D. looked pained. He hadn't thought of that. "You won't m-make me *stay*, will you, Mr. Jack?"

"Henry, I wouldn't stand in your way. You got something lined up? What are you going to do?"

Henry beamed. "I'm g-g-going to work at McDonald's, Mr. Jack. They're going to t-train me real good."

"Well, I wish you luck," I said. "I know you'll do real fine."

"You th-think I will?"

"I'm real sure you will."

Henry seemed relieved. He carefully put his socks back in the sack. I pulled up at his house. Henry D. didn't get out. He sat there a minute, his eyes shut tight, the muscles sort of twitching around his mouth. I had watched this scene before. He was trying to get the words out, trying to get it right. When he looked up at me, I thought he was going to cry.

"I got to d-do it," he said. "Mother says I got to get a r-r-real job, Mr. Jack. I got to m-make somethin' of myself. Checkin' doors, that's n-not a r-real job."

"Henry D., it's okay," I said.

"I guess I g-got to give back my deputy badge, Mr. Jack."

"You keep it, Henry. I don't need it back."

Henry grinned. "I sure like my badge. It's real nice."

He opened the car door and stopped. "Listen, you b-better buckle up, Mr. Jack."

"What?"

"You got to buckle up for s-safety. You shouldn't ought to d-drive, you're not buckled up."

"You're absolutely right," I said.

I watched him walk up to the house. He had a firm grip on his sack. He had two brand-new pairs of socks, he had the future in his grasp.

Henry D. was right. Checking doors was his job description and mine, and Uncle Will's lifetime career. Town constables have seen better times. Maybe Henry D. could get me into his trainee program. I could flip a burger as well as anyone else. I could learn to do the fries.

Earl showed up around six. I was having a Dortmunder beer and a grilled cheese sandwich on the porch. Earl stepped out of his bird-shit Lagonda and walked around my truck. He was wearing a wheat-colored English-cut suit, a blue shirt and a regimental tie.

"Good-looking truck," he said. "Bet it runs real nice."

"You'll never know if it does or not," I said.

"You got an unforgiving nature, Jack. A real narrow outlook on life. You got any more of that beer?"

"In the fridge," I said.

Earl walked inside. He seemed calm and unconcerned and that worried me a lot. Maybe he doesn't know, I decided. Maybe he hasn't been to Mrs. Stynnes's. Maybe I'd have to tell him and I surely didn't want to do that.

He came back with a beer. He sat down on the steps and lit a pencil-thin cigar.

"You are looking at me funny," he said. "Why you think you're doing that?"

"I'm not looking at you funny."

"It seems to me you are."

"Okay. I might be looking at you funny. I don't think I ever saw you in a suit."

"I been up to Dallas. You're black, you go up to Dallas in a suit. You don't want to look like a guy does the yard or sells dope."

"Well, you look fine," I said. "You're a credit to your race."

"One of us got to be. It sure isn't you." He flipped a little ash on the ground. "Cops think there's two kinds of niggers wear suits. There's lawyers and preachers. These are the niggers wear suits. You look like one of them, they're not so much inclined to haul you in. I guess you know about Emma Stynnes."

"I know about her," I said. "I wasn't sure you did."

"Uh-huh. You got this idea I can't control my inner self. I'm maybe prone to fits."

"Fits came to mind," I said.

"I run amok or something, it'll be a deliberate event. It won't be an accident."

Earl paused and gave me a long and searching look. He didn't do a lot of looks like that.

"I wrote her off, Jack," he said. "Pretty much right from the start. I told her momma different, but I knew she wasn't coming back alive, I knew that."

"Her momma likely knew that, too," I said.

"Likely did." Earl finished off his bottle and set it on

the porch. "I stopped by the house coming back. There were friends and neighbors everywhere. You see a mess of casseroles, you know something's wrong, you see that."

"I tried to call Doc Hackley. He isn't answering the phone. Ben's pretty good. If there's anything to find, Ben will. Listen, I guess you know you left me standing in the yard this morning, Earl. I didn't have a way into town. I don't consider that a neighborly act on your part."

Earl grinned. "You'd've got in the car, you'd have wanted to go along. Make me buy you a breakfast somewhere."

"Shit. You never bought me breakfast in your life."

"I have, you just forgot. Besides, where I was going you wouldn't fit, you being sort of tonally impaired."

"Tonally impaired."

"Lady I know in Waco's into that. Says we shouldn't call you whitey anymore. Says it's kinda demeaning. Says it isn't politically correct."

"I appreciate that."

"I got me some connections," Earl said. "I know a guy with the Dallas PD. I know a couple more who're into semi-legal enterprise. What I did, I found me a man used to work with Nate Graham. This fella was a waiter at one of the big hotels. Same time Nate Graham was working as a doorman there. Wore one of those admiral uniforms, get you a cab, hold open your door."

"Nate Graham was a doorman?"

"That's right. Worked there about two years. Fella said it's a real good job. You make good money in tips."

I tried to picture Nate Graham in the yearbook picture with Deke. I couldn't make him grow up. He had this doorman's uniform but he was still a little kid.

"The guy you talked to, he know Graham very well?"

"Knew him to talk to is all," Earl said. "Guy I talked to is black, you can figure they weren't best friends. Interesting thing is, my friend who's a cop told me this, Nate Graham quit about ten days before Max's dog got killed. Packed up and cleared out of the place he lived."

"Jesus." I felt a little tingle at the back of my neck.

"Uh-huh. Cops know all about him, except there's not a whole lot to know. Had a bunch of do-nothing jobs all his life and that's it."

Earl gave me a cryptic grin. "I know something they don't know. Something this waiter didn't ever tell the cops, 'cause he doesn't want his name on a list somewhere. Said he saw Nate Graham meet a guy out back one night, in the employees' parking lot. Said they had a long talk. Nate Graham quit about two days after that."

"He say what the guy looked like, the one who met Graham?"

Earl shrugged. "Said he was white, says you all look pretty much alike."

"Tonally impaired."

"He didn't put it nice as that."

"I can see your wheels turning, Earl. You're thinking it was Deke, don't tell me that you're not."

"Could've been. Could've been someone else. And you're right, I'm voting for Deke 'less you got another candidate."

Something moved under the house. Maybe Badger Bob. I wondered who he was eating since the chickens ran out.

"I *might* go along with you on Deke," I said, "but I won't buy your Millie-and-Deke conspiracy, Earl. You and I have been over that. Millie Jean might do in Max, she wouldn't be the first wife who did. But all that freaky stuff, forget about that. And she sure wouldn't harm Emma Stynnes."

"Okay. I might've been off base on that." Earl puffed on his cigar and looked off toward the creek. Dark was setting in and the night birds were darting in for early-evening meals.

"Say Deke's in it, and Millie Jean's not. Deke smells all that Coomer money down the line, he's stringing her along.

He figures this all blows over, he can get him some of that."

"Fine. And where does Nate Graham fit in?"

"Say Deke's using Graham. Got him a pet maniac. Got him all fired up to get back at all the people in Pharaoh didn't treat him right as a kid."

"Come *on,* Earl." I had to laugh at that. "No way Deke's going to do something crazy like that."

"Maybe Deke's crazy too."

"Deke's mean, he's not nuts. This guy, this waiter you're talking to. He say Graham ever acted kinda weird, anything like that?"

"I asked him. Said he wasn't much different than anyone else. See, your psycho fruitcake type, he doesn't have to act loony all the time. He's not hacking somebody up, he might act just like you and me."

"Thanks, Dr. Earl, that straightens it out for me."

"You're out of beer," Earl said.

"Imagine that. That cop who dropped in this morning, this Hess? He say anything he came down to see you? I mean, he mention anything about me?"

"Said you made good coffee. I got no respect for a man isn't smarter'n that." Earl showed me a lazy smile. "He's a cagey old bastard, isn't he? Wanted to know what I *did.* Acted like he didn't know, hadn't checked me out. Fucker asked me if I always paid my *tax.* I told him I got a tax man in New York scares the shit out of the IRS." Earl looked at me. "Didn't mention Nate Graham. Bet he didn't bring him up with you."

I hadn't thought about that. Earl was right. Maybe Hess was simply being sly. Cops think they hold something back you'll get nervous and wonder why.

Earl stood and brushed off his import pants. "You got nothing left to drink," he said. "No use me hanging around here. This Hess, he give you any trouble, Jack? Anything you can't handle by yourself?"

He looked somewhere else when he said it. He didn't look at me. He was trying to say that he knew I had reason to worry, and didn't want me to think he was asking why. He hadn't asked when he drove my truck off into the creek and he wasn't asking now.

"I think I'm okay," I said. "Thanks for asking, though."

"I'm sorry 'bout that Waxahachie doctor. How you going to figure a nice old man like that he's going to mess around with kids. I don't guess you ever know."

"I don't guess you ever do."

Earl took off his tie and walked out toward his car. Even with the bird-doo on it, his Lagonda looked better than my brand-new truck.

"Did Hess ask you if you shot up Deke's car?" I said. "I was wondering if he did."

Earl turned around. "Yeah, he asked."

"And you said what?"

"I said he asked me that again, I'd haul his honky ass into court like that. I said shooting up a cop car's against the state law."

"Good for you," I said.

Twenty-six

After Earl left I puttered around the house, mostly getting the bedroom back in shape, sweeping up glass and spackling bullet holes. Hess's people had left me a nice official note that said they'd been by. I hoped they'd had a lot of fun. I found a piece of plywood for the window that almost fit, did that, and threw out a broken lamp. It didn't look like your decorator bedroom, but then it never had. At least it didn't look like Sarajevo anymore.

What I was doing was killing time. I didn't want to read, I knew I couldn't sleep. Too much was going on inside my head. The house seemed empty without Alexander the cat. I kept looking for him everywhere he ought to be. I missed Cecily a lot. It wasn't like she was there all the time, it wasn't that. It was knowing there was something between us right now, and she might not be there again. I didn't like to think about that.

A little after ten I gave up, left the house and took off in my truck. It was a therapeutic drive is what it was. Wheels give the illusion that you've left all your troubles behind. We tell ourselves the magic only works one way. It never occurs to us we might be speeding toward a really shitty problem up ahead.

I liked my new truck. I liked the radio and the comforting soft-blue glow of the dash. The dash on my old truck had been on the blink for some time. I used to flick my lighter to see if I was running out of gas. I could've had the dash fixed. Instead, I made sure I kept a lighter in the cab at all times.

There was no one on the road, and it didn't take long to reach the outskirts of town. I spooked a jackrabbit with my new headlights. He looked at me with bright and startled eyes, and leaped into the darkness of the Pharaoh Cemetery grounds.

"Have a nice evening," I said, "and give my best to Max."

There were still a few lights on in town. Bedroom shades were drawn, and TVs flickered in the night. I called Doc Hackley from a phone booth on Main. He said he couldn't tell whether Emma Stynnes had still been alive when our lunatic cut her finger off.

"If she wasn't, she hadn't been dead very long," he said. "I'm guessing he made her watch. That's not a medical opinion, it's mine. You want to come on in for a drink? I'm here all by myself. A couple of starlets dropped by, but they had to get back to Hollywood."

"I guess not," I said. I hadn't told him I was calling from town. "I think I better get to bed."

"Suit yourself," he said.

I knew I wouldn't pass Ben's opinion on to Earl. Earl had enough imagination, he didn't need any help from me. It occurred to me then that I'd forgotten to tell him about the love nest at Eddie Trost's funeral home, or Billy McKenzie's calls from Nate Graham. It gave me a nice warm feeling, knowing I could spring this on him anytime. Sort of pay him back for leaving me stranded at the farm. If you don't keep score, what's the point of playing the game? Sparky Depp, who taught American history and coached the Pharaoh Asps, said that. He was real good at sayings, and led us through twelve straight seasons without a win.

I stood in the phone booth wondering what I ought to do next. Bugs circled drunkenly about the street lamps. Main Street was empty except for me. It was after eleven, so Henry D. had checked the storefronts. He made a chalk mark on every door he passed. That way, he wouldn't come back and check the same door again.

A drink with Doc Hackley was sounding a lot better than it should. I thought about Nate Graham's call to Billy, and that made me think about Phil. I wondered if he or George had heard from Graham again. He might not tell me, since we'd had our little tiff, but it wouldn't hurt to try.

Phil answered on the second ring and said fine, he was up, and I could come on by. He asked me if I knew where he lived, this a little dig to remind me that I wasn't yet forgiven for my sins.

Jesus, I thought, you are losing it, Jack. You could be in bed now watching bad TV. You've got to be lonely if you want to talk to Phil. Still, I told myself, if I wanted to learn anything, it was Phil by default. Talking to George was like talking to a post. I couldn't talk to Billy or Roy Burns. If those two remembered our encounters, they would surely know they'd talked too much and would henceforth shut up tight as clams. There was no use trying Eddie Trost. If I knew Eddie, he was scared out of his wits right now. Few would care to trust their dear departed to a man who ran his own girlie show.

So who did that leave? Deke? The lovely widow Millie Jean? Yeah, right.

Phil Eddels's house had that dusty, semi-shabby look that says a woman has lived here once but she surely doesn't live here anymore. Everything she'd done was still there, but nothing had been moved or added since. The artificial flowers on the TV set had been red at one time, but the Texas sun had faded them to pink. The slip-covered couch was stained with grease from a hundred lonely meals. I was certain if I lifted up the cushions I would find pizza crusts and petrified potato chips.

In a way, it looked a lot like my place, without the woman's touch.

"It isn't much," Phil said, "I kinda do for myself. George comes over to watch a game sometimes, but there isn't hardly anyone else."

"I know how it is," I said. I didn't, but it seemed like the right thing to say.

Phil got me seated in his only easy chair and disappeared down the hall. He said would I like a Dr Pepper or a Coke. I said a Coke would be fine.

There was a stack of paperbacks on the floor. I saw a Tom Clancy on top. A couple of CPA books. I was certain Phil had found the proper niche in life. I couldn't see him in a loud plaid coat selling cars. There were pictures on the mantel, over the false fireplace. Phil's parents in their thirties. Phil's mother looked grim. His father looked just like Phil, gawky and tall, with unruly yellow hair. I guessed the overweight woman in the tarnished silver frame was Louise. She smiled at the camera, a forced and clearly painful look, one she didn't use a great deal.

There were dead ancestors in faded sepia tones, ghosts from the past that we all keep around and can't identify. But the picture that caught my eye was a framed snapshot of a chubby little girl squinting at the midday sun. She was dressed in a princess costume, a frilly dress with flouncy sleeves and lots of pleats. She wore a sequined crown on her head and clutched a wand with a cut-out star. Her big smile told me a lot. She wasn't just playing like a princess, that's who she *was*. Maybe nobody else knew that, but she did.

"That's Elaine Ann," Phil said behind me. "Mother fixed her up for her birthday party. We had it out back under that big pecan tree."

I turned and saw him standing in the doorway. He had the Cokes on a tray and two glasses of ice. He wasn't looking at me. His eyes were back across the years.

"I figured it was your sister," I said. "I saw her lots of times when we were kids."

"You might've," he said. He set the tray down. "That picture was her eighth birthday. She was killed right after that. You try and do it, but it's hard to forget, something like that's in your head."

"I guess it is," I said.

Telling him I remembered her wasn't true, but I remembered when they'd found her in a ditch. Roy Burns's brother's collision with a Texaco truck, Billy's Christmas Eve, and the murder of Phil's little sister. The three bizarre events of that year. I had forgotten a lot about my time growing up, but I hadn't forgotten that.

"That was real awful, that nigger gal's finger turning up." Phil pulled up a chair and sat. "They got anything on it yet?"

"If they have, they wouldn't likely tell me," I said. "I don't guess there's much to know." I looked at my Coke. Phil had a Pluto jelly glass too.

"Listen, you had any more of those calls? You and George either one, from Nate Graham?"

"I wondered what you'd come by for," Phil said. "I figured it was something like that."

Oh, shit, I thought, we're going to drag it up again.

"Look, Phil, if you're still pissed off about that business out at the cemetery, I apologize. Sometimes you say something, it doesn't always come out right. Nate Graham didn't call *me*, he called you. You got to admit, you hear something like that it didn't happen to you, it's a little hard to take. I believe you now, okay? You had it right. The cops are on top of this too. They don't talk about it, but they're definitely after Nate Graham."

Phil showed me an awkward smile. "I get kinda worked up sometimes. George says I let stuff get to me, I guess I do. I try and work on that."

"Well, I think we all need to do that."

"I didn't act like that when Louise was around. A woman, she'll kind of keep you straight. And no, I haven't heard any more from Nate Graham, and neither has George. I hope to hell he leaves me alone. I don't need any more of that."

"I was thinking about that, driving around in town," I said. "I thought, Jesus, this guy could be anywhere, you know? I'm driving along, he could be right there, he's watching me I don't even know. I never felt that way in Pharaoh before. When we were kids, back then, you could go anywhere at all, you could do anything, you knew everything was okay."

"It wasn't like it is now," Phil said. "Isn't anything like it was then."

I looked at Phil. Even sitting back in his chair, sitting there easy, he seemed like an ungainly kid, all knobs and clumsy parts. Maybe he thought I still looked the same too, big feet and a semi-ugly face.

"You remember him any at all?" I said. "Nate Graham, I mean. I was trying to recall the guy, I don't remember much at all."

Phil grinned. "I remember when Max made him run around naked. I sure remember that."

"See, now I don't. We talked about that. I think George said he was there. I was in school but I know I wasn't there."

"Looks like you'd remember that."

I picked up my drink and then set it down again. There was something in the bottom of my glass. I wondered when Phil had washed it last.

"I'm having a little trouble with my past. Things that happened, I mean especially when I was a kid, they tend to sorta fade. I remember a lot of general stuff, like what a teacher looked like, but I can't remember what she taught or what grade; I sure as hell can't recall her name."

"I wish I could do that."

"Do what?"

"Forget about things. There's a lot of shit I'd like to forget about then."

"You had it kind of rough, Phil."

Phil shook his head. He leaned in toward me, his skinny arms resting on his legs.

"I'm not talking about my sister, what happened to her, I mean it did and I can't forget that, I'm talking about me. See, I remember Graham more than you do, Jack, 'cause I was kind of outside too. I mean, I wasn't like *him*, no way, I went to all the parties and stuff like everybody else, but I didn't feel like I was *in*. You know? Not like you other guys."

I had to smile at that When I did, Phil took it wrong and the color started rising in his face.

"Hey, hold it," I said. "What you're saying, right there, I got this picture of me, I'm at one of Max's parties, I think it was our sophomore year, and Max's folks they've got these lanterns hanging all around the pool, they've got a *live* band down from Dallas somewhere. And I'm standing, I'm standing on the edge of all this, I'm one of the guys like you said, you know? And I'm thinking, Jesus, I'm wearing these fucking white socks and my pants are too short, the guys in the band got better clothes than me, *everybody* has. I felt the same way as you did. I think a lot of us felt that way, except the one or two guys, their folks had money, you know? Even if you were Max's friend, you were always outside looking in."

Phil thought about that. "I guess," he said. "I always kinda thought it was me."

"It *was* you. All by yourself. That's the way we were. Anything we thought, we kept it locked up inside. Feelings like that, see, they hurt too much to tell anyone else. We were all sorta Nate Grahams then. We got to hang around with Max but we weren't even close to being him."

Phil looked down at his hands. He turned them over and

checked his palms, like he expected to find something there. When he looked up again, there was that shy and awkward grin he'd had since he was a kid.

"Nate Graham, he wasn't always by himself," Phil said. "He had him a friend sometimes."

"Who's that?"

The grin was still there. "You sit right here," he said.

Phil untangled himself from the chair and walked over to the bookcase by the TV, and I knew what he was going to show me, even before he grabbed the yearbook from the shelf. He scooted up his chair and laid the book in my lap. He had a strip of paper to mark his place, and when he opened the book there were Deke and Nate Graham.

"Well, I'll be damned," I said, and tried to look properly surprised. "Deke Glover and Nate Graham? You telling me they were friends?"

Phil tapped a finger on the page. "They look like asshole buddies or not?"

"I don't remember any of this," I said. "Why would they know each other, Deke and a guy like that?"

Phil beamed. "You really got this amnesia stuff, Jack. You don't remember? How Max used to kid Deke? Nobody else ever did because Deke would've beat the crap out of 'em if they did. Nate Graham did Deke's *homework* for him. If he hadn't, shit, Deke would've still been in high school, he would've got his ass kicked off the team."

I recalled that much. Deke wasn't all that swift in school. There weren't any of us headed for M.I.T., but Deke was extra dense. Either that, or he maybe didn't care. A little part of all this was coming back. Deke, really pissed off when he found out someone had snapped his picture with Nate and got it in the yearbook. I think he wanted to kill the kid who did it, but it turned out the photographer was a girl.

I felt the same way I had when I first saw this picture with Earl. Nate Graham and Deke in a photograph together is a very tenuous link. I might buy Deke tangled up in this mess somehow, like after Millie Jean's lovely body and the great pile of Max Coomer's dough, but I couldn't handle Earl's horror show, starring Deke and his pet lunatic.

"That's real interesting," I told Phil. "I don't ever recall seeing the two together. Likely no one else does either. It was a long time ago."

"There's a whole lot of yearbooks around," Phil said. "Anyone could look it up."

"Yeah, but there isn't any reason why they should."

"*I* did."

I picked up on that. "Are you making something out of this, Phil? I mean, Deke Graham and Nate?"

"I might. I don't know if I am or not."

"That's not telling me much."

"Me and George talked about this. We weren't going to say anything to anyone else." Phil hesitated. "Deke and Nate, they might've . . . known each other after that."

"You're saying you think they did."

"Max said he saw 'em together once."

"Max did. When was this?"

Phil shrugged. "Four, five months ago, I guess. It was at one of Max's barbecues. Before you got back. Max just made a joke out of it, you know? Everyone was having a couple of drinks. Deke, he was standing there and maybe Roy and someone else, I forget who. Max said something like, 'How are you and your fag buddy doing, Deke? He still doin' your homework for you?' Everybody laughed except Deke. He didn't think that was funny at all. I think he came about as close as he ever did to hittin' Max, but you know Max, he wouldn't stop, he'd get something going he wouldn't stop. He said, I don't remember exactly what, like, 'I hear ol' Nate still gives a pretty good blow job, that right or not?' That's when Deke turned around and stomped off."

"Jesus," I said, "Max, he just brings this up like that, he doesn't say anything else?"

Phil nodded. "I thought it was kinda funny, you know? Nobody *sees* this guy since high school, Max brings him up to Deke. Like he'd maybe seen Deke and Nate Graham together somewhere. Deke sure acted like that's what he did."

"You and George, you haven't said anything about this. Not to anyone else."

Phil looked alarmed. "Hell no, we haven't. Who are we going to tell it to? The sheriff? The fucking sheriff is *Deke,* for Christ's sake."

"I know who it is."

"Jack, you . . . broke a confidence with me and George. I don't guess you're going to do that again."

"No, Phil, I'm not. You got my word on that."

Phil ran a hand across his face. "I'm sorry, we've been over that, I don't guess I had to ask. This shit, it's just . . . hearing that guy on the phone . . ."

I stood, and squeezed Phil's shoulder. "You talked to that nutcase, you've got a reason to get upset. I would be if it was me."

"Yeah, right," Phil said.

He walked me down the hall to the door and clicked the dead bolt. Before he opened up, he switched on the porch light and peered through the little security hole.

"George says it isn't over yet. He says we're going to see some more of this shit before it's done."

"I think we kind of all feel that way," I said. "You can't hardly think anything else."

Phil nodded and opened the door and said something I didn't hear because the first shot hit the brick wall and sprayed mortar in my face and the second came right after that. I saw the funny look on Phil's face and he slid down his back against the wall and just sat there like he'd had a bad day, and I was diving for the shrubbery, bullets plowing dirt at my heels, and I'm thinking it's one of those fucking holly plants got stickers on the leaves, I'd maybe rather get shot than jump in that, but I didn't think about it very long . . .

Twenty-seven

I sat on the curbside and smoked a cigarette and watched Deke's deputies destroy the neighbors' flower beds. They were looking for the shooter, who clearly wasn't there, but they had gotten out of bed for all this and they felt they ought to try. The gunfire had come from across the street. I told them I hadn't seen the shooter. That if he took off in a car, I also hadn't seen that, as I was diving for cover at the time.

Phil was okay. I knew that when I crawled out of the shrubbery, hoping the guy was gone. Phil was yelling too loud to be dead. The bullet had grooved the flesh of his upper arm. There was a fair amount of blood, more than enough to launch Phil into a fit. The ambulance people had him calmed down some, and then Deke showed up and that set him off again. He was scared to death of Deke. I knew what was going through his head. Nate Graham had winged him, and Deke had come to finish him off.

Deke backed off and left Phil alone, and stomped out to the curb to hassle me.

"What the hell's he yelling about," Deke said. "Fucker didn't hardly get hit."

"Phil probably doesn't see it that way," I said. "He probably thinks he came close to getting dead. A lot of your civilian personnel, they're going to react like that. They're not old lawmen like you and me."

Deke pretended he didn't hear. "You and Phil just come

out of the door, the guy opens fire. Nobody sees a thing, nobody gets a look at the guy, that's it?"

"We've already done this, Deke. I think we did it twice."

"Yeah, well now we're goin' to do it again."

Deke squatted down and tipped his hat back on his head. "You think he was going for you or Phil? You said there was, what—four or five shots?"

"At least four. I don't know, maybe more than that. I wasn't in the mood to count."

"The first shot hit the wall."

"Right between us. It could've gotten him or me. How the hell do I know who he was shooting at? How about whoever he could hit?"

Deke stood and hiked up his pants. Cops do this a lot. He shook his head and scowled at the street. The word had gotten out, and half the population of Pharaoh was driving by the crime scene for a look. Neighbors were out on their lawns in pajamas and ratty robes. Several people walked their dogs.

"I'm thinking whoever did it was after you," Deke said. "He followed you here, and waited till you came back out."

"Why'd he do that?"

"Do what?"

"Wait until I came back out. Why not before I went in?"

Deke looked irritated. "Shit, I don' know, he just did."

"Why you figure me and not Phil?"

"Because you been shot at before and he hasn't."

"Right. He made sure he didn't hit me before. So he decides he'll take another shot and make sure he doesn't hit me again. I'm having a little trouble with that."

"I don't care if you are or not." Deke shot me a nasty look. "What were you doin' here, anyway? It's kinda late to be calling on friends."

"This is America. I can go anywhere I like."

"Fuck you, Jack." He pointed a big finger in my face.

"And stay out of this, you hear? I don't want it gettin' back to me you're doing any Dick Tracy shit."

"Be nice if one of us did," I said.

Deke turned and stalked off. I got on my feet and called him back.

"Now what?" he said.

"That business in the alley. That was a sucker punch. I wasn't ready, I should've been. It won't work that way again. Next time you're going to need your dental plan."

Deke cocked his head and gave me his John Wayne smile. "I'm ready anytime, asshole. You know where to call."

He walked off before I could tell him right now would be fine. The anger was suddenly there, I didn't even have to try. Every time I thought I'd put all the old crap with Deke aside, there it was again. I told myself getting knocked on my ass had brought it back. That it didn't have anything to do with finding out about Deke and Millie Jean. My return bout with Millie had knocked that fantasy out of whack, I had the sense to know that. Anyway, why did I need a reason? I didn't *like* the son of a bitch.

One of Deke's deputies let out a yell and started running across the lawn. A pickup truck came barreling out of the street, jumped the curb and smashed a picket fence. George Rainey stepped out. He looked wobbly and pale. His mouth was twisted funny; he was scared, and the muscles in his face were making gestures on their own. George marched across the lawn straight for Phil. A deputy got in his way. George went through him like he wasn't even there. George isn't all that big, but he's built like a stump. Probably from hauling that catfish money to the bank.

He talked to Phil on the porch and saw his friend was okay. He walked Phil out to the ambulance, and Phil got in the back. Phil turned and looked at me, like he might have something to say. An attendant closed the door and the ambulance drove away.

"They're going to give him a tetanus," George said. "He's going to be all right. He wasn't hurt real bad."

"George, I know that," I said, "I was here."

"Yeah, course you were." George showed me a silly grin and shook his head. "I'm not thinkin' straight, you know? Jesus, Sam Hooper calls, he drives the ambulance for his old man? He says, 'Listen, Phil's shot, get on over here.' He doesn't say he's alive or he's dead, he says you better get over here and hangs up. You okay, Jack? Phil says you didn't get hit."

"I maybe ruined my shorts," I said, "I haven't checked."

Deke was talking to a highway cop in the street. A car pulled up, and Hess and his cronies got out.

"Let's walk somewhere," I told George. "There's nothing more going on here."

We started down the sidewalk away from the house. There was still a little traffic in the street, but the neighborhood gawkers had disappeared.

"It was Nate Graham, wasn't it?" George said. "You get a look at him or what? Christ, this is bad. I told Phil something bad'd happen, I told him that it would."

"I didn't see anyone," I said. "Why did you tell him that?"

George hesitated. "What did Phil tell you? I mean, about the phone calls."

"He didn't tell me anything. He showed me the yearbook picture. What phone calls are we talking about here?"

George stuck his hands in his pockets. He was wearing overalls without a shirt. The overalls smelled like fish.

"Nate Graham called again," he said. "The other night. He told Phil a lot of real awful stuff. He said something dirty about Louise. You know, something with sex in it, like how she probably left him because he couldn't cut it. Stuff like a kid'd say, he don't know how to put it like a grown-up would, you know? He just says whatever he can think of, it sounds dirty. That's what Phil said. That he talked like a kid.

"Phil said he didn't care about that, about Louise, which isn't true 'cause the breakup hurt him a lot. It was—what Graham did was start talking about Phil's little sister, like did Phil remember if her . . . if her eyes had been cut out or not when they found her."

"Oh, shit."

"Yeah, right. Anyway, Phil gets mad I don't blame him for that, he said he told Graham off, told him to go fuck himself, stuff like that. I don't think he ought've done that, I mean I don't see that was a good idea, you tell a lunatic something like that. I figure that's why Graham came after him tonight."

"And you and Phil didn't mention this to anyone, of course."

George frowned. "I probably shouldn't be telling you any of this, Jack, if Phil didn't. And you don't say nothing about it either."

"Did Graham call you too or just Phil?"

"Yeah, he called. Right after he talked to Phil. If you're going to ask me what he said, just forget it. It wasn't real nice, I'll tell you that."

George stopped, looked back at the house and then at me.

"Phil's had a lot of hard luck in his life. His sister when he was a kid, and then Louise runnin' off like she did. He don't deserve something like this. I know a little how he feels. His folks passed away when he was, what, maybe twenty-five. My ma's still alive if you want to call it that, but Daddy went about the same time Phil's folks did. None of 'em were even fifty, you know? Me and Phil talked about that. You just get to know your people about then, you're a grown-up too."

"I know what you mean," I said. "I got a lot of that myself."

It occurred to me that quite a few people I knew in Pharaoh had had lousy luck with parents. Phil, George, myself—I thought of several others whose folks hadn't exactly reached a ripe old age. None left quite as dramatically as Billy McKenzie's, but they were gone nevertheless.

"Jack, you got to help us on this thing," George said. "Phil trusts you, even if you did do a Judas on us once, he's forgot about that. I guess I gotta trust you too, there isn't anybody else."

I looked at him. "Help you do what, George? What are you talking about?"

George reached out and grabbed my shoulders. "You got to *stop* this fucking maniac. There isn't anyone else going to do it. You're an officer of the law. You can do things me and Phil can't!"

I almost laughed at that. I was afraid George would deck me if I did.

"I'm not Batman, George, I'm the town constable. That doesn't mean shit and you know it. What's the matter with you?"

"You . . . you got the badge," George said. "You could use it if you wanted to. You just don't want to do it."

Desperation was working up to mad. I decided he might hit me yet. He wanted to strike out at something and I was all he had.

"I'm looking into some things," I lied. "If anything comes of it I'll let you know. There's not a lot more I can do."

George gave me a crafty look. "Deke's in this, Jack. You know that, don't you? Him and Nate Graham."

"No, George. I don't know that. And neither do you."

"Fuck I don't." George balled up his fists and did a nervous little hop, like he had to go and pee. "*Jesus,* Jack. We got a sheriff who's running this case and he's *in* it! You think he's going to bring in Nate Graham? Him and that loony are just like that."

"I got to get back," I said. "It's getting late, George.

Why don't you go and give Phil a ride home. I expect he's got his shot by now."

"I never did like you when we was growing up," George said, "you know that? You had that Captain Marvel shirt. You used to wear it all the time. Everywhere you went you were wearing that shirt. You thought you was shit on a stick."

"I wore it sometimes," I said. "I didn't wear it all the time."

"Hell you didn't. You wore it all the time. Listen, I ought to knock you on the ground."

"You got to get in line," I said.

Twenty-eight

On the way out of town I drove past Millie's place. All the lights were out, but the grounds were lit up like that other white house on Pennsylvania Avenue. Someone had told me a security firm from Dallas had come down to do a rush job—extra lights, new alarms, the works. I slowed down to look. A guy in a rent-a-cop suit stepped out from behind a tree. I tried to look suspicious and drove on by.

I wondered if all these precautions would stop Nate Graham if he wanted to get at Millie Jean. Probably not, but why would he bother anyway? All he had to do was ask his old pal Deke. Deke could let him in the bedroom door.

Maybe, I decided, I will simply give in and join the Conspiracy Club with Phil and George and Earl. It's easier if everyone goes along. Something comes up, you know right where to go. Bringing Deke in the picture would help solve a problem that had troubled me all along: Pharaoh isn't Big D., and there aren't a lot of places to hide. Everybody here knows everybody else. *So where does Nate Graham stay when he isn't playing sniper or cutting fingers off?* Your unstable person, he's got to eat and sleep like anyone else. He's got to go to the bathroom and have a place to watch TV. Deke doesn't have a wife to complain about guests, and he spends a lot of time at Millie Jean's. Nate could have the house to himself.

As I passed the cemetery on the road back home, another scenario came to mind. Nate Graham wasn't watching the tube at Deke's. He was creeping around the gravestones in the dark. He felt bad about what he'd done to Max. He thought he ought to bring Max back. *Tomb of Ligeia,* Vincent Price. 1965. In thrilling Colorscope. That Elizabeth Shepherd was a looker and a half. They don't make them like that anymore.

My broken heart sang. Cecily's Jag was at the house. So was Earl Murphy's bird-shit Lagonda and I didn't care for that. A man's been up in New York, you don't want him messing with your girl. Those people are into some pretty kinky stuff.

Cecily heard the truck and ran out on the porch. She met me on the walk and threw her arms around my neck.

"My God, Jack, you all right?" she said. "You're not *hurt* or anything?"

"I'm okay," I said. "Boy, you sure feel good."

Wrong thing to say. It quickly broke the spell. Cecily looked embarrassed and backed away.

"This *town* of yours is a cop show, Jack. I'd as soon hang out in L.A."

"It's usually pretty nice," I told her. "We're going through a bad time."

"You think so?"

Earl appeared in the door. "Mrs. Stynnes called me up," he said. "Said it wasn't you got shot. I thought I ought to come up anyway."

"You bring any beer?"

"I expect you're going to be asking that a lot, you spend all your money on a truck. What the hell happened in there? We under attack or what?"

"One of us is," I said.

I told them how we'd opened the door and the shooter opened fire and hit Phil. "I assessed the situation and dived into a bush. I doubt I'll get the Silver Star. I don't know if he was shooting at me or Phil or whatever he could hit. I don't think he gave a shit."

I went in the kitchen and got a beer, and brought one for Cecily. She took it without looking up. Her burst of affection had subdued her somewhat, and we weren't into eye contact.

I said Phil was okay. I said he'd stumbled on the yearbook bit by himself. Earl was pleased at that. I told them Nate Graham had called Phil and George again and what he'd said. When I got to the part about Phil's little sister, Cecily looked like she might throw up.

"He's pulling the same stuff he did on Billy McKenzie," I said. "This guy's got a real nasty curiosity about the dead. Likes to help you dig up those special fond memories from the past."

Earl looked puzzled. "What about McKenzie? I don't guess I heard about that."

"I tell you everything I know, you won't find me attractive anymore."

"I'm willing to risk it," Earl said.

"This one's going to cost you. This one's worth a quart of single-malt Scotch."

I explained about Billy's call and his seizure on the street, and what else that was really all about, which led into my talk with Roy Burns and the love-nest scene. When I was finished, Earl looked at his beer and didn't say a thing. Cecily wrapped her hands around her shoulders and made a face.

"You got a unwholesome atmosphere here is what you got," she said. "I'd move out of this place if I were you."

"Right. Get up to Dallas where the normal folks live." I looked at Earl. "What worries me is one of those good ol' boys maybe knows something. Or all three of 'em do. I don't think it's just the girlie-show business has got them up a tree."

"Max might've been up there 'fore he went and got killed," Earl said.

"Exactly that. One or all of them could've seen Max last. If they did, they're sure as hell not going to talk about it."

"Maybe it's more than that," Cecily said. "Maybe one of those jokers did Max."

"Jesus," I said, and gave Cecily a look, "don't say stuff like that in front of Earl. He's already got half the town in cahoots with Nate Graham."

"Nothing surprises me much in Pharaoh, Texas," Earl said.

"I've got one that will," I said. "This one you're going to like. Phil heard Max needle Deke. Something about Deke still hanging out with his old school buddy Nate. It really pissed Deke off."

"No shit." Earl showed his perfect teeth. "You're full of good stuff, aren't you?"

"I'm going to do a column. Try to keep everybody up."

"You do that. I'm going off to bed." Earl stood and kissed Cecily on the cheek. "He gets shot or something, you call me in the morning. After ten'd be best."

"We could do breakfast," Cecily said.

"That'd be good."

Conversation lagged somewhat after Earl Murphy left. A great deal was left unsaid, including why Cecily had shown up at the house when she was, I assumed, still supposed to be mad. For once I didn't ask. If this was Part One of our reconciliation, I didn't want to screw it up.

I had a brief moment of hope when she said that we ought to go to bed. Then she got a blanket and a pillow from the closet and dropped them on the couch. I suggested hot chocolate and she said she'd maybe pass on that.

"I'm glad you're here," I said. "I've missed you quite a lot."

"You saw me this morning," Cecily said.

"It seems a lot longer than that."

"I know what you're doing, Jack. You want to talk, you want to straighten things out. Please don't. I am not up to that."

"All right, I won't."

"Good. I'm glad you didn't get shot."

"We could kiss good-night. I mean, just do that, it wouldn't have to imply that we care for each other. We wouldn't have to think about romance."

"Jack, I'm going to drive off in my car."

"Okay, it was a thought. Good night, Cecily."

Cecily didn't answer. She turned her back to me and pulled the blanket over her head. She looked real good like that. The blanket was tight around her very shapely rear. A shrink-wrapped woman that I didn't know how to open up.

I checked all the locks and left the lights on in the kitchen and the bathroom and the hall. I put the Charter .38 on the table by the bed and tried my Elmore Leonard for a while. The chapter seemed familiar, and I realized I'd read it once before. In the drawer of my desk where I stuffed everything like bills and things I'd get to when I could, there were maybe a hundred bookmarks like they give you at the stores. I never had one for a book, they were always in a drawer.

A little after one I gave up and turned off the light. I thought I'd just lie there and do my insomniac bit but I went right to sleep. I dreamed that I woke up and saw her there, naked at the foot of the bed. She said she was sorry, that she'd acted like a fool. That there wasn't any man on earth besides me who could zing her into absolute bliss. Would I please chain her up and perform some base abnormal act? Anything at all, as long as it was vile, and included some mechanical device.

The phone rang at four. I started to let it go, then remembered I had a guest. I stumbled down the hall to the kitchen, wondering, once again, why I'd put the phone there.

I picked it up and said hello. A voice like gravel in a can said, "Hello, Jack. Hope I didn't get you up."

The chill started at the back of my neck and crawled up to the crown of my head.

"I'm here, what do you want?" I said.

The voice coughed up a laugh. "Bet you know who this is, huh? I bet you do."

"I know who it is."

"You diddling her right now, I bet, that girl drives the real pretty car?"

"Listen, pal—"

"I bet you suck her titties sometimes. Do you do that, Jack? You get 'em all, you know, all *wet?*"

I shut up right then. That's what he wanted, he wanted me to talk. That's how he'd done it with Phil and George, and Billy McKenzie, working them over, pulling them in, and I wasn't going to let him do that.

I listened to him breathe, to the static, to the ghost people talking on the line, the voices you can never quite hear.

"I'm still here," he said. "You there, Jack?"

I didn't answer. He didn't wait long, he didn't like that.

"That time you fucked Millie Jean, when we was in high school? A girl's doing that puberty thing, you know? She's maybe fifteen, they got any *hairs* around their—'round their *hole?* I saw one in a dirty picture show one time, she didn't look to be twelve, she didn't have any hairs at all. I was wonderin' about that, if they just . . . grow one hair at a time or if they—"

"I was wondering if you're still *fat,*" I said. "If you still look like a frog. Does a frog grow one wart at a time, Nate, or they spring out all at once? I was wondering about that."

"Shit-*fuck!*" Nate Graham screamed into the phone. I jerked the earpiece away.

"Shit-fuck-doo-doo-fuck-thingie glot-suckit-crap! Booga-fucka-ka-ka-digga—"

"Have a nice day," I said, and hung up.

I got a drink of water and sat down in a chair. The house creaked, settling in with an easy sigh. The faucet dripped, and I thought that I probably had a washer somewhere. Maybe in the drawer with my lifetime supply of bookmarks.

I decided I wasn't afraid of Nate Graham. Reason said I ought to be, but it was hard to be frightened of a guy who was still operating with an Archie-and-Jughead mind, a guy who might give you acne on the phone. It was hard to connect him with the lunatic who'd cut up Max and unfingered Emma Stynnes.

What bothered me the most, what stuck in my mind, was how he knew about my adolescent fling with Millie Jean. I'd never told anyone, which meant that Millie had. And who would she tell it to, something like that?

I couldn't help it. The name Deke Glover came to mind. It was the kind of thing you'd tell, lying there talking after making love awhile, sharing old secrets in the dark. It seems to draw you closer when you give another person a little of yourself, and you know they'll never tell, you know they wouldn't do that . . .

The phone rang again. Instant cardiac arrest. I jumped up and grabbed it. Yelled out, "You crazy motherfucker, don't you call me again!"

"Uh—Mr. Track?"

A woman I didn't know. Her voice a little shaky, used to a simple "Hello."

"I'm sorry," I said, "I've been getting crank calls. Who's this?"

"I'm Nora Sykes, Mr. Track. I'm a nurse at the hospital? I'm real sorry, Mr. Track. I'm afraid I've got some bad news."

"Uncle Will," I said at once, and I tried to open up and

let the proper feelings in, the sense of loss, the sorrow and regret, and there didn't seem to be much there at all.

"He passed on to his reward 'bout half an hour ago," the nurse said. "He went real easy in his sleep, Mr. Track, there wasn't any pain at all. We need to know about—arrangements, Mr. Track. I know it's real late . . ."

"Yeah, it is," I said. "I'll be over in the morning soon as I can."

"We're all real sorry," she said.

I told her I appreciated that. I hung up the phone. I wondered if Uncle Will had a cemetery plot. I thought he likely did. Nearly everyone in his generation gave a great deal of thought to being dead. I hoped he had a place over in the older part. I don't know why it mattered but it did, because I didn't want him in the new part, I didn't want him buried close to Max.

Twenty-nine

When I was a kid I had a book called *Mr. Good and Mr. Bad*. Mr. Good and Mr. Bad were these real little guys who lived inside your head. Mr. Good wore a clean white suit and a natty bow tie. Mr. Bad looked like he'd slept in a pile of shit. When you cleaned up your room and learned your Sunday-school verse, Mr. Good was in control. Mr. Bad was the guy who made you get all muddy and talk back to your mom, and eat Milk Duds until you urped.

The message was pretty clear: Mr. Good was a wimp and Mr. Bad had all the fun. I never shared this conclusion with my mother, but I suspect a lot of other kids got the point, too.

I hadn't thought about that book in some time. I did one night when I was shooting craps in Vegas at The Sahara. I was high on Scotch and I was thirty grand ahead. I had a brand-new suit and some unborn alligator shoes. Mary Zee was beside me and her hair was smelling fine. She was wearing this red satin dress that would drive a saint to sin. I looked around me at the glitter and pizzazz and I thought, "Fuck you, Mr. Good. I'll get muddy if I like."

This was my basic attitude in those years with Lloyd DeWitt and Mary Zee. You know you're doing wrong, you know that dealing dope's a crime. But Mr. Good's sedated somewhere and you're having yourself a time.

* * *

After my big initiation in the Arizona desert, I made a few contacts on my own, always with people I had already met through Lloyd. This went on for maybe nine or ten months, then the DEA shut down the Southwest in a clean-up drive that just happened to fall in a big election year. Lloyd dumped his operation overnight, and shifted his business to the Great Northwest. Soon, we were dealing with people in Seattle and Portland, and up in Vancouver as well.

I was left entirely out of that. The people Lloyd was dealing with were people he didn't know, and he was treading very lightly for a while. So I ran a few errands from time to time and played house with Mary Zee. And, as if Mary were not enough, there were other diversions as well. Showgirls and golden-skinned wives from Malibu. Teachers from Cincinnati on a spree. What it was was a time of dissipation and moral decay. My vessel was weak and the devil held sway.

Mary Zee didn't seem to care. She may have strayed herself. I didn't ask because I didn't want to know. It's that old double standard again: Be a strumpet when you're romping in my bed, Saint Theresa when you're not.

Six months after Lloyd started working his new territory, he sent me on a pickup by myself. He acted like this was a big promotion, but I didn't care for the deal at all. A contact is easy—you see someone and you set up a buy somewhere. There is no merchandise and no money on hand. All you do is talk. What Lloyd was asking me to do was pick up the dope and bring it back. Lloyd was a careful operator, and we almost never did that. The way it always went down was like the Arizona airdrop deal. Someone three or four steps removed from Lloyd took the risk of getting caught.

"This is somethin' special," Lloyd said. "I know this guy, he's okay. Hey, if there was any chance of a fuckup here I wouldn't let you close to it, pal."

If there isn't any problem, I thought, why don't you do it yourself? Of course the answer to that was that Lloyd never did *anything* himself if he could help it. Crime is like any other corporate enterprise. The more gofers you've got, the better you look to the other business guys. Lloyd was small potatoes, and he needed all the status he could get.

I didn't want to do it, but I did. I got the idea it was some kind of test, that I was being "blooded" in a way, and there wasn't any choice. Lloyd packed a briefcase full of bills. I didn't ask how much, but it was clearly one hell of a lot. Lloyd locked the case and kept the key, and made some asshole remark like, "Don't run off with all this," and drove me to the airport himself.

I flew from Las Vegas to Seattle, took a commuter flight to Bellingham, which is a nice little town in upper Washington State. They've brought back a little of the sixties there, and you can watch the reconstituted hippies, look at arts and crafts, and drink different kinds of tea.

My contact was a fat little guy with ketchup on his tie. I met him at a shabby motel. He had a key to the briefcase I carried, and he looked at the money and gave me the keys to his truck. His truck was a nondescript Toyota pickup that had seen better years. It was stacked high with household shit like mattresses and rusty lawn chairs. The fat man told me to drive the truck to Pendleton, Oregon, and not to stop off anywhere and to have a nice trip.

I waited until I was a hundred miles away and fairly certain no one was on my tail. Then I pulled off at a roadside park and unloaded all the crap from the truck. What I knew was I'd given the fat guy a lot more money than I should. There was absolutely no fucking way you could stash that much marijuana in a truck like that, so I was hauling something else.

It took me an hour and a half. It was stuffed in the false bottom of a wooden box full of dishes and pots and pans. Seven kilos of coke. More than enough to qualify me as a dealer and send me up for life. If Lloyd DeWitt had been there I'd have strangled the little bastard on the spot. So much for the myth I had let myself swallow that Lloyd only dealt in pot. Maybe I'd known all along, but I wanted to believe it, so I did.

I stood in the roadside park in the afternoon sun, somewhere in the middle of Washington. I told myself there was nothing about this deal that smelled right. I didn't know much, but I knew that no one but a certified moron would haul cocaine in a pickup truck. Lloyd had bad table manners and he didn't read a lot of James Joyce, but he wouldn't pull a stunt like that.

When the highway looked fairly clear, I took out one of the packets and made a little slit with my knife. One taste told me I was smuggling milk sugar instead of coke. I tried another packet, just to be sure. Then I put everything back like I'd found it and loaded up the truck.

My contact was waiting at a barbecue stand outside of Pendleton, Oregon. I gave him the truck, caught a plane to Portland, and eventually made my way home. The trip gave me plenty of time to think. There were only two answers to the Bellingham deal. One, someone had ripped Lloyd off and I knew it wasn't that. The other explanation was the one I had guessed from the start. The whole business was a fake. A setup to see how I'd react. Would I chicken out, take off with the money, or what?

Lloyd met me at the airport. He said, "Hey, you have a nice trip?" and that was that. We never spoke of Bellingham again.

During the next few months, I made a few contacts for Lloyd but it was all pretty standard stuff. I fell back into my routine, hanging out at the casinos, buying snappy ties and shoes. I got a deal on a Porsche from one of Lloyd's shady friends who assured me it wasn't hot. There were more acrobatics with Mary Zec. I took up tennis. I decided that I didn't care for golf.

In the middle of September, two bozos from Chicago flew down to talk to Lloyd. I knew they were important since Lloyd threw up all the time. After they were gone, Lloyd had a drastic personality change. He started acting nice to everyone. He didn't call the waiters "fuckin' fags." He bought everybody drinks. He was especially nice to me. He bought me a CD player and a case of good Scotch. He bought me two dozen pairs of cashmere socks with little racehorses on the sides.

I should have known something was wrong, but it didn't seem important at the time. I thought the big shots from Chicago had brought him good news, that he'd made a hot deal and was simply showing off. I never guessed this bastard's good cheer had much to do with me. That I had passed Lloyd's test, and thus very likely fucked any chance I had for a long and healthy life . . .

Thirty

There was no use trying to sleep after Nate's phone call and the news of Uncle Will. I dressed and left Cecily a note, told her I was off to Waxahachie and why. Low clouds had settled in, but I knew the sun would burn them off by noon and usher in another sultry day.

Everyone at the hospital told me how sorry they were about Will. I wondered how doctors and nurses could live like that, going through this every day, greeting the survivors who came to claim their dead. The answer is they get used to it, but I couldn't see myself doing that.

I called Eddie Trost in Pharaoh and got him out of bed. He said it was a terrible loss and that Will did indeed have a plot in Section One, Eternal Rest, and by the way, I had one too, and was I aware of that? I said no, I wasn't, and Eddie said he'd send someone right away for Uncle Will. I could come in later and we'd get the arrangements worked out. Had I given any thought to what kind of a service we were thinking about? I knew this was funeral talk for how much was I planning to spend, and I told him I'd be in around ten.

I had breakfast at the same place I always did when I came to see Will. They do a real nice cheese omelet and the coffee is good and I like the atmosphere, which is small-town Texas café. There are hundreds just like it, and you know them by sight if you've grown up here. This time, though, nothing seemed to taste right, and I wrote this off to the fact that Eddie had informed me I owned a small

acreage reserved for Jack Track. I figured my mother had
bought it and never thought to bring it up. She never got
her own life in order, but she liked to organize things for
everyone else.

I didn't like the idea that this somber piece of real estate
was *mine*. I felt it was a definite threat. If you don't have
one you're all right. If it's yours you've got to use it sometime. This doesn't make a lot of sense, but it fucked up
breakfast all the same.

I got through the funeral arrangements as quickly as I
could. I picked out a casket that Eddie said was "right" for
Uncle Will. I learned about gravestones and flowers and
perpetual care. I learned that you ought to buy a vault to
put your loved one's coffin in. This will protect the departed
from the "possible incursion of dampness over time." The
vault offered better insulation than I had at home, and I
said I'd maybe pass on that. What I learned is it costs a
whole lot to be dead.

Something else I learned was that Eddie Trost was nervous as a cat. He wanted to get me out of there, which told
me that he'd talked to Roy or Billy or maybe both. It was
clear that he was visibly relieved when I said I had to go.
He didn't have to worry. I was tired and depressed, and I
couldn't think of anything I wanted to know about his upstairs girlie show.

At the drugstore I stopped and called Phil. He said he
was fine, that George had brought him home the night before, that they'd had a drink and George had gone home.

"I know you don't want to hear this," I said, "but you
and George ought to give some thought to telling someone
about your latest phone calls."

"We did," Phil said. "We told you."

"I mean someone in authority, Phil. Let's not get into
that. Telling me, that won't do any good."

"And what good's it going to do to tell the law? What's *that* going to do?" I could hear the pitch rising in his voice, the irritation setting in. "Shit, Jack, they already know Graham's *out* there, they know he's cuttin' people up, he's taking pot shots at folks. What fucking difference does it make he does another freaky call!"

"All right," I said, "that's up to you and George. I'm not getting into this."

"Good. You just keep out of this."

"That's what I said, Phil. You hear me say that?"

"George and me was talking. I'd forgot about that Captain Marvel shirt. You sure ran that into the ground."

"I got to go," I said. "You think of any more high school shit you be sure and write it down."

Out on Main Street again, the sun straight up and the sidewalk hot enough to boil the soles right off your shoes. The good part about small towns is the way they retain their connection to the past; nothing seems to change, everything stays the way it was. The drugstore fan still whirs away the lazy afternoons; the paint still peels on the stores, which offer the same tired wares they sold fifty years ago. The bad part is, the folks who live here are stuck in this scenario as well. Constipation of the head is the key. Mental paralysis strikes down nine in every ten. George Rainey and Phil. They never think about Pakistan or AIDS, but they fondly remember Tom Mix.

I thought about buying a can of Turtle Wax and one of those products that keeps your vinyl seats looking bright. The new owner's vow to start right this time and keep his car clean. I could pick up some ribs and some beer and park the truck in the shade of my big pecan trees. Earl would drive by and watch. He would be overcome by shame and remorse, and beg me to help bring the bird-shit Lagonda back to life. I would say yes, if he brought his own beer, and we would while away the summer afternoon placing bets on the color of his car when we got past the crud and the paint showed through.

While I thought about this, a vision far stranger than Earl Murphy cleaning his car took shape before my eyes, Earl's car itself, attached to a tow truck from Herb's Exxon & Auto Repair, rolling past me down Main toward the courthouse square. Behind Herb's truck came a cop caravan— Deke Glover's car, two of his deputies after that, a highway patrol vehicle, and Aaron Hess. I stared at this scene, and thought what the hell is this?

I crossed the street in time to see the cars pull up. The cops bunched up in one spot, the way cops like to do. Someone opened a door and they dumped Earl out, hands cuffed behind his back, half a dozen deputies surrounding this felon in case he made a break to get away, a guy who weighed as much as your average cop's hat.

Halfway up the walk, Earl turned and said something to Deke. Deke went berserk and turned a florid shade of red. He went after Earl, big fists flailing in the air. It took four men to hold him back. The cops swept Earl off his feet and hurried him up the courthouse steps. Several other deputies led Deke around the other way.

Aaron Hess was left on the sidewalk by himself. He stuck his hands in his pockets and cracked a pecan beneath his shoe. He saw me and grinned and shook his head, as if we shared this little joke, we were totally detached from all this.

"Afternoon, Mr. Track," Hess said. "Man, this is some little town you got here. When it comes to peculiar, I'd say you got more than your share. You got some real cutups here, you got high jinks of every sort."

I had to give him points for that. You don't hear people say "high jinks" a lot anymore.

"What are they doing with Earl?" I said. "What's the charge?"

"Aggravated assault on an officer's car. Sheriff Glover says your friend shot his auto up."

"That's bullshit," I said. "Deke's got it in for Earl. This is harassment is what it is." Jesus, I thought, Earl has stepped in deep shit. Aaron Hess was watching me close and I hoped I looked sincere.

"Well, I sense animosity between those two," Hess said. "Doesn't take a lot to spot that."

"It isn't just Earl. Sheriff Glover isn't much of a hero in the black community here. Racial harmony isn't his strongest suit."

"I got nothing for or against your colored types." Hess showed me an easy smile. "Long as folks stay within the law, they've got no problem with me."

"That's a real enlightened attitude."

"Yeah, I feel it is."

Hess took off his glasses and wiped them on his tie. His tie was bright green, patterned with leaping trout. I could see him in his waders, dry flies hooked to his floppy fishing hat. A very patient man who was willing to wait for a fat rainbow to make a slip. One would do well to remember that, I thought.

"Slug we dug out of Mr. Eddels's door doesn't match the ones in your bedroom wall," Hess said. "That was a nine-millimeter Browning automatic. The bullet at Eddels's was from a twenty-two. Thought you'd like to know. Deke Glover isn't going to tell you that."

"But you will," I said.

Hess grinned. "You got a real suspicious nature, Mr. Track. Just because I'm breathing down your back, it doesn't mean we can't be friends."

"I know what you're doing. What I'd like to know is what for."

"Shit, I don't know. For whatever it is you did. You did *something,* friend. I intend to nail your ass."

"I don't care for this talk," I told him. "I think I'll slap you with a suit."

"See, you gave yourself away right there."

"How's that?"

"First thing your felon does, he'll try and hide behind the law."

"I didn't think of that."

"Don't let your guard down because I got on a store-bought suit. You're not messing with some fairy-ass cop on TV. You hungry or what? I'll spring for coffee and pie."

"I guess I'll stick around," I said. "I want to talk to Earl."

"I doubt they'll let you do that."

"Deke Glover keeps an ax handle in his car. He uses it to stamp out ethnic unrest."

Hess shook his head. "These are difficult times for us all, I'll say that."

He turned and walked away across the lawn. I had to give him credit, he certainly had a knack. Whatever he said, you could never be sure of what he meant. Maybe he didn't know himself. Maybe Aaron Hess had been a cop so long he had mastered the obtuse; he could talk all day and never say anything at all.

Hess was right about Earl. The deputy on duty said I couldn't see the suspect until later on that afternoon. He said the Sheriff's Department was questioning Mr. Murphy, that an official investigation was underway. Or words to that effect. What he said was, "Fuck no, you can't see him, Jack. Deke's got the nigger on the burner right now."

God bless America, I thought. Good will and fair play are still intact. The wheels of justice turn smoothly, as long as you don't have a flat.

I'd had the good sense to leave the windows open on my truck, but the seats were too hot to sit down. I made a mental note to get one of those cardboard things you stick up on the dash. Maybe they had one without printing on it. I didn't want one with those big eyeglasses. I sure as hell didn't want one that said, HELP! CALL THE COPS!

I wondered why I hadn't put a blanket or a towel in the truck. I wondered if I ought to go away and leave the air on for a while. I wondered why I wasn't fifteen anymore because Smoothy walked out of the drugstore then in crotch-hugging shorts, balancing a double-dip strawberry cone. Okay, not really *walking,* more like a hoppy little dance, a barefoot tiptoe act designed to outfox the heat, Smoothy going "Oh! Oh! Yikes!" every time she touched the hot cement.

What it was was the cover of *Underage Cutie* magazine. The sleaze behind the counter says, "Don't tell no one I sold you this, pal."

"Sheee-*it,* Jack! My feet are like burn-ing *up,* man!"

With that Smoothy screwed up her face and came at me and hopped up on my shoes. A charming little kid thing to do if you're four. With Smoothy it wasn't quite the same.

"Smoothy," I said, "now don't do that."

"Do what?" She tried to look dumb and scooted up real tight.

"That. What you're doing right now."

Smoothy grinned. "So how you been, babe? Haven't seen you since our big ol' farmhouse affair."

"We didn't have a big affair, Smoothy. We had an encounter is what we had."

"Yeah, right. A night with Mr. Fun."

"You're much too young to have fun." I looked around to see if we'd been spotted by adults. "You're not supposed to have fun for some time. You'll have fun when you're maybe twenty-one."

I picked her up by the elbows and set her on the street. Smoothy howled and started doing her little dance.

"You should've thought of that," I said. "You shouldn't go around without shoes."

"You'll make someone a good mother, Jack." She gave me a killing look. "So you going to give me a ride or what?"

"What'd you do with your car?"

"I haven't got a car. I got a ride from the house. One of those jerks Mother hired to watch the place. He said he'd give me five bucks if I'd take my shirt off."

"And what did you say to that?"

"I said *you* give me twenty, asshole, or I'll have your fucking job."

"Jesus, get in the truck," I said.

Smoothy hopped around the side and climbed in. She complained about the seat. I told her to hang from the roof for a while. I turned the air on high and backed out, burned a lot of rubber and got off Main Street as quickly as I could. It was very disturbing to be in the same county with Smoothy Coomer. Much less in the very same truck. You get a girl like Smoothy, she's sweating in your truck, you can get overcome by stupefying scents of every sort. Your head says this little honey is twelve; assorted manly parts say what do you care if she is or not? You can't give in to thoughts like that. Everybody did that, we'd be back in prehistoric times by Monday afternoon. The thing to do is drive and keep your mind on guilt, and try not to remember Smoothy lying buck-naked in your bed.

"I heard you got shot at," Smoothy said. "I guess you're okay, huh?"

"I got lucky," I said. "Phil Eddels got hit, but he'll be all right."

"This the same guy killed Daddy, you think? That's what Mother said."

Her voice was real different this time. The smart-ass kid part was gone when she talked about Max.

"It might be, Smoothy, I don't know. It kind of seems that way to me."

"I hope they catch him real soon," she said. "Doing that to Daddy . . ."

"That had to be awful hard on you."

"Me and him were awful close. He wasn't your average sitcom father, okay? He wasn't like anyone, I guess."

I didn't look at her. She went real quiet for a while. Three or four minutes, possibly a personal best. Then she slumped down in the seat, pulled out a smoke from somewhere and lit up. I gave her a look and she caught it, and stuck out her tongue.

"Don't get your ass in an uproar," she said. "It's not a joint, it's just a ciggie, Jack."

"Well you shouldn't be smoking those either," I said.

"Yeah, right." She giggled and stretched out her showgirl legs. "What you think of these *short*-shorts, huh? I mean, they're not *in* anymore, okay? I got to get 'em in this one real dumpy place."

"Smoothy, you're no slave to fashion," I said. "Anyone can see that."

"You like 'em, I bet."

"I don't think I'll comment on that."

"Uh-huh." Smoothy held her cigarette in her left hand, and licked ice cream off her right. "I'll tell you who likes me in shorts, you want to know. That old fart runs the funeral home? I mean, this guy sees me walking down the street, he goes nuts."

She got my full attention with that. "Eddie Trost? Is that who we're talking about?"

"Gee, I don't know. We got what, three or four hundred *funeral* homes in Pharaoh? Yeah, it might've been him."

I waited for the rest. Her eyes, the way she turned away when she spoke, told me there was something else to this. If there was, it was something she didn't care to volunteer.

"He just looks at you," I said. "He doesn't do anything else."

Smoothy shrugged. "He might've. Once or twice."

"Might've what?"

"I don't know. Said something. Made some kinda remark." Smoothy looked irritated. She rolled down the window a little and tossed her cigarette out.

"He was out at the house one time. A party or something, I forget. Him and Mr. Burns, some other guys. He was drinking, you know? Everybody was. This asshole, he was drinking a *lot*. So he said something to me, like, boy, I looked great, did I ever think about being a model, something like that. I *know* what he's talking about, right? Like I could have this *photo* opportunity, he could fix that up? Hey, I heard that one once or twice."

Smoothy rolled her eyes. "If Daddy'd heard him pull that model shit he'd have shot him on the spot. Jesus, all these old farts, they're waiting for the football season or a stroke, whichever comes first, they get some Dockers on, they get a drink, they're peeking up your pants."

I decided not to mention the fact that I was in the old-fart generation too, working up to forty and headed for the couch, that I would soon get overly excited watching golf.

We were getting real close to Smoothy's house. I pulled the truck off to the side of the road and stopped. Smoothy looked a little wary, like she might be under attack, a very non-Smoothy attitude, considering our nearly lurid past.

"Something else is bothering you, isn't it?" I said. "It wasn't just that. What Eddie Trost said."

"The guy came on to me," she said, "that's it."

"You don't have to say anything you don't want to, Smoothy. I'd like you to, though, if you would."

Smoothy folded up her legs in the seat. She looked out the passenger window. She wouldn't look at me.

"I said he was drinking, you know? Later on he was *really* whacked out, I mean, he couldn't hardly stand up. Mr. Burns, he was trying to quiet him down, they're fighting about something, Mr. Trost, he's really mad, he's swinging at Mr. Burns, he's getting all purple in the face. Mr. Trost says, he's talking real loud, he says, 'You want to wait'll Max fucks us *all* up, you go ahead.' He says, 'I'll fix the bastard 'fore that.' That's what he said. Exactly like that."

"He said, 'I'll fix the bastard.' He say anything else?"

"No. Mr. Burns told him to shut up. That's when he looked around and saw me. Mr. Burns, I mean. He saw me there and went all white like he was going to throw up. He got Mr. Trost out of there fast."

Smoothy turned to face me then. "I guess I wanted to tell you that. I didn't and I did. I thought about what he said a lot. It . . . kinda scared me, Jack."

"And you haven't told anyone else."

"Can we go now? I don't want to sit here anymore."

"All right," I said.

It was two or three blocks to the Coomer house. I waved at the guard and pulled up in the drive. Smoothy opened the door and got out before I stopped. She looked back at me once, looking twelve and looking scared. I watched her walk up to the house. I wondered if Millie was watching, and what Smoothy would tell her when she got inside. What she'd say was she'd seen me at the square and I'd given her a ride, and no, we hadn't talked about much.

I wondered when all this had happened, when this party had taken place. It wouldn't be hard to find out, and I could make a good guess. There had been a big gathering two or three nights before the business with the dead electric dog. I had begged off, because I hadn't seen Millie since I'd been back in town, and I wasn't quite ready for that. We're not quite ready for a lot of things that happen, I decided. But Fate doesn't seem to give a shit about that.

Thirty-one

"You are certainly a sorry sight," I said. "I hope the guys on Wall Street don't have to hear about this."

"They took my cigars," Earl said. "These people don't know squat about a person's civil rights. Every one of these clowns'll be crying in court, I'll tell you that. I heard about your uncle. I'm real sorry, Jack. I remember him coming to the farm when we were kids. He'd give me a nickel sometimes."

"I always got a dime."

"Shit. You never told me that."

"I never had the heart to tell you you were black."

"I kinda sensed there was something," he said. "Maybe that was it."

At least they didn't have him in a cell. I had seen the jail quarters in the courthouse basement several times. It was a damp and gloomy place with steel doors and granite walls, very much the way it looked when they'd built it in 1876. Dust motes suspended in narrow bands of light, the colors black and white. *The Man in the Iron Mask.* Louis Hayward, Joan Bennett, 1939.

Earl looked fairly contained, slightly irritated, a touch of defiance in the eyes and at the corners of his mouth. About as much defiance as your flyweight felon's going to get. We sat in worn library chairs in a high-ceilinged room on the second floor. There were boxes of ancient legal records stacked about, water-spot clouds on the walls. The fly-specked windows magnified the sun's atomic glare. No one had viewed the outside world from up here in some time.

"So what's this all about?" I said. "Hess told me they picked you up. You guilty or what?"

Earl frowned and nodded at the walls. "What's the matter with you? They likely got the place bugged."

"This is Pharaoh, pal. It isn't 'Top Cops,' it's 'The Andy Griffith Show.' "

"These bozos don't have a leg to stand on," he said. "They're tearing up my car and they're checking out my gun. Like I'd be dumb enough to keep some firearm around I shot a cop car with. Leave 'em a bunch of tire prints."

"You crime lords think of everything," I said.

"Damn right. I got me a phalanx of big-shot lawyers burning up the road right now. We got grounds for several suits."

Earl leaned back and showed me his Br'er Fox grin. "The thing is, friend, this shootin' incident is a sham is what it is. Deke knows he can't make it stick. Isn't why he picked me up."

"Do I want to know about this?"

Earl patted his pockets for the cigars that weren't there. "My understanding is the Dallas PD got one of those anonymous letters in the mail. Had that yearbook picture of Deke and Nate Graham. Some kind of intimation there might be a long-standing link between the two. That's how it got explained to me."

"Jesus, Earl." The room didn't have a lot of air, and I wiped my shirttail across my face. "You got a talent for stirring up trouble for yourself. Why you want to do this, you want to tell me that? Okay, dumb question. I don't know why I asked."

"I say I did it? I didn't say that."

"Yeah, right. I apologize. Who you think's going to *care,*

Earl? I mean besides Deke. Phil and George believe this horseshit but you're too smart for that."

Earl shrugged. "Doesn't matter if it's horseshit or not. Long as it causes ol' Deke a little grief. Besides, this isn't the fool idea you like to think it is. I looked it up in an abnormal-psychology book. There's evidence to bear me out. Normal folks utilizing some loony in a crime. See, what you got is the normal guy's supporting this wacko's basic need. He's telling this maniac his fantasy's real, what he's doing, that's fine. Maniac figures, all *right,* this other dude can't be crazy too."

"You read all this."

"I can give you cases if you like."

"No, thanks, it'd clutter up my head." I looked at my watch and stood. "I got some stuff to do. You going to be all right?"

"Lawyers have me out of this place in an hour and a half. I'll drop by, we'll have a drink."

I stopped at the door. "Outside when the cops brought you in. What did you say to Deke?"

Earl closed one eye in thought. "Might've been something 'bout his mamma, I don't recall exactly what. You go out, you ask those peckerwoods can I have my cigars back."

"I put it that way," I said, "I don't see how they can resist."

I hadn't been to Uncle Will's in some time. It looked the way it always had, an old man living by himself, keeping the past close by, shutting out the passing years. The house was stifling hot and I let the windows up. The unit in the bedroom didn't work. I plugged in some antique fans but they didn't seem to help.

It was clear when I walked in the door that a monumental task lay ahead. There were geologic layers of dusty magazines. *National Geographic, Collier's, Bluebook* and *Look.*

Hardly any were dated past 1946. In the kitchen there were unwashed dishes in the sink. Something like chili cement was adhered to a burner on the stove. A withered potato vine sat in the window above the sink, its roots like tangled dead spiders in the empty Mason jar. Will had been gone too long, and the summer had sucked the jar dry.

I wandered through the house, looking in closets and pulling out drawers. If Will had thrown anything away in eighty years it didn't show.

The closets were full of trunks and musty clothes. In one of the drawers, I found dozens of watches and old pocket knives. Another was full of empty Prince Albert cans. Great Jesus, I thought, there's a month's work here just sorting things out.

I went to the sink and washed my hands. Then I did the only thing any rational person could do. I closed the windows and turned off the fans. I left the house and locked the front door. All this would have to be done, but I wasn't about to do it now.

This is how one generation gets even with the next. We treasure this tradition and pass it down the line. What you do is live a very long time, then die and leave all your shit behind.

I was thinking how I ought to get a neighborhood kid to take care of Will's lawn when I heard the car honk and saw Millie pull up behind my truck. I waved at her and started off the porch and then stopped. My experience with Cecily of late had sharpened my senses somewhat. I had learned to spot a female storm coming up, and Millie Jean's tight light fists and the thrust of her chin said I ought to head for port. Too late for that, so I stood my ground instead. I said, "Hi there, Millie, what brings you to the neighborhood?"

"I am fucking furious at you," Millie said. She stomped

up the walk and jammed her hands on her hips. "I did not figure you for a mean-spirited person, Jack Track. I surely did not. It just goes to show you don't ever know a person real good, even if you've been with them in an intimate sense."

"Your car sure looks fine," I said. "I bet you been using that Turtle Wax."

"Shit." Millie blew a strand of hair off her face. "You put that colored guy up to it, Jack. Don't say you didn't, you son of a bitch, I know you did. I heard about your family loss. I'm real sorry 'bout that."

"Thanks. I appreciate the thought. Put him up to what? What are we talking about here?"

"You know *what*. Deke having something to do with that man who killed Max. That's the sickest thing I ever heard in my life."

"I had nothing to do with that," I said. "I heard about it is all."

"Well, somebody did." Millie used her tongue to get something off her lip. She was wearing a red T-shirt and tight designer jeans. Pre-faded and pre-ripped at the knees.

"What I thought was you were maybe pissed," Millie said. "Because of me and Deke."

"I'm not pissed, Millie Jean."

"You're not?" She looked surprised.

"You and Deke got something going, that's fine. What we had was more like an interlude. I expect Deke's the one who's mad."

"He didn't like it much."

"I don't imagine he did. He doesn't much like me."

Millie made a nervous little gesture with her hand. "I wish to hell this mess was over and done with, you know? I don't think I can take a lot more."

"I wish you and Smoothy'd get out of town. I still think that's a good idea."

"I'm thinking on it. I really am."

"If you're not going to go anywhere, I wish you'd stop flitting around. It doesn't do a lot of good, you got those clowns at the house, you're tooling all over town in a bright-red car. Millie, you ever get any phone calls? From Nate Graham?"

She looked up quickly. The question took her by surprise and she showed it in her eyes.

"Yeah, I got some calls. Couple of times since Max got killed."

"What did he say?"

"You know. Dirty talk. Real awful stuff."

"You tell anyone?"

"I told Deke. I talked to that Hess fella once, and some cops came down to see me from Dallas a couple of times. You shouldn't think bad things about Deke, Jack. I know you don't like him, but that doesn't mean he's mixed up in this business with Max. I know that."

"All right," I said.

"All right, what?"

"I'll think good thoughts about Deke."

Millie showed me a weary little grin. "No you won't. But you might think better of *me*, you know? Like you got an idea I don't have enough sense to know what kind of man I'm going with. Deke's got some faults, you don't have to tell me that. But I know him pretty good."

"If I said anything I didn't mean to hurt you," I told her. "I wouldn't do that, Millie Jean."

She looked at me a moment. "I don't guess you would," she said.

I watched her walk off. Whatever I had in my head about Millie it was still in there, and likely wouldn't go away. That was okay, because the high school frenzy, the hormone imperative was gone, I didn't have to do that anymore. At least not anymore today.

* * *

I stopped at the store and got some Spam, some Necco wafers, a six-pack of beer and some frozen éclairs, something from each of your basic food groups. Good nutrition is the key.

Back home I walked around outside the house and made a broad circle across the grounds. Everything seemed intact. No intruders, no strange footprints other than mine and Badger Bob's. I was eating a fried-Spam sandwich when Cecily called. She said she was sorry to hear about Will. She asked me when the funeral was and I told her tomorrow afternoon. She said she'd try and be there if she could. I listened for a hint of romance. She was into her power-person voice, and you can't do much with that.

Earl called a little after ten. He was up in Dallas so he wouldn't be by for a drink. No, he wasn't with his lawyers, he said, he was having what he hoped was a meaningless relationship. I said I was sure it would work out well for everyone.

Nothing was on the TV, so I burrowed through the books on the table by my bed. I found *The Viking World* and a book about the Celts, and Stephen Hawking's *A Brief History of Time*. I found *Secrets of the Jeopardy! Champions* and wondered where the hell I'd gotten that. I had tried the Stephen Hawking book a number of times, and never gotten anywhere. Some of us are quantum types. Some of us are Calvin and Hobbes.

I ate one of the frozen éclairs because I didn't want to have to thaw it out. I settled on Nero Wolfe and went to bed. The phone rang shortly after that. Doc Ben Hackley said they'd caught Fred Newcomb in the graveyard, attempting to dig up Max. Ben said he thought I'd like to know. He said Newcomb was captured with a chocolate-cream pie. He claimed he didn't mean any harm, all he wanted was to throw a pie at Max.

"What he did, the guy snapped," Ben said. "It's what we call fuckin' goofy in the medical biz."

I told him that a man who'd run the Pharaoh Brickyards for the Coomers thirty years had something coming to him, that a pie in the face didn't seem out of place after that. Ben said justice didn't hold much water at a sanity hearing; if it did Fred would surely get off.

I went back to bed and looked at my watch. It had stopped at eleven twenty-nine. Maybe I could call Stephen Hawking and get the right time.

It was an interesting night. Badger Bob married Millie Jean. Nate Graham popped out of a bloody wedding cake, and I danced the evening away with Nero Wolfe. Both of us were naked except for shower shoes. You are what you eat. Spam and éclairs are not the path to pleasant dreams.

Thirty-two

If you live long enough, you're not going to get a big send-off when you die. Everyone you know's already in the plot next door. Herb, from Herb's Exxon & Auto Repair, and two other old men I didn't know were on hand. The rest of the crowd were several generations removed from Uncle Will. I recognized some friends. The rest were folks who simply showed up. In your average small town, a funeral is more than just a somber event, it's somewhere else to go.

Roy Burns and Billy McKenzie were there. Phil Eddels and George. Millie Jean looked terrific in black. Smoothy had her own ideas about funeral wear, which included a red miniskirt and spike heels.

Earl stood beside me in his best Italian suit. I suppose we were breaking new ground. He was likely the first black man without a shovel in the Pharaoh Cemetery. The resting place for blacks was on the other side of town.

Cecily showed up late. She came up behind me and squeezed my hand. She said she was sorry that she couldn't be on time and I told her I was glad she was there. It felt good to have Cecily and Earl close by. A funeral is never any fun, and these two were all the family I had.

When the service was over, I shook hands with a preacher I'd never seen before. People came by and mumbled something nice about Will, then Cecily and Earl and I walked across the semi-dead grass back to the car. There were several small groups, all headed for the road like us. I spotted Millie Jean and Smoothy a little to the right and just ahead. You could make a D-plus in geometry and still figure out that we'd all reach the same point at once if I didn't steer us off, which is just what I did, sort of navigating Cecily a bit to the left with a subtle little touch.

"You can just stop that," Cecily said. "I want to meet her, Jack."

"Meet who?" I said. "Oh, you mean Millie Jean?"

"I guess that's who it is. She looks kinda different with a top."

"Oh, boy," I said.

Earl grinned over her shoulder. He was enjoying this a lot.

Millie saw us and stopped. She glanced quickly at me, and smiled politely at Cecily Benét.

"I hope I can get this right," I said, stumbling over someone named KENT. "I never can figure who gets introduced to who. Earl Murphy and Cecily Benét, this is Millie Jean Coomer and Miss, uh, *Millicent* Coomer."

"You remembered," Smoothy said. "That's real sweet, Jack."

"Jack is always *so* nice," Millie said. She nodded at Earl, anxious to get that over with, and beamed at Cecily Benét. "You can tell how a man's brought up. I believe he got most polite boy in fifth grade."

"Mr. Manners," Cecily said.

"Why, yes!"

They both got a laugh out of that. Earl went "Huh-huh-huh" and I punched him in the ribs.

"Well, I am glad I finally got to meet you," Millie said. "Jack talks about you so much."

"Is that right?"

"I understand you're in business for yourself?" Millie made it sound like Cecily had a snow-cone stand. "I think that is so fine."

"I like it," Cecily said. "It helps to pass the time. And what do you do, Millie Jean?"

"Just 'bout anything I want to, I guess. I'm *real* rich."

"No shit. So am I."

Millie shrieked and threw back her head. "You're fun, you know what? We got to get together sometime."

"We'll do that," Cecily said.

"Well, we got to get going," I said. I got a steel grip on Cecily's arm. "Thanks a lot for coming. You too, Smoothy."

"I'm just pleased I could," Millie said. "If there's anything I can do in your time of need."

"I appreciate that."

Millie Jean and Smoothy moved off through a stand of pin oaks to their car. I saw it was the black '57 Cadillac that had been in the family since Max was born. It still looked brand new. One rent-a-cop was driving. Another sat in the front.

"Jesus," Cecily said, "she is *gorgeous*, Jack!"

"She's kind of attractive," I said.

Cecily gave me a chilling look. "Worst lay you ever had. I believe that's what you said."

"Now why you want to get into that?"

"Because I've *seen* the lady, pal. That's why."

Cecily put her arms on Earl's shoulders and kissed him on the mouth.

"There. That'll give these rednecks something to talk about."

Earl grinned. "I loves you liberal white gals. I'd mow your grass for free."

"We'll talk about that."

Cecily marched off to her Jag. I recognized the walk. It was the same number Millie had used in her attack at Uncle Will's.

"You're something else it comes to social situations," Earl said. "I took me some notes."

"You were a lot of help. I'm grateful for the support."

"Shoot, what are friends for?"

Phil and George were waiting by my truck. They both had fresh haircuts and new shirts from Sears.

"I'm real sorry about your uncle," Phil said. "Anything I can do."

"You got our sympathy in this your hour of need," George said. "The wife would've come, but she and the kids are out of town."

I told them I was glad they were here. I introduced them to Earl. They seemed uncertain what to do. Finally they shook his hand and grinned. They showed the same grace and aplomb as Millie Jean, who had stared at Earl like he might be a Swazi girded up for war. They told me again how sorry they were and walked off.

"Can't help it," Earl said. "Sometimes I start missing those neighborly folks in New York."

"Me too," I said, "and I can't stand it up there."

It was getting close to four. The sun was intent upon its open-hearth-furnace imitation in the west. My truck was parked close to Earl's car. We were walking down the slope when I heard Billy's barnyard cackle and I turned and looked back and caught the punch line of the joke, caught it in a freeze-frame moment in the glare through the trees, saw Roy plant a kiss on the cheek of Eddie Trost, saw Eddie roll his eyes and go into his darky-shuffle bit. Everybody laughed, everybody broke up.

Earl caught it too. Something quick as lightning brushed across his face. It was there and it was gone.

"Fuck 'em," he said, "let's go."

He was absolutely right. Ignore the dumb bastards and go and get a drink. What I did was walk off and leave Earl standing there and head straight for Roy's car. Sometimes you listen to yourself, and sometimes you do what you want.

Billy McKenzie saw me first. His smile dropped away and he turned and said something to the others, and they all looked off and pretended they were doing something else.

"Real nice service," Eddie said, "I think everything went fine. I'll be getting that marker up later this week."

Billy looked down at his shoes. I turned to Roy Burns. He had loosened his tie and draped his coat on the fender of his car. I could see the outline of a flask in the pocket of the coat. Eddie's breath told me they'd been passing the booze around.

"It didn't mean anything," Roy said. "It was just a dumb joke."

"Yeah, it was," I said.

"I hope you didn't take offense," Eddie said. "There wasn't none intended, Jack. It didn't have to do with you."

"Who did it have to do with, Eddie?"

"Shit, you know." Eddie thought a grin might help.

"I got one for you," I said. "You tell me if you heard it anywhere. There were these three assholes figured they'd have a little fun, they'd bring some girls into town. Now I take that back, there were four. One of 'em ended up dead . . ."

"Jesus Christ, Jack!" Eddie took a step back. All the color left his face.

"There is no cause for this," Roy said. "You're upset, fine, I can understand that—"

I slapped him hard across the face. I used the back of my hand and it jerked his head around and slammed him up against the car. His hand went to his face. He looked at me and stared. He couldn't believe someone had hit him. Anytime he wanted to, he pissed somebody off. He had done this all his life and no one had called him down. He did all his fighting in the courtroom and that was okay, it didn't count.

"That is—*assault*," Roy said. His hands were shaking, and tears ran down the welt on his cheek. "You got a fucking *felony*, friend!"

He grabbed his coat and started around his car. I got the collar of his shirt and hauled him back.

"I'm not finished," I said, "you got to hear the rest."

Eddie and Billy hadn't moved. They didn't know how to deal with this. They decided not to try.

"These guys I'm talking about, they didn't think anyone'd find out. I mean, if someone did, they'd flat run them out of town. And if the cops found out ol' *Max* was mixed up in this . . . Anyway, that's not the funny part, *this* is the funny part: These bozos, they're trying to explain their little playhouse to their *wives?* Is that a punch line or what?"

A great deal of silence after this. In the solemn quiet of the Pharaoh Cemetery, it was hard to tell the living from the dead.

"Jack, now that's all over with," Eddie said. "Roy told you that. We don't any of us feel real good about it."

"But it felt real good at the time, I bet."

"Are you going somewhere with this?" Roy said. "You just talking or what? I'd like to know that."

"It's a joke, Roy. Like you said. I hope you didn't take offense."

"You can go fuck yourself," Roy said.

"Now Roy, you don't want to talk like that," Eddie said, "that isn't going to help."

"You shut your goddamn mouth," Roy said.

"You boys have a nice day," I said.

I turned away and left. I wasn't sure what I'd accomplished and I really didn't care. I had hit them where they lived, and maybe that was good enough. Roy would drown himself in bourbon, and Eddie would hit the Maalox. I wasn't sure what Billy would do. Eddie and Roy had done all the talking. Billy had stood there like a post. Like he might be on drugs or ought to be. Maybe he'd have another fit. Maybe he'd have a big end-of-summer sale on his over-stocked trucks.

When I got back to my pickup, Earl was gone. It seemed

to me the empty space where his bird-shit Lagonda had
been left a silent message behind. I decided I had probably
committed an offense. I regretted that at once. It was something that we'd have to work out, and I was sorry that we'd
have to do that. I knew what Earl was thinking, that his big
white buddy had rushed to his defense. In his eyes, my
schoolyard regression had protective and paternal overtones.
I hadn't meant it that way at all. Which didn't help much,
if Earl thought I did.

I didn't feel like going home. No one would be there but
me, and I had no reason to expect anyone. So I drove around
town in the early-evening dusk. There were three or four
cars at the square. The drugstore was open, and some high
school kids were hanging out. A single light was on in the
second floor of the courthouse, about where Ben Hackley's
office ought to be. Maybe he was up there, drinking bad
whiskey to while the night away.

Everything was dark at Millie Jean's, except for the security lights around the grounds. Rent-a-cops lurked among
the trees. As I passed the white house, a red Miata scooted
out of the drive, sprayed a little gravel and headed for the
east side of town. Blond hair whipped in the breeze, and
this time I knew it wasn't Smoothy but Millie Jean. A little
progress there. I was learning to tell the two apart in the
dark at fifty feet.

I eased back and followed. No good reason, except I
wanted to. She turned off at Fifth, went two blocks north
and then flicked off her lights. I watched her as she turned
in the drive and drove all the way back. Deke's house. A
late-night rendezvous, a chance for sweet romance. Millie
brings the wine. Deke hauls out the jalapeño dip.

Nice move, Jack. This makes the evening complete. You
want to follow old girlfriends around, that's what you get.

Thirty-three

Lloyd DeWitt's big spending spree lasted for a week and a half. All of us who worked for him in Vegas breathed a sigh of relief when the presents stopped coming and Lloyd was his old self again. It was surely not a moment too soon. Good cheer had nearly done us in. This cheap little bastard bearing gifts was a frightening thing to see.

I was still uncertain what had brought all this about. The Santa Claus bit had something to do with our visit from the two Chicago hoods. Just exactly what I couldn't say, and Lloyd wasn't giving any clues. Most of the time, I could read him like an inside straight, but he was playing it pretty cagey, keeping to himself. He wasn't doing business, he wasn't hanging out at his favorite sleazy bars. As near as I could tell, he wasn't doing anything at all except hiding in his zebra-striped room in the Sahara Hotel. He might be in his shorts. He might be in the last blue leisure suit left on planet Earth.

"So listen, what's he doing up there?" I asked Mary Zee. "He's not sick or anything, he's okay?"

"He's just fine," Mary said. "He's thinking is all. He's got a lot on his mind right now."

"Lloyd," I said. "He's up in his room all week, he's thinking up there. We're talking Lloyd DeWitt, right?"

"I don't know a lot of Lloyds," Mary said. "I maybe know two."

She was perched on a barstool in the lounge. She was

wearing this black body stocking made of fishnet lace. The back was cut out, and several other parts as well. Mary Zee got all her clothes ideas from Cher.

"I know where you're going with this," she said. She held me with a disapproving frown. "Something like, wow, Lloyd's *thinking*, I got to get a picture of that. He thinks a whole lot of you, Wayne. You shouldn't ought to talk like that. He gave you some real nice socks. They don't make 'em anywhere but New York, you know that? A guy gives you real nice socks, I'd show a little consideration, I was you, a guy thinks enough to do that."

"Hey, I like the socks. I like the socks just fine."

"Well, you sure don't show it. I'd show it I was you."

Mary Zee pranced off with a toss of sable hair. I watched her heels click across the floor. I wondered what had set her off. Most of the time, she didn't give a shit what I said about Lloyd. Most of the time, she had plenty to say herself.

I decided I would do well to take her words to heart. If Lloyd was truly deep in thought, something awesome was afoot. Mary Zee had leaped to his defense, but she knew as well as I did that thinking wasn't Lloyd's best suit. Lloyd would tell you this himself. He didn't like to think, he liked to do. Thinking was akin to wasting time eating food, or lying in your bed all night.

"You're sittin' there thinking, some other guy is doing," Lloyd had told me in the dark of an Arizona night. "This guy, he's doin' business. You're sitting on your butt, you're gettin' fucked."

So what did I know? It seemed to work for him just fine. He was the crime czar, I was just the jerk from the country who didn't have any taste in socks.

September passed into October without much incident. Lloyd stopped thinking, and seemed no worse for wear. I thought I detected a new sense of purpose in his step, but that might have been his leopard-skin shoes, which he ordered from an illegal outlet overseas. Fall was new-wardrobe time for Lloyd, a time of surprises for us all.

On Thanksgiving Day, Lloyd took Mary and me to dinner at one of the big hotels along the Strip. I don't remember which. I remember the revue, a great many tits and turkey feathers and voices raised in song. A very lively pageant the pilgrims and the Indians would scarcely recognize. Holidays in Vegas aren't the same as they are back home.

After dinner, Lloyd drove us out of town up 95. Sometimes he liked to listen to the radio and drive. He never listened to the radio unless he was driving in a car. He didn't like any kind of music unless it had a Mexican band. They didn't have a Mexican band, he'd turn it off. He wouldn't switch around the dial. The station was supposed to find Lloyd. If they couldn't, then fuck 'em, he'd look at the highway signs.

We stopped north of Indian Springs and pulled off on a road without a name. Everybody got out. As ever, the clear desert sky was full of stars. Vegas was a nuclear glow to the south.

"What we got is these guys," Lloyd said. "These guys are spics of the Mes'can persuasion's who they are. Morales is the dude who's running this bunch, he's a real heavy guy. They're running shit out of Hidalgo, which is south of Monterrey somewheres, I don't know exactly where it's at. These acquaintances of mine from Chicago, you met 'em a couple of months ago they come down here. What they been doing, they been working with the Morales outfit a long time, they got a real nice relationship, right? Everybody's happy, everybody's fine. The Mes'cans deliver, these friends of mine buy. Nobody fucks anyone around. You keepin' up with this or what?"

"Morales and Chicago," I said. "Nice relationship. Nobody fucks around."

"Right. That's what I'm saying A nice relationship. This is what they got."

This is the way Lloyd talked. He never led up to anything, he simply plowed right in. Like he'd picked up on a conversation you'd had a few minutes before. It was up to you to guess the part you missed. I wished I had a sweater or a coat. My import suit wasn't made for chilly nights. Mary Zee was dressed the way she always was, which was hardly ever anything at all. She didn't care if it was cold. She had her own supply of inner heat.

"What happens is, the guys from Chicago I know they find out there's another outfit. These guys are greasers too, they're workin' out of Veracruz. These guys are new, they want to do some bidness, they want to make a deal with somebody, you know? They got a good product, they got a good price. Only my guys can't see how they can deal with them too. They do that, they deal with these guys, they're gonna piss Morales off."

Lloyd paced about in the sand, wearing a little path from a big stand of yucca to the car. He couldn't stand still, he had to move. You stand still a minute, some guy'll sneak up and do a deal behind your back.

"This guy Morales," I said, "he knows about this other bunch, you think? This bunch in Veracruz?"

"Fuck yes, he knows." Lloyd gave me a look like he'd stepped in something with his new leopard shoes. "The guy's a moron or what? A guy he's a player, he knows all the other players, right? It don't matter he knows the guys from Veracruz or not. He *don't* know they're dealing with the people in Chicago. He don't know that. Somebody water this place it'd look like something, you know? They ought to do some grass. They ought to grow a fuckin' tree."

"I don't know, Lloyd," Mary said. "It's awful dry for trees."

Lloyd spread his hands. "What did I say? I said they

oughta water the place. They do some water they could plant a fuckin' tree."

Over the next few days, I learned more of Lloyd's plan. Bits and pieces fell in place. I learned a little in the elevator, a word here and there over lunch. I would run into Lloyd by the pool and he'd pick up where he'd left off. I learned something else besides the facts. Lloyd was in love with this deal. It had all the elements of criminal intent that he cherished in his heart—double-dealing and conniving, deception and deceit. What they had set up was your fairly basic fuck-your-buddy end-around run. Nobody knew Lloyd was in with the Chicago bunch. Which he wasn't, he was mostly connected in Detroit. But just in case anyone *did,* the guys in New York had loaned their pals in Chicago a name. For a piece of the action, Lloyd could use the name. The name would open doors in Veracruz. The guys in Veracruz would figure they were dealing with New York. That was Lloyd's cut-out number one. We were sitting at the bar in the Sahara at four on a Friday afternoon when he announced that his cut-out number two was me.

"Hold it," I said, "I'm a *what?*" I was suddenly aware that a chill Arctic breeze had swept into the bar. "What I'd like is, I'd like to know a little more about this, Lloyd. No, I take that back. I'd like to know a lot, since I don't know anything at all."

"There isn't anything to know," Lloyd said. He popped a handful of peanuts in his mouth. "It's perfect. It's slick as owl shit. *Nobody* knows *you.* Nobody never heard of Wayne Grosz. They don't *got* to know you. You got the guy's name from New York. The guy's name is good as gold. The spics from Veracruz, they see you got the guy's name, it's a walk through the park."

"A walk through the park."

"A fuckin' walk."

"What kind of walk are we talking here, Lloyd? I'm walking through Cleveland at noon, I'm walking in East L.A. in the dark?"

"Jesus, you and me on the same planet or what? I said it's a walk it's a walk."

"So where am I going to walk?"

"South Miami."

"Miami."

"Not Miami, I say Miami? South Miami's what I said."

"What's the difference?"

"One's fuckin' South Miami. One's not."

"And I got to do what?"

Lloyd shook the ice cubes in his drink. "What you gotta do is meet a guy. That's it. You give him the bag, he gives you the stuff. You say how's it hanging, how's your sister, pal? He says fine. You say have a nice day."

"What's with his sister?"

"There's nothing with his sister, I made that up. You don't say nothing. You do the deal, you walk away."

"I don't know why we got to do it in Florida," I said. "I don't like Florida very much."

Lloyd set down his drink. "Wayne, you want to do this or what? You don't, fuck it, I'll get somebody else."

"Did I say I wouldn't do it? I didn't say that."

"You want to do it or not?"

"I think I want to do it."

"Good. That's that."

"I want to think about it some. I'd like to do that."

Lloyd stood up and dropped a twenty on the bar. "So think about it," he said. "Think about it for an hour. An hour and a half. We got a plane to catch at eight."

I stared at Lloyd. I think I spilled my drink. "You didn't say tonight. We been here talking, you never said a thing about tonight."

"What's the difference tonight?" Lloyd said. "You got something going, you got a big event? I *know* your big event. It's the same one you always got, you're humpin' Mary Zee. No problem. She's going on the trip. You can do somethin' dirty on the plane."

"Lloyd, what you're doing you're intruding on my personal private life," I said. "I don't much care for that."

"Yeah, right." He gave me a nasty gangster smile. "Get your shit packed. Wear a nice suit. Take your good socks. Those fuckers cost me fifty bucks a whack."

Mary Zee slept on the plane. We did not perform unnatural acts, or any other kind. Lloyd told me I would make a lot of money, for very little effort or time. He said I was in for several points. I tried to look impressed. Points are very big in your criminal enterprise. You got points, you got a piece of the action, everybody knows you're not a hired hand.

Lloyd told me again how slick the deal was, how easy it would be. The third or fourth time he said "a walk in the park" my palms began to sweat. I wanted to tell him he could give my points to somebody else. That I did not feel qualified for something this easy. I would wait for something hard.

"What we got here's a get-together deal," Lloyd said. "They hand over a little merchandise, we give 'em a little bread. Forty, fifty grand. We see they got quality shit, they see we got the gold."

"And then we do what," I said, "what do we do after that?"

Lloyd grinned and poked me in the ribs. "I *love* this guy. What the fuck you think after that? We do *bidness* after that. We set it up regular-like with these Veracruz guys. We make more money than God's got in his checking account. And you got a nice piece of that, you got points is what you got."

I looked out the window at the clouds down below. I

didn't look at Lloyd. "How many points you think I got? I don't believe you said."

"Christ, all this time you ask me something like that."

I turned around to face him. Lloyd looked hurt. He looked like Nixon when they asked him about the missing tapes.

"I let you in on somethin' nice, you come up with something like that. I always tried to treat you right. You got a nice foreign car, you got some suits. Where the fuck you get all that, you play the fuckin' slot machines? You can fuckin' kiss my ass."

"Maybe I didn't put it right," I said. "I certainly didn't mean it like that."

"What a guy's maybe thinking don't count," Lloyd said. "What counts is the way it comes out."

"I can see that," I said. "I can see it didn't come out right."

"I don't want to talk about it," Lloyd said. He picked up a *Time* magazine. "I don't want you puttin' any more shit inside my head."

He was silent the rest of the trip. Sometimes he gave me a look. Sometimes he mumbled to himself. I never learned how many points I had. I don't know why the hell I asked, since I was already thinking how I might get out of all this without risking Lloyd's wrath. Several ideas came to mind. Bailing out over Kansas seemed the best.

Lloyd was playing it extra cool. Instead of Miami International, he routed us into Fort Lauderdale. He said he knew too many people in Miami, you could run into nearly anyone. Due to the nature of the deal, he didn't want to do that.

We rented a car, using a Visa Lloyd had that didn't say Lloyd DeWitt. We got a shabby motel off 95. Lloyd said no one anyone knew would spot us there. Mary Zee said there were roaches in her bathroom the size of small dogs. Lloyd said they didn't call them roaches down here, they called them Palmetto bugs. Mary said she didn't give a shit what you called the little mothers, she didn't like to be molested in the tub.

Everybody was tired. Everybody went to bed. We met for breakfast at a pancake house you could walk to from the motel. Lloyd was rested and full of good cheer. He'd made some phone calls. Everything was fine. The Veracruz guys were all set. We'd do the meet that night.

"And where's that?" I said.

"Where's what?"

"The place where we meet."

Lloyd gave me that same wounded look I'd seen on the plane.

"What do you care? You don't have to worry where. I'm taking care of that."

"Just thought I'd ask," I said.

"He's taking care of it, hon," Mary said. "You don't have to worry 'bout that."

"Yeah, I do," I said. "See, you're not going, I am. You're not going, and neither is Lloyd. I'm the one that's going. I'm the one that needs to know where."

Lloyd started to speak. He shook his head and pointed at his mouth. He swallowed and wiped a napkin across his chin.

"It's a place, okay? I never been there, you never been there, what do you care? I drop you off at Sixty-second Street. A guy I know, he takes you on from there. This guy, who he is is Tony D."

"Tony D. takes me to the meet."

"Tony D. goes *with* you to the meet. There's two of the guys from Veracruz, there's two of us. You and Tony D. Two and two, everything's kosher, everything's straight."

I set down my coffee. I looked at Mary Zee. She was wearing something trendy, what Cher would think was right for the beach. All the truckers in the pancake place figured she was in her underwear.

"This is what I'm thinking," I said. "I'm thinking, a guy goes with me, a guy with a name like Tony D., this isn't sounding like a walk in the park. This is sounding like it's maybe something else. Correct me if I'm wrong, okay? I figure this guy's not along for the ride, he's there for something else."

Lloyd shook his head. "You mean like he's got a piece, he's taking a piece on this?" He screwed up his mouth like he'd tasted something bad. "Jesus, Wayne, you got to stop watchin' TV. These guys aren't a bunch of crazies, they're fuckin' bidnessmen. I don't like how you're thinkin' on this, you know? You're thinking like this, you go in with a bad attitude, these guys are going to know it, you're going to piss somebody off."

"Lloyd, now he is going to do just fine," Mary said. She reached across the booth and squeezed my hand. She had done something funny with her eyes. She had purple contacts on, and she'd sprinkled something silver on her lids. I wondered if she'd decorated anything else. Sometimes she'd leave me a surprise.

"Wayne is a little uptight is all he is," Mary said. "You're a little uptight, aren't you, babe? Listen, you're going to be fine."

"You go in actin' like that, what you're going to do is fuck up," Lloyd said. "You think you're gonna do that, I got to get me somebody else."

"He isn't going to do that," Mary said, "he's going to be just fine. Wayne, tell him you're going to be fine."

"I'm going to be just fine," I said.

"Good," Lloyd said. "I am fucking relieved to hear that."

I was not going to be just fine.

I had known it on the plane, I had known it when I got

into bed the night before. I knew it for certain when I finally gave up on sleep about three. What happened is, fear reached out and clutched my heart in the dark and lonely hours of the night. This had happened once or twice since I'd gotten caught up in gangster life. I knew that I was wrong, that living on the wrong side of the law wasn't right. I knew that I might get caught. That if I did, my new best friend would be a person named Junior or Clyde.

And, always before, these phantoms of guilt and doubt had disappeared with first light. With the sight of my Rolex watch on the table by my bed, with the thought of my raw-silk suits. Most of all, with the wake-up vision of Mary Zee, slick and fine as milk. She was overwhelming proof that the good life wouldn't go away.

But Mary Zee wasn't with me in the night. She was in the shabby room next door. By silent agreement, we had spent the night apart. The situation being as it was, that and the setting and the Palmetto bugs, nothing seemed conducive to a night of carnal fun. I spent the night alone with the smell of sweat and mildew instead of nice perfume. And when I met Lloyd and Mary at the pancake place, all the fears of the night were still there. The more Lloyd talked, the more I was certain I was standing on the edge. The part about Tony didn't help a whole lot.

Still, I listened to what he said. I listened to Mary tell me everything was fine. And then I finished off my coffee and I told them I was going for a walk. I said it real casual like. I think I yawned and stretched. I tried to look confident and cool because the pancakes were churning in my gut and the sweat was popping out on my chest. I didn't want them to see that I was walking away. That I did not intend to ever come back.

Thirty-four

The lights of Lloyd's rental car vanished down the street. I stood with my attaché case on the corner in the dark, in front of the pizza joint. Next door was a doughnut shop. Across the street there were boarded-up stores. The Miami night was hot and still; I had been out of Lloyd's AC for a minute and a half and my suit stuck to me like a shroud. Not the best image, I decided, considering the business at hand.

Another two minutes. Maybe three. The black Mercury turned the corner and caught me in its lights. It pulled up to the curb and the driver leaned over and opened the passenger door.

"Get in," he said. "I'm the guy, I'm Tony D."

I shut the front door, opened the one in the back and got in. Tony D. looked over his shoulder and shook his head.

"Huh-unh," he said, "up front."

"I don't do that," I said. "I sit in the back."

He turned nearly all the way around and rested a burly arm on the back of the seat. The burly arm was attached to a burly neck. Tony D. was burly all over. He had an ex-fighter's face, a flat nose and a ridge of scarred flesh above his eyes.

"You didn't listen," he said. "I want you inna front. Guy gets in the car, I want him sittin' in the front."

"I get in a car, I'm sitting in the back," I told him. "I always sit in the back."

"What's the fuckin' difference?"

"My point exactly," I said.

Tony thought about that. He peered at me with eyes that had seen too many fights, too many right hooks and not enough time. No answer to his problem came to mind.

We got on the Expressway and headed down south. It was nearly eleven, but everyone in Florida was going somewhere. Off to the left, I could see the bright glow of Miami Beach. A million little sins, a million little lights. In the mirror, I could see the brooding eyes of Tony D. I moved behind his bulk and out of sight. My nerve ends were doing the cancan an inch above my skin. The last thing I needed was this palooka watching me like a chicken hawk.

"This is it," Tony said, "get out."

I looked around. There was nothing much to see. A darkened street with no one about. A few streetlights down the block. The ones near us were all shot out. I stepped out on the curb. Tony stood with his hands at his sides and sniffed the air.

"I think you got the wrong address," I told him. "I don't think anyone's here."

Tony didn't answer. He walked down the sidewalk checking doors. The building was dark-red brick. It was covered with graffiti and posters from ancient times. Tony stopped at a door that said 136. He turned and looked at me.

"You okay with this?" he said. "You gonna be all right?"

"I'm fine," I said.

"Don't do nothin' stupid. Don't do nothin' dumb."

That pissed me off a lot. It was clear he'd been talking to Lloyd.

Tony motioned me back, opened the door and went in. The place was big and empty and nearly dark. A plain wooden table was set in the center of the room. Over the table was a 20-watt bulb. Off in the dark, I made out the ghosts of old machinery, covered up with tarps. There was a dry, peculiar smell in the air, dust and something sweet, a smell that had lived in this place for some time.

"Tortilla factory," Tony said. "They used to make 'em here. They sent 'em everywhere. You go to a Mes'can place, I don't care where it is, the tortillas come from here. You like greaser food?"

"Sometimes I do."

"I can't eat that shit. Gives me gas."

Tony motioned me to stay where I was. He walked a few steps toward the light. For a big man, he moved real quiet. I looked up at the rafters. I thought I heard rats.

Tony D. stopped. He stood dead-still for a moment, then he raised both his hands a few inches from his sides and spread his fingers wide. I looked past him and saw them, two men walking out of the shadow at the far end of the room. They were tall, gaunt men with black hair slicked back and caught in ponytails. One, slightly taller than his friend, had a black patch over one eye. They both wore suits dark as night. Their shirts were high-collared, almost a phosphorescent white, even in the dim light. They had the thinnest ties I'd ever seen. I wondered how you got a knot in a tie as thin as that.

The guy without the patch carried an attaché case like mine. He stopped at the table and laid the case down and stepped back. The other guy looked at Tony D. and then at me.

"It's okay," Tony said, without turning around.

I walked up and stood beside him. The man with the patch looked at Tony and grinned.

"I don' guess you carrying, are you, friend? I don' thing you doin' that."

"I'm clean," Tony said, "him too."

"You don't mind if we look and see?"

Tony shrugged. He kept his fingers spread. Patch said something in Spanish to his friend. Friend walked up and frisked Tony, doing it quick and clean, then stepped up to me. I held my breath. I could feel my heart punching at my chest. I spread my arms wide, holding the attaché out in one hand. The man was wearing something strong. He smelled a lot like Mary Zee.

When he was done, he stepped away and nodded at the guy who wore the patch. Tony D. didn't move. He stood very still. I wondered why we got frisked, and Tony didn't get to check them. Maybe it was gangster etiquette. Like the other guys were hosts. It worried me a lot, but it didn't seem the right time to ask.

Patch stood by the table, his hands behind his back. He looked at me and grinned.

"You firs' time in Miami," he said. "You like it here okay?"

"I've been here once or twice," I said.

"You got the time, you wan' to go see them raze the togs. Tha's the thing you wanna do."

"Raze the togs."

"Sure. Raze the togs. They chasin' these rabbiss 'round the track, you know? They chase these fockin' rabbits 'round the track."

"Sounds like fun," I said.

"Hey, is a fun thing to do. No sheet." He looked down at my hand, glanced at Tony D., then back to me. "I think you got somethin' there for me. You wanna put these on the table, we get finished up with this, ever'body go home."

"Okay," I said.

I took a step and Tony held me back. "Hold it a minute," he said.

The guy with the patch looked at Tony. He cocked his head like he didn't understand.

"You say somethin'? You say somethin' to me, friend?"

"I was goin' to say, we'd like to see the merchandise is all," Tony said. "That's what I was goin' to say."

Patch spread his hands. "You gonna do that. You gonna see the merchandise."

Tony cleared his throat. "Yeah, well, see maybe your buddy, he could open up the case over there? My friend here shows you the money, you show the merchandise, that's okay with you."

"Tha's okay with me. That's fine." The guy smiled at Tony, a real big smile that showed a remarkable display of white teeth. He kept smiling at Tony. He didn't talk to him, he talked to me.

"These friend of yours, he is not considerate of other people's feelings, you know? Tha's a bad way to be, you don' thing of nobody but youself."

I took a deep breath. "I don't think he meant anything. I don't think that."

Tony looked pained. He knew the rules. He knew this wasn't how you played the game. "It's business," he said, "okay? You shouldn't take no offense."

"Hey, none tuken," the guy said. "What the fock, ever'ting is *bueno*, ever'ting is okay."

"Good," Tony said, "I don't want no—"

Patch shot Tony in the head. I didn't hardly see him move. His hand just slid beneath the table and his arm was straight out and the gun went *phhhht!* and Tony dropped like a wet side of beef.

"Jesus Christ," I said, "why'd you want to do that!" Something wet ran down my leg. "Why the *fuck* you do that!"

Patch pointed the gun at me. The big smile was gone. "These man, he was really impolite. You don' wanna be impolite, too." He gestured with the gun. "You put the case down, ever'ting is fine. Tomorrow, you go see them raze the togs."

"No problem," I said. I held the attaché case out straight. The guy grinned. I pulled the trigger and the Derringer jerked in my fist. Patch was maybe four feet away. The blinding yellow flame licked out and punched him solidly in the chest. The powder caught his hair on fire and turned his face black. I couldn't hear a thing. The blast from the gun was like a bomb going off inside my head. Patch was on the floor and the other guy was standing there looking like he wanted to cry or throw up. His hand clawed for something in his coat he couldn't find and then he turned around and ran. I held the case out straight and tried to keep my hand from shaking and I shot him in the back. He raised his arms above his head and took a leap like a runner when he hits the finish line, then everything got tangled and he dropped.

I tried not to shake. I noticed I was pissing on my shoes. I was grateful no one was alive to see that. I made myself go through Tony's pockets and find his keys. I didn't look at the other guys. I left the building where they made tortillas and ran to Tony's car.

I didn't know where the hell I was. The car was pointed west. I turned the corner and headed north. Cuba was south, I knew that, Miami was to the north. My lights swept the hollow red buildings, then glanced off the windshield of a car. The car was parked halfway up the block. My beams were on bright and I saw them as they raised their hands up to their faces to ward off the harsh white light. I passed them and whipped down the street and turned right. I knew they hadn't seen me, but I saw them. Lloyd and Mary Zee. Waiting down the block, waiting for the show to end.

By sheer blind luck, I stumbled onto 826, also called the Palmetto Expressway, in honor of the plants or the bugs of that name. The road ran into Miami International a few miles to the north. I pulled Tony's car into the long-term lot. Before I did that, I stopped at a mom-and-pop store that sold groceries and tackle, Hong Kong shirts and khaki pants. I changed in the car, and threw my nice suit in the trash. The butterfly skins his old garb and turns into something else. Wayne Grosz died in front of Bob and Lucy Mae's All-Nite, and Jack Track struggled back to life.

As I turned into the airport parking lot, sirens wailed going south. It could have been the mobster shootout I'd left behind. In Miami, it could have been anything else. A lot of bad shit goes on down there.

I took the first night flight out. I have tried to recall where it went. I do not have the slightest idea. I took several flights after that. On the TV shows, the guy doesn't leave a trail.

I finally got back to Philadelphia again. It had been nine years since I'd stumbled on Wayne Grosz dead in an alley, and borrowed his wallet and his name. I thanked him silently, and gave him back what belonged to him. I got all my Jack Track stuff out of the safety-deposit box. I took the money from the attaché case and mailed it to myself, in care of Uncle Will. I told him in a note to put the package away for me awhile. After that I hitched out of town. I got a ride to Harrisburg. Another after that, up the Susquehanna River somewhere. I slept beneath somebody's house. The local law hauled me in and let me go, and I bummed my way east out of town.

Part of what I told Aaron Hess was true. I worked odd jobs for six years before I landed in Vegas and took up a life of crime. I stayed there nearly three years, and spent another five on the road before I found my way home.

I've had a lot of time to wonder why I didn't leave Lloyd and Mary Zee at the pancake place. Just walk away and never come back. This is what I meant to do. I did not want to go and meet the guys from Veracruz. I did not want any points. What I wanted to do was run away and start a brand-new life.

This is what I always did. People ran away from *me*—why shouldn't I leave them? My father went and died. Mother took off, and I got even by pissing off college and going on the run. Maybe, I decided, as I walked through the Florida streets that morning, and into the afternoon, I would see something through this time, see how it all came out. Sit through the movie till the credits came on at the end.

I did it because I was scared. Because I was sure I'd chicken out, that I couldn't make myself go back. Okay, it was a hell of a time to make a stand. Nearly any other moment in my life would have been a better choice. As ever, timing is the key, and both hands are broken on my watch.

I didn't have a bit of trouble with the gun. If you're in L.A. or Miami or Detroit, all you have to know is where to look, you can find about anything you like. The pistol was a little under five inches long, a double-action Derringer with a satin stainless finish and a rosewood grip. I bought a can of paint and sprayed it black. It wasn't your ordinary hold-out gun. It would fire two .357 Magnum shells. This is a very big load, coming out of a barrel that is three-inches long. I knew it would kick like a horse. I also knew what it would do on the other end. I was not going to walk in a meet with these bozos with some little shooter that would tickle them in the ribs. The final point that sold me was the weapon was made by American Derringer in Waco, Texas. Practically my old neighborhood. Lloyd said the meet would go fine, the guys from Veracruz were businessmen. Bullshit is what I said to that. You want to meet some new folks, take along a friend.

I taped the pistol to the handle of my attaché case in the back of Tony's car. I've got pretty big hands, and when I wrapped my fingers around the handle and the gun, you couldn't tell anything was there.

I wasn't sure I could even use the thing. I have shot a lot of deer and popped a lot of tin cans. I missed all the wars, and never aimed at anything that might shoot back.

I dream sometimes about Patch and his friend. I see his hair on fire and his face turned black. Once, after I started on the hobo trail, I stopped at a library somewhere and looked up the story in the Miami papers. Those mothers weren't from Veracruz, I think I guessed that at the time. They were from the cartel in Colombia, a couple of real sweet guys from Medellín. Tony D. was from Iron County, Michigan, a place called Crystal Falls. He was local talent known to the police, a guy who would do odd jobs like drive a car or break somebody's knees. He died a long way from home. They listed some of his early fights.

The coke they found at the tortilla factory was very high-grade stuff. The papers said the cops were on the trail of "an unknown assailant who fled the scene." The incident was clearly a drug deal where something went astray. No mention of Lloyd or Mary Zee. No big surprise there. When things went haywire, they wouldn't hang around to watch the cops arrive.

There is no way to say just what was supposed to happen in South Miami that night. It wasn't any "get acquainted" deal like Lloyd said, I know that. There wasn't fifty grand in that case, there was close to two mil. Tight stacks of hundred-dollar bills. What I'm guessing is, the guys in Chicago told Lloyd to start easy, see how the thing went down. Maybe Lloyd meant to do it that way. Maybe he got to thinking how this might be a chance to make his big score. He would think about how he could turn nearly two million bucks' worth of coke into a wad that would set him up for life somewhere. I can see him sitting up in his room, talking himself into the deal. Maybe Mary Zee helped him along. He'd think how fine the deal would be. He wouldn't think about what might happen if something went wrong, or where he'd end up when the guys in Chicago discovered what had happened to their dough. Lloyd was pretty slick, but he wasn't real smart. With guys like Lloyd, greed is the key. This is fairly common in the criminal biz. Fuck everybody else is a basic way of life.

And this is where I came in. If Patch and his buddy didn't kill me, I'd walk out with the stuff, and Lloyd would pull off his big score. I have an idea I would not have lasted long after that. Tony D. and I would find a home several fathoms down. A deal like that, you can't leave a lot of witnesses behind.

If the deal went sour—as it did—Lloyd would have another plan. A carful of Tonys was very likely somewhere nearby. They would ambush the Colombians, take the money and the coke, and make a double profit for the day. I didn't see this carload of hoods, but I'm betting they were there. I wonder what sort of future Lloyd had planned for them. You can't kill everyone, but I guess you can try.

Maybe this is how it went down. Or maybe it was some other way. I don't know for sure what happened. I know how it ended up. I was scared out of my socks for five years, frightened every time I saw a cop or a guy in a big black car. Afraid that someone would learn Jack Track the road bum was the guy who used to be Wayne Grosz.

I am still scared now. Not like I was, but it's there. Something like that, it's not about to go away. I think it'd help if I could tell it all to Earl sometime. Maybe there'll be a night when the Scotch is smooth enough and the moon is just right. Maybe when I tell him, Earl, in his guise as The Nigger of Wall Street, can tell me what to do with the cash. I have sixty-seven packs of hundred-dollar bills, two hundred and fifty bills to the stack. One million, six hundred seventy-five thousand dollars, buried in the cornfield, thirty-seven yards from the back of the house. I am not real proud of the way I got it, but I figure it's mine by default. And it's better than being dead. It is better to be a live former gangster who is sorry for the sinful life he's led.

Thirty-five

Sowing and reaping seem to be the themes of life. The rest is just stuff Fate kind of tosses in as you stumble toward a patch of dead grass. I hadn't sown real good that day and I was reaping the benefits. There were only two people I really cared about and I'd pissed them both off. Earl would forgive me for my bit at the Pharaoh Cemetery. Sometime, but maybe not soon. For a while I would be Massah Jack, gone stand up for his poh darky friend.

I wasn't that sure about Cecily Benét. A pit bull will let go of your leg if you shoot it in the head. Cecily is not so forgiving as that. We were doing okay until she met Millie Jean looking stunning in black. I think this did more damage than spotting her that night without a top.

This is how you end up eating canned soup, and watching TV by yourself. Reruns are no substitute for friends. They cannot replace a person you care for scooted up beside you in bed.

I didn't dream about Cecily Benét. I dreamed about Mary Zee, and I hadn't done that in some time. I followed her through that hot Miami night in Earl's bird-shit car. She stopped at a cheap motel that looked a lot like my own farmhouse. Inside, it looked like Eddie Trost's place. I was on a stainless-steel table, stretched out naked, very cold and very white. Tubes ran out of every orifice. Nate Graham looked down at me and smiled. He had borrowed all the Black & Decker tools from Earl's place. Somewhere across

the room, Deke and Mary Zee performed an unlikely tra-
peze act. I don't think you could really spear a girl in midair
like that . . .

I was grateful for the knock that startled me awake in a
sweat. The clock said eight forty-five. The boy at the door
said, "Package for Mr. Jack Track." His blue uniform said
"Dallas Delivery" on the pocket, the same as it did on his
truck. I scribbled something on his pad, and he told me to
have a nice day. The boy showed a lot of tact. He always
kept his eyes on my face. These guys are used to people
in their shorts, and often less than that.

I didn't have to guess about the box. It had holes in the
top and made familiar plaintive sounds. I opened the lid
and lifted out the weightless fur ball inside. It squirmed a
lot and screamed and looked outraged and perplexed. Its
blue kitten eyes stabbed my heart. Its needle claws dug into
my chest. A card came with the box. It said, "This is Alexander Two. Love and Enjoy!" The card wasn't signed, but
of course I knew who.

What to make of this? I wondered. A sign of reconciliation, a peace overture? Cecily's way of telling me that all
would be well? Or, as they say on the quiz shows to losers,
"a lovely parting gift"?

I made a barricade in the corner of the kitchen and left
Alexander there with a hamburger ball and warm milk. He
gobbled everything up and wanted out. I called Cecily to
thank her, and possibly get some mood indicator from her
voice. Cecily was out. Of course they don't tell you that,
they say she's unavailable at the time.

I left my name and got dressed. Alexander yowled and
I picked him up and put him on my shoulder and carried
him through the house. A cat likes to get you trained early,
so you'll know how to act later on.

I was into my second cup of coffee when Aaron Hess

arrived. My heart gave a little start. I took a deep breath and tried to look indifferent as I let him in the house.

"Coffee smells good," he said. "What's that stuff you got in it? Vanilla beans or what?"

"Hazelnut," I said. "Pour yourself a cup."

"Like to." Hess shook his head. "Haven't got the time. Got to get on back to town."

He glanced at Alexander, who was crawling up my leg. He had the look people get who can't imagine why you'd have a cat.

I took my cup to the counter and rinsed it out. Alexander hissed at the water and I dropped him back into his pen.

"Do whatever you got to do," Hess said. "Close up or what. You're riding in with me."

I looked at him. "What for?"

Hess grinned at that. He was wearing his favorite trout tie. "I guess I've rounded up eight or ten thousand wrong-doers in my life. Likely more than that. They all say the same thing, Mr. Track. 'What for?' "

I tried to look bored, like I was very weary of this. "You keep doing that," I said. "That wrongdoer shit. I don't like it much. That's all in your head."

"Maybe, maybe not."

"So why are you taking me to town?"

Hess shrugged. "I'm not taking you anywhere. I'm asking you to talk to me awhile."

"I don't think that's what you said."

"Force of habit, I guess. No offense."

" 'Course not," I said.

We both knew it hadn't happened that way, that pushing me was no accident, that it pleased him to make a man jump. This is what he did, he had spent his whole life honing fear to an art, bringing this talent to a fine cutting edge. I had seen this skill before, in some of the men who came down to see Lloyd from Chicago and Detroit. Hess was on the side of right and they were not, but all of them clearly enjoyed their work a great deal.

"We got a real screwup in town," Hess said. "I sure as hell don't need it but I guess it's what I got. It's a burden I got to carry, seeing how there's nobody else."

He turned and looked at me. I was supposed to say, "What?" I gazed out the window at dry summer fields and skinny cows.

"What happened is, this Billy McKenzie, he's poundin' on my door about eleven o'clock. I'm having a drink, I'm watching that Jay Leno show. I enjoy that boy. This McKenzie, he looks like a ball of string that's coming undone. He says he wants to get it all off his chest. I say, 'What?' I'm thinking, I'm thinking to myself, I've got me the cut-up killer, only that isn't it. What it is is a real bunch of shit. He perches on a chair and he spills it all out. How him and these other jokers was keeping a bunch of honeys in town. He says he'll tell me all about it I promise to leave him out. I tell him I can't do that, I'll have to hear the rest, and anyway I want to get the sheriff over here before we get too far."

Hess shook his head and flexed his hands on the wheel. "McKenzie 'bout pees in his pants he hears that. He says I can't do that because Deke, he's mixed up in all this. He's the one that did the procuring, that the guy who was runnin' the girlie show was Max."

Hess gave me a sour look. " 'Course I'm not telling you anything you didn't already know about, Track. I mean, I got you to thank for bringing this load of crap out. McKenzie said he would've kept quiet if you hadn't scared the hell out of him yesterday afternoon. Said he went home and threw up, and figured he better get it all done."

"I'd heard something about 'em bringing girls into town," I said. "I didn't give it much thought. You can't rely on anything comes from those clowns. I sure didn't know about Deke."

"You didn't give it much thought."

"That's right."

"You took a oath of office, you got knowledge of a clear violation of the statutes in your town, *you* didn't give it much thought."

"For Christ's sake, Hess." I gave him a little wave that said this is nonsense, that we both knew better than that. "I'm the temporary town constable. People call me, they got a squirrel in the attic, a drunk's throwing up in the square. Don't put this oath-of-office crap on my back."

Hess didn't care for that at all. He went white around the mouth. His eyes were hard as railroad spikes. He jerked the car off the road and slammed it to a stop. I thought, hell, he's going to jump me right here.

"You son of a bitch!" He glared at me, and his hands tried to squeeze through the wheel. "Don't you hand me that country-boy jerk-off shit. I wasn't born in a Easter basket, boy. You got a real bad habit of keeping information to yourself, when you ought to be pursuing the law. Every time I turn something up, I run smack onto your trail. McKenzie told me 'bout his calls from Nate Graham. Which he'd *already* told *you* about. I'm guessing you heard about this yearbook business with Nate Graham and Deke. I got no doubt that anonymous letter come right from your fancy nigger friend. The Dallas PD knows he was sniffing around up there, asking about Nate Graham. He's got no business doing that. I expect Deke's right about who shot up his car."

Hess shook his head. He was running out of breath. "Damn it, Track. What the fuck's the matter with you? You think I'm a retard or what? You give me this stuff you're an outstandin' citizen who hasn't got a past, and all you do is kick me in the mouth."

"I had no intention of doing that," I said.

"Oh, hell, you didn't," Hess said.

"Listen," I told him, "all you've done since you busted in my house with your sunshade boys is climb up my back. You got a crazy hacker on the loose out there and you can't catch him so you mess around with me."

Hess thrust out his jaw. "I'm not the officer of the law who's neglecting his duties 'round here." He leaned out and poked a finger in my chest. "You know what you are, Track? You're a ordinary felon, is what. You got a criminal attitude. You can't tell the truth, even if it doesn't matter if you do. That's an inborn trait, is what it is. That is common to the criminal mind."

"Oh, come *on*," I said. I had to laugh at that. "You know who you sound like, Hess? You sound like Sherlock Holmes. 'Hark, Watson, the fucking game's afoot!' "

Hess looked solemn. "If you're thinking that's an insult, it's not. I got a lot of respect for the works of Mr. A. Conan Doyle. I don't approve of Holmes using hard drugs, now I can't excuse that. But I suppose those were different times."

Hess turned around and jammed his foot hard on the floor. We sprayed a lot of gravel and swerved back on the road.

"I am wasting my time, trying to shake some sense into you. I don't like you much, Track. But I know you're not an ignorant man. This whole girlie-show business wouldn't mean spit, if it wasn't for the fact that it has to do with Max. He was there that night, up in that room over Eddie Trost's place. Not long before he got himself killed. McKenzie said a girl saw someone looking in. No way to say if that means anything, but I can't dismiss the fact."

Hess looked straight ahead, squinting into the afternoon sun. "You knew about that. You knew Max Coomer was a part of that monkey business up in that room and you kept it to yourself. I fault you for doing that, Track. You can laugh off your badge if you like, but you neglected your duty there, boy. You took your dick out and you pissed on the law."

I didn't know what to say. I had to catch myself, because this jerk had me feeling *guilty* for a minute, like I was maybe Wyatt Earp and I'd taken a Clanton out to lunch. It made me mad, him pulling a stunt like that. I catch hell for tarnishing the badge, which shouldn't be a big surprise, since I've got this inborn trait, I got a criminal mind. This is what your cop'll try to do. He'll try to slick you any way he can. If you're not thinking straight, he'll get you real confused.

We didn't say much the rest of the way into town. At least, I didn't say much. Hess wouldn't shut up. He told me how he'd talked to Smoothy Coomer. He knew about Eddie Trost's drunken pursuit at the party, and what he'd allegedly said to Roy about getting rid of Max. He knew about Max making Nate Graham take his clothes off when we were kids. He even knew about Max baiting Deke about him maybe still hanging out with Nate. I wondered where he'd learned about that. I knew he hadn't pried it out of Phil. Phil was terrified of Deke. He wouldn't get within a mile of a cop like Hess.

Spilling all this, that wasn't like Aaron Hess at all, it simply wasn't his way. I knew what he was doing. He would never admit it to himself, but I had gotten under his skin. He had to tell me that he knew everything *I* did, that his was bigger than mine. It gave me some pleasure to see this crack in the armor of Hess the supercop.

Of course if I'd had any sense, I would've known that I'd have to pay for this. He'd figure out what he'd done, and I'd get another mark on his list. A man like Hess, you don't screw around with his pride. It doesn't make it any better if he brought it on himself.

* * *

It looked as if a major disaster had struck the courthouse. People stood around in the square and crowded up on the lawn. Cars drove around the block to see what was going on. There wasn't an empty parking space within half a mile of Main.

Hess honked his way through, waved at a trooper he knew and pulled up in the driveway out back. I was glad he had some clout. The media had sniffed out a story and they were all back in town, circling in for the kill.

"I got a rat's nest here is what I got," Hess said. We made our way to the elevators near the front door. More state troopers stood just outside. They weren't letting anyone in.

"Nobody knows shit, isn't anyone in charge. Deke's relieved of duty, and I'm handling things till the court gets somebody in. I don't know when that'll be. Everybody moves like niggers picking cotton 'round here."

Hess gave me a nasty grin. "You don't care for that, do you, Track? Me talking like that."

"No, I don't," I said.

"Good. You're a hard man to offend."

The elevator doors slid open. Hess punched the button for 2. A couple of lawyers tried to walk in. Hess told them to get the hell out. They didn't like that. Hess didn't care.

"You sure know how to get along with people," I said. "I can see why you've got so many friends. You got the knack, you just draw people in."

Hess didn't answer. The elevator jerked to a halt. Hess nodded me to follow down the hall. The sheriff's office was two doors down. Three or four deputies moped around outside looking grim. No one would tell them anything. They didn't know what to do next.

Hess stopped midway down the hall. "In there," he said, and pointed at a door.

"What for?" I said.

"Shit, there you go again." He was using that cop stare

again, hard as the bluing on a gun. "Here's what you're going to do for me, Track. You're going to go in there and sit. You're going to make an official statement for me, you're going to put everything down. I am talking fucking *everything,* friend. Anything you found out in your poking around. You leave anything *out* and I'll toss your ass in a cell for obstruction of whatever comes to mind. I might just do it anyway on the grounds that you piss me off. Is all that clear enough for you?"

"Are you arresting me or what? I'd like to know that in case I want to bring a suit."

Hess looked at me with total disgust and shut the door. I stood there and looked around the room. It had a table and a chair. A yellow pad and some ballpoint pens. I don't like that kind. I like the felt tips.

I wondered what they'd done with Roy Burns, Billy McKenzie and Eddie Trost. Had they charged them with anything or what? I wasn't sure bringing girls in town was illegal or not. I guess you'd have to prove they got paid. Maybe some of them were under age. If they were, those boys would be up shit creek.

Procuring, now that was something else. Deke would have a problem weaseling out of that. He'd lose his cushy job if nothing else.

I sat down at the table. I picked up a pen. For lack of something better, I wrote my name. I looked out the dirty window for a while. Somebody yelled somewhere. Glass shattered out in the hall. Someone yelled again. Something hard slammed against my wall.

I got up and ran to the door and looked out. Phil Eddels was sprawled on the floor. His hands were cuffed behind his back. He was yelling and shaking his head and there was an ugly bruise across his cheek. Broken glass was everywhere. A lot of it was in Phil's hair. A state trooper had hold of his feet and he was dragging Phil along the floor. George Rainey was a few yards down, near the sheriff's door. He was backed against the wall. His hands were cuffed as well, but he didn't seem to care. He was holding three troopers at bay. Blood ran down the side of his face. A trooper moved in and George kicked him in the crotch. The trooper folded and groaned on the floor. That pissed the other guys off. They sailed in and started clubbing George's head.

I looked down the hall. Hess was standing in the sheriff's door, staring at the sight. On this rare occasion, he and I were in accord. We both mouthed the words at once: Jesus, *now* what?

dots he was just touchin' ten. We called 'em 'dime-cups'...

Thirty-six

Phil looked haggard and subdued. He sagged in his chair and stared at the floor, clutching his legs with both hands, grabbing them just above the knees and holding tight. I knew what he was doing. He didn't want anyone to see that he was scared. He thought they wouldn't know if his hands didn't shake.

George didn't look subdued at all. He looked angry and ready for a fight. One eye was swollen shut and his lower lip was split. He was willing to go another round if anyone would take him on. The troopers didn't like the idea of having George in a room without his cuffs. Hess said they could shoot him if he moved. He said it looked bad on a report, you shoot a man he's all trussed up, he's wearing cuffs or restraints of any sort. He said some fag from the ACLU would climb your ass quick for doing that.

"You see 'em on the actual premises," Hess said, "or you *think* that's where they were coming from? You want to be certain what you're swearing to. I don't want any shit comin' back on this."

The big trooper had freckles and sandy hair. He looked at his partner, who was bald and very short. His partner nodded back.

Sandy-Hair said, "No, sir. Isn't any question where they was. Your perpetrator number one was in the driveway at the time. The mean sum'bitch, he had his butt out the window he was just comin' out. We called out 'Police!' and they took off and run."

"We begun pursuit of the suspects then," Shorty said. "Me in the vehicle and Gary on foot. We apprehended 'em both a couple of blocks down."

Hess frowned. "And no one was in the house. Where you think Sheriff Glover was at the time?"

"I don't know, sir," Sandy-Hair said. "He sure wasn't there."

Hess looked around. There were three other troopers in the room. *"Anybody* seen him? Goddamn it, he's supposed to stay *home."*

Nobody answered. Hess looked down at Phil. "You got any idea, Mr. Eddels, what kind of mess you're in? Breaking and entering's a crime. You can go down to Huntsville."

"I guess," Phil said.

"Isn't any guess to it. You boys'll draw ten to twenty years. That's a real long time."

Ten to twenty wasn't even close, but Phil probably didn't know that. He wasn't thinking tomorrow, he was thinking right now. All the troopers had him scared, five of these mothers in whipcord, Stetsons and boots. Five cops in one room is all you need.

Hess shook his head and looked sorrowfully at Phil. "You want to tell me what you and your friend were doing there at Sheriff Glover's house? I'd like to hear about that."

Phil showed Hess a fierce and defiant look. As fierce and defiant as he could get. "Someone has to do something. Someone's gotta *act!"*

"What's that supposed to mean?"

"Just what I said."

"Well, shit, it doesn't mean anything to me." Hess leaned down in Phil's face, close enough to bite his nose. "Now you get off this crap and tell me what you were *doing* breaking into that house. I am tired of fucking with you."

"Leave him alone," George said. "You don't have to tell him nothing, Phil!"

"*You* shut up," Hess said. "I got you on B and E and aggravatin' assault."

George came out of his chair like something at a rodeo event. The troopers had been waiting for this. One on either side grabbed him by the shoulders and slammed him down again.

"I will have you severely restricted, you try that again," Hess said.

"I'm going to do it," George said.

"You better *not* do it, friend."

"I am. I'm just tellin' you that. I could spring up any time."

Hess stared. "Are you feeble or what? What's the matter with you?"

"You don't have to state your mental health. I'd advise against it. My clients are going *sub silentio* here and now."

Hess turned at the unfamiliar voice. "Mister, we got private business in here. I'll ask you to step on out."

The man in the doorway smiled. He was a tall, dark-haired man with gray eyes. He wore a well-cut suit, a Daffy Duck tie, and Tony Lama alligator boots. He stuck out his hand to Hess.

"Garner T. Marcos," he said. "Met you in Austin one time, over to Annie Richards' place. I'm representing Mr. Earl Murphy downstairs. We're filin' a bunch of suits. Sheriff Deke Glover, Pharaoh County, *et alii*. False arrest, harassment, violation of civil rights. Whatever else comes to mind."

Hess looked perplexed. Marcos stepped past him and nodded at George and Phil. "You gentlemen charged with anything, you under arrest? These fellas bother to read your rights? Damn, I sure hate to see this. I'd say my clients have suffered undue use of force. Don't you clean 'em up.

I'll want some color photographs. Shit, we got us a *coram non judice* here, we got a kangaroo court."

Marcos looked solemnly at Hess. "I'd advise you to finish up here and get these boys downstairs. We'll be making bail."

"Who will?" said Hess.

"No offense. That's none of your concern at this time. *Cave canem.* Have a nice day."

Marcos nodded to us all and walked out. It occurred to me he'd never stopped smiling all the time that he was there.

"What the fuck?" said Hess. He looked a little dazzled, slightly out of sync. "I don't much care for this."

"He say I'm his client? Where's he get that?" Phil looked upset. "What do I need a damn lawyer for?"

"I'd get me two or three, I was you," one of the troopers said.

I finished up my statement for Hess. I wrote down everything he'd told me coming over in the car. I left out everything else. Hess was out of pocket, so I left my statement with one of the idle deputies who were wandering about. Overnight, these poor souls had become the lepers of the courthouse square. They had all the status of a Patriots quarterback. People sent them out for sandwiches and Cokes. They didn't seem to care.

They wouldn't let me talk to Phil and George. With Deke in disgrace, Hess and his troopers were running the show, and everyone was real uptight. I caught Doc Hackley on the stairs and he made a quick call. Phil and George had been officially charged. If Marcos came through as he'd said, they were likely already out on bail.

"What the *hell* got into those two?" Doc wanted to know. I told him I didn't have a clue, that Phil and George saw through a glass darkly sometimes. Doc said he didn't care for literary crap that early in the day, that he could handle it better at night.

When I walked out back, Earl was leaning on the fender of his bird-shit car, lighting up a thin cigar. He was wearing a great-looking charcoal semi-summer suit, European cut. Blue work shirt buttoned at the collar, no tie. Blue-striped Nikes, no socks.

"You looking for a ride, I bet," Earl said. "Never knew a man had such a talent for bein' somewhere without a car."

"If you're going back home, I'd be grateful for your help. And don't talk to me about cars."

"Get in," Earl said.

He was parked in a spot that said RESERVED FOR COUNTY JUDGE. He backed out and hooked down the driveway toward Main. A covey of reporters took pictures of the car. They didn't know who we were or much care.

"I appreciate your lawyer stepping in to take care of Phil and George," I said. "I don't feel those two got paddles to go with their canoes. They can use all the help they can get."

"Clerk downstairs said they'd done something to Deke. I said that's good enough for me. Told Garner to go try and get 'em out."

I opened the window to let Earl's cigar smoke out. There were dark clouds off to the west. I wasn't real impressed. Clouds in north Texas in the summer tend to dry up or go somewhere else.

"He looks like a good man," I said. "Like he's got a lot of confidence."

Earl grinned. "Ol' Garner could've got Hitler off. Could've got him thirty days in a halfway house. What'd those fuckers do, get themselves beat up like that, they aren't even black?"

"Breaking and entering. Got into Deke's house."

"What for?"

"I can't answer that. Phil and George, they see through a glass darkly sometimes."

"Say they do?"

"They been like that since they were kids. Listen, you and me going to be okay? I'd like it if we could."

"I expect we maybe will. I got you on ignorance is all. You're pure in heart. I'm not charging intent."

"I'm apologizing," I said. "Don't push it much further than that."

"Not pushing you anywhere, Jack." Earl looked at the road. He didn't look at me. "Don't say anything you don't *want* to say to me. I don't care about that."

"What I'm saying is I'm sorry for what I said. I thought that'd be enough. All I do is apologize. I don't do penance, Earl."

"Shit. Nobody asked you to."

"I was thinking that you did."

"Nobody said nothing like that."

"See, I thought you did. What it sounded like to me, it sounded like you were thinking I got to be contrite. Like sorry won't cut it, you want to string it out. I maybe go on a quest, I got to go and find a grail. I'll maybe get off I do that."

Earl slammed on the brakes. My seat belt cut me in half.

"You got good timing," he said. "We're right close to your house."

"What are we doing, you're letting me out? I can't believe you're doing this. This is a real immature thing to do."

"I'm glad we could talk," Earl said. "Sorta straighten things out."

"Well, fuck you, Earl."

"Going to rain like hell about dark."

"No it's not. This is real shitty, you know that? You get a ride with a black guy, he's going to do something like this."

"You got that right," Earl said.

I got out and Earl drove off. It was a quarter mile to the house. I didn't mind that. It was the principle of the thing, making me get out and walk. I was right. He'd got something stuck in his head. Like I was going to have to regain my honor somehow. Maybe do a joust. I hoped he wasn't going to hold his breath.

Alexander Two had gotten out of his pen and disappeared. I heard him crying out. He sounded far off, down in a hole somewhere. I panicked for a minute. He was trapped in a pipe. He'd drown, if Badger Bob didn't find him first. I found him behind the kitchen cabinet. He was wearing a lint-ball overcoat. He was hungry and extremely pissed off.

By the time I fixed a sandwich it was three. I thought maybe Cecily would call. I thought I'd lie down for a while. Not a real nap, just rest and close my eyes. I did what I always did, I completely crapped out. Not even the usual dippy dream, just deep and heavy sleep, down there dead as a stump until lightning hit out in the yard, punching the ground like a German eighty-eight and sending Alexander up the wall.

Thunder nearly shook the house apart, rattling the windows and pounding on the walls. All the lights went out. Alexander yowled. I felt my way into the kitchen, following the strobic bursts of light. The raw smell of ozone was heavy in the air. I couldn't find a flash. I grabbed a bunch of candles and the kerosene lamp. Left one candle going in the kitchen, one in the living room, and went back down the hall. Alexander was under the bed, too terrified to come out.

Lightning struck again, an explosion that split the air and left a ringing in my ears. This time I was sure it had hit the house. I wondered if I had a lightning rod. Did they do any good? The clock said only a quarter after six, but it was black as Satan's heart outside.

I thought I heard the phone. The rain was pounding the roof, drowning out every other sound. I ran back to the kitchen. The phone rang again.

"Anybody there?" I said.

"Jack, I been trying to get you. Where the hell you *been!*"

"Phil? I haven't been anywhere, I been here. It's raining like hell."

"Jack—got to—talk—you—"

"What?" His voice crackled in static, coming and going in quick little bursts. "Listen, I can't hear you real good."

"I got to *talk* to you, Jack. I got to   "

"Phil, what's wrong? You don't sound too good." Even with the static I could hear it in his voice, the desperation and the fear. "Are you okay? What is it, Phil?"

A burst of sound, a sizzle that burned up the line. I jerked the phone away. "Hey, are you still there?"

"He won't answer. He won't answer the phone."

"Who won't?"

"George. He won't answer the phone . . ."

"Well, maybe it's out. All this lightning and—"

"We found something, Jack."

"You what? What are you talking about, you found what, Phil?"

"I got to . . . get out there . . ."

"Where? You mean out to George's place? Jesus, you don't want to do that. You don't want to get out in this."

"Jack . . ."

A sound came over the line that sent a chill up my back. Like he was hyperventilating, gasping for breath, so goddamn scared he was choking to death.

"Phil, just stay right there, okay? I'll try and get in, I don't know if I can. Don't go anywhere. Phil? *Phil!*"

He didn't answer. Nothing there but that awful gasping

sound. I hung up the phone. I called the sheriff's office, thinking they could get someone to drive by. That didn't make any sense. They'd have their hands full with this storm going on. There wasn't any ring. The phone shrieked like a million volts were trapped in the line.

I couldn't find my raincoat anywhere. I dug Alexander from under the bed and dumped him in the closet. He wouldn't like it in there, but I'd know where he was while I was gone.

It was the dumbest thing I could possibly do, getting out in a storm like that. It was worse than I thought. The wind was up to sixty or sixty-five, maybe more, and howling up the scale. A big pecan had snapped in the yard. Lightning had opened a raw and twisted wound. The rain was slanting in sideways now, slashing at the truck. I wondered how Earl was doing at the bridge. The banks were pretty high, but if this kept up, a flash flood could roll down the creek and tear everything up.

I leaned into the wheel and drove as fast as I could. There was crap all over the road, dead leaves and scraps of wood, tangled sheets of corrugated tin from someone's shed. I wondered if a tornado had hit somewhere. The radio just said damaging winds and heavy rain, but the guy was in a studio in Dallas, he wasn't out here.

There were lights still on west of town, but everything south of Main was gone. I saw a trooper's blinking lights. He was stopped by an electric-company truck. He spotted me and ran out in the street in his yellow slicker, trying to wave me off. I drove on past him and turned right for Phil's.

The rain let up for a minute, then struck with a vengeance again. I hoped to hell Phil hadn't tried to get out in this. It was bad enough if you were thinking half straight. If you were goofy when you started and scared half stiff . . .

Phil's lights were out. I pulled up behind his car, relieved to see it was there. He had a garage in the back, but he'd left the car out front. I got out and bent low, squinting against the driving rain. I stepped out between the front of my truck and Phil's car and the headlights caught me, a harsh and cutting glare that seared my eyes. I threw a hand up before my face and it hit me in a quick half-second that the light was still coming, that it didn't intend to stop. I yelled out something and threw myself back against the fender of my truck. It came right at me, a coal-black pickup whipsawing crazily out of Phil's backyard, the motor shrieking with the strain, the tires whining on the grass and slinging mud. It hit the side of Phil's car, ripped at the door and swerved off. I leaped for the hood of my truck. The pickup caught my leg and the pain shot up through my belly to my head. I howled and twisted over on my back. Lightning shredded the sky, etching everything in a cold electric white, and in a bright quick instant I saw the driver's shadow, hunched against the wheel. I saw the black pickup plow across the yard, hit the curb and slam hard into the street.

I slid off the hood and watched the pickup vanish down the street without lights. I knew I'd never catch it, even if my leg would let me drive. The pain was angry and alive and I wondered what the hell to do next.

I limped for the house, hoping Phil's phone wasn't out. The front door was locked. I started around the back, holding on to the house and wiping the rain out of my face. The kitchen door was wide open. Water was rushing in like a river on the floor. There was a concrete step and I missed it in the dark, slipped and grabbed for the side of the door and something hit me in the face. I ducked and beat at it with my hand, thinking spiders or a goddamn bat and my leg gave way and I fell in the mud on my ass. I looked up and saw it then and it wasn't any spider, it was a finger hanging on a string, the rain jerking it around in a tight little circle and pointing down at me. Everything came up in my throat and I sat there and emptied my cookies in my lap. You got to do something like this, it's better to do it in the rain. You can get sick and get cleaned off without wasting any time.

Thirty-seven

The first troopers were there in three minutes. Four more cars arrived seconds after that. Sirens whoopahed in the night. Red and blue halos blinked through the rain, and guys in yellow slickers were running everywhere. We had sound, we had lights, we had special effects. As soon as the director arrived we could shoot our big scene.

Hess got there in eight minutes flat. He found me in the living room, cuffed to a straight-back chair. I was soaked to the bone, my leg hurt like hell. I was yelling at these redneck fuckers, telling them they better get off their fat butts and get out to George's fast. They were telling me I had the right to get kicked in the nuts, I had the right to go to jail. That I'd better talk fast and tell them where the body was, what I'd done with Phil.

I've got to hand it to Hess. He bulled through the bozo squad and told them to shut the fuck up. I told him what had happened. I'd had a lot of practice by then.

My cuffs came off. A trooper helped me up, gave me his slicker and helped me outside to Hess's car. The rain lashed out, coming in hard from the north; then, an instant later, shifting without warning from the south. A trooper shouted over the wind that a funnel had touched down between Ennis and Palmer, a few miles to the west. There were no reports yet but it didn't look good.

"Why the *hell* didn't you call me after you talked to Eddels," Hess said. "God*damn* you, Track!"

He struck the steering wheel with his fist. It was the first time he'd said a thing to me since he'd walked in Phil's house.

"I called the sheriff's office," I said. "I didn't know how to get you, I didn't know which motel. Nobody answered at the courthouse. I got a lot of static is all."

Hess gave me a furious look. "Bullshit you did. I can check on that."

"You do whatever the hell you like."

"I by God will. Don't you worry 'bout that."

He leaned into the wheel, squinting to see out. The wipers didn't do any good. One trooper was ahead of us, another behind. I could hardly see their lights.

"You didn't *see* Eddels in that pickup truck," Hess said. "You don't know if the killer took him off in that or not."

I looked at Hess. "The guy tried to run me down getting out of there," I said. "I think it's a pretty good guess."

"*Guessing* isn't what the law's about, Track. We deal in evidence and facts."

"Yeah, right."

"Anyway, he'd be alive if you'd called someone. That's on your head. You can live with that, fine."

"I am real tired of listening to this. You're lucky you're too old to hit, I'd knock you on your ass."

Hess turned and gave me a wicked smile. "I don't believe you could."

"I *know* I could."

"I feel I could take you pretty quick. A lawman's got a natural force of strength he can call on he needs to bring it out. It's there when you want to get it out."

I stared at him. "You think you got a force?"

"You heard what I said."

"I don't guess I heard about a force."

" 'Course you haven't. You violated your oath, you're not going to have it. You wouldn't even know about that."

"Jesus. I'm riding in the Batmobile."

"You make a joke if you want," Hess said. "There's a lot of things you don't know, you're not on the side of right."

What worried me was whether Hess was putting me on or not. He had never made a joke of any sort. I didn't know which was worse, he wasn't or he was.

George Rainey's farm was only six miles from town, but it took forever to get there in the rain. It wasn't like I remembered it from the past. Catfish had made George rich, and he had put in good gravel roads from the highway to his house. Through the rain I could make out the checkered array of walkways and ponds that had turned poor farmland into gold credit cards.

No lights were on at the house. George's truck was in the yard. A late-model Lincoln was in the garage. I had told Hess what George told me at Will's funeral, that his wife and children were out of town. There was room in the big garage for several cars. There was no way to know if they were back or still gone.

Hess told me to stay in the car. He got out and held a quick conference in the rain. Two troopers took off into the dark. The other pair hunched in their slickers and followed Hess up to the house. Hess knocked once or twice, then picked up a brick and broke a window and slid it up. One of the troopers went in. Everybody had their weapons out. Lights went on and the trooper opened the door. I got out of the car and went in.

Hess glared at me, but didn't bother to send me back.

"Eddels didn't give you any idea what they found, what we're looking for?"

"He said they found something. That's it."

"Didn't say where they'd got it, either, I don't guess."

"You know where they got it, that commando raid on Deke's house."

Hess shook his head. "That's a natural assumption, but we don't know that."

"Holmes would know that. He'd know it right off."

Hess didn't answer. I followed him into the kitchen. A trooper was poking through cabinets and drawers. We walked down a few steps into the den. The room had an elegant but easygoing look. There were several nice paintings of mountains, and one wall of books. Someone knew how to spend money and not look overdone. Cecily Benét says that's real hard to do. In this house, the credit had to go to George's wife or a good decorator. I was certain it wasn't George. Money hadn't taken him out of overalls.

Hess stood in the middle of the room and looked around. I knew what he was thinking. If George and Phil had found something, it could be anywhere. We didn't know what it was, or even if it was here. It might have been at Phil's. If it was, whoever hauled him off had it now. Phil was frightened out of his wits when I talked to him. He wouldn't have held out for a minute, he would have told the killer anything.

I didn't like to think about that. The poor bastard sitting there, maybe looking up at crazy Nate, and Nate Graham telling him he'd be okay if Phil gave him what he wanted, Phil wanting desperately to believe that and knowing he was wrong, that I wouldn't make it in time, that he didn't have a chance in hell. Something else I'd like to block out that wouldn't go away: Whether Phil was alive when that son of a bitch cut his finger off.

"Mr. Hess? You . . . better come and see this." He didn't have to tell us, it was there in his face.

Hess let out a breath. We followed the trooper down the long hallway. There was a small half-bath just off the back porch. A 100-watt bulb in the fixture turned the room a harsh and antiseptic white. There was blood on the floor. George's clothes were in a pile in the corner by the shower stall. Picture wire was wrapped around the john, at the bottom and the top. The wire was cut. The seat was up. Some-one had sat there, wired to the john, and filled the bowl in his fright. Blood and shit were spattered everywhere.

"We got us a body somewhere," Hess said. *"Goddamn all this!"*

"You want me to call this in?" the trooper said.

"I want you to stand here," Hess said. "I don't want you to do anything, all right?"

The other trooper who was with us walked into the room, coming in quick and nearly bumping into Hess. He was the big, freckled-faced lout who'd been in the room when Hess was questioning Phil and George. He took one look and turned white and stumbled back. He said, "Oh, Jesus, Jesus Christ!"

"Stop that." Hess glared at him. "Get your head on straight."

Hess pushed him roughly aside and stalked out. He got on the phone in the den and talked to someone for a while. I wondered if George had anything to drink. I wondered what Mrs. Rainey would do with the catfish farm. Maybe she'd sell it and retire to southern France or Wichita Falls. I was thinking on this and other things when the troopers walked in from outdoors and looked at Hess, and Hess looked up at them and quietly put the phone down. No one had to say a thing. We all got into our slickers and went back out into the rain.

It had slacked off to a drizzle. The storm was far off to the west; lightning flashed on the horizon and you knew someone was catching it over there. The troopers had left George where they found him. He was lying in two feet of water face up. The heavy-duty flash lit everything brighter than anyone cared to see.

They didn't look like a whole bunch of fish, they looked like one big gray and swollen creature, something fat and awful from a fifties horror show. They darted in and out in a frenzy, a thousand or a million flat heads and red eyes, wriggled in for little nips, for hurried little bites. There were more fish to the left of the body than the right, so the body moved around in a slow cartwheel, everyone hanging on, everyone having fun on this grotesque carnival ride.

Hess took in the scene for a minute and a half. "What are you standing around for," he said. "Get him out of there."

"I got a camera in the car," one of the troopers said. "Forensics likes us to—"

"Get your damn picture, then get him out of there." Hess turned to scowl at me. "You want to throw up or anything before we get in the car? I want to know before you do."

I wasn't listening anymore. I was slogging through the mud to the house. I was having a preview of a coming nightmare. *Revenge of the Catfish,* mostly starring George. These hungry little mothers were going at his eyes and his mouth, tugging at his vital parts. It was bad—but not as bad as it would get when it showed at my house.

At the courthouse I had to do statements again, everything Phil had said to me on the phone, and what I'd said to him, and what time, and everything that happened when I got to the house. I had to do it three or four times. Hess always found something he thought I'd left out. He wasn't real happy with me. What he wanted was to figure out some way this was all my fault.

There was an all-points bulletin out on a black pickup. I told Hess I didn't think it had plates. He was certain that it did. That a person with inborn criminal traits wouldn't bother to take it down. A real lawman, he said, would get the plates. Never mind I was being attacked in a blind fucking rain by a lunatic driver intent on taking off my leg. Eliot Ness wouldn't dream up a flimsy excuse like that.

One thing I didn't put in my statement was the fact that I was certain Nate Graham had made another call to Phil. Nothing else would have scared him like that. Either Nate Graham or Deke. Phil was terrified of Deke. I didn't want to get on that conspiracy business again, but it was hard to ignore the fact that Deke wasn't anywhere around. Hess had suspended him from duty and told him to stay around his house, and no one had seen him since. He wasn't there when George and Phil broke in and he wasn't there now.

Hess wasn't pleased with this. Deke's disappearance posed an irritating question that he didn't want to face: Was Deke on the lam because he was involved in the girlie-show farce, or was it maybe something else? Hess didn't actually *tell* me he was thinking this way, but it wasn't hard to guess. He twitched every time someone mentioned Deke's name.

Several things happened between the bleak hours of midnight and four. They found George's family and told them the awful news. Doc Ben Hackley reported that Phil Eddels's finger had been chopped off while he was alive. Ben hadn't finished the autopsy on George. A quick examination told him several things we already knew, and a few things we didn't. After he was wired to the john, George had been tortured for a while. There were marks from an ordinary pair of pliers on his flesh. These were mostly in the area between his legs. What he'd finally died of was a single gunshot in the back of the head. We hadn't noticed that, since George had been floating on his back. Max had been shot the same way, but we'd have to wait for a ballistics test to see if both bullets had come from the same gun.

There was still no sign of a black pickup—at least, not the one we were looking for. The search was hampered by the fact that every state, county and local cop in this end of north Texas had his hands full. The storm the night before had spawned four tornadoes that left heavy damage in several towns, and picked up an entire trailer park. At least five people were dead.

A little after three, the troopers reported in from George's house. They had found two pictures between the pages of a Joe Lansdale book. The pictures weren't very good, but they didn't have to be. One showed a young girl playing an old familiar tune on Eddie Trost. You could only see the back of her head, but Eddie's face was clear. He looked dazzled and intent. Somewhere between agony and terminal bliss. Another man was in the picture, standing stark-naked just behind the girl. He was cut off at the waist and the knees. I knew it wasn't Max, the guy wasn't fat enough. It could have been Billy or Roy Burns. I could certainly not identify their parts.

The second picture was, if possible, even more explicit than the first. It would take some time to describe the scene in depth. The various acts and positions were somewhat complex. The characters were two girls and Max. There was possibly a mechanical device. It was not the sort of picture Max would pick for the Coomer Christmas card.

Hess looked at the photos with disgust. "I'm supposed to be catching the loony that whacked your local hero, make everybody happy in Austin and up in D.C. Something like this got out, every big shot that came down to the funeral's going to wish he'd stayed home. They're going to have to blame someone, and by God that'll be me.

"Track, you better hear me straight on this." He gave me that look cops practice till they get it just right. The one that strikes fear in your average felon's heart. "You didn't *see* this picture. You didn't see it, the damn thing doesn't exist. The troopers found this stuff, I can break their backs, they know that. Anything gets out, it came from you."

"Hey, I'm a crime fighter too," I said. "You can count on me."

Hess muttered something I didn't hear. He told me to get the hell out and go home. I certainly didn't care for the man, but I had to feel sorry for him then. He was out on his feet, he looked a hundred years old. He had spilled a lot of coffee on his tie. It hadn't been a really good day.

It was getting light out. Branches littered the courthouse lawn and there was water everywhere. By noon it would be like a sauna outside. I was getting in my truck when the two troopers pulled into the lot. I knew them both from the night before. They informed me that Billy McKenzie had put on his worst plaid coat and his wing-tip shoes and gone over to his lot. He had gotten in the seat of a '93 Buick Century Sedan, 4-door, power locks and cruise control, and blown his head off. I didn't have to ask. I knew he had used the same 12-gauge Remington pump that had worked for Mom and Dad. You can't beat tradition. That's what makes our great nation the country it is today.

Thirty-eight

When I got to Earl's unbuilt house by the bridge, he was letting bacon sizzle on the camp stove while he stirred up a batch of scrambled eggs. Earl does pretty fair eggs. They're not as good as mine, but that's because he doesn't use enough cheddar cheese. With scrambled eggs, cheese is the key. Cheese and some salsa and a dash of Tabasco sauce.

I walked up the slope past the shingles and the lumber and the pipe, everything covered up with tarps against the rain. The creek was nearly back to normal now, but it had risen a good six feet in the night. Brush and broken branches were tangled on the bank about eighteen inches below the bridge.

"Looks like you had a little luck," I told Earl. "Another couple of feet, you'd be on your way to Galveston."

Earl knew I was there but he didn't look up. He was wearing white boxer shorts and rubber shower shoes. He looked like a dipstick with a Band-Aid stuck around "Full."

"Got real interesting a little after two," Earl said. "Got a lot of wind but didn't damage anything."

"I can see that. I can see everything's okay." I knew better than to mention that you couldn't damage something that wasn't there. What you could do was float a lot of power tools and lumber down the creek.

"I lost a good tree," I said. "Snapped right off. At least it didn't hit the house."

"One of those pecans."

"The big one north of the house."

"Damn shame to lose a big tree. Lose something that old, it's flat gone."

"That's the thing. You can put another one in, it won't do you any good. A tree like that, it'll start looking good about twenty, thirty years."

"That's a fact," Earl said. "It's gonna take that long."

This fascinating talk had little to do with trees. What it had to do with was making amends, getting easy with each other again. You talk about things that don't matter, you work yourself up to things that do.

Having breakfast helped. Earl didn't ask me to stay but he handed me a plate. He didn't mention once how I always seemed to be on hand for meals. I didn't mention that the eggs were short of cheese.

I waited until we were finished and had everything washed up. We took our coffee and walked out on the bridge and watched the crap floating down the creek. I told him everything—from Phil's frantic call and what happened at his house, and the way we found George. I told him what Billy McKenzie had done and that Deke had disappeared, then I filled in anything I'd left out.

When I was done, Earl looked at me sideways a minute, not real sure I wasn't making this up. Finally, he shook his head and stared down at the creek.

"Lyin' there with a bunch of damn *catfish*. I wouldn't care for that."

"I doubt if George minded at the time. What he minded was the stuff before that."

"Uh-huh." Earl lit the stub of his cigar. "I thought you looked a little beat. You kind of had yourself a night."

"Well, it was that or watch PBS. They had *Birds of South Dakota* on again. I guess I've seen it twice."

"Man can't look at a whole lot of birds," Earl said. "There's more to life than that."

He was still gazing down at the creek. I waited awhile until he looked back at me.

"I know you won't do it," I said, "but I'm going to say it anyway. Nobody knows where Deke is. They haven't got any idea. I don't see him running off like this if all he's mixed up in is hauling those girls. I think he ran because he's into the other thing. If that's true, you don't know what the hell he'll do. He might decide he's got nothing to lose, and go after everyone he doesn't like."

"Meaning me," Earl said.

"Your name comes to mind."

"I appreciate the thought. I don't see me going off somewhere. He comes around here, he better bring some help." Earl studied me and closed one eye. "I can think of someone else going to be on that list. Isn't just me."

"I've considered that."

"So where you running off to?"

"I thought I'd stay up at the house. Bolt all the doors. Possibly get under the bed."

Earl grinned. "Maybe we could build us a fort. Get some ladies to come and stay in."

"Let's get some who can shoot."

"I hear that," he said.

Earl walked me down to my truck. I told him about my new cat. He said he'd surely get up and meet him real soon. I said to bring some single-malt Scotch, that Alexander Two would like that.

We didn't have to say it and never would. The ice was broken now and everything was fine again. Which is good, because you're going to build a fort or get drunk with someone, it ought to be someone you like.

Alexander was still in the closet and still pissed off. A hearty meal took care of that. He ate until he couldn't stand up and went to sleep in my lap. Sleep sounded like a good idea, but I was too hyped up for that. Everything that had happened in the night and all the shit before that kept churning through my head. Max getting killed, the girlie show up at Eddie's place. Someone taking porno shots. Phil and George finding those pictures and getting themselves knocked off.

It all fit together but it didn't somehow. I didn't know exactly why. One of the girls thought she saw someone at the window. The pictures say she did. So who *took* those pictures, Nate Graham? Why not, taking a picture isn't hard. Your average lunatic could do that as well as anyone else. On the other hand—why? Maybe for a sexual thrill, but I couldn't see Nate being happy with a dirty snapshot. He wouldn't be satisfied with that. He liked to get close to his victims, talk to them, touch them, then do the things he did.

Say it wasn't Nate who took the pictures, it was someone else. Like Deke. He procured the girls, he knew when they were there. He takes the pictures, thinking he'll blackmail Max. With a shot like the one I saw, he could bleed Max dry. But before he has a chance to do that, Max turns up dead . . .

The thought brought a little chill. It was one of the pieces that didn't fit. Why does Deke want to kill Max? Max is the guy who can pay him big bucks to get the picture back. I wondered if we were looking at the whole thing backward, if we maybe had it wrong. Nate kills Max and Max's dog. He kills Emma Stynnes and chops her finger off. In his fucked-up head, he's got a good reason for this. Max treated him bad when they were kids. Max had everything he didn't have, and this is a way of getting back.

And Phil and George—what if Nate had nothing to do with that?

The guy who took the pictures wants them back. He chops off Phil's finger and tries to make him talk. Maybe Phil does, the loony's going to kill him anyway. Then he goes through the torture routine again with George, and even shoots him in the head. We've got the maniac's signature all spelled out, so we blame it on him.

I leaned back on the couch and closed my eyes. George's pale face appeared and I opened them up again. It *could* have happened that way, I thought. Two different killers, murders only connected by circumstance. You got a jerkwater town like Pharaoh, Texas, one maniac is enough, you're not going to look around for two.

I got up and went in the kitchen for a beer. It all sounded real good until you ran it through your head a few times and then some ragged holes appeared. Would Deke waste his time in a penny-ante blackmail scheme? What for? He'd be a lot better off with Max dead, the road free and clear to the very rich widow Millie Jean. But *someone* took those pictures, and I didn't have any doubt at all that Phil and George had found them at Deke's. That opened up another can of worms. With Max Coomer dead and in the ground, a compromising picture of Max lost its clout. Who cared? It wouldn't bother Millie Jean a great deal. She'd pay about twenty-nine cents to get it back.

That left Roy Burns and Eddie and Billy McKenzie on the list. They wouldn't want those pictures around, even if everyone knew what they'd done. Billy was dead. There wasn't any picture of Roy. At least, none that we'd seen. I'd thought about that, and I imagined Aaron Hess had, too. The troopers only found two pictures. That didn't mean there weren't any others around. Maybe there were, and Roy Burns or Eddie had them now. Or maybe someone else did, someone who'd meant to blackmail *them*.

There were enough unanswered questions to drive Holmes to one of those morphine shots, I decided. Phil's and Earl's yearbook fantasies were starting to look real good. Deke and Nate were pals. They'd decided to whack out everyone in town. Couple of weeks, they'd have Pharaoh all to themselves. Deke could be mayor and sheriff and live in Millie's big white house. Nate could handle any stray dogs or drunks that might wander into town.

Sleep wouldn't come. I tried to watch TV, then went through my stuff and found some football tapes. I settled on the Eagles and the Saints. I watched Byner slam into the line and get dumped. I watched Hebert pop short quick passes off to Early and Smart, making it look real easy for a while, until the Eagles decided they didn't want to lose this game.

I woke up with the screen spitting static and my neck in a permanent crick. The phone was ringing and my Mickey said twenty after six. I had slept five hours, making up for my overactive night.

Doc Hackley was on the phone and he wanted me to know that the bullet he'd taken out of George hadn't come from the same gun that'd been used on Max. George was shot with a .22 long from an old Colt Woodsman. One of the eight handguns, five rifles and three shotguns George owned himself. A trooper found the .22 tossed in a laundry basket. No prints. This didn't rule out the possibility that one person had killed both Max and George, Ben said. Only that he'd used a different gun. I told Ben I had figured that out for myself.

"Billy McKenzie and George'll be buried on Tuesday," Ben said. "The families are both usin' funeral homes up in Dallas. Eddie's temporarily shut his place down. I doubt if anyone'd be inclined to give him their business right now."

I said I could understand that. He said Roy Burns and Eddie Trost were staying home and wouldn't talk to anyone. Eddie's wife had instantly filed for divorce and taken off for Fort Worth.

"Roy's old lady's still there. I don't expect Roy's enjoying a lot of marital bliss."

"I expect Roy's having a drink or two," I said. "I doubt if he knows she's there."

"Yeah, he does. I met her one time. Isn't any way you wouldn't know that woman's there."

Ben paused a long moment. I could hear him breathing into the phone. "Jack, they haven't caught Deke yet. Doesn't anybody know where he is. You want to take care."

"I'll do that," I said.

"You got a firearm out there, I hope."

"I've got my trusty thirty-eight."

"Jesus, Jack. I'm not talking fuckin' toys, I'm talking firearms. I got a Thompson submachine gun here, belonged to Clyde Barrow once. You're sure welcome to that."

"Thanks. I think I'll be all right."

"You make sure you are," he said, and hung up.

I didn't ask Ben Hackley what he was doing with such an exotic weapon in the house. People in Texas tend to have firearms of every sort, everything from old Colt .44s and buffalo rifles on up to the modern stuff. I know a man in the Hill Country south of Austin who has an authentic Gatling gun in his den. His wife puts a big plant on it when her friends come over for bridge.

I thought about Billy McKenzie and George. I wasn't sure I could stand to go to any more rites at the Pharaoh Cemetery. I wondered if anyone could. Max and Uncle Will, and now these two, all in a matter of days. And that didn't count the unburied dead, like Emma Stynnes and Phil. Earl had told me Emma's mother refused to have a service for her daughter, that it wouldn't be right when all you had to put in the casket was a finger. That God would let her know if Emma was truly dead.

I hadn't finished talking to Ben two minutes when Cecily called. She said she'd been worried sick, she'd been calling all day, that all they'd had on the TV was awful stuff about Billy and Phil and George.

"I guess I didn't hear the phone," I told her. "I was pretty knocked out all day, I had a real bad night."

"My Lord, hon, I guess you did. You sure you're all right?"

"I'm fine," I said. "Just a little tired."

Hon sounded good. Was this friendly concern, I wondered, or genuine and passionate distress?

"I'm coming down there," she said. "I got a couple calls to make, I'll leave right after that. You got anything in the fridge besides beer and old cheese?"

"Cecily, I don't want you doing that," I said. I said it real quick, before I could change my mind. "I want you to stay up there. I'll come up to Dallas next day or two. You can take me out somewhere nice."

"Jack . . ." A little catch in her voice, a little auditory twitch. I'd tried to sound easy but she knew me much better than that.

"Jack, you listen to me—"

"Cecily, everything's okay. I'll see you Thursday, no later than that."

"You get yourself up here now. You and Alexander both."

"I can't do that."

"Yes, you can, too. Isn't any damn reason you—God, Jack, it's that Deke Glover person, isn't it? The TV says he's on the loose. You think he'll come after you!"

"Cecily, I'm just being cautious is all. I'm not concerned about Deke."

"It's okay for you down there, it isn't safe for me. That doesn't make a lot of sense."

"Cecily, I got to go now."

"Don't you hang up on me. You better not."

"I care a whole lot about you," I said and hung up.

I stood by the phone a long time. There was a lot more I wanted to say, but that wouldn't help me keep her from coming down. I wanted to see her, but I wanted her far away from here until all this was over and done. And when would that be? I wondered. Maybe the killer out there had other things to do. Maybe he really didn't give a shit about my social life.

It was a little after seven. Alexander yowled and climbed my pants. Every three minutes was dinnertime to him. If I didn't get some kind of schedule going, he'd outweigh me in a month. I gave him something to shut him up, and fixed myself a tuna-fish sandwich and a beer. I got another beer after that and took Alexander outside, thinking, as a kind of afterthought, that I ought to stick the pistol in my pocket just in case. It seemed like a dumb thing to do, and I wondered why I felt like that. I'd been shot at in my own bedroom, and again at Phil's house. Someone had tried to run me down. Still, none of this seemed very real. I just couldn't feel threatened in my own front yard.

The outside world spooked Alexander good. He'd never seen anything like that. He skittered sideways and arched his back, and hissed at dead leaves. He tried to climb a tree and got scared. I peeled him off the bark and took him back inside.

The phone rang and I hoped it wasn't Cecily Benét. I didn't think I could hang up on her twice.

I didn't get a chance to say hello. Ben Hackley said, "Jack? It's me. Jack, he's got her. He's got Millie Jean."

I gripped the phone hard. Something turned over inside. "Who's—who's got her, Ben? What happened?"

"Jesus, I don't know who, Deke—somebody—he's got her, he took her off, he's got her in a car, I don't *know,* Jack!"

Ben was yelling into the phone and I could still hardly hear him. All hell was breaking loose at the courthouse. He got it out as well as he could. A state trooper had skidded into Millie's drive going fast, panic lights blinking and siren on full. He got out and pounded on the door and Millie let him in. A minute after that, they both came out again and got in the car, and the trooper took off. The rent-a-cops out on the grounds thought it didn't look right, that maybe Millie didn't want to go. They went inside and called Hess. Hess blew his stack. Nobody had sent a car to get Millie Jean. All this had happened, Ben said, half an hour ago. They'd found the trooper the car belonged to. He was dead in a ditch on I-35.

"I thought you'd want to get in here," Ben said. "Don't tell Hess I called, he'll have my ass if you do—"

I hung up. My hands were shaking and my knees wouldn't work. *Oh, Christ, Millie Jean . . .*

The phone rang again and I picked it up quick and said "What?" thinking it was Ben. Deke said, "You want to come where I tell you to, Jack. You want to do that right now. Take that cutoff north of the old Hamil place. Go three-point-five miles north and then right. You'll see the place."

"Deke . . ." My throat went tight and I tried hard to get the words out. "Deke, don't do anything to her, you don't want to do that."

"You shut the fuck up. I'll do anything I like!"

"Okay, Deke, all right."

"I guess you got the sense not to *call* anyone. Anybody comes out with you, Millie gets hurt real bad."

"I don't think you'd do that," I said, as calmly as I could. "Someone else, all right, I don't think you'd hurt Millie Jean."

Deke laughed, a sharp explosive sound that hurt my ears.

"No, I sure wouldn't do that. But see, I got me this ol' boy out here, he wouldn't mind at all. He'd as soon cut her up into KC steaks and cook her ass on a grill. You want to do what I say. You want to get the fuck *out* here, Jack . . ."

Thirty-nine

There's all kinds of scared. You hear somebody say, "Boy, was I scared," you don't know what they're talking about. They might've had a misgiving or an ordinary qualm. You got a qualm, that isn't too bad, it's not like you had a real quake or it's up there close to a dread. The worst I ever had was a flat-out total scared stiff. That was the night I walked into the tortilla works with Tony D. I knew I'd be facing something awful in there but I didn't know what. That was pretty grim. But it didn't come close to the scared I was feeling driving down that dark dirt road. I *knew* who was waiting for me there, it was Deke and Nate Graham, and Millie maybe already gone, and if I couldn't stop them I'd wind up a dead electric Jack.

That's what I was feeling, that's the kind of scared I had. I was bone-cold crap-in-your-trousers fucking petrified . . .

I found the Hamil place. I remembered it from when I was a kid. They used to run some dairy goats but there was no one living there now. I took the cutoff and started checking the miles on the dash. I'd never been this way before. It was a part of the county where the rock came right up to the surface and the soil wasn't good for anything. If it wasn't for the rocks, someone could've raised some catfish.

I checked the .38 in my belt to make certain it was there. The odometer on the dash read two-point-five and I turned off the lights. What I had in mind was I'd try to get close, pull off the road and walk, see if I could find where they were holding Millie Jean. There couldn't be much on that road. There weren't any farms, there wasn't anything to do.

I lit a match and saw two-point-nine and started looking for a spot to pull off, and that's when I looked up and saw him loping toward me down the road, running in that gangly awkward gait like a scarecrow on the loose. Even in the pitch-black dark I knew that it was Phil.

I braked the truck and got out. The light went on in the cab and I shut the door quick, trying not to do it loud. Phil stumbled and fell. I ran to him and helped him up. He grabbed my arms and held on and I got him to the truck. He made an awful noise like he might throw up and collapsed facedown on the hood. He lay there gasping for air, his mouth all twisted out of shape, like every breath hurt him somewhere.

"It's all right," I said, and reached out and touched his shoulder, "you're okay now."

"Jack . . ." He shook his head and pulled himself up. "Got to get . . . back there . . . got to . . ."

"Just take it easy, Phil."

He pushed me away, a look of total desperation in his eyes. "I tried to help her, Jack, honest to God I did. I couldn't—I couldn't *do* anything!"

I felt a surge of hope at that. "She's alive, then, they haven't hurt her."

"There's a . . . a big barn," he said. "They went out there. That's where they've got her. I was in . . . some kind of closet in the house. They left and I got out. If they come back in and I'm gone . . ."

"What's the best way to get in?" I tried to picture the setup in my head. "How far's the barn from the house?"

"Maybe . . . twenty yards, shit, I don't know. There's cover in the trees for the truck. They won't see it if they're still in the barn."

I looked at him. "Is that a good idea? If we go in on foot—"

"D-damn it, Jack, I been *in* there, all right? We haven't got time to talk about this!"

Phil's voice broke. It was clear he was starting to come apart. He was driving himself, pushing himself to get through this.

"Can you make it all right?" I said. "You could stay here, you can give me the layout, I can go in."

"I think I got to do this," he said.

I let out a breath. "All right, get in. Watch the light in the cab. Shut the door easy as you can."

As soon as I opened the door I pushed the little button in the jamb to douse the light. I wished I had some tape. I found a box of matches in my pocket and I broke a few off and forced them tight against the button and prayed they'd hold.

Phil sat up straight and gripped the seat and stared out into the dark. For the first time, I saw the dirty bandage wrapped around his hand, the empty space where his index finger used to be. Dirt was smudged on his face, and he filled the cab with the smell of sour sweat.

"You shouldn't have come here by yourself," he said. "You should've got some help."

"The National Guard came to mind," I told him. "I was afraid they'd find out somehow, they'd do something to Millie Jean."

Phil turned to me and stared. He hadn't thought about what I was doing here, how I'd found the place. "That's it, they told you where they were?" He covered his face with his hands. "Oh, Lord, they'll be w-waiting for us, Jack."

"They know I'm coming. But they didn't figure on you, that I'd know my way around. Maybe that'll help."

"You got a gun or anything?"

"I've got my thirty-eight."

"You got to take 'em quick," he said, "you gotta do that. You give those fuckers a chance we're all dead."

"I know what to do," I said.

I wondered what he thought I was going to do. I was scared down to my socks but I knew what I had to do if I got the chance. A *High Noon* showdown with Deke and Nate Graham never even crossed my mind.

I was grateful for the pitch-dark night. Low clouds scudded across the sky and masked the moon. If Phil hadn't told me exactly where to go I would have missed the turnoff to the left. It was overgrown with weeds. Only the ruts on either side betrayed it as a road.

There was a thick stand of hackberry trees on either side, and Phil had me pull in to the right. We got out quietly and didn't shut the doors. Phil pointed and led me down the road for twenty or thirty yards, then took off through a thicket beneath the trees. No one had ever been through this damn place with a mower or pruning shears. Low branches whipped my face. I bent low and tried to keep Phil in sight and I stepped on a piece of dry wood. It snapped like a bomb going off. I stopped dead and took a breath. The fear caught me standing there and hammered at my chest. They could both be out here anywhere, waiting in the dark. They'd discovered Phil was gone and they'd killed Millie Jean and now they were going to kill me . . .

Phil squeezed my arm and I nearly came out of my shoes. His face told me he was scared too. The two scared guys meet the two maniacs. A bad B-movie, one I didn't want to see.

From the cover of the trees I could see the barn and the house, black shapes against a greater dark. The road we'd left behind curled in between the buildings to the right. I could just make out the cars beside the house, a black pickup and a '91 or '92 Chevy, fairly beat up. Behind that, the dull reflection of the panic lights on top of a trooper's car.

"The door to the barn's over on the other side," Phil said, close to my ear. "You can't see it from here."

"There's not another way in, another door somewhere?"

"I left pretty damn quick, Jack. I didn't have time to look around."

I couldn't argue with that. We kept low as we left the brush and sprinted for the barn. If that was the only way in, that's how we'd have to go.

There was no light anywhere, and no way to tell if they were still in the barn or in the house. That was something I desperately needed to know, and couldn't see how to find out. One of them, I was certain, would be waiting for me to show up. I'd thought about that, what I'd do in their place, and decided I'd have someone up by the road. They could see just who came in, and if I'd come by myself. So where were they, then? I had an idea I'd gotten out here quicker than they figured that I would. Which meant no one had gone up there yet, or they'd walked up the road while Phil and I were cutting through the woods. Whichever way it was, it was too damn close.

I had noticed the sound from our cover. It was even more obvious now. A deep, steady thrum, like some kind of machine, a sound you could feel in your chest. I touched the side of the barn and I could feel the vibration in my hand. A generator, maybe. I hadn't checked for poles or wires. It was possible they didn't have power out here.

Phil peeked around the corner of the barn, and motioned for me to stop. I waited. I held the revolver so tight my hand hurt. Finally, Phil waved me on.

"I don't think they're in the house," he said. "Whenever they were in there they'd turn on a light. I could see it under the closet door. I think there's a little light coming from the barn. I can't tell. That's what it looks like from here."

"We'll have to go with that," I said. "We haven't got a lot of choice."

I slipped past him and looked around the side. That's in the rules. The guy who's got the gun gets to go first.

Phil was right. There was a dim yellow glow, a thin stripe, like a door that isn't completely shut. I took another breath and went in low, keeping close to the wall. The door was maybe fifteen feet away. I stepped carefully over a pile of rusty pipe, pressed my face against the weathered wood and looked in. A 40-watt bulb on a string, a dirty wooden floor. I couldn't see much more than that. I gripped the edge of the door and hoped it didn't squeak. They could both be in there, to the left or the right. I would have a split second to spot them and squeeze off a couple of shots. Jesus, I thought, what if they aren't together? What if one of them's close to Millie Jean?

My heart tried to slam through my chest and I eased the door open an inch and then Phil said, *"Jack!"* and I jerked around fast because I wanted to tell him he was much too loud and then the light went out.

Not the one in the barn. The one inside my head. . . .

Forty

I came up out of it thinking that it didn't make sense it was already light, because I couldn't remember even getting into bed or doing anything else before that. It didn't matter if I didn't or I did because the goddamn sun was right *up* there tossing red-hot hammers at my head. I shut my eyes tight but it wouldn't go away. Someone had a cigarette burning little holes through my lids. Someone put the cigarette out, and something cool and wet and pleasant touched my face.

"Jack? Jack, you all right, pal?"

"I'm—I'm just fine," I said, "I'm okay."

"You lie real still. Don't try and move or anything."

"That's a real—good idea."

I squinted up at Phil. The cool rag felt good. The sun shrank to a 40-watt bulb. Some of the lint in my head cleared away. Why was I okay? I wasn't *supposed* to be okay.

I sat up fast. Phil pushed me back down.

"Now you just take it easy," he said, "you got hit pretty hard."

"Damn it, don't you think I know that? I know that." I sat up again and pushed him off. "What the *hell's* going on here, Phil? I don't . . ." My head was still fuzzy. They had Millie Jean, at least I thought they did. She was in here somewhere, we had to get her out . . .

I grabbed Phil's shoulders. "Deke and Nate Graham, you

think they're up at the house? We better find her and get
the hell *out* of here!"

Phil grinned. "Don't you worry 'bout them. You just get
to feeling better, Jack."

"Don't *worry?*"

"Don't worry. I'll be right back."

He grinned at me again and got up and tossed the wet
rag aside and walked off across the room. I decided the
strain had hit him hard and he'd completely flipped out. He
stopped and brushed the dust off his knees. I blinked to
make certain my eyes were working right. We'd been too
close together on the floor, but now I could see he wore
baggy black pants with blue satin stripes down the side.
The pants were three inches too short. White socks and
black shoes, and one of those god-awful T-shirts they print
up to look like a tux. Black coat and white dickey with
studs. A black bow tie and a flower in the lapel, and in that
instant another ball of lint fell away and let a spark of reason
through, and reason said if someone hit me they'd have hit
Phil too and they'd still be *here,* and oh, dear God, there
was no one in the place but us . . .

Something bad started crawling up my belly to my throat,
and I came up off the floor fast, keeping low and going for
his knees. Something jerked me to a stop. I yelled and
grabbed air and hit the ground hard. I pulled myself up and
spit dirt. My leg hurt like hell. I grabbed it and saw the
steel cuff around my ankle and the chain attached to that.
I gave it a yank. The other end was attached to an eyebolt
in the wall. I looked up at Phil. Phil looked at me.

"I told you to take it easy," he said. "You're going to
hurt yourself, actin' like that."

"I don't much like this," I said. "I don't know what
you're doing, I am trying not to think about that because
what I'm thinking doesn't make any sense and I don't want
it to. I think we ought to talk about it, Phil. I think you

ought to get out of that shirt. I don't think we can talk real straight, you're wearing that shirt."

Phil looked hurt. "I got to have it for the party," he said.

"What party's that?"

"You feeling okay now?"

"Never fucking *mind* how I'm feeling. Damn it, Phil, you *talk* to me!"

Phil didn't answer. He walked off out of the light. When he came out of shadow again he was dragging a rocker with a patched cane back. He was also carrying a sawed-off shotgun, the kind troopers like to carry in their cars.

He sat down in the rocker and laid the shotgun across his lap. He looked at me and smiled. He said, "Hi there, Jack. You doin' okay over there?"

"I'm not going to try and figure how you're mixed up in this," I told him. "It hurts my head to try. I can't see you and Deke and Nate Graham. I can't, but I am chained to the wall over here and it's kind of hard to overlook that. Are you going to tell me or am I supposed to guess?"

"Deke and Nate are fine," Phil said. "They'll be along in a while."

"I didn't ask you how they were. I don't give a fuck how they are, Phil. Where's Millie Jean? What have you done to her, you better not have done anything."

"Millie Jean's okay."

"I want to see her."

"You're going to see her, Jack."

"I want to see her right *now.*"

Phil shook his head. "Isn't time for the party. You don't want to see her 'fore that."

"I want to *see* her, Phil!"

He gave me that same silly lopsided grin he'd had since we were kids but it didn't seem funny anymore.

"Ol' Deke, he wanted to see her too. Said he had to know she's all right. I said I'd let him have a peek if he'd make the phone call. He said let me see her first and I did, then he tried to back out. Said he didn't like you but he wouldn't bring you into something like this, he wouldn't do that to anyone. He came around, though." Phil laughed to himself, like he'd just recalled a good joke. "Isn't like on your TV shows where the hero hangs in there no matter what. You hold one of those bolt cutters 'round a guy's dick, he'll say about anything you want."

Oh Christ, Phil, I'm not hearing this . . .

Something came up in my throat and I tried to push it back. I felt the funny chill you get when the phone rings and you know something real bad's happened before you pick it up. A sound came to me from the shadows just past the cone of light. The click of a timer, then the steady hum of some machine. For an instant, the bulb overhead flickered and nearly went out. I was sure it was the same sound I'd heard outside, but it was louder, more distinct in here. I wondered where they had Millie Jean. Maybe she wasn't here, maybe they had her in the house. Maybe Phil was lying and she wasn't still alive.

"You okay, Jack? Everything all right?"

"No, Phil, I am not okay. Everything is not all right."

"You're real surprised, I bet. I mean, you didn't *know,* didn't anybody even guess." He leaned forward in the rocker. "See, that's the thing, Jack. I know what you're thinking, you won't come out and say it but you are. Old Phil's the last person ever, no one'd figure he'd do *anything,* shit, no one ever did. I'd be at a party, we were kids? I could've painted my ass bright green, wouldn't anybody even look up. I got a goddamn lifetime of that, nobody ever lookin' up."

"Now that isn't true," I said, as calmly as I could, "it wasn't like that. We were talking, over at your house that night? There were lots of us weren't in Max's bunch, it wasn't just you. I remember lots of times I'd—"

"That's *b-bullshit* is what it is!" Phil came out of his chair. He was shaking like one of those kids you see on

MTV. "I know what you said, you said we were both out-
siders, that made me real mad, Jack, 'cause people could
see you, and *I* wasn't even there, didn't anyone in that suck-
up crowd know I was alive. And you know wh-what? You
get started off like that it don't change any, it keeps going
on, you grow up it's all the same. Me and George'd go to
Audie's didn't anyone know we was there drinkin' coffee,
didn't anyone care. I spent a whole fuckin' *life* doing that
and I didn't have anyone to talk to except maybe George,
and he's worse than me, he's fucking pathetic is what he
is! You think after he got stinkin' rich he'd ever give any
help to me, I get strapped or somethin', I need a buck or
two? He kept hanging around, though, sure, 'cause his
money didn't do him any good with Roy and them, it didn't
mean shit. Didn't any of those bastards want a catfish king
in their fucking coffee crowd!"

"I can see your point," I said, "I can see how you feel
that way." It seemed like the right thing to say. He was
marginally calm, slightly in control of himself, and I wanted
him to stay that way. "It's good you're talking like this,
talking it out, I think that's going to help."

Phil cocked his head and looked off somewhere. "I got
tired of that, Jack. Being left out and you want to get a date
you got to ask some *fat* girl'll go with anyone she can to get
out of the house, you get a date she hasn't got B.O. she's got
a unsightly rash somewhere. That's how I got ol' Louise, you
know? Didn't anyone fight me over her, you can bet on that.
I'm sick to death of taking everybody's scraps. You didn't
have to worry 'bout *girls* any, Jack, you don't *know* how it
is they don't even see you, they're p-p-prancing around
showin' off their ass to everyone like those little *whores* Max
and them brought up to Eddie's place. I *saw* what they were
doing up there, they'd do anything you w-wanted them to do,
you could stick your th-thing in 'em anywhere, didn't matter
what you did and I got pictures of them, too. I may be just
nothing, you know, okay? But I didn't pay anyone to do a

bunch of dirty stuff, I didn't do that, those assholes aren't any better'n me 'cause I never did *that . . . !"*

I didn't move or blink because Phil didn't see me anymore and I didn't want him to. He was out of his chair now, stalking about, jerking this way and that, talking to the shadows, talking to the walls, mingling at his nightmare party with invisible guests, and I hoped to God he wouldn't remember that I was the only son of a bitch who'd shown up. Only God was out to lunch right then because Phil stopped jerking around and turned back to me.

"You doing okay, Jack? You need anything?"

"I'm just fine," I said, "everything's okay, Phil."

"I don't guess it is. I bet everyone's going to be real mad about this. I bet I pissed a lot of people off."

"Hey, now you don't know that. People are a lot more understanding than you think, you give them half a chance."

"You think?"

Phil looked hopeful for a moment, then his face turned weary and sad. He was worn down and flat bone-tired. He had razors in his head and they were ripping him apart, and he wanted someone to know why. That was important, I could see that, he wanted someone to understand.

"Listen, I'm not one of those crazies or anything," Phil said, "don't go thinking that. I just got things I have to *do,* okay? Something you got to get done, you got a right to do that, it don't mean you're some kinda mental case."

"No, now it sure doesn't, Phil." I tried to look earnest and sincere. "Something you have to do, anyone can understand that."

"You scared of me, Jack?"

"I'll be honest with you. Yeah, I really am."

Phil sighed and ran a hand across his face. "It was so damn *easy,* you know? I figured someone'd see it, only all they ever saw was old Phil the fuckin' nerd like they always did."

He looked at me a moment, then a silly smile played

across his face. He turned away and dropped his head into his hands. I thought, what the hell is this? He mumbled to himself, ducked his head between his shoulders, then jerked around and faced me again, a cartoon hunchback doing his monster act, rolling his eyes and twisting his hands into claws.

"Boo! Boo! BOO!" he said, and did a little Igor trot, "Nate Graham is goin' to *git* you, Jack!"

I backed up and nearly tripped on my chain. He looked so totally stupid, Bela Lugosi in a tux T-shirt, but it scared the living hell out of me, I couldn't help that. I had only heard that gravelly voice on the phone one time, but seeing it come out of Phil was something else.

"You ought to see your face!" Phil laughed and clapped his hands. "Man, you should've heard old Billy and George. They didn't *want* to talk to Nate Graham. Every time I'd get 'em on the phone they'd 'bout shit. *How's the old lady, doing, George, you stick it in her again?"*

Phil shook his head and started doing his stalking bit again. "That fuckin' George. You know what that dumb sum'bitch did? You and me was talking at my house, I go in the kitchen, get us something to drink? I call George and say, get on in here and take a couple of shots, you know? That'll stir things up, and Jack, he'll maybe take Nate more serious after that, we get us some help around here, catch that mother 'fore he does something awful to *us*. George, he doesn't much want to do that, but he's scared to death of Nate Graham."

Phil stopped and gave me a painful look. "He isn't supposed to *hit* anyone, the fucking moron, he shoots me in the *arm!* Listen, you want something to drink?"

"Yeah, I could use something," I said.

"I got Dr Pepper and orange. They're hard to get in bottles anymore. I don't like a soft drink it comes in a can."

Phil walked off into the shadows. I thought if he kept doing that, racing up and down the dial, doing crazy, then doing something else, I was going to go nuts myself. Maybe that's how it worked, I decided, how they pulled it off. You could go around acting real normal, then kick in the loony gear again. I made a mental note to ask Doc Hackley—in case I ever got the chance.

I heard him back there, pulling bottles out of an ice chest. He'd left the shotgun leaning on the seat of the rocker. I had about eight feet of chain. If I got down on the ground and stretched, I'd miss the stock by a foot and a half.

He came out holding two bottles dripping ice. When he saw me he stopped and got that lopsided grin, like he knew what was going through my head.

"You better back off some," he said. "You don't get a cold drink unless you do."

I backed off and sat. Phil leaned down and put a Dr Pepper on the ground. I crawled up and got it and backed off again.

"That's a top name-brand chain," Phil said, "it isn't going to come loose. George wouldn't spend an extra nickel to get something good. Got more money than God, he puts ten-dollar retreads on his wife's Cadillac. Shoot, her and the kids could've run off a bridge." He took a big swallow of his orange. "You don't mind if I work while we talk? I got a lot of stuff to do."

"Uh, what kind of work is that, Phil?"

Phil looked real irritated. "For the party, Jack. I *told* you 'bout that."

"Right, I forgot."

"You just sit there and have your cold drink." He wiped his mouth and walked off into the dark.

I looked at my watch. It was a little after twelve. I knew Aaron Hess had every cop in the state out looking for Millie Jean. Maybe they'd get around to looking here. I thought about the cars in the yard. Hess would have the choppers out. That trooper's car was a dead giveaway, if anyone got close enough to look. Maybe Phil was too busy with his nutso party to think about that.

I heard him humming back there, moving something about, dragging something heavy across the rough wooden floor. In a moment, he came out backward, into the light. He was pulling a straight-back chair, and Millie Jean was sitting there, rigid and wired up tight, the wire cutting into her legs and her arms bent painfully back. Her mouth was taped shut and her eyes were enormous with fright. She was dressed for the party, ready for the lunatic ball. Her costume was crude and homemade and didn't fit, but I knew what it was because I'd seen it in a picture at Phil's, the little princess in her frilly pink dress and the cardboard crown with the sequins on her head, and I knew who the party was for. We were having his little sister's eighth and her very last birthday again . . .

"Phil, you're going to have to stop this shit right now," I said. "Just let Millie go. You do that, everything'll be fine, nobody's going to get pissed off."

Phil blinked. He'd forgotten I was there.

"You want another cold drink? I don't know if I got a Dr Pepper or not."

"I don't want a drink, Phil. I want you and me to talk. We can have a real good talk and you can let Millie loose from that chair, it isn't going to hurt anything you do that. She can just sit there and you and me can talk. There isn't any need to tie her up like that."

Phil looked perplexed. "I can't do that. I got to get her ready for the party, Jack."

"You don't have to get her ready. She looks fine now."

"Shoot, she isn't near ready yet. I got a lot of stuff to do."

"Damn it, Phil, you *listen* to me!"

I stretched the chain as far as it would go. I wondered how hard it was to chew your foot off. Animals did it all the time.

Phil wasn't listening. He walked into the dark end of the barn and came back with an old suitcase and a brown paper sack. He put the suitcase on the rocker and tossed the sack at me.

"What the hell's this?" I said.

"It's your stuff for the party," Phil said. "You can be getting it on while I'm fixing Millie Jean."

I emptied the sack. It was an old pair of jeans and some sneakers and a white T-shirt. Phil had drawn something on the shirt with red and yellow crayons, a stick figure with a yellow bolt of lightning on its chest, something a little kid would draw.

"I couldn't get a Captain Marvel shirt," he said, "like the one you used to wear? I don't think they make 'em anymore."

I stared at him. "You think I'm going to wear this stuff, is that it?"

"You *got* to." Phil frowned and shook his head. "It's for the party. Everybody's got to l-look right."

"What, like you? You got a mirror in here, you looked at yourself? You're buggy, Phil, you got some kind of shit in your head, and it doesn't help your image you're wearing a goofy T-shirt."

Phil blinked. "You better take that back. There isn't nothing wrong with my head!"

"Okay, you're right. Forget the buggy part, we can work around that."

"You gotta wear a costume, Jack."

"No, now I don't either, Phil, that's not how they do it anymore. You go to a party, you can wear a costume or not. You want to, you can wear a suit. Can we get *off* the costume business a minute, can we do that?"

I took a deep breath because I didn't want to do this, I didn't want to find out but I knew I had to try.

"I want you to tell me something," I said. "I want to know what you're going to do with us, Phil. See, I feel you've got something that's possibly harmful in mind. No offense, it just looks that way to me. What I want you to do, I want you to think about that. I think the Phil I knew is still in there somewhere, I don't think he wants to do this, I think he wants to work this out."

"I got to get Millie ready," Phil said. "I got to go and do that."

"Phil, I'm not finished here, you listen to me!"

He turned away and walked over to the rocker and I knew that I'd lost him, he was off somewhere. He put the shotgun on the floor. He dragged the rocker close to Millie and opened up the suitcase. I couldn't see what was in there but it was clear that Millie could. Her eyes got huge and the sweat popped out on her brow. She thrashed around and strained at her bonds, jerking like someone had wired a million volts through her chair.

Phil slapped her hard. Millie shut her eyes against the pain, and tears rolled down her face.

"You crazy son of a bitch, you get away from her. Don't you touch her again!"

Phil turned on me and his eyes were broken glass. "Don't you t-tell me what to do, Jack! It wasn't for you and her, everything'd be fine. I would've been all right!"

"What?" I stared at him. "What the hell are you talking about?"

"I could've stood it," he said, "but you and her made it *hard,* Jack. I didn't even know what they *looked* like with all their clothes off and you and her's lying down by the river and I'm comin' home from school and you put your th-th-thing in her. I saw you *do* it! God, I couldn't even get to sleep knowing what she looked like!"

Oh, Phil . . .

"She got to be Max's girlfriend and I knew they were doing it too, I didn't see 'em but they did. She did it with Deke, too, you know that? I watched them a couple of times. And then you c-come back and you st-stuck it in her again. I bet you stuck it in her daughter, too, I bet you did that."

"No, I didn't, Phil. I wouldn't ever—"

"Oh, Lord!" Phil tore at his face, trying to rip the hurt away. "I *told* Elaine I just wanted to *look,* I wasn't going to *do* anything—I just wanted to see, and she got all scared and said she was goin' to tell Mama what I did and God, I didn't want to *hurt* her or anything. All I ever get to look at is f-fat Louise. You got a d-damn whale spreadin' out on the bed, how you going to g-g-get it up you got somethin' like that? I didn't *want* to see you and Millie doin' that, Jack. You're not *supposed* to be watching dirty stuff like that!"

He looked at me once, and all the pain and the fury was there, all the shattered fragments of his life, there in his face and in his eyes, and then he reached in the suitcase and drew out something that glittered sharp and cold in the light. He smiled real sad at Millie Jean and ripped the tape off her mouth. Millie's scream came out. She kept screaming and couldn't stop, and Phil looked at her like he couldn't understand why she'd want to do that, why she wasn't acting right.

I yelled at him and jerked on my chain and called him a fucking lunatic and he didn't hear any of that. He stopped and looked blank and kind of stared around the room like he knew there was something he forgot. Then he walked off into the dark and all the lights came on in the barn and the music blared out of the walls and I saw that I was wrong: Millie and I weren't alone . . . The other guests were already there. The birthday party had begun, and we were all invited to Phil Eddels's looney-tune decorator hell . . .

Forty-one

The barn was ablaze with lights, he had lights every-where, hanging from the ceiling and the walls. He had strobe lights and headlights he'd taken off cars, he had dance-hall mirror lights that stabbed shards of color in your eyes. He had Christmas lights strung everywhere. He had the kind that blink, my mother wouldn't let them in the house. She said they made her dizzy and they weren't dig-nified. He even had the kind that bubble, I don't think they make them anymore. Lights flashed and glared and shim-mered, trapped in a tangle, in a web of strings and wires, like some goofy spider had a hard-on for psychedelic flies.

But that was not enough for this mother of all bad taste, there was dime-store crap dangling down from the ceiling and pasted to the walls. Cardboard Santas and Valentine hearts, turkeys and bunnies and crepe-paper fold-out Hal-loween cats, and every fucking holiday there is. And to make this madhouse complete, there were tinny speakers screeching from the walls and I thought, sweet Jesus, what else, it's the theme from *Star Wars*.

That was the fun part. The bad part was just coming in from the far end of the barn . . .

Double doors clattered open like the waiter's going to march in with your lunch. A whisper, a soft sigh of air, and a cloud of frost rolled into the room. A breath of winter reached out and chilled me to the bone. It might have been that, or it could have been the party guests suddenly appearing through the fog, bumping and swaying, their feet hanging just above the ground. They didn't look real good, but you hardly ever do when you're dead. It doesn't help if your skin's turned blue, you've got frost in your beard, you got a big icicle up your nose. You got all that, you got a meat hook in your back, it's kind of hard to look your best.

Nate Graham was first in line. I knew who he was, he was wearing his doorman's outfit, gold buttons and natty epaulets. Little wires ran from a pulley that was screwed into his head. Now and then he tipped his funny hat. He had a cheery frozen smile. He had a tiny tape recorder on his chest. He said, *"Take your bags—take your bags—take your bags—"* and passed me by, jerked to the left and started back the other way. I squinted up through the lights and saw the oval track overhead. It circled the barn to another set of doors, and back into the freezer, back into the winter wonderland.

Emma Stynnes was in her maid outfit. Her feather duster moved in jerky little motions through the air. Her tape said, *"Get you anything, Miz Millie?"* Her dark sad eyes said she wished to hell she had another job.

Fat Louise was a surprise. The Eddelses weren't entirely divorced, as we'd been led to believe. She banged on a skillet with a spoon. She said, *"Time for supper, dear."* She didn't look pleased. But then it couldn't be easy, living with a guy like Phil.

Deke looked a little better—maybe a little worse—than the rest. He had come to the party late, and there hadn't been time for the cold to freeze him up. Phil had done the best he could. Deke had a tinfoil star on his chest. It was held there securely by a screwdriver, driven in up to the hilt. It might have been a Phillips or the ordinary kind, I couldn't tell. Deke didn't have a lot to say. He looked a little tired. He looked right at me and he wasn't even mad anymore.

There was one last entry in this grisly parade, a very small bundle in a dark plastic bag. I was grateful that I couldn't see inside. A wand was pinned to the bag. The wand had a cut-out star. There was glitter on the star and it shimmered in the light.

Everybody swung by to the tune of *Star Wars*. Out through the door and back into frosty air, and Millie is screaming going out of her mind, she's got a double horror show. She's got a bunch of dead folks, she's got Phil. She's screaming at everyone. I'm going hoarse screaming at Phil. Phil is jumping up and down. He thinks his party's going fine. He's lunging at the air with his knife, he thinks he's maybe Errol Flynn.

The door popped open and the Popsicle people started out again. Phil stopped prancing around. He cocked his head and blinked at the lights. He looked at Millie Jean. He knew he had something to do and he remembered what it was. He squatted down in front of Millie, grabbed a handful of cloth and started cutting off her skirt.

My throat closed up tight. I said, "Oh shit, Phil, *don't* do that!" I called him a fucking lunatic, I called him everything else. Phil couldn't hear, he was busy at his work. He sliced the frilly skirt up across her thighs. The knife slicked over her belly and up between her breasts. Millie screamed and jerked in her chair. I ran back to the far wall and got down on my butt and put both feet up on either side of the bolt that held my chain. I knew it wouldn't give but I knew I had to try. Something pulled loose inside. I gritted my teeth against the pain and tried again. A hernia doesn't matter if you're dead.

To hell with that. I got to my feet and picked up the shirt and jeans Phil had given me to wear. Nate Graham was swinging by again and I stretched out as far as I could go. I lashed out at him with the jeans, trying to hook his arm, anything I could. I flailed out again and again and he tumbled on by. He was two feet past my reach, as good as a hundred miles away. I tried again with Emma Stynnes. One leg of the jeans caught her hand for a second and fell away.

Millie Jean screamed. I looked at her and my heart nearly stopped. Phil had her costume off and he was cutting it into shreds, laying little pink ribbons across her breasts. I stepped back and whipped the belt out of my pants. Fat Louise jerked by, banging on her pan. I leaned out and tried to snake the belt around her arm. All I did was knock the spoon out of her hand. I tried again. The belt fell away. The third time it stuck, the buckle catching on her dress. I held my breath and gave the belt a steady pull. She was nearly past me then and I thought, oh shit, Jack, this is not going to work, you're going to end up on a hook in your Captain Marvel shirt.

The belt held. Louise's frozen corpse leaned slightly in my direction. I risked another pull and let her go. She swung away, then arced back again. I reached out and caught her dress and wrapped my arms around her waist and hung on.

A motor clattered somewhere, keening up to an uneasy whine. Motors like to go, they don't like to stop. I peered around Louise's ample waist. Phil jerked up. His mouth fell open and his eyes got big as poker chips.

"Stop *doing* that," he said, "you're going to sp-spoil everything!"

I held on tight. The motor groaned and tried to set things right again. Screw that. I wasn't about to let go of Louise. Phil stuck his knife in the wall and went for the shotgun on the floor. His eyes were full of colored lights. He brought the gun up to his waist and I buried my head in Louise's big butt. The blast took her full in the chest. Pellets dug into my hands and I yelled and let go. Louise was suddenly free. Two hundred pounds of frozen fat rushed at Phil. Phil blinked and threw up his arms and Louise kicked him solidly in the chest. Phil yelled and slammed into the wall. The shotgun dropped from his hands. He shook his head and came to his knees.

He didn't need his Igor imitation anymore. The light in his eyes said guaranteed fucking lunatic.

Louise and her crew rumbled by. Phil picked the shotgun off the floor. His hands shook with anger as he brought it up and aimed it at my head. My life didn't pass before my eyes. I thought about barbecued ribs. I thought, oh man, this is going to hurt a lot.

"Oh God, Phil, I sure want it bad, come over here and *do* it to me, hon, come stick it in me, Phil!"

Phil blinked. He turned around real slow and stared at Millie Jean. He didn't see me. All he saw was Millie Jean. All he saw was a naked holy vision wired to a straight-back chair, all he heard were the words that he'd never heard before.

"I really *mean* it," Millie said, "I *got* to have it, babe, I want that big ol' thing of yours in me just as *far* as it'll go!"

Phil's eyes glazed. He said, "Whaga-whaga-doo."

Millie kept gabbing, the worst dialogue I ever heard, a porno director would've fired her on the spot, but Phil didn't seem to care. He said, "Fooga-fooga-whah," or words to that effect. A funny grin slid across his face and I leaned down slowly and picked my Dr Pepper bottle off the floor. God, I thought, if you're listening, this is not the time to put me in my place. I held the bottle by the neck and threw it like a knife, the way Eastwood does it when he's got to knock off a Nazi guard.

Phil went *"Whoofa!"* and dropped like a sack.

Millie looked at Phil. Then she looked at me. Tears started pouring down her cheeks. "Oh, shit, get me out of here. You get me out of here right this minute, Jack!"

"I'm not real sure how I'm going to manage that," I said. "I haven't got a key to this thing. It's probably in his pocket somewhere, and I'm about four feet short of chain."

"Is he dead? I hope you killed the little prick."

"I don't know if he is or not. I think he's just out."

There was a blue lump rising on the side of Phil's head, but I was sure he was alive. I didn't want to tell Millie Jean. The shotgun was way out of reach. For me, not for him.

Millie seemed to get the idea. She looked horrified. "Oh Lord, you do something, Jack. You do something real quick. He wakes up he's going to be awful pissed off."

"Just shut up," I said. "I'm thinking, all right?"

"You don't do something, I'm going to pee in this chair, Jack Track. I've never done that in my life."

"I don't think any of the folks here'll care, Millie Jean."

Millie gave me a furious look. "Well, *I* care. You better just—oh *God!*"

Phil groaned. He opened one red eye and blinked. Millie screamed again, which didn't help a lot, it seemed to wake him up. Phil just looked at me and raised his head and reached out and found the shotgun. He didn't say a thing, maybe because there wasn't much to say. He turned over on his side and swung the shotgun in my face. Earl Murphy's fine Italian shoe appeared and sent it skidding off across the floor.

He looked at me and Millie Jean. He stared at the Popsicle people who were rounding the far turn again.

"God A'mighty," he said, "I seen some kinky shit in New York one time, I don't think they got a thing like this."

"We're catching up," I said. "We're closing the culture gap fast."

"I hear that," Earl said.

Forty-two

"I might get me one of these Chester Cheetah skateboards," Earl said. "Says here it's got a suggested retail price of sixty bucks. You can get it for thirty-one ninety-nine and five proofs of purchase off the sack."

"I'd give thirty-one ninety-nine to see you on a skateboard," I said. "I might go the retail price."

Earl frowned at the sack. "What you figure canola oil is? I never heard of that."

"Life was simpler when we just had lard. You knew where everything came from back then."

We were sitting in the kitchen after dark drinking Dortmunder beer and eating Chee-tos. We'd been at it some time, and our fingers had turned bright orange. Earl had some ideas on reducing the national debt. I threw in a science fact I'd seen on PBS. This one program said the praying mantis fucks a lot better after his mate cuts off his head. As soon as his brain stem is severed, it quits sending out these inhibition signals and he gives his lady friend a real thrill. Earl said he wondered what kind of inhibition a praying mantis had. He said he didn't think a bug would store up a lot of guilt.

We narrowed down our ongoing list of movie stars who had class. Finalists were Ingrid Bergman, Lena Horne, Patricia Neal and Lauren Bacall. I nominated that girl who does the GUESS ads, and Earl said absolutely not. She wasn't old enough and she wasn't a movie star. I said I didn't care if she was or not.

All in all, it was an evening of personal growth. When the beer was all gone Earl left, and I fed Alexander and put him out. Cecily had fallen asleep with the light still on, a book called *Killer Corporations* in her hand. She looked very lovely and fragile lying there, not at all like a woman determined to swallow all her rival yogurt chains. *Forbes* had put her on the cover the week before. The caption read, *Cecily Benét: Freeze-out Time in Big D.* She was real pleased with that.

I turned out the light and she opened her eyes and said, "What time is it? Earl gone yet?"

"He just left," I said "It's after twelve. I'm sorry I woke you up."

"Wasn't asleep," she said, and turned over and put a pillow on her head.

I walked out quietly and closed the bedroom door. All things considered, I decided we were doing fairly well. She still brings up Millie Jean sometimes, but I've learned to live with that. I keep hoping for a memory lapse, but the woman's got a real sharp mind.

We weren't exactly where we'd started, and I kind of missed that, but you can't expect things to stay the way they are. I thought where we were was on hold, neither of us sure where we were, both of us wanting to hold onto the good things we had. This wasn't an easy thing to do. She was fast becoming a mega-yogurt queen, and I was still uncertain what I wanted to do with myself. Neither of us talked about this, but it was there.

I turned off all the lights and walked outside on the porch. There isn't much real fall in north Texas. It's hot all day, and cool sometimes after dark. I had a light sweater on, and that was fine for a late-October night.

* * *

It didn't seem that long since Pharaoh's summer of discontent. A few short months, and it was hard to tell that anything had happened there at all. This wasn't true for everyone, of course. George Rainey's widow wouldn't likely forget that summer, nor the mother of Emma Stynnes.

Main Street and the courthouse look the same. Eddie Trost's Hardware & Funeral Home is still there, but it's closed up tight, and Eddie's off to parts unknown. No one sees much of Roy Burns. He goes to his office and drinks and goes home. He's still an asshole, he just isn't an asshole lawyer anymore.

I see Henry D. from time to time. He works at Six Flags Over Texas in Arlington. He's got a jazzy uniform and he sells lemonade and hot dogs. He never forgets to remind me that this is a real authentic job, not like the one we shared before. I tell him this is true, that I hope to make similar strides someday myself.

Millie's in Switzerland, or Italy or France. She moves around a lot. She doesn't have Smoothy in school, she keeps a tutor with her and doesn't let Smoothy out of sight. I think Millie's harrowing experience brought the two of them close. I saw her once or twice before they left town. She told me she would never forget what might have happened if she hadn't sent Smoothy up to Dallas and made her stay with friends. If she'd been there in the house, Phil would have taken her too.

People still go to Audie's and the drugstore and rehash our maniac spree. But this is the end of October, and football is the topic of the day. Everyone wants to know if the Cowboys can make it to the Superbowl again.

My personal barometer of "when we'll get back to normal life" is Earl. I make a little mark on my calendar every time he tells me how he saved my life. It has been nine days now, a record so far. The story changes a little every time. Basically, it seems he hears me drive off in the night, and follows in his bird-shit car. He follows because he "senses danger in the air." He says black people have an inborn talent for this, that they are far more sensitive than whites.

As Earl tells the story, he loses me awhile, then picks me up again. He says I'm lucky that he trashed my old truck, that the new one has brand-new tires with the tits hardly even worn off. They make a distinct impression on the country dirt roads, and he's able to follow my trail. Right about here there is usually a part about Zulus tracking lions, how he's close to the pulse of Mother Earth. If he's had a lot to drink, the Zulu stuff gets muddled up with Indian lore. If he's drinking single malt instead of beer, the Great Black Father comes in there somewhere.

I don't know how Earl found me. I am eternally grateful that he did. I will be more grateful still when he comes to the end of all this.

Several things have come out about Phil's escapade. It is very likely some things never will. It is clear that his obsession had been simmering in his head for some time. He bought the house and the barn some eight years back. It formerly belonged to a man who stole and butchered cattle and sold the meat to Dallas restaurants. He made a lot of money and retired. After the dead electric dog turned up, and then Max, the cops checked everyone around north Texas who owned something bigger than a household freezer: Deer lockers, butcher shops, ice-cream plants. Of course nothing turned up. The freezer in the barn had been part of an illegal enterprise, and hadn't been in business since 1976.

An interesting side note here: The man who ran the meat business was a cousin of Herb, of Herb's Exxon & Auto Repair. That whole clan was into crime of some kind, and still is. Herb never liked his cousin, and he might have told the law just what was out there. If he happened to remember. If anyone happened to ask.

Doc Ben Hackley and two pathologists from Dallas confirmed that Phil dug up his little sister about the same time he bought the place out of town. No one knows exactly how he did in Louise. There really was a divorce and she did move out of town. Some people got postcards for a while, then no one heard a word after that.

A week or so after things cooled down, a trooper found a bedroll by the river, and some of Deke's things. He'd camped out there to get away from everyone after Hess kicked him out. There's no way to say how Phil found him there. Except that Phil *wanted* to know where we all were. That's all he had to do.

No one knows how Phil got on to Nate Graham, but it's easy to make a guess. I think he spent a lot of time with that yearbook. I think it was the focus of his need to get back at everyone he felt had left him out. That wasn't the beginning, of course. The terrible thing he'd done to his sister was probably the start, or at least the first act of the madness that was festering there. He couldn't carry all that guilt himself. He had to find a reason for his pain, and he found it in us—Max, Millie, Deke, me, everyone. He hadn't plunged himself into that dark and awful world. We had put him there.

Maybe he found the picture of Deke and Nate together, and tracked Nate down somehow. Or maybe he happened to spot him at his doorman's job, and found the picture after that. It's sad to think that Nate was probably glad to see Phil. He'd grown up as a loner, too.

I can't help thinking about what Phil said to me that night. *It was so damn easy . . . I figured someone would see it, only all they ever saw was old Phil . . .* He was dead right about that. We swallowed the Nate Graham story, just as he knew we would. If things slowed down, Phil was there to stir them up. A few phone calls, some flowers on a grave.

A rumor about Nate and Deke that Phil knew would get back to Max. And he was always there. The outsider, the invisible man.

Like I said, there are some things we know, and some we never will. Phil knows the answers, if he still knows who he is. The doctors at Rusk, where we lock up the criminally insane, say Phil's probably out of it for good. He never says a word to anyone. The only indication that he's there is an incident that happened some two months ago. The attendants got careless for a moment, and Phil nearly tore off his own private parts before they could get him restrained.

It's an odd observation on life that everyone in Pharaoh is pissed off at Phil for different reasons than you'd think. I've heard them talking at Audie's sometimes. They were convinced Nate Graham was our raving lunatic, that he and Deke were likely in cahoots the whole time. They didn't think Phil had any business being nuts. They didn't appreciate that. They felt he'd betrayed them somehow . . .

It was getting a little chilly and I thought about going back in. Cecily would be asleep, but sometimes if I made the right moves she didn't object to waking up. I looked around to see if Alexander might want to come in. If the hunt was going well, he'd spend the night out, then yowl to get in about four.

He wasn't in the front, so I walked around the side of the house. I thought I saw him out by the dead peach trees. I called a few times, then turned and walked back. That's when Aaron Hess stepped out of the dark and stuck a big gun in my face.

I jumped about a foot, like anyone would. I said, "What the hell is this, what are you doing here!" or something dramatic like that.

"Just walk," Hess said, "go on out back and don't try

anything, Track. You got any weapons concealed on your person you better not try and bring 'em out."

"I don't have any weapons, I'm in my own backyard. What's the matter with you?"

"Shut up. Get up against the wall and assume the position, boy."

"What position's that? I hope you aren't thinking romance."

Hess didn't answer. He frisked me quickly like he'd done this once or twice. We walked past the house to the edge of the cornfield and stopped. He told me to sit and I did. Hess perched on a stump that I used to cut wood.

"I told you I'd get you," he said. "It took me a while but I did. I got a lot of friends in the law-enforcement trade. I sent a bunch of your pictures around. One of 'em paid off. A guy works for DEA called me Thursday afternoon. I flew to El Paso and talked to this Mes'can he's got in the jail down there. This fella's looking at heavy time and he'd like to get a little chopped off. He ID'd you right away. Said you didn't have a beard back then but it was you. He met you on a dope deal in Arizona once. You were working with a guy named Lloyd DeWitt. I did a check on him. He did a year in Leavenworth before he had an industrial accident. Someone put an ice pick in his back. The word is, he pulled a sneaky on a deal in South Miami and pissed off some friends back East. A couple of Colombians got themselves whacked down there, and left a lot of coke lying about. Whoever did 'em took the money and ran. At his trial, DeWitt said the guy was Wayne Grosz. It turns out that was you, Track."

"I was in Florida once," I said. "I think it was '79. That was Orlando, though. All I got was a Mickey Mouse hat."

Hess waved his gun and grinned. "It was you, all right, there isn't any doubt about that. Jesus, I had you pegged from the start. You got that wrongdoer attitude. A lawman can always spot that."

"You are out of your fucking mind," I said. "I didn't take any money from anyone. I don't know any Lloyd DeWitt, I don't know what you're talking about."

"They all say that," Hess said. "I can see you're guilty, the way you move your eyes."

"It's dark out here. You don't have any idea what I'm doing with my eyes."

"This DeWitt had a partner. A real pretty gal named Mary Zee. Lloyd skipped out and they couldn't find him, so they laid the whole mess on her. The girl wouldn't give 'em anything. They convicted her and sent her to the Federal facility at Lexington, Kentucky, for a while. She took a good look at the ladies in there and turned around on DeWitt real quick. They got her in the Federal Witness Program. She's doing fine, got her own boutique. Don't ask me where it is. That's confidential, strictly need to know. I showed her your picture the other day. Said she'd never seen you in her life, said you didn't look a thing like Wayne Grosz. Of course I knew better'n that and so did she."

Hess hesitated. He rested his gun hand on his knee. "Where you got the money hid, Track? Lloyd and Mary Zee both testified it was close to two mil. I don't figure you bought savings bonds, it's probably right around here."

"I haven't got any two million dollars," I said. "I don't know any of these people you're talking about."

Hess stood and scratched his rear. "There's two ways we can go about this. I got enough on you to build a pretty good case, whether we find that money or not. I think I can get you close to life. The other way to do it is you find the money, and we work something out right here."

I didn't get it for a minute, then I did. I stared at Hess and laughed. "Am I hearing this, am I getting this straight? I can't believe I'm hearing this, a lawman of your standing violating his oath. I'm real disappointed in you, Hess."

Hess gave me a look. "I don't want any shit from you on this. I don't need some goddamn felon tellin' me about a oath. I don't feel good about this, it goes against the grain with me. I'm getting put out early, the state's cutting everything back. I can't live on the pissant pension I'm going to get. I played it straight all my life. I never took a cent from anyone."

"Right. But you're willing to make an exception for me."

"That's not stealing, taking anything from you. Stealing's when you rob an honest man. You didn't earn that money. That's ill-gotten gains is what it is."

"I'm glad you explained all this," I said. "I understand it better now. I'm the Sheriff of Nottingham and you're Robin Hood. The only thing is, I haven't *got* the money, Hess. You've got the wrong man. What I'd like you to do is stop this crap and get off of my farm."

Hess shook his head. He held the gun straight out and I heard him draw the hammer back. "Now this just isn't going to cut it, Track. Either way we do this, you're going to get the ass-end of it, I don't see why you can't understand that. That's just how it's going to be."

"No," I said, "here's how it's going to be. You can shoot me right here but I don't think you will. I think you're up the creek and you'd like to eat steak instead of beans. Well, fuck you. Nobody asked you to work for the state, you should've known better than that. It's not my fault you did that. You think you can shoot me, go ahead, I'm going back to the house and go to bed."

I didn't look at Hess. I got up slow and turned around and started walking back.

"Damn it," Hess said, "why you got to make things difficult, Track?"

"It's an inborn criminal trait," I said. "You told me all about that."

"You're sure quick to take offense, you got to bring up everything somebody said. Listen, I can come back here with a carload of Feds. We'll smoke you out."

I turned around and stopped. "I can go in and phone up a Mafia don in New York. I'll tell him I want you whacked."

"You don't know any Mafia dons in New York."

"You don't know if I do or not. If I was Wayne Grosz, I'd know a bunch of dons, I could call 'em right up."

"That isn't even how you do it," Hess said. "You don't call a don, you call somebody else. Track, I don't see why we can't talk about this. There isn't any harm in that."

"There's nothing to talk about," I said. "You figure out what you want to do. You can shoot me or turn me in or forget about this."

"Shooting you's not my first choice."

"It's good to know that. What's number two?"

Hess let out a long breath. He put his gun away. "I'm not through with you. Don't think I am. I might come back in force."

"You won't make any money like that."

"Does that mean I might?"

"I didn't say that."

"I'm getting cold out here. You got anything to drink?"

"Not for you I don't."

Hess put his hands in his pockets. He looked real tired. I was tired too.

"I didn't think you'd act like this," he said. "I'm surprised you got any friends. You've got a shitty attitude."

"That's what everybody says."

"I want you to think about this. You do, I think you'll do what's right."

"I expect I will," I said.

He looked at me to see if he could make anything out of that, then he turned and walked off toward the road. I watched until I heard his car start and saw the taillights vanish in the dark. I knew I couldn't go to bed. I went back in the house and got a drink and smoked one of Earl's cigars. I sat on the porch until two, then I walked out back again and made a wide circle around the cornfield. I stayed out of sight as best I could. I knew the farm better than anyone else. I'd know if Hess decided to hang around.

At a quarter after three, I got a shovel from the garage and paced off thirty-seven yards from the back of the house and walked out into the corn. The package was three feet deep. The ground was fairly soft and it didn't take long. I had wrapped the money in a heavy grade of plastic, and sealed that with wax. Then I'd put the whole thing in a waterproof canvas bag. I didn't think Hess would come back, but I wanted that stuff out of there. I wasn't sure what I'd do with it then, but I didn't want to leave it in the ground.

I put down the shovel and squatted down to work with my hands. I felt the rough surface of the canvas, and ran my fingers down along the sides. I touched something that didn't feel right. It felt like canvas if you took it apart and saved the threads. I poked underneath it and touched something hard. I worked it loose and brought it out. What I had was a chicken bone. It might have been a former wing, or it might have been a thigh. I reached down again and came up with some feathers and some bones, and a lot of green paper in the handy shredded size. Real good for packing things, you want to send a dish to someone.

I wondered if I still had Will's old shotgun in the house. It was clear someone had done me wrong. Someone had done me great harm. Someone had totally wrecked my future life. I would never be the Honky of Wall Street now. I would have to drink very cheap Scotch, I'd have to buy my suits at Sears.

Oh, Sweet Jesus, what I'd have to do is *work,* and I was certain that I couldn't handle that . . .

Forty-three

Fuck you too, Badger Bob . . .

HORROR FROM HAUTALA

SHADES OF NIGHT   (0-8217-5097-6, $4.99)
Stalked by a madman, Lara DeSalvo is unaware that she is most in danger in the one place she thinks she is safe—home.

TWILIGHT TIME   (0-8217-4713-4, $4.99)
Jeff Wagner comes home for his sister's funeral and uncovers long-buried memories of childhood sexual abuse and murder.

DARK SILENCE   (0-8217-3923-9, $5.99)
Dianne Fraser fights for her family—and her sanity—against the evil forces that haunt an abandoned mill.

COLD WHISPER   (0-8217-3464-4, $5.95)
Tully can make Sarah's wishes come true, but Sarah lives in terror because Tully doesn't understand that some wishes aren't meant to come true.

LITTLE BROTHERS   (0-8217-4020-2, $4.50)
Kip saw the "little brothers" kill his mother five years ago. Now they have returned, and this time there will be no escape.

MOONBOG   (0-8217-3356-7, $4.95)
Someone—or some*thing*—is killing the children in the little town of Holland, Maine.

AMANDA HAZARD MYSTERIES
BY CONNIE FEDDERSEN

DEAD IN THE CELLAR   (0-8217-5245-6, $4.99)

DEAD IN THE DIRT   (1-57566-046-6, $4.99)

DEAD IN THE MELON PATCH   (0-8217-4872-6, $4.99)

DEAD IN THE WATER   (0-8217-5244-8, $4.99)

THE MYSTERIES OF MARY ROBERTS RINEHART

POLITICAL ESPIONAGE AND
HEART-STOPPING HORROR. . . .
NOVELS BY NOEL HYND

CEMETERY OF ANGELS   (0-7860-0261-1, $5.99/$6.99)

GHOSTS   (0-8217-4359-7, $4.99/$5.99)

THE KHRUSHCHEV OBJECTIVE   (0-8217-2297-2, $4.50/$5.95)

A ROOM FOR THE DEAD   (0-7860-0089-9, $5.99/$6.99)

TRUMAN'S SPY   (0-8217-3309-5, $4.95/$5.95)

ZIG ZAG   (0-8217-4557-3, $4.99/$5.99)

REVENGE   (0-8217-2529-7, $3.95/$4.95)

THE SANDLER INQUIRY   (0-8217-3070-3, $4.50/$5.50)

Available wherever paperbacks are sold, or order direct from the Publisher. Send cover price plus 50¢ per copy for mailing and handling to Penguin USA, P.O. Box 999, c/o Dept. 17109, Bergenfield, NJ 07621. Residents of New York and Tennessee must include sales tax. DO NOT SEND CASH.

READ EXCITING ACCOUNTS OF
TRUE CRIME FROM PINNACLE

A PERFECT GENTLEMAN   (0-7860-0263-8, $5.99)
By Jaye Slade Fletcher
On October 13, 1987, the body of 16-year-old Windy Patricia
Gallagher was found in her home in Griffith, Indiana, stabbed 21
times and disemboweled. Five months later, 14-year-old Jennifer
Colhouer of Land O'Lakes, Florida, was found raped and also
slashed to death in her own home. But it was the seemingly un-
related cold-blooded murder of a Beaumont, Texas police officer
that sparked a massive, nationwide manhunt across 5 states and
2 continents to apprehend one of the most elusive—and charming—serial killers who ever lived.

BORN BAD   (0-7860-0274-3, $5.99)
By Bill G. Cox
On a lonely backroad in Ellis County, TX, the body of 13-year-old
Christina Benjamin was discovered. Her head and hands were missing. She had been sexually mutilated and disemboweled. A short
distance away was the badly decomposed corpse of 14-year-old
James King face down on the creek bank. He had been brutally shot
to death. This ghoulish discovery would lead to the apprehension of
the most appalling torture killer Texas had ever seen. . . .

CHARMED TO DEATH   (0-7860-0257-3, $5.99)
The True Story of Colorado's Cold-Blooded
Black Widow Murderess
By Stephen Singular
Jill Coit spread her lethal web of sex, lies, and violence from one
end of the country to the other. Behind the beauty queen smile
was a psychopathic femme fatale who took a fiendish delight in
preying on innocent men. With fifteen aliases, countless forged
birth certificates, and a predatory allure, she married ten men,
divorced six, and always stayed one step ahead of the law in a
poisonous spree of bigamy, embezzlement, and murder that lasted
nearly 35 years.

Available wherever paperbacks are sold, or order direct from the
Publisher. Send cover price plus 50¢ per copy for mailing and
handling to Penguin USA, P.O. Box 999, c/o Dept. 17109,
Bergenfield, NJ 07621. Residents of New York and Tennessee
must include sales tax. DO NOT SEND CASH.